# Snow in August

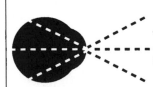

This Large Print Book carries the
Seal of Approval of N.A.V.H.

# Snow in August

## PETE HAMILL

DISCARD

**Thorndike Press • Thorndike, Maine**

Published in 1997 by arrangement with
Little, Brown and Company, Inc.

Thorndike Large Print ® Basic Series.

The tree indicium is a trademark of Thorndike Press.

The text of this Large Print edition is unabridged.
Other aspects of the book may vary from the original edition.

Set in 16 pt. News Plantin by Rick Gundberg.

Printed in the United States on permanent paper.

**Library of Congress Cataloging in Publication Data**

Hamill, Pete, 1935–
   Snow in August : a novel / Pete Hamill.
    p.  cm.
   ISBN 0-7862-1221-7 (lg. print : hc : alk. paper)
   ISBN 0-7862-1222-5 (lg. print : sc : alk. paper)
   1. Friendship — Fiction.  2. Baseball — Fiction.
3. Jewish way of life — Fiction.  4. Brooklyn (New York,
N.Y.) — Fiction.  5. Large type books.  I. Title.
[PS3558.A423S66  1997b]
  813'.54—dc21                        97-28017

THIS BOOK IS FOR

*my brother John*

AND IN MEMORY OF

*Joel Oppenheimer*

*who heard the cries of*

*"Yonkel! Yonkel! Yonkel!"*

*in the summer bleachers of 1947.*

*Now faith is the substance of things hoped for, the evidence of things not seen.*

HEBREWS 11:1

*A Jew can't live without miracles.*

YIDDISH PROVERB

# 1

Once upon a cold and luminous Saturday morning, in an urban hamlet of tenements, factories, and trolley cars on the western slopes of the borough of Brooklyn, a boy named Michael Devlin woke in the dark.

He was eleven years and three months old in this final week of the year 1946, and because he had slept in this room for as long as he could remember, the darkness provoked neither mystery nor fear. He did not have to see the red wooden chair that stood against the windowsill; he knew it was there. He knew his winter clothes were hanging on a hook on the door and that his three good shirts and his clean underclothes were neatly stacked in the two drawers of the low green bureau. The *Captain Marvel* comic book he'd been reading before falling asleep was certain to be on the floor beside the narrow bed. And he knew that when he turned on the light he would pick up the comic book and stack it with the other *Cap-*

*tain Marvels* on the top shelf of the metal cabinet beside the door. Then he would rise in a flash, holding his breath to keep from shivering in his underwear, grab for clothes, and head for the warmth of the kitchen. That was what he did on every dark winter morning of his life.

But this morning was different.

Because of the light.

His room, on the top floor of the tenement at 378 Ellison Avenue, was at once dark and bright, with tiny pearls of silver glistening in the blue shadows. From the bed, Michael could see a radiant paleness beyond the black window shade and gashes of hard white light along its sides. He lay there under the covers, his eyes filled with the bright darkness. A holy light, he thought. The light of Fatima. Or the Garden of Eden. Or the magic places in storybooks. Suddenly, he was sure it was like the light in the Cave of the Seven Deadly Enemies of Man. That secret place in the comic book where the faceless man in the black suit first took Billy Batson to meet the ancient Egyptian wizard named Shazam. Yes: the newsboy must have seen a light like this. Down there, beyond the subway tunnel, in that long stone cave where the white-bearded wizard gave him the magic word that called down the lightning bolt. The lightning bolt that turned the boy into Captain Marvel, the world's mightiest man.

Michael knew that the magic word was the same as the name of the wizard: *Shazam!* And he had learned from the comic book that the letters of the name stood for Solomon, Hercules, and Atlas, Zeus, Achilles, and Mercury. Ancient gods and heroes. Except for Solomon, who was a wise king from Bible days. Mighty symbols of strength, stamina, power, courage, and speed. They weren't just names in a comic book either; Michael had looked them up in the encyclopedia. And their powers were all combined in Captain Marvel. On that night in the mysterious cave, the wizard named Shazam told Billy Batson he had been chosen to fight the forces of evil because he was pure of heart. And no matter how sinister his enemies were, no matter how monstrous their weapons, all he needed to fight them was to shout the magic word. *Shazam!*

Alas, on the streets of the parish, the magic word did not work for Michael Devlin and his friends, and for at least three years they had debated the reasons. Maybe they needed to get the powers directly from the Egyptian wizard. Maybe the word didn't work because they weren't pure enough. Or because, as his friend Sonny Montemarano put it, Captain Marvel was just a story in a fucking comic book. Still, Michael insisted, it might be true. Who could ever know? Maybe all they had to do was believe hard enough for it to happen.

Michael was snapped back into the present by the sound of the wind. First a low moan. Then a high-pitched whine. A trombone choir, then a soprano saxophone. Tommy Dorsey's band, and then Sidney Bechet. The names and music he had learned from the radio. It sounded to Michael like the voice of the light. He sat up, his heart pounding, wondering what time it was, afraid that he had overslept, and swung his feet around to the floor. They landed on the *Captain Marvel* comic book.

I wish I didn't have to do this, he thought. Sometimes being an altar boy was a huge pain in the ass. I wish I could just lie in bed and listen to the wind. Instead of dragging myself all the way to Sacred Heart to mouth a lot of mumbo jumbo in a language nobody even speaks. I wish I could fall back into this warm bed, pull the covers around me, and sleep.

But he did not sink back into the warmth. In his mind, he saw his mother's disappointed face and Father Heaney's angry eyes. Worse: he felt suddenly alarmed, as if he had come close to the sin of sloth. Even Shazam warned against sloth, listing it among the Seven Deadly Enemies of Man, and Shazam wasn't even a Catholic. The word itself had a disgusting sound, and he remembered a picture of an animal called a sloth that he'd seen in a dictionary. Thick, furry, nasty. He imagined it growing to the size of King Kong, waddling wetly through the city, stinking of filth and laziness and animal shit. A dirty goddamned giant *sloth,* with P-38s firing machine guns at it, the bullets vanishing into the hairy mush of its formless body, its open mouth a pit of slobber. Jesus Christ.

So Michael did not even raise the black window shade. He grabbed his trousers, thinking: The antonym for sloth must be self-denial. Or movement. Or a word that said get off your ass, get up and go. When the priests, brothers, and nuns were not drilling them in synonyms or antonyms or the eleven times table, they were forever hammering away about self-denial. And so, buttoning his fly in the dark, he refused himself the pleasure of pulling the shade aside, or rolling it up, and thus revealing the source of the luminous light. He would wait. He would put off that vision. He would offer up his discomfort, as his teachers commanded him to do, for the suffering souls in Purgatory. Be good. Be pure. Accept some pain and thus redeem those who are burning for their sins. He could hear the chilly orders of his catechism teachers as clearly as he could hear Shazam.

Shirtless and shoeless, he hurried through the dark living room and past his mother's closed bedroom door to the kitchen, which faced the harbor of New York. The fire in the coal stove had guttered and died during the night, and the linoleum floors were frigid on his bare feet. He didn't care. Now he would deny himself no longer. He lifted the kitchen window shade, and his heart tripped.

There was the source of the light.

Snow.

Still falling on the rooftops and backyards of Brooklyn.

Snow now so deep, so dense and packed, that the world glowed in its blinding whiteness.

The thrilling view pebbled his skin. It had been snowing for two days and nights, great white flakes on the first day and then harder, finer snow driven by the wind off the harbor. The boy had seen nothing like it. Ever. He could remember six of his eleven winters on the earth, and there had never been snow like this. This was snow out of movies about the Yukon that he watched in the Venus. This was like the great Arctic blizzards in the stories of Jack London that he read in the library on Garibaldi Street. Snow that hid wolves and covered automobiles and crushed cabins and halted trolley cars. Snow that caused avalanches to cover the entrances of gold mines and snow that cracked limbs off trees in Prospect Park. Snow from a mighty storm. The night before, someone on the radio said that the blizzard had paralyzed the city. Here it was, the next morning, and the snow was still coming down, erasing the world.

He stepped into the narrow bathroom off the kitchen, closing the door behind him. The tiles were colder than the linoleum. His teeth chattered. He urinated, pulled the chain to flush, and then washed his face quickly in the cold water of the sink, thinking: I will go into it; I will face the storm, climb the hard hills, push into the wind of the blizzard to the church on the hill. Father Heaney, a veteran of the war, will celebrate the eight o'clock mass, and I will be there at his side. The only human being to make it through the blizzard. Even the old ladies in black, those strange old biddies who make it to church through rainstorms and heat waves, even they will fail to make it through the storm. The pews will be empty. The candles will flicker in the cold. But I will be there.

His heart raced at the prospect of the great test. He didn't care now about the souls in Purgatory. He wanted the adventure. He wished he had a dogsled waiting downstairs. He wished he could bundle himself in furs and lift a leather whip and urge the huskies forward, shouting, *Mush, boys, mush!* He had the serum in a pouch and by God, he would get it to Nome.

He combed his hair, and when he stepped out of the bathroom, his mother, Kate, was raking the ashes in the coal stove, her flannel robe pulled tightly around her, worn brown slippers on her feet. Steam leaked from her mouth into the frigid air. A teapot rested on the black cast-iron top of the stove, waiting for heat.

"Let me do that, Mom," the boy said. "That's *my* job."

"No, no, you're already washed," she said, in her soft Irish accent, a hair of irritation in her voice. Raking the dead ashes was one of Michael's chores, but in his excitement over the blizzard, he'd forgotten. "Just go and get dressed."

"I'll *do* it," he said, taking the flat shovel from her and digging the ashes out of the bottom tray. He poured them into a paper bag, a gray powder rising in the air to mix with the steam from his breath, then shoveled fresh coal from the bucket onto the grate. The fine ash made him sneeze.

"For the love of God, Michael, get *dressed*," she said now, pushing him aside. "You'll catch your death of cold."

Back in his room, at the far end of the railroad flat, he pulled an undershirt over his head and a dark green shirt on top of it, shoving the tails into his trousers. After tugging galoshes over his shoes, he finally raised the blackout shade. The snow was piled against the windowpane at least two feet above the steel slats of the fire escape. Beyond the steep drift, snow swirled like a fog so dense he could not see across Ellison Avenue. He hurried back into the kitchen. A fire was burning now in the coal stove, its odor staining the air like rotten eggs. He wished his mother would buy the Blue Coal advertised on *The Shadow*; it was harder — *anthracite*, they said in school — with almost no smell. But she told him once that they couldn't afford it and he never asked again.

"I'm sure you could stay home if you like, Michael," she said, the irritation out of her voice now. "They know how far you have to come."

"I can do it," he said, combing his hair, choosing not to remind her that the church was eight blocks from 378 Ellison Avenue. From the backyards he heard a sound that he was sure was the howling of a thousand wolves.

"Still," she said, pouring water for tea, "it's a terrible long way in this storm."

He followed her glance to the wall clock: seven twenty-five. He had time. He was certain that she also looked at the framed photograph of his father. Thomas Devlin. Michael was named for his mother's father, who had died in Ireland long ago. The photograph of his own father was hanging beside the picture of President Roosevelt that she'd cut out of the *Daily News* magazine when he died. For a moment, Michael wondered what she thought about when she looked at the picture of his father. The boy didn't remember many details about the man she called Tommy. He was a large man with dark hair and a rough, stubbled beard who had gone off to the army when Michael was six. And had never come back. In the framed formal photograph, he was wearing his army uniform. The skin on his smiling face looked smooth. Much smoother than it actually felt. His hair was covered by the army cap, but at the sides it was lighter than the boy remembered. That brown hair. And a deep voice with an Irish brogue. And a blue Sunday suit and polished black shoes. And a song about the green glens of Antrim. And stories about a dog he had as a boy in Ireland, a dog named Sticky, who could power a boat with his tail and fly over mountains. His mother surely remembered much more about him. The boy knew his father had been killed in Belgium in the last winter of the war, and thought: Maybe the blizzard reminds her of Tommy Devlin dead in the snow, a long way from Brooklyn. Maybe that's why she's irritated. It's not my lolly-gagging. It's the snow.

"I wish you could eat something," she said, sipping her tea, but not pouring a cup for Michael because she knew he could neither eat nor drink before serving mass.

"I've got to receive Communion, Mom."

"Well, hurry home. There'll be bacon and eggs."

Usually he was famished and thirsty on mornings before mass, but the excitement of the storm was driving him now. He took his mackinaw from the closet beside the front door.

"Wear a hat, lad," she said.

"This has a hood, Mom," he said, "and it's real warm. Don't worry."

She took the starched surplice from the clothesline and covered it with butcher paper, closing the wrapping with Scotch tape. Then she kissed him on the cheek as he opened the door to the hall. Halfway down the first flight of stairs, he glanced back, and she was watching him go, her arms folded, her husband smiling from the wall behind her, right next to the dead president of the United States.

I wish she wasn't so sad, he thought.

And then, leaping down the three dark flights of stairs to the street, he braced himself for the storm.

# 2

As the boy stepped out of the vestibule, into what Jack London called the Great White Silence, he felt as if his eyes had been scoured. Down here, in those first moments on the open street, the snow wasn't even white; here in its whirling center the storm was as gray as the crystal core of a block of ice. Or the dead eyes of Blind Pew in *Treasure Island.* Michael blinked again and again, his eyelids moving without his command, as the tears welled up from the cold. He rubbed his eyes to focus and felt cold tears on his cheeks. He rubbed until at last he could see. The only thing moving was the snow, driven wildly by the wind.

He plunged his hands into the mackinaw's pockets. And his gloves were not there. Goddamn. He remembered leaving them to dry beside the kerosene stove in the living room. Wool gloves, with a hole in the right forefinger. Thinking: I should go upstairs and get them. No. I can't take the time. I'll be late. Can't be late. And wishing he had a watch. I'll just keep my hands in my pockets. If they freeze, I'll offer it up.

Then he started to walk, the wrapped surplice under his right arm, hands in his coat pockets. In this block of Ellison Avenue he was sheltered in part by the four-story buildings, and he stepped lumpily through the drifts piled against the tenements, wishing he had snowshoes. As he squinted tightly and saw better, a phrase that he had memorized from Jack London rose in his mind — *sole speck of life journeying across the ghostly wastes of a dead world* — and he tingled with excitement. These were ghostly wastes. This was a dead world. He was the sole speck of life.

The fallen snow was up over the tops of parked cars. It covered the newsstand outside Slowacki's candy store, which for the first time in memory was dark. All the other shops on the block were dark too, their doorways piled with snow. There wasn't even a light in Casement's Bar across the street, where Alfred the porter usually mopped floors before the start of business. Michael could see no sign of a trolley car, no traffic, no footprints in the snow. Somewhere, the wolves howled. Perhaps, up ahead, he would find the Malemute Kid.

Or Sitka Charlie. He would build a fire on the frozen shores of Lake Lebarge. Up ahead were the wild bars of Dawson. And the Chilkoot Pass. And the lost trail to All Gold Canyon. Here on Ellison Avenue, Michael Devlin felt like so many of the men in those stories: the only person on earth.

He was not, however, afraid. He had been an altar boy for three years, and the route to Sacred Heart was as familiar as the path through the flat he'd just left behind. Wolves howl, the wind blows, there is no sky. But there is no danger here, he thought. Here I am safe.

Then he stepped past Pete's Diner on the corner of Collins Street and the wind took him. No simple wind. A fierce, howling wind, ripping up the street from the harbor, a wind angry at the earth, raging at its huge trees and proud houses and puny people. The wind lifted the boy and then dropped him hard and tumbled him, whipping him across the icy avenue. Gripping the surplice with one hand, Michael grabbed with the other for something, anything, and found only ice-crusted snow.

He rolled until he was thumped against the orange post of a fire alarm box.

"Holy God," he said out loud. "Holy God."

He gasped for breath, sucking in darts of snow, his nose clogged with ice. But if he was hurt, he was too cold to know what part of him was broken. Still holding the surplice, he skittered on hands and knees and braced his back against the leeward side of the fire alarm box and huddled low, where the wind wasn't so strong. No pain. Nothing broken. He looked around, keeping his head down, and realized he'd been blown across all six lanes of Ellison Avenue. He saw the heavy neon sign above the entrance of Unbeatable Joe's bar dangling from a wire, tossing and shaking in the wind, then crunching against the side of the building. But he couldn't see very far down Collins Street, not even as far as home plate on the stickball court. Everything was white and wild. Then he saw that his mackinaw was coated with snow, and he remembered how characters in those Yukon tales always froze to death if they remained still, or if they fell asleep. They huddled with dogs, they held tight to wolves; anything for warmth. Or they rose and walked. I have to get up, he thought. If I don't, I will goddamn well die. Michael shoved the surplice under his mackinaw, stuffing it into his belt. Then, crouching low, he began to run.

He ran into the wind, and made it across

Collins Street, grabbing for the picket fence outside the factory of the Universal Lighting Company. The building rose above him like an ice mountain from the Klondike, one of those treacherous peaks that killed men in winter and drowned them in spring, washing their bodies into the Yukon River. The black iron pickets were so cold they seemed to burn his bare hands, and he was afraid the skin would be torn off his palms. But his skin held, and he pulled himself along until he was free of the hammering force of the wind.

At Corrigan Street he repeated the process: head down, crouched, falling once, then up again, until he reached the shops untouched by the wind. Away off, about three blocks, he could see the ghostly shape of a trolley car. Its lights were on but it wasn't moving. High above the avenue, the cables that gave the trolleys their power were quivering like bowstrings. Michael paused under the shuddering marquee of the Venus, gazing at the showcards offering *The Four Feathers* and *Gunga Din*. He'd seen both at least three times and tried to conjure warm images of India or the vast deserts of Africa, with Fuzzy Wuzzies charging in the dust and British soldiers sweating in the heat. The images only made him feel colder. And for the first time, he was afraid.

I have to go now, he thought. I have to turn this corner and go up Kelly Street, past the armory, past the Jewish synagogue, have to cross MacArthur Avenue, have to turn right at the park. I have to do this now. With the wind at my back. I must go. Not just to serve mass. No. For a bigger reason. If I turn around and go home, I'll be a goddamned coward. Nobody will see me turn and run for home. But I'll know.

He turned the corner into Kelly Street. There were three-story houses to his left, the humped shapes of parked cars to his right, and around him and under him and above him he heard a high, thin, piercing whine, the savage, wordless wolf call of the wind: penetrating him, lifting him and dropping him, driving him past the soaring drifts that concealed buried cars. The whine was insistent and remorseless. Who are *you*, Michael Devlin, the voice said, to challenge *me?*

Then he looked up and his way was blocked. A giant elm had been smashed to the ground from the front yard of one of the houses. As the tree fell before the wind, it had crushed the fence of the house and collapsed the roof of a parked car, and it was now stretched out to the far side of the street. The branches of the tree seemed to reach toward the white sky in protest. Snow gathered on the dying trunk. The windows of the crushed car had exploded, and snow was drifting onto its seats. The boy thought: If the tree had hit me instead of the car, I'd be dead.

Holy God.

He pushed through loose waist-deep snow between two parked cars and crossed the street, skirting the murdered tree, until he reached the side of the armory. This was no refuge. Behind its barred windows, the armory housed a boxing ring and dozens of old jeeps and National Guardsmen called "weekend warriors." But its sheer redbrick walls rose a forbidding six stories above the street, and no doorways offered shelter. The boy saw now that the armory's copper drainpipes had burst. High above the ground, shoving their way from the ruptured seams of the drainpipes, giant icicles stabbed at the air, defying the wind. They were thick, muscular icicles, a foot wide at the root, sharp as spears at the tip. Michael Devlin remembered photographs in the encyclopedia of stalactites, gray and dead; these icicles looked just as primitive and ancient and evil. And all of them were aimed at him.

He turned his eyes away from the icicles

and trudged on, wishing again that he had a wristwatch. Seems like hours since I left the house, he thought, but maybe it's only been minutes. I don't really know, and the storm doesn't care anything about time. He thought: Maybe this is crazy. What if the church is closed too? What if Father Heaney took one look at the storm and decided to celebrate mass alone in the rectory? What if the electricity has failed and the altar is dark? And suppose another tree falls, or a monster icicle, and hits me? Without warning. Nobody to shout: Watch it, kid. It would just happen. And I'd be left here in the drifts, without a dog or a friend or a scout from the mining camp. My mother would have to bury me and she'd be left completely alone. Or I'd end up crippled, a drag on her and everyone else. In one of the Jack London stories, a prospector broke his leg in a storm and his best friend was forced to obey the wisdom of the trail by shooting him in the head. Otherwise both of them would die.

Then, moving over a piled ridge, Michael imagined his father in the snows of Belgium. Many Americans had been killed there by the Germans in what was called the Battle of the Bulge. Thousands of them. He saw his father in full uniform, with a helmet and heavy boots, carrying a gun, and the snow driving even harder than this Brooklyn blizzard, and the wind whining, with the goddamned Germans somewhere up ahead in the blinding storm: as close, maybe, as MacArthur Avenue, as near as the synagogue. Unseen. Hidden. Ready to kill. Did Tommy Devlin think about turning around and running home? Of course not. He wasn't a goddamned coward. But did he have a friend with him? Or was he alone when he was shot, his blood oozing red into the white snow? Had he lost all feeling in his hands and feet before they killed him? Did he cry? Did he hear wolves? Did he think of Mom? Home in the top-floor flat on Ellison Avenue? His blue suit? Did he think of me?

Suddenly, Michael Devlin heard a voice.

A human voice.

Not the wind, but the first real voice he'd heard since he left home.

He stopped and gazed around at the deserted world.

And then, through the slanting sheets of icy snow, he saw a man peering from a door on the Kelly Street side of the synagogue. A man with a beard. And a black suit. Like the man in black who called to Billy Batson from the dark entrance to the subway. He was waving at Michael.

"Hallo, hallo," the bearded man called, his voice seeming to cross a distance much wider than the street. "Hallo." As if coming from another country.

Michael stood there. The man was beckoning to him.

"Hallo, please," the man shouted. "Please to come over . . ."

The voice sounded very old, muffled by the falling snow. A voice as plain and direct as a spell. Michael still didn't move. This was the *synagogue*, the mysterious building in which the Jews worshiped their God. Michael had passed it hundreds of times, but except for Saturday morning, the doors were almost always closed. In some ways, it didn't seem to be part of the parish, in the way that Sacred Heart was part of the parish, and the Venus, and Casement's Bar. The synagogue rose about three stories off Kelly Street, but Michael always felt that one dark midnight, it had been dropped on the corner from somewhere else.

That wasn't all. To Michael there was something vaguely spooky about the synagogue, as if secret rites, maybe even terrible crimes, took place behind its locked doors. After all, didn't everybody on Ellison Avenue say that the Jews had killed Jesus? And if they could kill the Son of God, what might they do to a mere kid in the middle of a blizzard in Brooklyn? Michael had a sudden image of the bearded man tying him up, then heaving him into an oven, or bricking him up behind a wall, like the guy in "The Cask of Amontillado." He saw a headline in the *Daily News*: BOY VANISHES IN STORM. And started to walk on.

The bearded man called to him again. "Please."

Michael stopped. There was a note in the man's voice as he said the simple word *please*. The sound of distress. As if a life could depend upon what Michael did next. There was pain in the word too. And sadness. Maybe the bearded man was just that: a bearded man, calling for help in a blizzard. Not some agent of the devil. They were like two men in the trackless Arctic, specks in the ghostly wastes of a dead world.

If I walk away, Michael thought, it will be for one reason: I'm afraid. The Malemute Kid wouldn't walk away. Neither would Billy Batson. Shit, if Billy Batson had walked away from the man in the black suit he would never have become Captain Marvel. And my father, Tommy Devlin, he would *never* walk away. Not from a thousand god-damned Nazis. And definitely not from a man who said *please* in that voice.

The boy crossed the street, struggling again for balance, found the wall of the synagogue in the twisting snow, and inched his way to the side door. The bearded man's face was clearer now. Under his heavy black hat, he had blue eyes behind thick horn-rimmed glasses. His small nose made his beard seem larger, more solid, as if it were carved from wood instead of made of hair. The beard was dark, with touches of rusty red and gray, but the boy could not tell how old the man was. He was standing just inside the door, a heavy dark tweed coat hanging loose over his shoulders. Everything else he wore was black.

"Please," he said. "I am the rabbi. I need a help. Can you give me a help?"

Tense with fear, Michael stepped closer. The wind abruptly died, as if pausing for breath. The boy stared at the bearded man, noticing his dirty fingernails, the ragged cuffs of the tweed coat, and wondered again if dark secrets lay behind him in the synagogue.

"Well, you see, Rabbi, I —"

"One minute, it takes," the rabbi said.

Michael fumbled for words, trembling with fear, curiosity, and the cold.

"I'm an altar boy up at Sacred Heart,"

he said. "You know, a Catholic? And I'm late for the eight o'clock mass and —"

"Not even one minute," the rabbi said. *"Bitte."* He pulled the coat tighter. "Please."

Michael glanced past him into the unlighted vestibule. Wood paneling rose about five feet from the floor, topped by a ridge. The rest of the wall was painted a cream color. He could see nothing else in the gloom. What if he's Svengali, he thought, the bearded guy in the movie who could hypnotize people? Or like Fagin in *Oliver Twist,* who made the kids steal for him? No: his voice doesn't sound like those bastards. The wind suddenly attacked again, like a signal of urgency. Besides, the boy thought, I can always push him down the steps. I can knock off his glasses. I can kick the door open. Or kick him in the balls. One false move. *Boom!* Knowing that he was talking to himself to kill his fear.

"Okay," Michael said abruptly. "But it's gotta be fast. What do you want me to do?"

The bearded man opened the door wide and Michael stepped in, suddenly warmer as he left the wind behind. There were three steps leading down. The boy stood uneasily on the top step.

"A little light, is good, yes?" the rabbi

said, waving a hand around the dark vestibule.

"I guess."

"There," the rabbi said. "You see?"

Michael moved down a step and peered through the dimness toward the wall to the right. A switch was cut into dark wood paneling. The rabbi gestured nervously, as if flicking the switch, but he did not touch it.

"You mean turn it on?" Michael asked.

The rabbi nodded. "Is . . . uh . . . it's dark, no?"

Michael was suddenly wary again.

"Why don't *you* turn it on?"

"Is not . . . permitted," the bearded man replied, as if groping for the correct word. "Today is *Shabbos*, you see, and — is simple, no? Just —"

He brushed the air with his hand to show how easy it would be. Michael took a breath, stepped down, and flicked the switch. The space was suddenly brightened by an overhead globe. They were in a small vestibule; three steps up on the far side, there was another door. The creamy ceiling paint was cracked and peeling. The boy exhaled slowly. No bomb had exploded. No steel walls had descended to imprison him. No trapdoor had opened to drop him into a dungeon. The light switch was a light switch. The rabbi smiled, showing uneven yellow teeth, and looked pleased. Michael felt loose and warm.

"Thanks you, thanks you," the rabbi said. "*A dank.* Very good boy, you are. *Du bist zaier gut-hartsik* . . . Very good."

Then he pointed to the ridge along the top of the wood paneling.

"Is for you," he said. "Please to take. For you."

It was a nickel, gleaming dully in the light.

"For you," the rabbi said.

"No, it was nothing, I don't need it. . . ."

"Please."

Michael was anxious again, about the time now and the four blocks he still had to journey through the blizzard. He picked up the nickel and slipped it into the side pocket of his mackinaw.

"Good-bye," the man said. "And thanks you."

"You're welcome, Rabbi."

The boy opened the door and rushed into the storm, feeling taller and stronger and braver.

# 3

Father Heaney looked as if he too wished
he had stayed in bed. His halo of uncombed
gray hair combined with his wild black eyebrows and unshaven chin to create a vision
of distraction and carelessness. Only his eyes
seemed to belong to the man whose war
record made him a hero to Michael and
some of the other altar boys. His slits of eyes
were more hooded than ever, causing Michael to imagine him posing as a Japanese
submarine commander spying for the OSS.
This was not too absurd a possibility; they
had heard from other priests that Father
Heaney had been a chaplain in North Africa
and Sicily and Anzio; he had gone into Germany with General Patton. He had not been
in the Battle of the Bulge, although when
Michael asked him about it, he said, in a
tight-lipped way, that he'd known men who
died there. In his sermons, or in the mornings in the sacristy, Father Heaney never
talked about the war. But Michael was sure

the war hung over him like a dark cloud; after all, less than two years ago, he was giving the last rites to dying soldiers.

To be sure, Father Heaney's silences were not confined to the war. He was silent about most things. In the mornings before mass, he seldom said anything to the altar boys, but on this morning he was more silent than ever. He grunted when he saw Michael arrive breathlessly at ten after eight. He grunted at Michael's apologies. Then he grunted and motioned with his head for the boy to precede him out to the altar.

The priest's style was to say the mass very quickly, like a man announcing a horse race, and the other altar boys always joked that he was in a hurry to get back to his bottle. Michael had never seen him drinking, or even smelled whiskey seeping from his pores, but on this arctic morning, Father Heaney's impatient, hurtling style hadn't changed. He raced through the mass in the cold, empty church while Michael tried valiantly to keep pace. Usually there were two altar boys, but Michael's partner had been defeated by the blizzard, and Michael made all the Latin responses himself. At one point, Father Heaney cut Michael off in midsentence; at another, he completely dropped a long piece of Latin. It was as if even the words of the ancient ritual were more than he wanted to say. Michael moved the heavy leather-bound missal from one side of the altar to the other. He did what he was supposed to do with wine and cruets. As the priest mumbled before the tabernacle, with a plaster statue of the bleeding Christ above him, Michael tried to pray for his father in his Belgian grave and the souls in Purgatory and the starving people in Europe and Japan. But only the impulse rose in his breast; the actual words of prayers did not follow. Father Heaney wouldn't let them, driven as he was to cross the finish line. The priest blessed the great dark space of the church and skipped the sermon, while far above, the steeple of Sacred Heart of Jesus R.C. Church shuddered and creaked under the assault of the wind.

Then Michael remembered the injured tone of the bearded man's voice: that *please.* And he decided that the rabbi had been desperate. That he needed Michael to turn on those lights or he would suffer for the rest of the day. There was raw pain in his voice. Not pain that had to do with the light switch. Some other kind of pain. Coming from that man. That rabbi. That Jew.

Then he heard a phrase: *Domine non sum dignus . . .*

And a whisper from Father Heaney: "Pay attention, boy. We've got two customers."

They had reached the moment when the priest hands out Holy Communion, and somehow, from the vast wind-creaking darkness, two old women in black clothes had made their separate ways to the rail of the altar. Michael quickly lifted the gold dish called the paten and followed Father Heaney to the railing and the kneeling women, wondering: How did they get here? Did they walk through this blizzard that knocked me flat? Did someone drive them in a car? Maybe they *live* here. Mumbling Latin, his left hand holding the gold chalice known as the ciborium, Father Heaney deposited a host upon each outstretched tongue, while Michael held the paten under their chins. This was so that no fragment of the host, which had been transformed into the body of Jesus Christ during the Consecration, would fall upon the polished floor.

The first woman's eyes were wide and glassy, like the eyes of a zombie from a movie. The other closed her eyes tight, as if fearful of gazing too brazenly at the divine white wafer. The second one had a mole on her chin, with white hairs sprouting as if from the eye of a potato. They each took the host the same way: the lips closing over it, but the mouth stretched high and taut to form a closed little fleshy cave. To chew the host, after all, was to chew Jesus. Bowing in piety and gratitude, they rose and went back to the dark pews to pray until the host softened and they could swallow.

Then Michael knelt on the altar, and Father Heaney placed a host on his tongue too. Michael squinted but didn't shut his eyes. He saw that the priest's thick fingers were yellow from cigarettes. And he remembered the rabbi's dirty fingernails. And thought: Maybe the pipes in the synagogue have frozen and burst, like the drains at the armory, and there isn't any water. Maybe he's not permitted to wash his hands. Like he wasn't permitted to turn on the lights. But helping the man had to be what the catechism listed as a corporal work of mercy, right? Even if he was a rabbi. A Jew. That still must count. You were supposed to help the needy. The poor. The sick. The man looked poor, didn't he? And he needed someone to turn on the lights. For some mysterious reason. *Is not permitted.* . . . The mystery of the brief moment in the synagogue grew larger as Michael swallowed his own softened host. The rabbi wasn't Svengali. He wasn't Fagin. But he was strange and mysterious, like someone from a book, a bearded guardian of secrets. And Michael thought: I want to find out those secrets.

Finally the mass ended. Father Heaney muttered *Ite, missa est,* and Michael answered *Deo gratias,* and the priest strode off the altar, with Michael behind him. In the sacristy, with its marble counter and ceramic sink, Father Heaney began removing his garments: the chasuble and stole, the maniple and cincture, the amice and alb. Under all of these, the priest was wearing a tan turtleneck sweater and black trousers. His black shoes were stained from dried rock salt. He sighed, took a pack of Camels from his trouser pocket, and struck a wooden match on the sole of his shoe to light up. He inhaled deeply. The smell of the cigarette filled the air.

"Thanks, young man," he said, his eyes moving under the hooded lids. "And, hey: How in the hell did you make it here this morning, anyway?"

"I walked, Father."

The priest inhaled deeply, then made a perfect **O** with the exhaled smoke.

"You walked, huh? How many blocks?"

"Eight."

"No wonder you were late," he said, his black eyebrows rising. "Well, you can offer it up to the souls in Purgatory."

"I did, Father. During the prayers."

"I hope you included me," the priest said, without smiling. And then grabbed his army overcoat and walked out to cross the snow-packed yard to the rectory.

Michael's duties were not finished. This was the last mass of the day, and so he went back to the altar to extinguish the two candles with a long-handled device the altar boys had named the "holy snuffer." The old women were gone. They seemed to have ascended into the darkness like the waxy smoke from the candles after he capped them with the brass bell at the end of the snuffer. For a moment, staring into the darkness, he imagined the rafters full of smoky old women with hair sprouting from their chins. Hundreds of them. Thousands. Whispering in Italian and Polish and Latin about dead husbands and dead children. Like angels grown old but not allowed to die. He could smell them: the odor of candles.

Quickly, Michael came down off the altar, genuflected, and returned to the empty sacristy. He pulled the surplice over his head, hung the cassock in the closet, and changed into his street clothes. Before leaving, he flipped the switches of the altar lights, peer-

40

ing out to be sure he had turned them all off. Then, from the dark upper reaches of the church, he could hear the moaning of the wind. And through the wind, a voice.

*Please,* it said.

*Please to help.*

# 4

That afternoon in the howling white world, while his mother worked her shift as a nurse's aide at Wesleyan Hospital, Michael Devlin was alone in the living room of the flat, lying on the linoleum floor beside the kerosene heater. A pillow was folded under his head. His stack of *Captain Marvel*s was beside him. After mass and the promised bacon and eggs and his mother's departure, he had searched for the issue that told the story of Billy Batson's first encounter with Shazam. Or rather, he'd found the retelling of the story, because he didn't own the precious first issue of Whiz Comics, the one published long ago, near the beginning of the war. In the retelling, for a special issue of Captain Marvel's own book, the man in the black suit was there with his hat pulled down to mask his face. But except for the black clothes, he didn't resemble the rabbi from Kelly Street, and neither did the wizard Shazam. The wizard was much older, with a white beard instead of a dark one, dressed in a long, flowing robe. The rabbi was younger, heavier, and with his blue eyes and horn-rimmed glasses looked more like a schoolteacher from the Wild West than an Egyptian wizard. Somebody who could have taught Abraham Lincoln.

After a while, Michael put aside the *Captain Marvel*s and started reading a comic book named *Crime Does Not Pay*, all about the terrible killer Alvin Karpis and his bloody career and bloodier end. This comic made Michael feel very different from the way he felt reading *Captain Marvel*. *Captain Marvel* was about magic words and mad scientists and tigers that talked, about bullets that bounced off chests and a hero with a gold-trimmed cape who could fly through the air. But the crime comic was full of real gangsters in real cities. No capes. No magic words. Just robbing and shooting and dying. Bullets didn't bounce off chests, they went through them; and nobody went flying through the air, high above the skyscrapers. The crime comics were about men who were once good kids in places like Brooklyn and came to bad ends. Like the men from Murder Incorporated, Lepke something and Gurrah. Pretty Boy Floyd. Dillinger. They died in ambushes. They died outside movie houses. They even died in the snow, like Tommy Devlin died in Belgium, but without being heroes. They didn't ever die for their country. They died for money. Or women.

Partway through the story of Alvin Karpis, Michael realized that the wind had stopped. He listened hard, fearing some trick from the storm, and then heard shovels scraping against sidewalks and knew that it was over. He wanted to tell his mother the news, but she was working at the hospital. So he dressed, and grabbed his dry gloves, and dashed down the stairs to find his friends.

Sonny Montemarano was already there, testing the snow with big mittened hands. His dark face was shiny, his eyes bright.

"You ever seen anything like this?" he said.

"Never," Michael said. "They got icicles up at the armory that look like rocket ships."

"We couldn't get out my door," Sonny said. "It's frozen shut. We hadda jump out the fucking window."

"This morning, the wind threw me across the street," Michael said. "Like I was a goddamned feather."

"I never seen anything like it. What a fucking storm."

Sonny always said *fuck*. Michael loved

hearing Sonny talk, but he still had trouble using the forbidden word, afraid it would become such a habit that he would say it in front of his mother. He used *goddamned.* None of them said the worst word of all: *motherfucker.* Sonny had tried it one time last summer, but Unbeatable Joe, who ran the saloon on the corner, heard him, grabbed him by the shirt collar, and said, "Don't ever use that fucking word, you hear me? Only *niggers* use that fucking word."

Then Jimmy Kabinsky arrived, with a big wool hat pulled down to his brow. He was a DP, a displaced person, and a figure of much amazement in Sacred Heart School because he'd learned English in three months. Nobody was more amazed than Sonny Montemarano; his grandmother had come from Sicily forty-one years ago and still didn't speak much more than *Sonny, come uppan eat* or *Sonny, you shut up.*

"They got snow like this in Poland?" Sonny asked.

"They got snow in Poland goes up three flights," Jimmy said. They started walking together toward Collins Street.

"You're shittin' me," Sonny Montemarano said. "Three flights? You'd have nothing but dead Polacks, you had that much fucking snow."

"I swear," Jimmy Kabinsky said. "My uncle told me."

"Oh," Sonny said, rolling his eyes at Michael behind Jimmy's back. "Your *uncle*. That makes sense."

Jimmy's uncle was a junkman. He made a living picking up old newspapers, broken bicycle wheels, ruined radios, then piling them into a pushcart and taking them off to some warehouse on the waterfront. During the last year of the war, the kids rode him without mercy. For one thing, his arms were very long, his shoulders sloped, and his body was always pitched forward at an angle, even when the pushcart wasn't dragging him down the hills of the parish. For another, he had no wife and no kids and never went to the bars with the other men. Finally, he was very ugly, or so everyone agreed: his eyes were buried under a clifflike brow, his wide, potato-like nose was always flared in anger, his ears were like a pair of ashtrays, and his teeth were yellow. The kids all called him Frankenstein, except when Jimmy was around. When Jimmy came to live with him, because DPs all needed sponsors, he became Uncle Frankenstein. The kids didn't rag him when Jimmy was around, out of respect for Jimmy, whose parents died in the war.

"How high you think the snow is in Ebbets Field?" Jimmy said.

"Upper deck," Sonny said, winking at Michael. "My grandmother heard it on the radio."

"Upper *deck?*" Jimmy said. "Come on, that's like, what, six flights?"

"Deeper than fucking Poland!" Sonny said, shoving Jimmy into a pile of snow. "And they got the wind out there, blowin' to left field. Swear to Christ."

Soon they were romping in the snow, falling facedown into its whiteness, hurling snowballs at each other and at strangers. Kids emerged from the tenements with sleds, heading for Prospect Park. A trolley car slowly pushed its way along Ellison Avenue. A few cars arrived from nowhere, their tires encased in chains. Then Unbeatable Joe, thick and burly with a fur hat and a heavy army coat, came to look at his saloon, gazing at the sign that was smashed on the sidewalk. He shook his head and kicked the sign. Then he unlocked the door and went inside. He was back in a minute, holding two shovels. He shouted across the street.

"Hey, do you worthless, lazy bums wanna make some money?"

They took turns, two of them shoveling while the other warmed his hands. Michael shoveled around the fallen sign, which was two feet high, three feet wide, about a foot deep. The neon lettering was smashed, the tin sides bent, the steel cables torn; that was some goddamned wind. Then he started cutting a path for pedestrians, pushing loose snow out toward where the gutter was. That was the easy part. But there was a layer of hard-packed icy snow beneath the fine snow that had fallen near the end of the storm. The packed snow wouldn't move.

"Lemme try," Sonny said. He took the shovel from Michael, forced the blade under the packed snow, put a boot on the top of the blade, and shoved hard. The snow peeled back. "Ya see? Ya gotta get *under* it."

"I'll finish it, Sonny," Michael said.

"No, no, I enjoy this." He laughed. "Help Jimmy."

When the job was done, Unbeatable Joe came out again.

"You bums oughtta sign up with Sanitation right now," he said. He took a dollar from his pocket and handed it to Sonny. "Go get laid."

He turned and kicked the sign one more time.

They went past Slowacki's candy store, which was too crowded, and walked another block to Mister G's. In this smaller, darker candy store, Sonny bought a Clark bar, Jimmy chose a bag of peanuts, and Michael picked a box of Good and Plenty. Behind the counter, Mister G was reading the *New York Post*. He was an old man, short and dumpy, with very little hair and sad eyes behind rimless glasses. He was an oddity along Ellison Avenue; it was said, for example, that he was a Giants fan and that his kids had gone off to college. That was strange; Michael had never known anyone but Dodger fans and nobody at all who had gone to college. It was also strange that Mister G read the *Post* in a neighborhood where men swore by the *Journal-American*. And that he lived with his wife in a tiny apartment at the back of the store. It was said of her that she "went to business," which meant she had a job in an office and rose early and went to the subway in a suit or a dress. It also meant that they could afford a regular apartment but were too cheap to move from the back rooms of the candy store.

Mister G said nothing as he rang up the sale on a heavy gilded cash register on a shelf behind the counter. He gave Sonny change from the dollar while flipping a page of the newspaper in a distracted way. Mister

G's silence was not odd, for there was no need for chat. Kids were in and out of the store all day, buying penny candies from the boxes on the counter, or nickel candies from the three-tiered rack. And the store was not only for kids. Grown-ups used the pay phone in the back. Or bought newspapers. And in neat boxes on the right of the counter, Mister G had built displays of cigarettes and ten-cent cigars.

"Man, I hope it snows s'more tonight," Sonny said. "I hope it snows for a *month*. We'd be rich."

He was dividing the change when Frankie McCarthy walked in.

Sonny shoved the change in his pocket and started examining the comics on the standing rack against the wall. *The Spirit. Batman. Jungle Comics.* Michael was suddenly nervous. Frankie McCarthy was one of the older guys, at least seventeen, and the leader of the gang called the Falcons. He scared Michael. He had dark red hair, wet now from the snow, freckles, slushy blue eyes with very small pupils. He kept his lips pulled tight over his mouth to hide a broken front tooth. The summer before, Michael saw him punch out a drunken man on the sidewalk in front of Unbeatable Joe's, battering him until the man's face was a smear of blood. The scene was terrible, but Frankie McCarthy seemed to enjoy it. So did his boys on the Falcons. They all cheered as Frankie walked away from the fallen older man like he was Joe Louis. And he *enjoyed* it. That's what scared Michael.

"Whatta you got in your pocket, kid?" he said to Sonny.

"Nothin', Frankie."

"You're lyin' to me, kid," he said, turning to Michael. "He's lyin', ain't he? I seen yiz shovel the sidewalk in front of Joe's. I seen Joe put somethin' in this guinea's hand." He smiled in a chilly way. "And it set me thinkin'."

Michael turned away from the slush-eyed gaze. Mister G looked up from his newspaper, peering over his glasses.

"What I'm thinkin'," Frankie McCarthy said, "is this. I'm thinkin' you should buy me a soda, kid. And a pack of Luckies too. I'm thinkin' you're a nice, generous kid and would be only too happy to do this for a neighborhood guy just come outta the snow."

Mister G cleared his throat.

"Hey, leave the kid alone," he said in a reasonable voice.

"What?" Frankie McCarthy said. "Wha'd you say?"

"I said leave the kid alone," Mister G said, annoyed now. "Kid broke his ass shovelin' snow, let him keep his money."

"This is none of *your* fuckin' business, pal."

"It's my candy store," Mister G said. "I don't like extortion going on in my store."

"You Jew prick," Frankie McCarthy said, ignoring Sonny and moving to the counter. "How'd you like me to turn this place into a fuckin' parkin' lot?"

Michael moved away, toward the rear of the store, his back to the pay phone. Something bad is about to happen, he thought. I wish I could stop it. I wish I was bigger and stronger. I wish I could step over and grab Frankie McCarthy by the neck and throw him into the goddamned snow. I wish.

Jimmy Kabinsky was near the door now, and Sonny gestured with his head for Michael to follow them out into the snow. Michael started to ease behind Frankie McCarthy.

"Stay right there, kid," he said to Michael, his nostrils flaring. "I wanna show you how to deal with a Jew prick like this."

Mister G slammed the counter. "Don't you dare call me a Jew prick, you . . . you Irish son of a bitch!"

Frankie McCarthy exploded. With one hand he swept the tiered rack of candies off the glass-topped counter. Pivoting, he used the other hand to sweep the cigar boxes onto the floor. Then he stomped on the cigars, his lips curling, the broken tooth showing. He turned and jerked the comic rack off the wall, littering the floor with *Blue Bolt* and *Sheena* and *Captain Marvel*. He kicked at the comic books, driving them into the air. Michael tried to say a word, but it would not come.

Then Frankie saw Mister G lifting a telephone and he leaped for him, grabbed the phone, and smashed the top of the counter, splintering the glass. He wasn't finished. He turned and hammered Mister G with the phone. The eyeglasses dangled from one ear. Blood spurted from the old man's nose, and he held his face in pain, hunching before the next blow. Sonny and Jimmy opened the door and rushed out. The door slammed behind them. Michael didn't move.

"That's how you deal with a Jew prick like this," Frankie McCarthy said, smiling through tight lips.

Then his eyes widened again in a kind of frenzy, and in the tight space behind the counter, he kicked and stomped at the fallen man, who made small whimpering sounds of futile protest while Frankie screamed: "You cocksucker, you Jew cocksucker! You motherfucker!" Then Frankie jerked the ornate cash register from its shelf, grunted as he raised it over his head, and hurled it down on Mister G. The cash drawer sprang open with a jangled sound and change rolled on the wooden floor.

In a calm way, Frankie picked up some bills and change and then turned to Michael.

"You didn't see a fuckin' thing, did you, kid?"

Michael said nothing.

"*Did* you?"

Michael shook his head no. Then Frankie McCarthy smiled and reached over for a pack of Lucky Strikes. He hefted them and went to the door.

"All I wanted from this Jew prick was some cigarettes, for chrissakes."

He went out, leaving the door open to the cold air. For a long, heart-thumping moment, Michael did not move. He wanted Sonny and Jimmy to return, to help him decide what to do. They didn't come back. Slowly, Michael walked around the counter and saw that Mister G was weeping, his face to the wall, wet blood on his hands. The cash register lay on its side on the floor beside the scattered pages of the *New York Post*. Mister G's eyes were shut. The boy touched his elbow.

"Mister G, I'm sorry," he said. "Can I help you? Maybe —"

Mister G moaned, but did not speak. Michael backed away. Then he took the rabbi's nickel from his pocket, went to the pay phone, and dialed the operator for an ambulance.

# 5

That evening, as his mother ladled tomato sauce over two bowls of spaghetti, Michael Devlin tried to explain what had happened in Mister G's candy store. The words spilled out of him. He described what was said, leaving out the curse words, and the way Sonny and Jimmy ran outside, and how Frankie McCarthy wrecked the store and tried to destroy Mister G. She smiled thinly when he told her about calling for an ambulance, but the smile faded when he told her how he ran out of the store, panicky, afraid the police would think he had something to do with hurting Mister G. Jimmy and Sonny had vanished, he said, but Michael stood in the doorway of 378 Ellison Avenue and saw the ambulance coming slowly through the boulders of frozen snow, followed by the first of three police cars. All of them parked far from the doorway of Mister G's candy store because of the huge piles of snow. Men came out of Casement's

Bar to watch, and Michael joined them. They smoked and talked about the way this kind of crap was ruining the parish, and Michael felt safe in their company. The men wouldn't let Frankie McCarthy harm him.

Then he saw Mister G's wife coming along the snow-packed sidewalks from Garibaldi Street, a small, thick woman in overcoat and boots, with a large bag of groceries in her hands; saw her pause a block away, as she squinted at the ambulance; saw her suddenly hurrying, slipping and jerking on the packed snow. And then, as Mister G was carried out on a stretcher, the attendants straining and heaving to lift him over the snowbanks, Michael could hear her scream and saw her run, and the grocery bag fell from her hands and broke open and cans of Campbell's soup and a box of Wheaties and two rolls of toilet paper spilled across the snow.

He told his mother all of that, and she pressed his shoulders to her warm body, then took a small glass from a shelf and poured herself some of the sweet wine she liked, a dark purple wine called Mogen David.

"Holy God," she said. "That poor woman. That poor man."

Michael did not tell her about his own confusion.

On the street and in the schoolyard, he'd heard all the stories about Jews being greedy and sneaky Christ-killers. But when this man, this Jew, poor Mister G, had been beaten so savagely, Michael had felt no elation. If Jews were bad, then Frankie McCarthy should be a hero. But in that candy store, it was Mister G who had spoken up to defend Sonny. And in return Frankie had been as scary and vicious as any gangster, while Sonny ran away. Michael struggled with that confusion. He also couldn't express his own fear, the shameful cowardice that had stopped him from trying to help the old man. He could not get around one awful fact: while Frankie McCarthy was battering Mister G, Michael said and did nothing. Sonny ran; he thought, but I froze. And when it was over, and Mister G lay bleeding, and Frankie had told me to forget what I'd seen, I just nodded my head.

"He's a bad fella, that McCarthy," Michael's mother said. "He comes from bad people and he'll end up in the gutter."

"I think he's a little crazy, Mom."

"He might be," she said. "Stay away from him."

"But why would he *do* it?" the boy asked. "Why would he hurt Mister G so *badly?*"

"Bad people do bad things," she said, curling her spaghetti on a fork, using a large spoon to control it.

"Was it because Mister G is a Jew?"

"I hope not." She paused. "But from what you say, son, it sounds like that was part of it."

She talked about Hitler then, and how he hated Jews so much he killed millions of them. The Nazis were crazy Jew-haters, she said, and before they were finished, millions of other people were dead too. Not just the Jews.

"But *why* did they hate Jews?" Michael said.

"Och, Michael, most of it's plain old jealousy, if you ask me," she said, taking a sip of wine. "They'll give you a lot of malarkey about killing Jesus and all that, but the same idjits don't even go to church. Hitler didn't go to church. Neither does Frankie McCarthy, I'd bet." She paused, picking her words carefully. "The Jews get educated, that's one thing. Maybe that's what makes ignorant people so mad at them. Their kids do their homework. They go to college. A lot of them, their people came here without a word of English and they ended up doctors and lawyers. I wish to God our people would do that."

"I heard Mister G has three sons in college," Michael said. "You know, the ones who work in the store in the summer?"

"There you go," she said. "You'll never hear about any of the McCarthys going to college. They're a worthless lot." She looked at him. "Don't, for God's sake, be like them."

They finished the spaghetti. His mother sipped the last of the wine, then rose, took the plates, and laid them in the sink. In a quick, busy way, she fixed tea, with milk and sugar, and some Social Tea cookies, humming an Irish tune that he didn't know. Michael thought she looked relieved to be finished with the discussion about Jews and what had happened to Mister G and he did not go on with it, even though pieces of the scene in the candy store still scribbled through his mind. When she asked Michael what else his friends were talking about, besides the blizzard, he was relieved too. The subject was all too confusing and scary. He mentioned that the Dodgers were thinking about bringing up a minor league player named Jackie Robinson, who was colored. But everybody down on the avenue said he could never make it in the major leagues.

"They say colored players aren't as good as white players," the boy said. "They don't work as hard, or something."

His mother knew little about baseball; she glanced at the photograph of Private Tommy Devlin as if wishing he were there to talk to Michael.

"Well, they wouldn't be giving him a chance," she said, "if he didn't work hard to get it." She sipped her tea and restrained him from dunking his biscuit into his own cup. "You can be sure he wasn't standing on some street corner, making remarks, when they signed him up."

They did the dishes together, her face very tired. As Michael dried the plates and glasses, and stacked them in the cabinet, she walked slowly into the living room. For weeks, she had been reading a fat book by a writer named A. J. Cronin, and when Michael was finished with the dishes he followed her into the living room. She was sitting in a large gray armchair with a standing lamp beside it, lost in the book. The kerosene heater made the room feel hot and close. The windows were opaque and filmy. Michael drew faces in the steam with his fingers and stared down at the snow-packed streets and wished she would tell him some Irish stories, the way she did when he was small.

Those stories were even better than the comics, better than the books at the library on Garibaldi Street. Magical tales of Finn MacCool, the great Irish warrior, who in the midst of some bloody battle had reached down, grabbed at a hill with one mighty hand, and heaved it at his enemy. Finn was so big and powerful and the hunk of earth so gigantic that when it landed in the Irish Sea it became an island, the one now known as the Isle of Man. Or Usheen, his son, who followed a woman with golden hair to the Land of Youth, where he lived for three hundred years, never growing old, until at last he grew homesick for Ireland. He was told that his white horse knew the way home but if he once dismounted, he could never return. Trying to save some poor men who were about to die under the weight of an immense flagstone, he fell from the horse and instantly became a withered, blind old man. It was like that movie he'd seen at the Venus, *Lost Horizon*, where everybody lived in a valley called Shangri-La and stayed young forever but got old if they left.

Or she could tell him again the story of Balor, who had an evil eye so huge that it required eight men to pry it open; when it was open the eye paralyzed every enemy warrior who dared to gaze upon it. If Balor had only been at Mister G's, he could have paralyzed that goddamned Frankie McCarthy. And Finn MacCool could have thrown him to New Jersey. When Michael was five and six and learning to read, his mother told him of giant pots in ancient Ireland where the food was never exhausted, of silver trees with golden apples glistening in the sun, of spells cast by wizards that made men sleep for forty years, of magical swords that always found the enemy's neck, of rainstorms turned into fire by druids and women transformed into mice, mice into warriors. There was a magic cauldron, found in a lake, into which dead warriors could be plunged to emerge alive, though unable to speak. Or she told tales of the great Cú Chulainn, who had seven pupils in each eye and seven fingers on each hand and seven toes on each foot and had the power to move one eye to the back of his head to watch his enemies. Or she told him about the great bull of Cooley that could carry fifty boys upon its back. All of this in Ireland, where she came from, across the foggy seas.

But Kate Devlin was tired now, her shoes off, her feet swollen and sore. He tried to remember whether his mother was there when his father told his stories of Sticky, the magic dog. No. We were in the park. It was summer. On a bench. He saw his mother nod and then snap suddenly awake. She looked at him and smiled.

"Was I asleep a long time?" she asked.

"Maybe ten seconds," he said.

She shook her head.

"I started drifting off," she said. "I thought I was in Ireland."

She looked again at her book.

"Mom?"

"Yes, son?"

"The stories about Ireland," he said. "You know, Finn MacCool and CúChulainn and Balor and all. Are they true?"

"Of course."

"Seriously?"

She chuckled. "Well, when I heard them from my father, God rest his soul, I was told they were true."

"So where did they all go, Finn and Usheen and all of them?"

"I asked just that question," she said, "and my father said they didn't go anywhere, they were still there, hidden, invisible, and when Ireland needed them, they'd be back."

"So why didn't they come when the English invaded?"

"Maybe they didn't want to get their hands dirty," she said, and laughed.

He was glad to see her happy and left her with her book and retreated to his room. He gazed out the window facing the snowy fire escape, wondering how Mister G was doing in his hospital room, and where Frankie McCarthy was at that very moment, and whether the rabbi up on Kelly Street knew what had happened in the candy store on Ellison Avenue. He imagined CúChulainn on a mighty horse, a *steed*, as they called them, his eyes all red and his beard like fire, a sword as thick as a door in his belt, coming through the snow on Ellison Avenue to find Frankie McCarthy and punish him.

Then he sat on the floor, with his back to the bed, thinking about the *Captain Marvel*s scattered on the floor of Mister G's candy store, and how, when a real man was being hurt, he could utter no magic words to ward off evil. He started reading *Crime Does Not Pay*, wondering if someday they'd run a story about Frankie McCarthy. Written by Charles Biro. Drawn by Norman Maurer. The story would start in Brooklyn, and they'd show him stomping a drunk outside Unbeatable Joe's, then hitting Mister G with the telephone, the blood spurting, calling the old man a Jew prick, then towering above the stricken man with the dead weight of the cash register. Then Frankie would graduate into the rackets, and have big cars and sharp clothes, surrounded by dames in New York nightclubs. And then he'd go too far: the cops would chase him down and catch him, and he'd go weeping to the hot seat.

Yeah.

Except they never used the word *prick* in comic books.

Or the word *Jew*, either.

He lay there thinking about this and saw through the window that the snow was falling again, very softly. And he remembered the rabbi, calling to him that morning through the snow and wind. He couldn't believe now that he had been so scared about entering the darkened vestibule of the synagogue and switching on a goddamned light.

Abruptly, Michael got up. He stepped quietly into the living room. His mother was asleep in the chair, the book on her lap, a thumb wedged in the pages where she'd stopped reading.

He went past her to the bookcase where they kept the blue books of the *Wonderland of Knowledge*. This was an encyclopedia his mother bought by sending coupons away to a newspaper, enclosing a dime for each volume. He picked out the volume marked *Jes–Min*, with a drawing of construction workers on the cover, one welding steel beams, the other carrying stones in a basket on his bare back, with pyramids in the distance. He turned to "Jews" and found the entry on page 2080.

*Persecution, hardship, and war have marked the long story of the Jews, a Semitic people who trace their ancestry back to the days of Babylonian and Egyptian civilizations. The 16,000,000 Jews in the world today have retained a racial purity hardly equaled by any other division of man, but their valuable contributions to the world have been of an international character. Greatest of these contributions is in the realm of religion. As the oldest people to believe in one God, the Jews laid the foundation of Christianity and other faiths based on this principle. . . .*

Amazing: first came the Jews, and *then* the Catholics! As he read the text, his excited eyes moved from a statue of Moses, heroic, stern, as muscled as Tarzan, to a picture of a beautiful woman named Judith. The caption told him that Judith entered a city called Bethulia accompanied only by her handmaiden, murdered the Assyrian general, and seized the town. In the picture she was wearing a headband, her long black hair tied in pigtails, and jeweled bracelets on her wrists, along with necklaces and earrings. She was walking proudly, swinging her arms. Behind her on the left was a bearded guy on a horse. Obviously he was behind her because Judith was the boss, the commander. On the right was a bare-shouldered woman in a striped dress, her head downcast under a shawl, carrying a bag. She must be the handmaiden, Michael thought, some kind of a maid, the one who polished Judith's bracelets and necklaces and earrings. There were more horses and a lot of guys with spears, and off in the distance there was the outline of a walled town. Bethulia.

It was like a scene from a movie.

Michael could see it now, in Technicolor, on the screen at the Venus. Hedy Lamarr slips into the town. She and the maid walk around, the general sees her, he looks at her in that certain way they have in the movies and he tells the maid to wait outside. The general takes her to his room. He's telling her stuff and offers her wine, and as he lifts his own goblet to drink, taking his eyes off her, *Hedy Lamarr cuts his goddamned throat!*

The movie scene vanished. Michael read

on, all about how God gave Moses the Ten Commandments, thus setting up the laws we were supposed to live by, most of them the same ones he had to memorize from the Baltimore Catechism. There was nothing about turning on light switches. And none of what he was reading was like the stuff he heard on the streets. There was no mention of the Jews killing Jesus. There was nothing about Jews being greedy and sneaky and vengeful. Were the people who wrote the encyclopedia *hiding* something?

The story in the blue book did say that the Jews, who were nomads, also set up laws about health and cleanliness. And they gave the world the Bible and the first alphabet. The goddamned *alphabet!* And music too!

*The music of the Jews also has come down to modern times as a special contribution to art. It is a unique form of music — full of pathos and melancholy melody, yet beautiful and tender.*

Michael realized he'd never heard Jewish music. He knew Catholic music, like "Tantum Ergo" and "Mother Dear, O Pray for Me." He knew all the words, in English and Latin. And he had come to love jazz music, listening to it on the radio, wishing he could play some instrument. A piano. Or a trumpet. But Jewish music . . . what did it sound like? He read the words again — *full of pathos and melancholy melody, yet beautiful and tender* — and thought it must sound like the blues.

He glanced out at the falling snow, saw the blurred red neon sign of Casement's Bar, and again felt a sudden darkness in his mind. What if the encyclopedia was lying? Maybe this was a terrible trick. Maybe a Jew wrote the story in the book. Or paid someone to write it the way the Jews wanted it to appear. To fool the Christians, make them let down their guard. That's what they'd say down on Ellison Avenue. That's probably what they'd say if he took the blue book across the street to Casement's and said: What do think of *this,* pal?

But that couldn't be. This was an *encyclopedia;* if it was full of lies, someone would write to a newspaper or the mayor or some other big shot; they'd expose the lies. If they were lies. Maybe the stuff he heard on the street was the real lie. He would have to ask his mother about it. Or Father Heaney. Father Heaney was tough, but he wasn't mean. He didn't say much, but shit, neither did Gary Cooper. Father Heaney would tell Michael the truth. The boy didn't completely trust what he heard on the street. The grown-ups knew a lot more than he did about most things. But he also knew that some of what they had to say was what they all called bullshit. Until he died, they talked lots of bullshit about President Roosevelt. They were talking bullshit now about Jackie Robinson. Maybe they were also talking bullshit about the Jews.

He turned from the falling snow and resumed reading through the entry, his eyes glazing over the details, seeing words like *Talmud* and *Torah*, and a long history of dates going all the way back to 722 B.C., about things that were done to the Jews and how, in spite of everything, they continued to survive. He wanted to find out more about Judith, but there was nothing else. Down near the bottom, his eyes widened.

*Today persecutions and oppressive measures are still carried on in some European nations. In Germany the dictatorship of Adolf Hitler has deprived Jews of political and civil rights which they previously enjoyed. The result has been a gradually increasing exodus of Jews from Germany. Poland, where oppressive measures have existed for many years, has more than 3,000,000 Jews. . . .*

Hitler was now dead, so this must have been written before the war. He looked at the small type in the front of the book. Copyright . . . 1938? That was almost *nine* goddamned years ago. So even then, long ago, before the war, in *1938,* when Michael was three years old, people knew what Hitler was doing. And what he was going to do. His mother was right: Hitler hated Jews and killed millions of them. But if people knew, why didn't anyone stop him from doing it? Why did they wait until it was too late? Better: why didn't some Judith go in and cut his goddamned throat?

*The United States, where religious and political freedom have attracted Jews from all lands where they have been oppressed, has the greatest number of Jews,* the blue book said. *In the forty-eight states and possessions there are 4,229,000, of whom nearly 2,000,000 live in New York City.*

Michael suddenly realized that he knew almost no Jews. There was Mister G, of course, and Mr. Kerniss, the landlord, who was about seventy years old and came around every month to collect the rents from the super. Now there was this rabbi on Kelly Street, but he didn't really know him. He'd *met* him, but he didn't *know* him. He didn't even know his name. Almost everybody else in the parish was Irish, Italian, or Polish, or as some of them said, Micks, Wops, and Polacks. They were Americans, of course. But they described themselves on the basis of where their parents or grand-parents came from. Michael was Irish. Like his mother, who came from Belfast in Northern Ireland. Or his father, who came from Dublin. And Sonny Montemarano was Italian. And Jimmy Kabinsky was a Polack. No matter where their people came from, almost all of them were Catholic. There were a few Protestants around too; they went to the public school and the Protestant church on White Street and played in the street like the others. But they were just plain Americans; their parents never talked about the Old Country; they acted as if they had been in Brooklyn since Indians roamed in Prospect Park.

But there were no Jewish kids at all. Even Mister G's three kids were like phantoms. They didn't hang out in the parish. They didn't play on the streets in summer. They were just blurry faces in the back of the candy store. Michael had never seen any young people going in or out of the syna-gogue on Kelly Street. Not one. On Satur-day mornings, there were only a few old men and women on the sidewalk. How could that be? If there were two million Jews in New York City, where did they live? Where were their kids? Did they play stick-ball? Were they Dodger fans? Did they pitch pennies in the summer and trade comics and read about Captain Marvel? Why weren't more of them around *here?*

He wanted to wake up his mother and ask her all these questions. He wanted to tell her about his discoveries, about the Jewish laws and the health codes and the alphabet. He wanted to ask her why all those Jews had been killed by Hitler if *even before the war* everybody knew what he was up to. He wanted to ask her if she'd ever heard Jewish music and where those two million Jews lived in the city of New York.

But she looked exhausted, tired from the long hike through the snow to the hospital and the harder walk back, when the snow was deeper. Her jaw hung slack, her mouth open. He touched her forearm. Her eyes opened.

"Mom," he said, "you better go to bed."

She looked startled. "What time is it?"

"It's late," he said. "Go to bed."

In his own room, with the door closed, his teeth brushed, warm under the covers, Michael lay awake. The walls glowed brightly from the freshly falling snow. There was no wind and no sounds as the snow fell all over the parish. In the back room of the candy store, while the snow piled up on the sidewalk, Mister G's wife was probably weeping. Her husband had been taken away in an ambulance, unconscious, his face a swollen, bloody mess. Everybody saw the ambulance and the police cars and nobody said anything. At the synagogue on Kelly Street, the snow was gathering on the doors and the front steps and the roof, while the bearded man with the sad eyes listened, Michael was sure, to Jewish music, beautiful and tender.

The rabbi was from over there. Somewhere in Europe. Michael knew that from the accent. He wasn't from here. But how did he escape? The newspapers said that maybe six million Jews were killed. Why wasn't he one of them? Was he from Poland too? Did the Nazis come to his door? Did he hide in an attic or a closet? Did he pick up a gun and fight? The rabbi had to have a story, and Michael wondered what it was.

Just before sleep came, he thought about what it would be like to meet Judith, with her bracelets and earrings and jeweled hair, and touch her golden skin. Then he pushed her from his mind too, as an occasion of sin, whispering the words of the Hail Mary to keep himself pure as a snowy hill in Prospect Park.

# 6

In the morning, after mass, Sonny and Jimmy rang the bell and Michael bounded downstairs to meet them. Sonny embraced him in the hallway.

"We didn't leave you flat, Michael," Sonny said. "That fuck Frankie McCarthy was all over the place with his boys, the fuckin' Falcons, so we had to hide out."

"We stayed up the house," Jimmy said. "Listenin' to the radio."

"That's what I figured," Michael said, wanting anxiously to believe that he had not been abandoned in Mister G's store. He didn't tell them how he'd felt, and didn't mention to them that he had called the ambulance. That was yesterday; today was today. They started to walk toward the park. The air felt cold and clean. Michael thought that the snowbanks were like mountain ridges now, and they began to name the tall piles on the corners, shoved into peaks by the city snowplows. Mount

Collins. Mount MacArthur.

"Fuckin' mountains will last 'til summer," Sonny said. They laughed, and watched smaller kids burrowing like miners into the sides of the snow hills. It was hard for Michael to imagine these streets sticky with summer.

They walked into the park, following the kids lugging sleds and others draped with ice skates. At a food stand beside the zoo, Sonny bought a hot chocolate and shared it with Jimmy and Michael. The only animals in sight were the polar bears, and Michael thought they looked happier than he'd ever seen them.

"How do you figure Mister G is feelin'?" Sonny said at last.

"How could he feel?" Michael asked. "Frankie hit him with the goddamned cash register."

Sonny shook his head and looked off at the snowy forest beyond the zoo. "I know how I feel," he said. "I feel fuckin' awful. The guy was stickin' up f' *me*, remember?"

Michael remembered.

"It's over," he said.

"Like hell it is," Sonny said.

For the next two days, Mister G's candy store remained closed. At all hours, Michael and his friends saw detectives moving around the snow-packed streets of the parish in an unmarked police car. These were the cops they called Abbott and Costello, because one was tall and thin and the other short and fat, like the movie comedians. They were not comedians. Most of the kids had heard what they did to bad guys in the third-floor squad room at the precinct house on McGuire Avenue and didn't want such things to happen to them.

Around noon on the second day, Abbott and Costello stopped in front of Unbeatable Joe's and went in together and drank beer at the bar for a while and then left. Costello did the driving. Then they pulled up in front of the Star Pool Room, across the street from the Venus, and hurried in. They came out talking to each other, shaking their heads. Costello waddled into the Venus, while Abbott waited outside in the snow, his right hand inside his gray overcoat. Michael saw him spit into a snowbank. Then Costello came out of the Venus and they got in the car and drove away.

"They're lookin' for Frankie," said Sonny. "For beating the shit outta Mister G."

The boys were standing in the doorway of the variety store next to Slowacki's candy store, stamping their feet to keep warm.

"I saw them go up his house too," Jimmy said.

"I hope they get him," Michael said. "I hope they put him in the goddamned can."

"What?" Sonny said. "You hope they *get* him?"

"What he did to Mister G was rotten," Michael said. "*He's* the prick. He's a coward, Sonny, a goddamned jerkoff, beating up an old man like that. Besides, he was defending *you.*"

Sonny paused. "Yeah," he said, "but you better not say nothing. You don't want to end up with the mark of the squealer."

"What's that?" Jimmy asked. Little puffs of steam issued from their mouths when they talked.

"They take a knife and they dig in the point *here*," Sonny said, twisting his forefinger into his cheek at the hinge of his jaw. "They make a hole, see? And then" — he pulled the finger down his cheek to the corner of his mouth — "then they cut it all the way down to your mouth. So everybody knows you got a big mouth. They know that for the rest of your fucking life."

"Jesus," Jimmy said.

Michael shuddered.

"It's real bad," Sonny said. "Very bad. The mark of the squealer."

"Still . . . ," Michael said.

"The bulls come askin' you questions, Michael, you didn't see nothing," Sonny said. "That's it. For you. For all three of us."

Michael remembered what Frankie McCarthy had said as he was leaving with his pack of Lucky Strikes. You didn't see nothing. One of the rules.

"Okay," Michael said. "But what happens to Frankie?"

"Nothing, probably."

"That's not right, Sonny."

"No, but that's the way it is."

"You mean, he can just do that and not get punished? He beat the crap out of an old man. He *could*'ve beat the crap out of *us*. So who punishes him?"

"I don't know. God, maybe."

Jimmy Kabinsky smiled. "My uncle said Mister G got what he deserved."

"What do you mean?" Michael asked.

"He's a Hebe," Jimmy said. "My uncle says back in the Old Country they would have killed him."

"For what?" Sonny said. "Resisting assault?"

"No, just, you know, in general."

"Your uncle is a goddamned jerk," Michael said.

"What do you mean, a jerk? He's —"

"Hey, come on, knock it off," Sonny said. "What do we gotta have an argument over Jews for? Jesus Christ."

"My uncle says the Jews killed Jesus and they gotta pay."

"Jesus was killed, what? Five thousand fuckin' years ago?" Sonny said. "I guarantee you Mister G wasn't there that day."

"Yeah, but —"

"No buts, Jimmy. Look, I don't like Jews any more than the next guy. But it don't make no fuckin' sense to beat the shit out of Mister G because of something he had nothing to do with."

"Right," Michael said. "It wasn't about Jesus. It was about *us*."

"Well . . ."

"Come on," Sonny said, "let's go shovelin'."

They wandered along the snowy ridges and icy hills of Ellison Avenue, repeating jokes they'd heard at school before the Christmas break, discussing the possibility that if it snowed at least one more time they'd never go back to school, arguing about who invented the telephone and wishing they had one, and stopping in shops, where they offered to shovel snow. The shopkeepers had their own shovels, and some of them had kids who were doing the work. But they earned sixty cents anyway and then went to Slowacki's and sat at the counter and ordered three hot chocolates.

"You know, I gotta confess something," Michael said.

"*You* beat up Mister G," Sonny said, laughing.

"No," Michael said. "Something else."

He told them about his visit to the synagogue on Kelly Street and how the rabbi appeared in the blizzard and called him over and asked him to turn on the lights. He couldn't exactly describe the sound of the man's voice, or admit to his fear when he stepped into the vestibule. But he did say that he thought the rabbi was a pretty good person.

"That's *it*, that's why you got so pissed off before," Jimmy said. "You're in with them."

"All I did was turn on the goddamned lights," Michael said, sipping the thick, sweet cocoa. Mrs. Slowacki was busy with other customers; with Mister G's closed, she was busier than ever, selling candy to kids and cigarettes to men.

"That's how they get you," Jimmy said.

"What, to trick me and drop me through a trapdoor? Jimmy, here I am, alive."

"How do you know he didn't hypnotize you?"

Then Sonny put up his hands, palms out.

"Wait a minute, wait a minute," he said, halting the argument. "This could be good."

Michael turned to him.

"What do you mean?"

"The treasure."

"What treasure?"

"Don't tell me you never heard of the treasure, Michael. Everybody knows about it."

"I never heard of no treasure," Jimmy said.

Sonny lowered his voice and leaned close to Michael and Jimmy. "All the Jews, they give money and jewels and rubies and gold and shit like that to the rabbis. But these rabbis, they don't put it in banks. They bury it. They hide it. They keep it there, so if one morning they gotta run, they pack it all in a bag and get the fuck out of there."

Michael thought about the rabbi's frayed coat, his dirty hands, the peeling paint in the vestibule.

"They always talk about the treasure up the synagogue on Kelly Street," Sonny went on. "My uncles, my aunt Stephanie, they all heard about it. It's hidden up there. Jewels, diamonds, gold, everything. A long time ago, before the war, my cousin Lefty even busted in there one night with some friends, trying to find it. But the rabbis got it hid pretty good."

He paused, his eyes excited, gazing around to be certain that nobody in the candy store could hear him.

"So?" Michael said.

"So Michael, you got your foot in the door now. Go all the way in. Find the fucking treasure."

Michael's heart tripped.

"You mean, so we could *rob* it?" he whispered.

Sonny turned his head to the side, his eyes drifting toward the rack of comic books and pulp magazines.

"Nah. Not rob it. Take it back is what I'm thinking. It's all money they got from rents and charging too much in stores and shit like that."

"Come on, Sonny," Michael said. "That's just stealing."

"So what if it is? Wouldn't you like to get a house for your mother? Out in Flatbush or someplace? You know, with a yard and a tree and a garage with a car in it? You wouldn't like to say to her, Ma, no more working at the fucking hospital, I made a score?"

"She'd laugh at me. Or she'd call the goddamned cops."

"That's bullshit and you know it, Michael," Sonny said. "Money is money. You make up a good lie and she'd take it. Nobody calls the cops on their own kid."

"You don't want your share," Jimmy Kabinsky said, "you give it to me. My uncle wouldn't call the cops."

"I saw the rabbi," Michael said. "He's poor. His clothes are raggedy. The tops of his shoes look like burnt goddamned bacon. He has a treasure in there, why doesn't he buy a coat?"

"Maybe he don't even know the treasure is there," Sonny said. "He's new, right? You never seen him before, right? Maybe the last guy died and never told this guy about the treasure."

"And maybe there's no treasure."

"So find out."

Costello, the fat cop, came in, wheezing as he stood before Mrs. Slowacki and ordered a pack of Pall Malls. The boys stopped talking. The detective gave them a look and walked outside, peeling the cellophane off the cigarette pack. Abbott was sitting in the police car, which was raised on one side on a hummock of frozen snow. He nodded when the fat cop slipped in behind the wheel.

"That tub of shit," Sonny said.

"Big tough guy," Jimmy said.

"So what about it, Michael?" Sonny said.

"I just don't believe the story," Michael said, wishing he'd never told them about his visit to the synagogue.

"You believe in Captain Marvel and you don't believe this?" Sonny said.

"Who says I believe in Captain Marvel?"

"You told me last year maybe it could be true."

"That was last year."

"So this year, go up the fucking synagogue and see what you can find out."

Michael finished his cocoa.

"Let me think about it," he said.

# 7

On New Year's Eve, horns blew and church bells rang and pots were banged on fire escapes, but it wasn't like the year before, the first New Year's after the war. There was too much snow, muffling the sound, and there were too many men and women who had lost their jobs in the war plants. As 1947 arrived, Michael stayed at home. His mother went downstairs to a party in Mrs. Griffin's flat on the second floor, and he was alone when Guy Lombardo played "Auld Lang Syne" on the radio at midnight. He wondered what the words meant. *Auld* was easy: old. But what did *lang* mean? Or *syne?* He couldn't find them in the dictionary and hoped he would remember to ask his mother about them in the morning. He read *The Three Musketeers* in bed, thinking that he and Sonny and Jimmy Kabinsky were like Athos, Porthos, and Aramis, and that they needed one more guy to be D'Artagnan. The title of the book wasn't really accurate because there were actually four musketeers, but in the end, that didn't matter. What mattered was their slogan, their motto: All for one, and one for all. That's the way he and Sonny and Jimmy were. Even when they disagreed on some things, they were together. Friends. Musketeers. Forever. He was thinking about that when he fell asleep.

On the following Saturday, on the last weekend of vacation, Michael was assigned to serve the seven o'clock mass at Sacred Heart. The snow had ended. But cars were still frozen in reefs of black ice, and on Kelly Street the icicles were even more menacing as they aimed their frozen snouts from the burst copper drains of the armory. The giant toppled elm had been shoved to the side by a snowplow, but the smashed fence and the ruined car were still there, encrusted with ice. Michael saw them as he turned past the Venus, shoved along by the hard wind off the harbor.

When he reached the synagogue, the door was closed. He heard no voice saying *please* from the dark interior, and he felt a certain relief. All week long, Sonny had pushed him to go back to the synagogue as a spy. To befriend the rabbi. To locate the secret treasure. In short, to betray the man with the sad voice and the frayed cuffs and the story Michael wanted to know. For a moment, Michael hesitated, thinking he should knock and ask the rabbi if he was needed to turn on the lights. He did not knock. He kept walking, all the way to the church on the hill.

But for the entire mass, as Father Heaney raced through the liturgy, Michael thought about the rabbi. He knew he should be meditating on the Passion of Christ, giving personal meaning to the memorized Latin phrases. But Michael couldn't get the rabbi out of his head. Not only because of the treasure. Maybe there was a treasure and maybe there wasn't, but Michael still could not see himself entering the synagogue at night to carry it away. And besides, if Jews were bad because they were sneaky and treacherous, wouldn't he be just as bad if he was sneaky and treacherous too? For a moment during the offertory, he heard his own voice arguing with Sonny, telling him he couldn't do what Sonny wanted him to do. Sonny, it's wrong. Sonny, we can't even think about doing this because it is just goddamned well wrong. He heard Sonny laugh. He saw Sonny shrug. He heard Sonny remind him that their motto was all for one and one for all.

Then it was time for Communion, and

the old ladies came up from the pews, and some young women too, and two older men, and he held the paten and then imagined the rabbi's face. Maybe he was still sleeping, he thought. After all, last week I served the eight, not the seven, so maybe he'll be waiting for me at ten to eight. But then maybe he's sick. Or maybe he heard about what Frankie McCarthy did to Mister G and he's afraid to open the door. Michael brooded, while Father Heaney deposited the host on various tongues. For a moment, Michael hoped that someone else had come along to switch on the lights, and then felt a stab of jealousy. Nobody else should do that job. I did it last week, I should do it again today.

The Communion ended. Father Heaney rushed to the conclusion, muttering his blunt Latin phrases, while Michael returned his automatic responses. But the boy's mind wasn't on the mass; he was too full of his own hard questions. Why did I keep walking? Was it because I was afraid of being late for mass? Or because I was so cold? Of course not. I was afraid of going in there to case the joint. Of being tempted to find the treasure and then being too weak to resist the temptation. But, hey: what the hell would we do with a treasure anyway? Answer me that, Sonny. Would we take it to Stavenhagen's Pawn Shop and sell it? Bring it to some fence down on Garfield Place? If three kids showed up with diamonds and rubies, the cops would know in two hours. It's a goddamned joke. And another thing, Sonny: The synagogue is a house of God. And the Christians came from the Jews. The same God! And those people wrote the Bible, man. It says so in the encyclopedia. Before Jesus, there were the Jews. They invented the goddamned alphabet, Sonny! It would be like robbing a *church*, Sonny. He could hear Sonny laughing. Worse, he could see Sonny turning away from him, their friendship over.

But maybe there was another reason, he thought. A much simpler reason. Maybe I kept walking because the bearded man was a Jew. Maybe it was as simple as that.

After mass, Michael hung his cassock in a closet, folded his surplice, grabbed his mackinaw, and hurried down the passage connecting the altar boys' room with the priests' sacristy. He wanted to talk to Father Heaney. The eight o'clock mass had already started, and he could hear Father Mulligan out on the altar, saying the mass in his more sedate, high-pitched voice.

Father Heaney had removed his own vestments and was sitting on a folding chair, his feet wide apart, deep in thought and smoking a Camel. He didn't look up when Michael entered the sacristy. The boy eased over and stood in front of him. Father Heaney said nothing.

"Father Heaney?"

The priest looked up. "Yes?"

"Can I ask you a question?"

"Sure, kid."

"Did the Jews kill Jesus?"

The priest looked directly at him now, and Michael noticed that his hooded eyes were red and watery.

"Why are you asking me such a dumb question at this hour of the morning?" he said sharply.

"I, uh, well, some kids say, you know, down on Ellison Avenue, they say that the Jews killed Jesus, and —"

"They're jerks."

"The Jews?"

"No, the idiots you're talking to down on Ellison Avenue."

The priest stood up, pulled a final drag on his Camel, and turned on the water tap in the sink. He held the cigarette under the water and then dropped the drowned butt down the chute used for dead flowers. He cupped some water in his hands, splashed it on his face, then turned off the tap and reached for a towel. He dried his face and rubbed his eyes. Every movement seemed part of a ritual.

"The Romans killed Jesus," Father Heaney said, with disgust in his voice. "They were the big shots in Jerusalem, not the Jews, and they saw Jesus as a threat to their power. Like most politicians. Or better, like racket guys. So they bumped him off. Just like racket guys do it. If your idiot friends on Ellison Avenue could read, they'd know that."

Michael loved the way Father Heaney talked; if Humphrey Bogart were a priest he'd talk about Jesus being bumped off too.

"Besides, Jesus was himself a Jew," Father Heaney said. And then sighed. "Although you'd never know that, the way the world has turned out."

He reached into a closet and grabbed his army overcoat, pulled it on, and walked to the door.

"Find someone else to hang out with, kid," the priest said, and then was gone.

Michael was excited. Father Heaney had confirmed it: the encyclopedia was right. Jesus was a Jew. And if that was true, then everything else in the blue book must be true. About Jews. About other subjects. He glanced through the open door to the altar and saw parishioners assembling for Communion. He went out by the sacristy door into the sanctuary, passing the old ladies with their bowed heads, breathing the air thick with the smell of incense and burning candles. He reached the front door without looking back and then stepped into the street and gulped the clean, cold air of January.

*The Romans killed Jesus!*

As he moved down the icy hill, he remembered pictures of the Romans doing the deed. Men with iron helmets jabbing spears into the side of the crucified Jesus. And other Romans gambling for his robe. In his mind, they resembled Frankie McCarthy. A bunch of nasty pricks.

When he reached the synagogue, Michael went directly to the side door and knocked hard. He waited a moment, and then the rabbi opened the door. When he saw Michael, his face brightened and he smiled. He was dressed in the same frayed tweed overcoat, the black hat clamped on his head, the horn-rimmed eyeglasses dangling on a string from his neck. Behind him, the vestibule was dark.

"Did you find someone?" Michael said. "You know, to turn on the lights?"

The rabbi smiled. "No," he said. "A *Shab-bos goy* I didn't find."

"A what?"

"A *Shabbos goy*. Today is *Shabbos*. In English, the Sabbath." He opened the door wider. "Come in. Please to come in. *Koom arayn, bitte . . .*"

Without being asked, Michael reached to his right and flipped the switch. The ceiling light came on. The rabbi's blue eyes twinkled, and he closed the door on the snows of Kelly Street. "Thanks you," he said. Then he started up the three steps on the far side of the vestibule, gesturing for Michael to follow.

"Come in, please," he said. "Here, is very cold."

For a moment, the old fear rose in the boy. Maybe now the rabbi will spring the trap. Maybe that's why he's smiling. What could be beyond this second door? Why should I trust him? Maybe Father Heaney is wrong, maybe the lies are all true, maybe . . . Michael hesitated for a moment, fighting down the impulse to back away and run home. And heard Sonny, urging him to be a spy.

"A *Shabbos goy* I need in here also," the rabbi said. "To make tea I need a stove and . . ."

His voice trailed off as he opened the door. Michael took a breath and followed him into a boxy, low-ceilinged room that smelled of pickles. Newspapers lay open on a table in the center of the room, with a red pencil beside them and a thick book that looked like a dictionary. There was a sink against the wall to Michael's left. Beside it was a gas stove with a chipped oven door. The rabbi gestured at it, making a twisting gesture with his right hand, until Michael turned on a gas jet under a pot of water.

"Is cold," the rabbi said. "So is better we have now a glass tea. You like tea? Good hot tea on cold day."

"Okay."

"*Gut.*" The word sounded like *goot.*

"Rabbi?"

"Yes?"

"What was that word you said before?" Michael said. "Sobbis?"

The rabbi pondered this, then brightened. "*Shabbos!* The Sabbath, you say. Friday night it starts, and goes all day Saturday. God's day. The day of rest."

"And the other word?"

"*Goy?* Is a word . . . it means a person not a Jew. Like you. Shabbos goy is a person not a Jew who comes on Shabbos to turn on lights or stove or boiler, like that. We can't do it."

"How come?"

The rabbi shrugged. "That's the rules. A Jew like me, he can't work on Shabbos. Is the rule. Some Jews, nine days a week they work. Me, I'm a Jew that I go by the rules. Turning on a light, work. Turning on a stove, work. A letter, writing it is work. And money you can't put a hand on. That's the rules. To honor God."

Michael thought: This is the dumbest goddamned rule I ever heard of.

"So how come I can do it?" he said.

"You are a goy," the rabbi said. "A goy, is okay for him to do this. Not a Jew."

"But it's the same God, right? I mean, I read in a book that Christians came from the Jews. They worship the same God. So if it's the same God, why does he have one law for Jews and another law for the goys?"

"*Goyim.* More than one, goyim."

"Why a different rule for . . . goyim?"

"Good question."

"But what is the answer?"

The rabbi turned away, to see if the water was boiling.

"This I don't know," the rabbi said. "Some questions, we got no answers."

The rabbi gestured again and Michael

turned on the water tap for him, thinking: This is why his hands were dirty last week; he couldn't turn on the water. The boy tried to imagine a priest, even Father Heaney, admitting that to some questions there were no answers. Impossible. While the rabbi washed his hands, Michael glanced at the newspaper, which had certain words circled in red. Words were also circled in the dictionary. He looked around and saw two more doors. One was thick, with brass handles and an elongated keyhole. The other was smaller, cracked open an inch. And he thought: Maybe the big door opens into the treasure room.

Against the opposite wall, there was a small unmade bed, and a packed bookcase. Wedged into the top shelf was a framed browning photograph of a woman. With an oval face. Hair tied back. Liquid dark eyes. Michael drifted toward the books, glancing again at the woman's face but trying not to be too interested. He ran his fingertips over the spines of the books and remembered some movie where a detective pushed at a bookcase and it suddenly swiveled, opening into a secret room.

"You like my treasures?" the rabbi said, and Michael's heart slipped.

"What?"

"My books," the rabbi said, his own hand touching the books on the second shelf, below the photograph of the dark-haired woman. "Is all I have, but treasure, yes?"

Michael's heart steadied as he peered more closely at the books. Their titles were in languages he did not know or letters that he did not recognize.

"You like books?" the rabbi asked.

"Yes," Michael said. "I love books. But are these books written in Jewish?"

The rabbi pointed at the leather bindings of the thickest books.

"Not Jewish, *Hebrew*, these here," he said. And then he touched some smaller books, with worn paper bindings. "These are Yiddish."

"What's the difference?"

"Hebrew is, eh, the, eh . . ." His eyes drifted to the dictionary. "Language of Yisrael."

The word came out *lan-goo-age,* the last syllable rhyming with *rage.* Michael pronounced it correctly for the rabbi, who nodded, his bushy black eyebrows rising in appreciation.

"Eh, language." He said it correctly. "Good, I need your help. Please tell me when I make mistake. Language, language.

Good. Anyway, Hebrew is language of To-rah and Talmud —"

"*The* language," Michael said, remember-ing the endless drills in grammar class. "The *the?* It's called an article," Michael ex-plained. "A definite article, they call it. *The* language, *the* table, *the* stove."

The rabbi smiled. "The tea!"

He went to the stove and lifted the boiling water and poured it into a pot.

"We soon have *the* tea!"

"What are those other books?" Michael said. "You started to say —"

"Yiddish," the rabbi said. "The language of the people. The ordinary people. Not the rabbis. The ordinary people."

"What are the books about?"

The rabbi stood before the bookcase.

"They are about the everything," he said, lifting a volume. "Religion. The history of the Jews." He hefted a volume. "But also Balzac. You know Balzac?"

"No."

"Very good, Balzac. A very smart France-man. You should read the Balzac. He knows everything. And this, this is Heinrich Heine. Very good poetry. And here, Tolstoy, very great."

Michael squatted down, took a dusty book off a bottom shelf, and opened it.

"Is this Hebrew or Yiddish?"

The rabbi perched the glasses on his nose. "Yiddish."

"What's it say?"

"Is a very funny story. Very sad too. Good Soldier Schweik. A Czech soldier, he knows the war is crazy. I am sure all are in the English books too."

The rabbi turned away and found two glasses on a shelf above the sink. He poured the tea. Then he folded the newspapers and moved them aside and set the glasses on the table and gestured for the boy to sit down. Michael had never had tea in a glass before. The rabbi then placed a sugar bowl and a spoon between them. Suddenly he reached forward awkwardly, offering his hand. Michael shook it.

"I am Rabbi Hirsch," he said. "Judah Hirsch."

"Michael Devlin," the boy said.

"You are kind boy," the rabbi said, rhyming *kind* with *kin*. Michael repeated the word, rhyming it with *rind*. Then the boy lifted the tea and sipped. The glass was hot in his hand.

"This is great," he said, putting the glass down to let it cool.

"Is hard to get the good tea in America," the rabbi said. "Maybe the water?"

So he *was* from Europe, where the water was different. Michael remembered the blue books and said: "Are you from Poland?"

"No. From Prague. You know where is Prague?"

"I know about the Infant of Prague. It's a statue of Jesus that's supposed to work miracles or something. They sell little copies of it up at Sacred Heart. But I'm not sure exactly where Prague is."

"In Czechoslovakia," he said. "Beautiful city, Prague. *Shain. Zaier shain.* . . . Most beautiful city in all of the Europe."

Sadness surged in his voice then, and he seemed guarded, and Michael thought of his mother when she would sing certain songs about the Ireland she'd left behind. The Old Country, she would always say. While living in the new country.

"Why you think I am Polish?"

"I read in a book that before the war there were three million Jews in Poland."

"True. Now? None left. All dead."

Abruptly, he shifted his eyes to the newspaper.

"English, very strange language."

"Are you going to school to learn it?"

"No. No. Teaching myself. But is very hard." He held up the back page of the

*Daily News* and pointed at the headline. "Look, what is this mean?"

The headline said: FLOCK SIGNS ROB-BIE.

"Well," Michael said. "It's about base-ball."

For the first time, and not the last, Michael began to explain the mysteries of base-ball to the rabbi from Prague. He started with the word *flock*, which meant the Brook-lyn Dodgers. The reason they were called the flock, he said, was that years ago they were called the Robins. And robins were birds. So even after they changed their name they remained a flock of birds.

"But nobody ever calls them the flock," the boy said, "except in the newspapers. Here we just call them the Dodgers. Or dem Bums."

The rabbi's eyes looked quizzical.

"Dem Bums?" He paused. "What it means?"

"Well, a bum is like a tramp, a worthless person."

"So they don't like them?"

"No, we love them. But when they lose, here in Brooklyn, we call them dem Bums. *Dem* is a Brooklyn word for *them*. We should say 'those Bums,' but — You see, Rabbi, it's like a Brooklyn way of saying things. In the movies or on the radio, they talk different . . ."

Michael's voice dribbled into frustrated silence; in some ways, baseball was really too hard to explain. He could never explain any of it to his mother. You probably had to be born to it. The rabbi stared at the boy, his brow furrowed, as if he were realizing again that learning English would not be simple. Then he pointed at the other word.

"What is Robbie? Is a Bum?"

"We don't know yet."

Michael explained that Robbie was a baseball player named Jackie Robinson. He was a colored man, a Negro, and there had never been a Negro player in the big leagues before. So the headline meant that the Dodgers had signed a contract with Jackie Robinson and if Robinson got through spring training he should be playing in Ebbets Field by the middle of April. This year. Nineteen forty-seven. The first Negro in the big leagues.

"What is the big leagues?" Rabbi Hirsch said.

"Well, there are two major leagues, which is another way of saying big leagues. The Dodgers are in the National League. So are the Giants, who are over in Manhattan in a place called the Polo Grounds. But the Yankees, who are up in the Bronx, they're in the American League. Then there are a lot of minor leagues. The best players are in the major leagues, especially now that the war is over. . . ."

He struggled to make all of this simple. But the rabbi's face became a tight grid of concentration.

"I must to learn all this," he said, shaking his head. "If I am to be in America, I must to learn." He looked up at Michael. "Maybe you can teach me."

"Aw, gee, Rabbi, I don't know. I'm still learning it myself."

"No, no, you speak good. You could teach me. I know this."

Michael felt suddenly trapped; the rabbi was asking him to do something a lot more complicated than turning on a light switch.

"Money, I don't have, to pay you with it," the rabbi said. "But Yiddish I could teach you. You give me English, I give you Yiddish."

Michael glanced at the bookcase. The rabbi looked poor. This room was as poor as any room on Ellison Avenue; by comparison, Sacred Heart was a palace. If the rabbi had a secret treasure, he certainly wasn't using it for himself. But he did have this other treasure, right here in front of him: these mysterious books with their strange alphabets. For a moment, Michael felt people rising from the books, bearded men and dark-haired women, a soldier who hated war, a Frenchman who knew everything, all of them speaking languages he had never heard. They rose from the bookcase like a mist.

He wanted to speak to them and for them to speak to him. And perhaps that could be done. In this deep and endless Yukon winter, there was nothing much to do in the afternoons, no ball games to play, no aimless journeys around the parish with his friends. He had time on his hands. Too much time.

"You really think you can teach me Yiddish?" he said.

"Sure thing," the rabbi said, pleased with his use of the American phrase.

"Well, we could try," Michael said.

The rabbi smiled broadly.

"Good! Very good!" He drained his tea, then wiped his mouth with his sleeve. "Yiddish is very great language, but not hard. Not hard like the English is hard. You can learn." He slapped Michael on the back. "How you say it? Is a deal!"

Michael finished his tea and looked around for a clock. There was no clock.

There was no radio either. He glanced at the heavy door in the corner.

"Is the church out there?" Michael said, feeling like a spy.

"Yes," Rabbi Hirsch said. "But not a church. We say —" He leafed through the dictionary, ran his finger down a page. "Sanctuary." He pronounced it *sank-TOO-uh-rye*. Michael said *sanctuary* for him. The rabbi repeated it several times.

"Can I see the mass, or whatever you call it? I mean, it's not secret or anything, is it?"

"Yes, yes, is not the secret. You come sometime."

So it was not a door to a treasure house, with gold ducats spilling from chests, and rubies and emeralds gleaming in the dim light. It was just a church. All he had to do now was convince Sonny. He turned to go and then saw the picture of the woman again.

"Is her name Judith?"

"No." The rabbi paused. "Leah. Her name is Leah." He stared at the framed photograph for a long time. "My wife."

"She's very beautiful."

"Yes," said Rabbi Hirsch. "But she's dead."

"I'm sorry, Rabbi," the boy said.

"Is hard for a boy to understand, death."

"My father's dead too," Michael said. "He was killed in the war."

The rabbi turned away from his wife's photograph.

"Excuse," he said. "I am a fool. I think I am the only person with someone dead."

"It's okay, Rabbi," Michael said.

"No. Death, is not okay for someone so young. At least I, I . . ." He couldn't find the words. "I am very sorry."

"Forget it," the boy said. "I'm sorry about your wife, you're sorry about my father. So next week we start English lessons."

"Yiddish lessons," the rabbi said.

"Both," Michael said.

"Yes, both."

# 8

January was full of storms.

In the first week, Michael saw a truck arrive outside Mister G's candy store, its narrow hard-rubber wheels lurching over the scabbed ice and fresh snow. Mister G's sons carried out cartons, a table, suitcases, clocks, a bed, and a couch and then climbed into the truck with all that had belonged to them and drove away. They did not look back, nor did Frankie McCarthy come around to say goodbye.

A few days later, Unbeatable Joe assembled some of the regulars from his bar and produced ladders and planks and a winch and started the process of raising his sign to its former glory. The men worked. They drank whiskey. They heaved and groaned and cursed. They drank more whiskey. Michael, Sonny, and Jimmy watched from a warm vestibule across the street, snickering and making remarks. Unbeatable Joe and another man climbed to the planks and examined the steel rigging that was to hold the sign. Unbeatable Joe gestured down at the other men. Then the sign was raised on high, like a declaration of triumph.

But the wind began to blow hard, as it always did on Collins Street, and the men cursed and pulled on their ropes and backed up and rushed forward, and then the giant sign flew up in the air and came down with a tremendous crash, bringing the ladders, the planks, and Unbeatable Joe with it. The boys laughed and left the warmth of the doorway to watch Unbeatable Joe hopping on one foot and holding the other. The rest of the men were cursing and drinking whiskey from a bottle to stay warm.

And then Unbeatable Joe limped out of the bar with a huge fire axe and began to chop at the sign in a maniacal rage, his eyes wide, his hair rising in spikes, his nostrils flaring, and when he was exhausted, he handed the axe to one of the other men and that man chopped at the sign and passed it to another, who gave it to another, and back to Unbeatable Joe, and now there was a crowd, all cheering, guys from the factory across the street, women with shopping bags, kids from over on Pearse Street, urging the men on, raising fists. A police car came along and stopped and the cops got out, but the men just kept battering and smashing and splintering the sign until there was only a pile of broken pieces left, and the crowd roared, even the cops.

"Get me a broom," Unbeatable Joe said. "We gotta sweep up this fuckin' sign."

When Michael told Rabbi Hirsch about this a few days later, his blue eyes danced and he laughed from his belly.

"The goyim are crazy," he said.

Michael didn't tell Rabbi Hirsch that some of the goyim were crazy in a different way. On the day of the destruction of Unbeatable Joe's sign, Michael sat in the hallway beside the roof door with Sonny and Jimmy. It was too cold now to play in the streets. And Michael had begun to understand what Jack London meant when he described cabin fever.

"So what's the story?" Sonny said.

"What do you mean?"

"The synagogue. What'd you find out?"

Michael sighed.

"There's nothing to find out," he said. "The rabbi's poorer than we are, Sonny. He's got no telephone, he's got no radio, he lives in one small room like a goddamned pauper."

"That could be a, whatta you call it, a disguise."

"Come on, Sonny. If there was a treasure, he could just take it over New York, sell it, and go somewhere that's warm. Florida or someplace. What's he need to be in the synagogue all day in his overcoat for?"

"To fool us," Jimmy said.

"You mean fool *me*," Michael said. "He doesn't even know you and Sonny are alive."

"It's the same difference," Jimmy said. "All for one and one for all, right?"

"Right, but . . ."

Sonny leaned forward.

"Maybe *he* don't know there's a treasure there."

Michael and Jimmy looked at him.

"Maybe . . . it was buried, or put in the fucking walls or something, and the last rabbi, he knew where it was, or had a map, or some secret code, and then *that* rabbi died before he could pass it on. Maybe that's why he acts like it ain't there."

Michael stiffened. A week ago, he was thinking the same thing.

"But if that's the case, what do we do?" he said. "Tear the building down?"

"Nah, nothing drastic."

"Then what?"

"Keep your eyes open, that's all. Wait."

He said this as if Michael had agreed to

a conspiracy, and Michael did not object. This silence made him feel treacherous. He had come to like the rabbi. He liked his accent. He liked what seemed to be his good heart. He liked the way he didn't treat him like a kid and the way he was unafraid to make mistakes in his new language. But he didn't say this to Sonny Montemarano. He didn't want to be forced to choose between the rabbi he barely knew and someone he'd known since first grade. He said nothing, but he knew that Sonny would take his silence as an agreement. The way he had agreed, without words, to Frankie McCarthy's reminder that he had seen nothing in Mister G's candy store. So he said nothing. He would keep his eyes open anyway, as he got to know the rabbi, and in that way he could keep his word. But if he saw nothing, he would have nothing to report to Sonny.

Later, when he saw the rabbi to begin their lessons in Yiddish and English, Michael didn't discuss Sonny and the rumors of hidden treasure. Instead he made the rabbi clap his hands in delight by counting to five in Yiddish. He told the rabbi about his schoolwork and the rabbi said study, study, study, and Michael thought about his mother explaining that the Jews always did their homework and maybe that's why they were hated.

The rabbi listened carefully when Michael told him about his mother and how she had come to New York from Ireland after her mother died, long ago in 1930, and how she had met Tommy Devlin at a dance a few years later, which was about all that Michael knew about their story. His father, Tommy Devlin, was from Dublin, but he loved America so much he joined the army before he got drafted. He was an orphan too, the boy explained, just like his mother; and so Michael had never met any uncles or aunts or cousins.

"In the world, all over, there are people with no cousins and no uncles," the rabbi said. "But your mother you got. You are lucky."

Michael didn't speak about Mister G or Frankie McCarthy either, or some other things that happened on Ellison Avenue. One Saturday night the snow came down hard again, although not as hard as it did during the great blizzard after Christmas. By early afternoon the parish men were drinking and singing in Casement's, which Michael's mother told him was named for an Irish patriot named Roger Casement (just as Collins Street was named for Michael

Collins, another Irish martyr). Before he went to bed that night, Michael glanced down at the yellow light of the saloon and saw a blur of men through the glazed windows. There were no women there. And he thought: My mother has no man and those men have no women. Somehow the arithmetic doesn't add up. She's pretty. She's smart. She works hard. Why won't one of them ask her to go to a movie down at the Grandview? Why can't one of them take her to a goddamned dance?

In the morning, there was a great crowd on Collins Street and a police car with its doors open. Michael ran over. One of the uniformed cops told him to stand back, and a woman grabbed him by the arm and jerked him aside and said, "Don't look at this." But he looked anyway and saw the frozen body of an old man, wedged between two snow-covered cars. Michael could see rotten brown teeth in the man's open mouth. The eyes were wide and scared and had no color. Snot was frozen in his nostrils. Someone said, "Name's Shields, Officer. Jack, or Jimmy, I can't remember. A wino from down the Hook." The cop wrote this in a notebook. Michael stared at the dead man, whose arms were half-raised, his clothes too frail for the snow that covered them, and wondered if he'd had a wife or children.

Then in his mind he put his father's face over the face of the dead man and he left Brooklyn. He saw his father sprawled in the snow in a frozen forest in Belgium. The trees around him had no tops. Ruined tanks were everywhere, covered with snow. Other soldiers were leaning down to look at his father's face. *Don't look at this,* a woman's voice said in the snows of Belgium, but there were no women to be seen. Michael stared at his father's eyes. They were seeing him, knowing him, full of need, as if he were trying to say words. And then he was gone and Michael was back in Brooklyn.

At Sacred Heart School, he could not explain to Brother Donard that image of the dead man in the snow and the way it was mixed up with the face of his father. He did not even try. Nor did he decide to mention it to Rabbi Hirsch, who had heard enough about death. Instead, he worked hard in class, doing homework during study periods, making notes while Brother Donard spoke. Most of the other kids didn't bother with notes. They stared out the window. They drew airplanes. They made faces at each other, trying to provoke laughs. But Michael had discovered that making the notes helped him to remember things. If he wrote down a word, then a memory of it was stamped in his brain. When he needed it, the word appeared. He didn't know why. The brothers didn't teach them to do it that way. But it worked for Michael. And besides, when the time came to study for a test, he could look at the notes and all the words would come back to him. It was a form of magic. The words were gone, vanished, disappeared from the world, and then suddenly — *Shazam!* — they were there when he needed them.

Words themselves had a special power and mystery to Michael. In Latin or Yiddish, they were like those secret codes used by spies, or members of secret societies, which he sometimes wrote down while listening to *Captain Midnight* on the radio. But even in English, a word wasn't as simple as it looked. The letters *H-O-R-S-E* were combined into *horse.* But what kind of a horse? Which horse? Gene Autry's horse Champion? Roy Rogers' horse Trigger? And that other cowboy, Ken Maynard, had a horse named Tarzan even though they didn't have any goddamned Tarzan books in the Wild West. There were big police horses and the small horses people rode in Prospect Park in the summertime and the racehorses that the men in Casement's Bar bet on with

Brendan the bookmaker. There were colts and stallions and ponies and yearlings, pintos and broncos, steeds and mustangs, and those were just horses he'd learned about at the movies in the Venus. And down at the lumberyard at the bottom of Collins Street they used sawhorses, which were made of wood! Sometimes, words didn't name things very clearly. They could get confusing.

Michael would think these things late at night, trying to sleep. The right words helped drive out the terrible occasions of sin, those images of women that kept swimming through his head: Judith with her golden skin and Hedy Lamarr and a French woman he saw in a Tarzan movie in the Venus. Denise Darcel. Their eyes and skin and hair and teeth would come from nowhere into his mind and he would feel strange and his penis would get hard and he would want to touch it. Then he would try to resist with words. Magic words. Europe. Steeples. The Vatican. Japan. Horses. Hallways. Pigeons. Jeeps. Each word was like the cross held aloft to confront Dracula. Each word was like the magic amulet employed by Tiny Tim in the Sunday comics of the *Daily News*.

Words had assumed another importance

too. He was thinking about them in new ways because of Rabbi Hirsch. There were words he knew without having any memory of learning them; he just knew them, the way he knew baseball. But Rabbi Hirsch didn't know these words in English, so he had to explain them, spell them, look them up in dictionaries. And when he had given those words to Rabbi Hirsch, the man made them his own. If Michael corrected his pronunciation, the rabbi never again made the old mistake. He repeated the word, wrote it into a school composition book, tried it out in sentences. The rhythms of those sentences were often wrong; the verbs were in the wrong place. But the rabbi treated words as if they were jewels. He caressed them, handled them with his tongue, repeated them with delight, turned them over for a view from another angle. Sitting with the rabbi on January afternoons, watching him plunge into words, Michael couldn't believe he was ever afraid of the man, and he wished everyone in the parish could see how hard the man was working at becoming an American.

The rabbi also taught by example. Michael realized that he had never done with Latin what the rabbi was doing with English. He barely knew what the Latin words meant, and he certainly could not speak Latin. And neither could the priests at Sacred Heart. They all spoke English to each other. The priests and the altar boys *recited* Latin, like actors in some play. The priests often read the Latin prayers from books, while the altar boys called up the replies from brute memory. And Father Heaney raced through the Latin prayers as if they were a bore. Michael did love the sounds of the Latin words, the flowing vowels, the abrupt consonants. But they were part of a code he didn't fully understand.

Spurred by the example of Rabbi Hirsch, he went to Father Heaney and borrowed a translation of the liturgy of the mass, and within days the Latin code was partially cracked. But the new knowledge made him feel deflated. What was being said in the ceremony of the mass no longer seemed as mysterious. *Ite, missa est,* for example, meant Go, the mass is finished. *Deo gratias* meant Thank God. He laughed when he read that, because that's how he sometimes felt, after a long, slow, drowsy mass. Thank God this is over, he would think, because now I can pick up the buns at the bakery and go home to breakfast. *Deo gratias.*

But Michael's sudden interest in Latin wasn't as impassioned as his growing desire to learn Yiddish. At first, he had agreed to learn the rabbi's language out of politeness; that agreement had even felt like a trap. But then the lessons began to feel like part of an adventure. Not like visiting the Taj Mahal, the way Richard Halliburton did in those fat books he saw at the library. Or like Frank Buck going after man-eating tigers in India. But Michael did feel that learning the language was like entering another country.

There was another thing too. In some way, because he had heard it all of his life, Latin was familiar. It was like the parts of the parish that everyone else knew: the church, the factory and the police station, the Venus and the Grandview. But Yiddish was strange, secret, special; in the world of the parish, it would be *his*. After all, the Egyptian wizard didn't give Billy Batson a magic word in English or Latin. It was a private word in a private language. And even if Michael did master Latin, he couldn't speak it with anybody. As a language, it was dead. The blue books said so. *By the end of the eighth century after Christ, Latin was no longer the common spoken language, and was diverging into Spanish and French and other forms. . . .* Yiddish was different. Right there, on page 3067 of the *Wonderland of*

*Knowledge,* was the entry.

*From Eastern Europe has come Yiddish, an extremely flexible language spoken principally by Jews. It is based mainly on the German of the Middle Ages, but the inclusion of Aramaic, Hebrew, and Slavic words and phrases has made it quite distinct from the language spoken in Germany today. Although Jewish scholars once frowned on Yiddish as a vulgar tongue, it is now accepted as a language of wide literary merit. Numerous high-grade works of literature have been written in Yiddish; first-rank writers have used it as their medium; and there are a number of newspapers printed in Yiddish. Russia, Poland, and the United States have produced the principal Yiddish literature. . . .*

If he could learn Yiddish, he could read the newspaper that Rabbi Hirsch sometimes had on his table, the *Forvertz,* and find out what they said about the goyim in a language the goyim could not read, and how they would cover the arrival of Jackie Robinson. And he could borrow books from Rabbi Hirsch's bookcase and read them. He was thrilled by the example of Balzac. He wrote his books in French, which came from Latin, and here they were in Yiddish, which came from German, and wouldn't it be something if an Irish kid could read those stories after they had traveled all the way to

Brooklyn? It would be like reading Latin, French, German, and Yiddish all at once, and turning them into English in his head. There were some books by Balzac on the shelves in the public library, but Michael did not even try to read them. He wanted to hold off until he could read them in Yiddish, the way he had held off looking at the snow on the morning of the blizzard. But more than anything else, he wanted to have a secret language. Among his friends and classmates, among the priests and the shopkeepers, in a world where Frankie McCarthy swaggered around with the Falcons and old rummies died in the snow, Yiddish would be his.

By the end of January, he had established a routine with the rabbi for their classes. Saturdays were out. The rabbi had to preside over the downstairs sanctuary. A small group of old people would arrive early, and sometimes stay all day, and the rabbi had to be available for discussion. Michael did show up early on Saturday mornings to be the Shabbos goy, refusing money from the rabbi but always accepting a glass of tea. Sometimes he brought the rabbi a sugar bun from Ebinger's Bakery, where the day-old pastries were only three cents. Sometimes they talked quickly about the weather. But then they would say goodbye until Tuesday. The lessons now were on Tuesdays and Thursdays, after school, which still gave him time to see his friends.

But it wasn't only the rabbi's obligations that made Saturday lessons impossible. The rhythm of Michael's week was changed one evening near the end of the month. He came up from the streets and found his mother happy and whistling as she listened to Edward R. Murrow on the radio.

"I've got great news," she said, turning down the volume on the radio. "We're going to be the janitors. And I've got a new job."

She turned the hamburgers in the frying pan on the coal stove while she spoke, and stirred the boiling carrots. The McElroys were moving out of the first floor, his mother explained, going to Long Island, and Mr. Kerniss, the landlord, had asked her if she wanted the job of janitor. She had accepted.

"The first thing he's going to do is take out the damned coal stove and give us a gas range," she said. "How do you like that?"

"No more rotten egg smells!" Michael said.

"And we won't have to pay any rent," she said, her face happier than he'd ever seen it. "We'll have to sweep and wash the halls once a week, and make sure the garbage cans are set out, and change the lightbulbs. And put coal in the furnace in the cellar for the hot water. It'll be hard work, but with your help, Michael, we can do it."

Michael felt a surge of emotion that he could not name. For the first time he was being called upon to do man's work. He would be able to help his mother in a way that he could never do when she worked at the hospital. Then she gave him the rest of the news.

"I'll be leaving the hospital on the first of February," she said, her face telling him this was good news, not bad. "And I'll start work as a cashier at the RKO on Grandview Avenue. It's a bit more money, and with us not having to pay rent, we'll be in the chips." She smiled broadly. "Well, not really. But 1947 will be a lot better than 1946."

She seemed abruptly close to tears, and for a moment, Michael wanted to hug her. He wanted to tell her that as far as he was concerned 1946 wasn't so bad. They hadn't gone hungry. They didn't go on relief, like the Kanes or the Morans. He'd done well in school. And right at the end, he'd met Rabbi Hirsch. That was a good year.

But he said nothing and realized how

proud he was of the changes in their lives. The RKO Grandview, after all, was one of the big movie houses. It wasn't like the Venus, where the same movies returned year after year, *Four Feathers* and *Gunga Din*, *Frankenstein* and *Bride of Frankenstein*, along with the serials and cartoons and coming attractions. The Venus was a small, rowdy place that wasn't very clean. In fact, most people in the parish called it The Itch, implying that you could get fleas just by sitting in its hard seats.

But the RKO Grandview was like a palace. The lobby alone was bigger than their flat, with paintings of old Romans rising along the side walls, the men playing flutes while women with bare shoulders gazed at them like they were heroes. Some of the women resembled Judith from the encyclopedia, or at least Hedy Lamarr. There were hundreds of seats in the orchestra, sloping toward the stage and the movie screen, and when you walked in, the first twenty rows had a mezzanine above them, with boxes like the ones where Lincoln was shot by that actor, and above the mezzanine was the balcony. Michael had no idea how many seats there were in the balcony. It just climbed and climbed into the darkness, with cigarettes burning like dozens of fireflies, and the distant ceiling farther away than the roof of Sacred Heart.

To be sure, Michael had been there only three times. Once, on his fifth birthday, his mother took him to see *The Wizard of Oz.* That was long ago. Before the war. They came home after the movie, his mother skipping and singing one of the songs about going off to see the wizard, and then in the kitchen he sat on his father's knee and felt his rough chin and breathed the tobacco odor and tried to tell him about the Tin Man and the Cowardly Lion and the Scarecrow who talked. His father laughed, and then turned serious, and told him about the time Sticky the dog swam to Africa and enlisted the lions and elephants to fight for Ireland.

"The monkeys built a boat, bigger than Noah's Ark," he said, "and they'd have eaten the king of England if it weren't for the bloody bad weather. It was so cold, the lions and the elephants jumped in the water and swam back to lovely Africa, and Sticky had to sail home alone. . . ."

His father took him to the dark movie palace the second time, after the war had started, and they sat in the vast balcony so Tommy Devlin could smoke, and together they watched *They Died With Their Boots*

*On.* Errol Flynn played a soldier named Custer and the end was very sad. Michael had never before seen a movie where the hero died. He wanted to cry but didn't, because his father didn't cry, and he was sure his father would laugh at him for crying. On the way home, Tommy Devlin said he would take him to the Grandview again, when he came home, but he never did. That Monday, he went away to the army and never came back.

His mother took him one more time, when his father was in North Africa. She didn't smoke, so they sat in the orchestra and saw a musical called *The Gang's All Here.* But all through the movie, Michael kept thinking about his father. He wished he could go up the carpeted stairs, past the candy machines and the bathrooms and the entrances of the mezzanine, all the way to the balcony. He wished he could go up and down the aisles and find his father sitting alone. Smoking a cigarette. Wearing the blue suit and black polished shoes that were still in the closet at home. He wished he could hear his deep voice. He wished he could jump on his lap and hear him tell a story.

For a long time after that, and after they knew that Tommy Devlin was dead, he did not want to go to the Grandview. His mother never mentioned her dead husband when they talked about a movie at the Grandview. She just said it was "too dear." Ninety cents to get in, while the Venus was only twelve cents on Saturdays and Sundays before five o'clock. Still, Michael longed for the Grandview the way he sometimes longed for his father. He passed it on long walks and gazed in at the murals; he studied the showcards in their glass cases, telling of coming attractions. John Garfield. Betty Grable. Humphrey Bogart. John Wayne. At the Venus, all the movies were old; they returned over and over again, the images ragged and often scratched. At the Grandview they came straight to Brooklyn from the movie houses of Manhattan. Now it might be different. No more *Four Feathers*! No more *Frankenstein*! Now he could see the new movies at the Grandview out of loyalty to his mother, even if there was a ghost in the balcony.

"Will we get in for free?" he asked.

"We'll see about that," she said, and chuckled. "First let me do the work."

The deal was done. Three men arrived one Saturday morning and took away the coal stove, using hammers and chisels to separate it from the crusted cement foundations that kept it steady, pulling the stove-pipe out of the wall and patching it with a circle of aluminum. Then they brought in the gas range: white, gleaming, with four jets on top, an oven, legs that looked like the legs of women, and even a clock. They connected it to the new gas line that ran up the side of the building, tested the jets and the oven, and then thumped down the stairs, leaving behind bits of broken iron, torn linoleum, drifts of coal dust, and a chisel. When the other tenants could afford to spend a hundred and thirty dollars for a gas range, they could be connected too. For the moment, the Devlins had the only one in the house, and it was free.

"Well," Kate Devlin said, "let's have a cup of tea. We can clean up the mess later."

They divided the janitorial work. His mother changed the hall lightbulbs when they burned out and polished the brass mailboxes every other week. Together they rolled the battered metal garbage cans from the back of the hall to the sidewalk for pickup. They struggled with the much heavier ashcans, filled with ashes from the coal stoves that remained in the other apartments and from the coal-fired hot water boiler in the cellar. The other tenants came in to examine Kate Devlin's wonderful gas stove, but they still used coal stoves for cooking and heat in the kitchens, while kerosene heaters warmed their living rooms. The women expressed envy and hope that they would have such a glory soon, if only their husbands would stop wasting money in Casement's Bar, or if they could finally win the Irish Sweepstakes. Mr. Kerniss sent word that he would install central heating the following year — steam heat! — but would have to raise the rent to pay for the new boiler, the pipes, and radiators. For now, the coal stoves produced their many pounds of ashes. Since Michael was usually at school when the sanitation trucks came by on weekday mornings, his mother returned the empty cans to the back of the hall. Each evening before dinner, Michael would go to the cellar and shovel coal from the coalbin into the furnace, so that everyone in the building would have hot water. If there was snow, Michael shoveled the sidewalk and sprinkled ashes on the pathways so nobody would slip on the ice.

He worked hard at these chores, but one other task filled him with a kind of mindless joy: cleaning the halls. Every Saturday morning, after serving mass, after stopping at the synagogue on Kelly Street to turn on the lights, after greedily consuming buns and hot tea in the company of Rabbi Hirsch, he would race to Ellison Avenue. He would start at the roof door with a broom and sweep his way down four flights to the ground floor. He was always amazed at how much litter would be dropped in seven days: soda bottles, bunched newspaper, candy wrappers, pebbles, birdseed, dirt he could not name. Michael never saw anybody drop this stuff: that was the mystery; it just seemed to erupt and *be* there. But no matter where it came from, his job was to deal with it. On the ground floor, he would sweep the litter into a dustpan and drop it in a paper bag which he then shoved into a garbage can.

Then he would start again at the top with a mop and a bucket of hot water. When his mother first took the job, Mr. Kerniss bought them a new aluminum two-gallon bucket with a roller at the top and a great thick ropy mop. After Michael swept, his mother would descend the stairs splashing Westpine disinfectant from a bottle, and the pungent scent would fill Michael's head as he moved behind her with the mop. Once the odor was so strong he had to turn away, gasping, and return to the apartment to wash his eyes with cold water and blow his nose. But he actually loved the smell: its clean, cutting odor erased the smells of food and stale beer, dead roaches and unwashed bodies.

And while Michael washed the hall, his mother was sweeping the apartment, straightening up, changing the bedsheets and pillowcases, washing underwear by hand in the sink, and all the while listening to Martin Block on the staticky old radio. Usually with the door open. Music made the work easier for Michael, smoother somehow, a *pleasure,* the mop moving to the rhythms of a dance band, his body bending and twisting, his skin beaded with sweat on the coldest days. The static didn't matter. He hummed along with Benny Goodman and Glenn Miller, sang the words with Bing Crosby, Buddy Clark, and Frank Sinatra. It was like being in a movie, where people always had music in their lives. Music came from the other apartments too — opera music from Mr. Ventriglio, classical music from Mrs. Krauze — and sometimes Michael would wonder again what Jewish music sounded like, what songs the rabbi would sing when he was alone, what songs he had heard while dancing with his wife, long ago in Prague.

# 9

The rabbi was cleaning the stove, scrubbing hard with a rough cloth. While he did this, he murmured a litany of his jeweled new English words: *stove, cleaning, teapot, cleanser, oven, range, jet, matches,* with Michael occasionally correcting his accent. There were now scraps of paper Scotch-taped around the room, naming each object in English: *door, table, sink, wall, bookcase,* with the Yiddish word written underneath in English letters. *Tir, tish, vashtish, vant, bikhershank.* They were there for Michael. Occasionally the rabbi would stop in mid-sentence and point at a door and Michael would shout back: *Tir!* Or he'd touch the low ceiling and Michael would bark: *Sofit!* Their lessons were continuous and practical, with an undertone of magic; like magicians, they were showing each other that nothing was what it seemed to be, that one name for a thing might be hiding another name. A secret name.

One afternoon, Michael squatted down and eased a tall leather-bound book from the bottom shelf of the bookcase. He opened it and saw an illustration of a huge, looming castle, its spires rising into fog. It looked like the place where Dracula lived, in the movie that had sent Michael running for the sunshine one Saturday afternoon from the slithery darkness of the Venus.

"Is this Prague?" he asked, turning the open book to the rabbi. The words were all in Hebrew.

The rabbi slipped his glasses to the tip of his nose.

"Yes," he said. "Prague."

He looked at the drawing, then leaned closer.

"That is St. Vitus Cathedral, in Hradčany," he said. "The Castle."

"Man, it's scary-looking."

"Yes."

"Was Prague a scary place?"

"Sometimes," the rabbi said. "In the bad times." He took the book from Michael, holding it open with both hands. "But also beautiful."

He laid the open book upon the table.

"Yes," he repeated. "Beautiful."

The cleaning stopped now, and the rabbi sat down and tried to explain faraway

Prague to the boy from Ellison Avenue. Michael listened as the man talked about how it was on Prague mornings in spring, walking along the banks of the Vltava with the trees budding and the light a pale green. Michael began to visualize the crowds on the bridges in summer. "Always pretty girls, with boyfriends," the rabbi said. "Priests. Old rabbis . . ." As he slowly turned pages, Michael walked with him through the palace where the Hapsburgs stayed when they came over from Vienna. He gazed at the guards who marched outside in polished boots and plumed hats and gold scabbards, even when the kings and queens were gone. He strolled with Rabbi Hirsch through the royal gardens where the Hapsburgs grew their tulips in vast dazzling rows. They peered together at the orange tile roofs and cobblestoned streets and weeping willows of the Mala Strana, at the foot of the Castle on the left bank of the river, and saw the old aristocrats and the rich artists and heard their horses trotting on the wet stones after a summer rain.

Michael went with the rabbi to the 1920s, and the rabbi's father was with them as they took long walks and heard about history and stopped before houses that were built in the thirteenth century. Imagine: on these very streets, Schiller once strolled with his head full of poems. And there, down that path where the rabbi's father was pointing, just beyond the gurgling fountains and the beech trees, there are the Waldstein Gardens.

"Waldstein, he was a *meshuggener*, a crazy man, a general, one of those, how do you . . . men of destiny?" He smiled. "The Thirty Years' War, he started with a murder. No: *three* murders! Three of his enemies he had thrown out from the window in the Castle. But it was a happy ending his story, that you would like. He was killed by an Irisher! A dragoon that put a dagger in his heart!"

"What was an Irishman doing in Prague?"

"Making a living," the rabbi said. "Killing, in those days, it was a job."

Then they were together on another street in the Mala Strana, and in that corner house lived the violin makers, and up the street was the Italian Hospital and the Lobkowicz Palace, and Michael imagined nuns in starched white habits moving down bright corridors and a princess walking barefoot on marble floors in the moonlight. And there, that small house? That was where Mozart stayed when he came to Prague for the world premiere of *Don Giovanni*.

"The first time *Don Giovanni* I saw," the

rabbi said, "I am your age. I have never see anything like it ever before. The music. The beauty."

Michael didn't know who Mozart was or what *Don Giovanni* was about, but he listened carefully and pictured the orchestra with the musicians all in tuxedos and the balconies full of powdered women, and chandeliers glittering on the ceiling, like in *The Phantom of the Opera* with Claude Rains. And there in the crowd, beardless, smaller, his blue eyes wide, was Rabbi Hirsch. Then they were walking together on a weekday along the river in Prague and crossing into the little island young Judah Hirsch said was called Kampa. They were the same age, and they watched the young women washing clothes on the banks of the river. Or it was Sunday and families held picnics on the grass. There were artists everywhere, a forest of easels pitched along the riverbank, men in berets painting the bridges and the turrets of Charles University across the river, and the sky above them all.

"And the birds," the rabbi said. "Thousands of birds, getting lunch in the river."

The rabbi turned a page now and pointed beyond some small houses and told Michael that in the old days there had been a Jewish cemetery there. Then it was dug up and replaced by buildings. Now it was lost to history, the graves and the names of the dead long forgotten.

"The old people, they used to say that the spirits from the lost graves, all the souls, they floated up in the sky forever, trying to get home," he said. "Now they have plenty of company."

Michael saw them now, hundreds of them, floating in the air, cartwheeling, swooping, men searching for women, and children searching for parents, high above the spires of St. Vitus, mixed in with Finn MacCool's lost followers, the *fianna*, all of them careening like birds, like a lost flock of robins. And as he listened to the rabbi recall his own childhood fears, he was standing in Kampa, watching as the spires detached themselves from the cathedral and slowly rose into the sky and circled Prague, like knobby rockets reaming the air, scattering ghosts and angels and fianna, before driving hard and ferociously through the flock of ghosts into the Jewish Quarter.

The rabbi's eyes were drowsy with the past, his face loose. And then he was a young man, taking Michael with him into the cellar cafés, the air blue with cigarette smoke, and Mucha posters on the walls full of women with thick coils of hair and red lips, and all of them, Judah Hirsch and Michael Devlin and their friends, talking about naturalism and symbolism, Mallarmé and Nietzsche and Rilke. The names meant nothing to Michael as he listened hard, trying to shape the rabbi's life in his own mind, living it with him.

"This is a time, the first time I try to live without God," the rabbi said, his eyes drifting to the door that led to the sanctuary. "Is a surprise, a rabbi can try to live without God?"

"Yes," the boy said.

"We are, *were* young," the man said.

He kept talking, as much to himself as to Michael, trying to explain a time in the 1920s when he and his friends and most other Czechs believed that culture would unite them all. Michael didn't exactly understand the word *culture;* it made him think of pictures of rich people he'd seen in the *Daily Mirror.* But the rabbi spoke about a time, in those cellar cafés, when all of them thought that culture would be the cement of Prague, strong enough to bind together Christians and Jews and atheists, men and women, old and young. Culture would end the ancient quarrels of Europe, preventing bloodshed and bitterness and cruelty.

"God we didn't need," he said, "if we

had Vermeer. Or Picasso. Or Mondrian. On every wall, we had their pictures pasted."

None of this talk made pictures in Michael's mind, nor carried him high above the distant city to share the sky with ghosts. But he could see himself with young Judah Hirsch, sitting beside the first radio in a smoky corner of the Café Montmartre on Celetná Street, smoking cigarettes, listening to words coming through the air in other languages. Michael could not tell one language from another but knew that there were Germans speaking, and Slavs, and Austrians and Russians, and he wished that Father Heaney was with them, because he had been to Europe and could help sort them out.

Then the rabbi talked about the arrival of the phonograph record in Prague, and Michael saw his friend Judah Hirsch winding up a Victrola and putting the needle on the record and heard him telling his friends that in this new Czechoslovakia, this new Europe, this place free of hatred and war, they would drown together in the music of Dvořák and Mahler and Smetana. Names that Rabbi Hirsch pronounced as if they were saints. Names that Michael did not recognize, could not even imagine how to spell. The rabbi made the boy long to hear their music. He wished his mother would save up and buy a phonograph, even a windup Victrola from the St. Vincent De-Paul Society, where things were cheap, so he could hear the music of these men, and *Don Giovanni* too. And suddenly he realized that the rabbi, who spoke about music as if it were played by God, lived here in the synagogue without a radio, without even the company of Bing Crosby and Benny Goodman.

"Modern, we all were," the rabbi said, with no music in his voice. "That was the new religion. Modernism." He paused, and glanced at Michael's puzzled face. "Too modern for believing in God, we were."

Such talk made Michael uneasy. He could not imagine how a man of God, a rabbi, could admit that once upon a time he did not believe in God. The priests in Sacred Heart could have no such doubts. They seemed born to be priests, chosen by God himself. Or if they had the doubts, they surely would not tell Michael. But when Rabbi Hirsch spoke of his doubting youth, Michael felt even closer to him, for Michael had his own unspoken doubts, his own questions.

"Eh, you are a boy," the rabbi said, as if understanding that he had wandered too far from the streets of Prague and the names of buildings and streets and rivers. "I am saying too much of grown-up things."

He returned to the pictures in the book, like a man examining a map, tracing paths into the New Town Square and showing Michael the astrological clock on the walls of the church, with the apostles moving through two windows every hour, hour after hour, so accurate that even the passing Jewish businessmen would look up and check their pocket watches. Then Michael and young Judah Hirsch were gazing up at the lacy facade of the Palace of Industry. Its clock tower seemed to float in the air above its roof, and the facade's pattern of intricate iron grills and repeated circles turned yellow in the August sun. Stone flowers sprouted from other buildings or curled around each other in stained-glass windows, and then Michael was on the steps of the National Museum, standing with Judah Hirsch and his father as they looked out over Wenceslas Square and listened to the great leader Masaryk speak about democracy and hope to half a million roaring Czechs.

"How can you remember all these things?" Michael said.

"A Jew, he must watch, and he must remember," the rabbi said, and smiled in a detached way. "If he wants to live."

"Like the Irish with the English," Michael said, remembering the tales his mother told him of British soldiers on the streets of Belfast in 1923, when she was a girl.

"Yes," the rabbi said. "Like that."

He turned a few more pages, and there, finally, among the drawings of Old Town and the Jewish Quarter, was the house where he had lived with his father and mother. In a street called U Prasne. In his mind, Michael saw the father's face: grave, severe, with a trimmed gray beard and pince-nez glasses, checking his pocket watch as he passed the clock where the apostles appeared every hour. Michael was beside Judah Hirsch when his father came home through the winter snows from the clothing store, to slump gray-faced in a chair beside the fire, sitting in the same way that Michael's mother sat in the living room chair with her book by A. J. Cronin. Then Judah's mother began to play Mozart on the piano, and the color slowly returned to his father's face.

"Perfect, it wasn't," the rabbi said. "But some nights always I remember it."

"Do you have pictures of them?"

"All lost."

"Your mother —"

"Home from school I comed, *came,* one day, and she is gone," the rabbi said. "Clothes gone. Jewelry gone. To Vienna, they tell to me. My father that night . . . he said never again her name is to be said in the house. Thirteen years old I am at this time. In bed, when I finished crying, I heared him in his room, crying too. And never again we say her name."

"I'm sorry, rabbi. I didn't mean to —"

"Is okay. In the life, worst things happen."

That day, the rabbi told no more stories of Prague. He closed the book and returned it to its shelf and then asked Michael for the latest news about Jackie Robinson.

But at home in the darkness of his room, Michael wondered what it must be like to have your mother disappear, her name erased from all conversation. He could not conceive of his mother leaving his father and going off to Boston or Chicago or the Bronx, never to return. He imagined himself as the rabbi when he was a boy, Judah Hirsch lying in his room in Prague, knowing he would never see his mother again. And knew that Judah Hirsch must have felt the way Michael felt that night in early 1945, after the two soldiers had come up the stairs to their door and talked to his mother, and she had wept without control for the first and last time, and then had to tell the boy that his father wasn't coming home.

That was only two years ago. It seemed like a hundred. He had bawled like a baby that night, and she had to console him, and hug him, and tell him that someday he would see his father in Heaven. And she told him that he must pray for his father, Private Tommy Devlin of the United States Army, God rest his soul, and offer up his own pain for the souls in Purgatory. But he had prayed for his father every day during the war and still he had died, so Michael did not know why he must keep praying for him. After all, he said to his mother, Daddy can't be in Purgatory: he died for his country. But she said they must still pray for him, and if Private Tommy Devlin of the United States Army didn't need the prayers he would give them to someone who had no prayers at all. There were orphans who died in the war, and babies who had never been baptized, and Jews and Chinese and Russians. All sorts of people are dying in this awful war, she said, and we must pray for all of them.

When he was finished crying, his mother dried his face and told him that now he must be the man in the family, that he must not show his grief to strangers, that they must keep their feelings behind the door. And he had done that, refusing to ask for pity from his friends, embarrassed when a teacher at school told the class that they must pray for Michael Devlin's father, who had died in the war.

But alone behind the door of his room, he would make his father come to life again, with his muscled arms, and his deep voice, and his booming laugh. He would hear him sing. He would walk with him in the park and see a flock of robins. He would sit with him in the balcony of the Grandview. And when he had remembered all the Sticky stories his father had told him, Michael would invent others. He would hit a soft grounder past second base, and Sticky would appear and he would ride the great dog around the bases. A bully would wrestle him to the ground in the schoolyard, and Sticky would seize the bully by the belt and hurl him fifty feet. He would see his father as alone as Custer, surrounded by Germans in the whirling snows of Belgium, and through the forest Sticky would come running, to snatch him away and take him home to Brooklyn.

Michael did not cry in front of others, and his mother was his strongest model: he had never seen her cry again. On this night more than two years after she had last cried, as he thought about the somber voice of Rabbi Hirsch when he explained his own mother's departure, Michael was glad he had come to know this strange bearded man. The rabbi did not cry. The rabbi did not ask for pity. At least not in front of others.

On a frigid Thursday a week later, the huge leather book about Prague was back on the table, and the rabbi was showing him the routes he took each day to school when he was the boy's age, moving easily into the Jewish Quarter called Josefeva. Now the rabbi's words were full of magical images, as if he had remembered them during the week. Michael walked with the rabbi past black suns and black Madonnas, heading for Josefeva. In Old Town Square, Michael pictured Jews tied to the stake among soaring flames in the fourteenth century, their screams filling the air along with the odor of scorched flesh. Men in black robes piled on the wood. Children wept.

Then he was coming out of the house with Judah Hirsch, and the young man crossing the street was Franz Kafka, who was some kind of a writer. Kafka's father ran a haberdashery right there, around that corner, in a building called the Kinsky Palace, and maybe that's why Kafka always appeared in a black suit and a tight necktie and sometimes even a bowler hat. Then the boys went to inspect the glories of Pariszka Street. The name meant Paris in Czech. A Paris it wasn't, the rabbi said, but it was pretty good anyway. They saw Kafka's father, shouting, arguing with Judah's father . . . what was the word? *Debating.* Michael heard Kafka's father's voice, high-pitched, angry, always right while everybody else was wrong, and his anger made Michael laugh. Then they were playing beside a fountain, with Kafka's sisters. Ottla, Valli, Elli. Younger than the man who was some kind of a writer.

"All three die in the camps," Rabbi Hirsch said, his eyes suddenly milky. "Kafka himself, he was lucky. Before Hitler he died, of the TB. The girls, they went to the camps."

There was a finality to the last sentence that made Michael feel clumsy, as if his own curiosity had led the rabbi somewhere the man did not want to go. Maybe the spell had been broken. Maybe now the rabbi would close the book and leave Prague. Michael didn't know what to say, but he did not want the rabbi to stop talking. Finally he stammered a few words.

"Tell me about Josefeva."

The rabbi shifted in his chair, cleared his

throat as if gathering his strength, turned to another page of the book, and then reached into the past. He talked about a street called U Stareho Hrbitova, a street that was there in the book, and how if you hugged that gray stone wall, right there, and kept going, you would come to the heart of the old ghetto. Michael knew the word *ghetto* from the blue books. The rabbi talked about how Jews had been there since before the Czechs, perhaps from as far back as the time of the expulsion from Jerusalem. But the walls that sealed the Jews into the ghetto were not built for another thousand years. He described the wall to Michael, its porous stone and mossy base, the huge wooden gates, and how within the gates everything was separate from the rest of Prague. There was a Jewish court, a Jewish jail, even a Jewish post office.

"That was dumb," Michael said.

"Yes, but a long time the dumbness lasted, right up to about 1850," the rabbi said. "You know what is the most stupid? When the Christians sealed us *in*, they sealed themselves *out*."

"From what?"

"From learning. From tradition." A pause. "From miracles."

Michael knew he couldn't mean Catholic

miracles, like the one about the loaves and the fishes or the water turned into wine at Cana.

"You mean, like . . . magic?"

The rabbi looked up from the book, and raised an eyebrow.

"Maybe," he said. Another pause. "Magic, you like to hear about?"

"Yes."

The rabbi took a deep breath, turned a page, and took Michael into another Prague, one that could not be described by geometry or science. A magical city of goblins and ghosts and doppelgängers ("a kind of bad twin," the rabbi explained). In that city, Michael looked up and saw angels. Not fat little pink cherubs from greeting cards. Great silvery creatures with wings as wide as buses, dancing in clouds, swooping behind the spires. As big as Finn MacCool. In a narrow street called Golden Lane, he saw a man in a dark robe covered with silver stars, a man who looked like what the wizard Shazam might have looked like when he was young. Rabbi Hirsch said he was called an alchemist, part scientist and part astrologer. Michael knew an astrologer was a guy who could read the stars and make horoscopes like the ones in the *Daily News* that claimed they could predict the future and never did.

These alchemists, the rabbi went on, were always trying to turn cheap metal, like lead or zinc or iron, into gold.

There were hundreds of them in Prague, brought from all over Europe by a mad emperor named Rudolf, who lived in the shadows of Hradčany Castle because his face was made of fruits and vegetables. There was even a painting of him showing radishes and carrots and onions where his nose and chin and ears should have been. One of Rudolf's alchemists had invented a magic mirror where the future revealed itself through smoky glass. Another, bent and old, had spent his entire life searching for the philosopher's stone, a single object, made of the hidden minerals of the earth, that would contain all wisdom and the secrets of eternal life. Another wore a silver nose and traveled with a dwarf and claimed to be 312 years old. All carried vials of sulfur and mercury. They studied stars and meteors and the movements of planets. They prayed to gods without names.

Wandering with Rabbi Hirsch in this ancient Prague, Michael felt mystery and wonder on all sides. They watched a man disappear in a puff of smoke. They passed the bodies of two alchemists who made gaudy promises to Rudolf and then failed to deliver; as punishment, they were covered with tinsel and hung with gold-painted ropes from gold-painted scaffolds. An innocent man was heaved from the upper story of Hradčany Castle and then two angels dove to his rescue. A slatternly woman was transformed into a cow. A bird became a soldier. Donkeys danced. Metal trees bore iron fruit. Snow fell in August, the rain rose from the Vltava and hurled itself at the clouds, and once the sun appeared at midnight. Stars exploded and showered the earth with crystals. Ravens circled the evening sky and flew in and out of the gates of Hell.

"Magic everywhere," the rabbi said. "In the Jews too. Maybe even more in the Jews."

"What kind of magic?"

He stared at his hands.

"In the Jews, the magic of the Kabbalah," he said.

The word itself sounded magical to Michael Devlin, lush with images of exotic places and gorgeous costumes, men with curved swords and women with bare bellies, in lands where minarets glinted in the sun. Turhan Bey and Sabu and Yvonne DeCarlo . . . Kabbalah, Where She Danced.

Those movie images were wrong. He returned in his mind to Prague and listened as the rabbi spoke of formulas passed across the millennia, whispered from one Jewish wise man to another from the time of Adam. Kabbalah, meaning the secret wisdom. And how the Kabbalah contained special alphabets and magic words, the most important of which, the most powerful, the most awesome, was the secret name of God.

"What *is* the secret name of God?" Michael asked.

"If I tell you, it's a secret?"

"No, but why does He have a secret name? What's the matter with just 'God'?"

"God you don't ask why He does things."

Kabbalah was the true philosopher's stone, as real as this drawing, in this leather-bound book, of a very special place Judah Hirsch had often visited with his father. Michael wanted to hear more about the Kabbalah and the secret name of God, but Rabbi Hirsch turned away from both subjects and traced a finger across the next drawing.

"This, right here, this is the Old Jewish Cemetery," he said, and his voice grew hushed. "Not the one dug up for a building. The cemetery where the dead still sleep."

In the drawing, Michael saw hundreds of tombstones. No, not hundreds. *Thousands.* As he moved among them in the tight walled space of the cemetery, with Judah Hirsch as his guide, the stones were jammed together in jumbled disorder, some sinking into the earth, the coffins going twelve layers down, the rabbi said, each bearing words in blocky Hebrew. Michael's shoes were thick with mud, and then he was sinking into the graveyard and felt a sudden terror; he could sink all the way down, twelve layers deep, to the rotting corpses or bony skeletons of the dead. He lifted a foot with all his strength and the mud made a sucking sound, and then his friend Judah grabbed his arm and pulled him to the safety of a gravel path. A silvery rain began to fall. Some stones bore symbols, which the rabbi explained: scissors on the grave of a tailor, a mortar and pestle for a man who sold medicines, a book to memorialize a printer. Michael could not read the names or the dates on the wet tombstones because all were in Hebrew. Even if he could read Hebrew, the task was impossible; the edges of the letters had been worn away by rain and snow, sun and time. In the Old Jewish Cemetery, not only God had a secret name.

The rabbi pointed to a statue of a man rising dramatically above the tombstones. In the drawing, the man was wearing furled robes and a bucketlike hat, his eyes and face in darkest shadow. Like a true wizard. Not some fake of an alchemist. Michael was certain he could see the eyes burning a bright blue through the shadow.

"This man, very important man," the rabbi said.

"Who is that?" Michael asked. "He's got the biggest tombstone in the cemetery."

The rabbi paused.

"That," he said, "is Rabbi Loew."

"L-O-E-W?" Thinking: Like Loew's Metropolitan on Fulton Street?

"Yes. Judah Loew. I am named for him."

"Why does he have a separate picture?"

"Because he is the most famous rabbi in the history of Prague."

"Did you know him?"

Rabbi Hirsch laughed. "No. He is from the sixteenth century and I am born in 1908."

Eight from forty-seven. Nine. Carry the one. He's thirty-nine, Michael thought, gazing at Rabbi Hirsch. Maybe thirty-eight, if he was born after February. Just a few years older than my mother. But he looks much older.

"Why was he so famous?" Michael asked.

"A long story," the rabbi said. "A great story. A . . . what is the word? *Terrible* story.

But a story that it's too long to tell you tonight."

Michael didn't want to leave. He didn't want to walk out of the dark wonders of Prague into the ordinary streets of Brooklyn. He wanted to know more about the amazements of the world.

The name of God.

Kabbalah.

Magic.

But he heard himself saying good night.

# 10

The cops came to see Michael one Monday night while his mother was working at the Grandview. He was at the kitchen table, rushing through homework before getting to a new *Captain Marvel* and a *Crime Does Not Pay* that he had traded for with Jimmy Kabinsky. There were books on the table, his canvas schoolbag open on a chair. His fingers were stained with ink from the leaky fountain pen. The stew his mother had left in the pot was still warm on the stove, his plate in the sink, to be washed and dried before she came home. WNEW played quietly on the radio. Harry James. "Ciribiribin." He finished the long division and was halfway through the English grammar homework, glancing in a longing way at the cover story on Pretty Boy Floyd in the crime comic, when he heard heavy steps in the hall outside the door. Then a baritone murmur. Two sharp knocks.

"Who is it?" he called.

"Police," came the voice. "Open up."

Michael's heart thumped. This was the first time the police had ever been to their flat. He wished his mother were there.

"Let's go," the hard voice said. "We ain't got all night."

He opened the door and saw Abbott and Costello, the two detectives who had been moving around the parish for weeks. Up close, Costello was very fat, with slabs of pink flesh framing a small mouth and tiny nose. Abbott had gray skin, deep black circles under his eyes, a flattened prizefighter's nose, and an unlit cigar wedged between his fingers. Each wore an overcoat. Each wore a gray fedora.

"You Michael Devlin?" Costello said.

"Yes."

"Your mother home?"

"No. She's at work."

"What about your father?"

"He's dead."

They gazed warily past Michael into the kitchen.

"You're alone?"

"Yes."

They stepped past him, one on either side, and Abbott closed the kitchen door behind him. Their bulk made the kitchen smaller.

"We're detectives," the fat one said. They

remained standing, eyes moving around the kitchen and into the dark rooms beyond.

"You know Mr. Greenberg? Yossel Greenberg? Guy they call Mister G?"

"I used to go in his candy store. But he moved away."

"He moved into a hospital, kid," the gray-faced one said. He put the cigar in his mouth, snapped a lighter, and took a drag. Blue smoke drifted from his mouth. "His skull is fractured in two places. He might never come out alive."

"We understand you was in the candy store the day he got beat up by this bum Frankie McCarthy," Costello said.

Michael said nothing. He could feel the knife entering his cheek at the hinge of his jaw and the slash that would give him the mark of the squealer for the rest of his life. He stared at the floor. If he stared long enough, maybe they would be gone when he looked up.

"Well?" the gray-faced Abbott said.

"I don't know what you're talking about," Michael said.

Costello sighed. He put a fat finger on Michael's catechism book.

"You're a Catlick, right?" he said.

"Yes."

"Me too," he said, wheezing sadly. "And

160

I see a surplice on a hanger over there, so you must be an altar boy, right?"

"Right."

"I was one too," he said. "Years ago. *Ad Deum qui laetificat* and all that."

"Two altar boys," the gray-faced cop said. "Fancy that."

Costello stood over Michael. He picked up the book and dropped it again.

"And I see you study the Baltimore Catechism."

"Yes."

"So you know lyin' is a sin, don't you?"

"Yes."

"So why are you lyin', Michael?"

The boy was quiet for a long moment.

"Maybe you should come back when my mother's here," he said in a low voice, looking away from them.

"You think your mother would tell you to lie? She's a Catlick too. And a brutal crime has been committed. Your mother would understand we can't put this Frankie McCarthy away unless we got witnesses. And you're a witness, kid. According to our sources. . . . So why would you lie?"

"Maybe this explains it," Abbott said. He was holding up a small Yiddish-English phrase book. Costello took it from him and held it in his short, pudgy fingers.

161

"A *Yiddish* phrase book?" Costello said. "I see, said the blind man. I see. It comes clearer. Like maybe you was helpin' yourself to some stuff in Mister G's when Frankie was beating him into a pulp?"

"No!" Michael said. He lunged for the phrase book, but Costello held it out of his reach.

"Where'd you get this, then?" the fat cop said.

"Rabbi Hirsch gave it to me," Michael said.

"Who the hell is Rabbi Hirsch?"

"From the synagogue on Kelly Street," Michael said. "I'm the Shabbos goy there."

Costello turned to the gray-faced detective. "Well, whattaya know? An altar boy that speaks Hebe."

Abbott chuckled.

"Maybe he can say in Hebe: You're going to the fucking can."

And then the fat cop slammed his hand against the icebox door.

"You love the fuckin' Jews so much," he shouted, "then help us catch the bum that beat one up!"

Michael wanted to cry, but he held back the tears. He felt himself trembling.

"Mister G is in Kings County Hospital," the fat one said. "His head is broke. He

162

could die. You know what that means? It means a murder rap against Frankie McCarthy. You know what it means to *you?* It means you could be an accessory after the fact. You keep your mout' shut, you're guilty too. Of coverin' up a *homicide!* You and your friends that were in the candy store that day. Alla yiz. And I'll see that yiz get put away."

"That would be some disgrace," Abbott said, dragging on the cigar. "Break your mother's heart."

The fat one pointed at the framed photograph on the wall.

"That your father?"

"Yes."

"He die in the war?"

"Yes."

"Where?"

"The Battle of the Bulge."

Costello sighed.

"The worst battle of the war."

"Much worse than Pearl Harbor," the gray-faced cop said. "You think he died for nothin'?" Costello asked, poking a finger in Michael's chest.

"*No!* He died for his country!"

"You think he died so a shithead like Frankie McCarthy could beat up a Jew?"

"No."

"You think he'd be proud of you, you cover up for a bum like that?"

The door opened behind them, and Kate Devlin stood there, her face surprised. Michael went to her, trying very hard not to cry.

"Jesus Mary and Joseph, what *is* this?" she said. "Who the hell are you two bozos?"

The fat cop reached into his back pocket for a wallet. Michael could see his gun, polished blue steel in a worn leather holster.

"Sorry, ma'am," the fat one said. "We're detectives." He showed his badge and handed her a business card. She didn't take it, and he laid it on the table. "We're investigating the beating of Mr. Greenberg, from the candy store. He might die, y' see. And —"

She glowered at them.

"Get out of my house," she said.

"Listen, we think that your son knows —"

"If you don't get out," she said, "I'll throw you out."

The two cops tipped their fedoras to her and eased around toward the door. Kate Devlin continued hugging her son.

"We'll be back," the gray-faced cop said.

"I'm sure you will," she said sharply. "Good night."

She locked the door behind them. Then

164

she exhaled and separated from Michael and sat down hard at the table.

"What was *that* all about?"

He told her. When he was finished, she shook her head sadly. And then got up to run water into the teapot.

"You're more Irish than I thought," she said, almost proudly. "In the Old Country, there was nobody lower than an informer. Scum of God's sweet earth, informers. The bloody British used them against us for centuries. They corrupted weak men, they destroyed families." While the teapot simmered on the gas range, she started washing Michael's plate. "It goes all the way back to Judas, who took his money and informed on Jesus. Many's a gutless man took the king's shilling and left for Australia or London, leaving a load of misery behind him. I'm proud of you, son."

"But what about Frankie McCarthy?" Michael said. "He *did* it."

"If the police don't get him," she said, "God will."

She poured two cups of tea.

"Open that window, Michael, will you?" she said. "I can't stand the smell of a cigar."

# 11

They called their meetings classes, and at the next few classes, Michael pressed Rabbi Hirsch to tell him about the mysterious man whose statue stood so dramatically in the Old Jewish Cemetery in Prague. The sixteenth-century rabbi called Judah Loew. The man who knew the secrets of the Kabbalah and gazed from the shadows like a wizard. Rabbi Hirsch put him off. He acted as if there were more important matters to discuss: the rules of baseball or the words for work or the names of former presidents. What was a base on balls and what did they mean by "blue collar" and how did you pronounce Coolidge? He made Michael feel that the story of Rabbi Loew would require more energy than Rabbi Hirsch could summon. Or that the story needed a certain kind of weather, or music, or mood.

And then one rainy afternoon, Rabbi Hirsch made some tea and, using some of the leather-bound books as references, began to tell the story. Michael soon felt as if he were in some drafty stone building in Ireland or Prague, with the rain pounding on the roof, and a fire in what the storybooks always called the hearth. The words flowed. Michael was swept away.

He was in Prague again, this time in the fearsome years of the sixteenth century, when Jews were in peril throughout Europe. Rabbi Loew was presiding over the Old-New Synagogue in the Jewish ghetto, then called the Fifth Quarter. Rabbi Loew was lean, serious, careful, kind to his wife and daughter, generous to the poor, living in a modest house with a small walled garden. Next door was the synagogue, where Rabbi Loew spent most of his time; if he wasn't in the house of God he was in his study, surrounded by books. Everybody knew that Rabbi Loew had no interest in the riches of the world; if he needed some new volume to add to his knowledge, he would give up eating for a week to pay for it. And he was so respected in Prague that he was not restricted to the streets of the ghetto.

He was most respected, perhaps even feared, by Emperor Rudolf himself. Michael saw Rudolf in Hradčany Castle, tall and wild-eyed like the actor John Carradine, moving among his strange collections of art, animals, and rare objects. Look: in the private zoo, a two-headed alligator, snakes with legs, a cow with tits on its back. And look: two nails from Noah's Ark! And dirt from a place called Hebron where God made Adam in His own image! And the horn of a unicorn!

And there was Emperor Rudolf, his face covered with a white mask from Japan, clopping over cobblestones in a stagecoach through the foggy midnight streets of Prague. Going to see Rabbi Loew. To enter the book-lined study, where the rabbi closed the drapes and lit candles, and listened to the Emperor's tales of woe: treacherous alchemists, spies sent by the greedy English, fighting on the borders with the Turks. The Emperor himself, listening to advice, nodding, embracing the wise rabbi, hurrying back to the fog-shrouded Castle.

But it wasn't just Rabbi Loew's wisdom that drew the Emperor to him. The rabbi possessed something else that the Emperor could not buy, could not collect, something that he wanted and feared.

Magic.

The magic of the Kabbalah.

Michael saw Rabbi Loew in his big green chair in the study, a fire burning low in the hearth, a sheet of paper on a book in his lap, a hand to his temple, his eyes closed, and knew that he was communicating with rabbis all over Europe. His hand held a feathery pen and began to move, and words appeared on the paper in a language nobody knew. The words told of planned campaigns against Jews, the kidnapping of Jewish women, of forced conversions and burnings at the stake. Rabbi Loew's advice was sent out to Russia and Italy and Belgium, without a word being spoken, without Rabbi Loew even once opening his eyes. Magic.

And as if he were at a movie, Michael saw him displaying his other powers. There was, for example, the first time that the Emperor came to the rabbi's house. A jealous associate of the rabbi, short, fat, greedy, sweating heavily on a winter day, forged an elaborate letter to the Emperor, inviting him to a formal banquet at the rabbi's house. The clear intention was to embarrass Rabbi Loew, whose cramped and book-strewn quarters were fine for his family but obviously could not accommodate a formal dinner for a goddamned emperor. The Emperor sent word that he accepted. And Rabbi Loew understood that it could be very bad for the Jews if he canceled the invitation. So he turned to the Kabbalah.

Michael could see him in the study, consulting the magic alphabets, his face deep in concentration, murmuring words in a private language. And then on the evening of the so-called banquet, as Emperor Rudolf prepared to leave his castle in disguise, so that nobody in Prague would know where he was going, Rabbi Loew stepped outside and scanned the skies. There, visible only to him, a great flock of angels appeared, carrying an entire marble palace, lifted from a distant kingdom.

Angels. Hovering in the air. Wings beating. Muscles like cords and cables.

The angels set the palace upon an empty lot in the Jewish Quarter, and suddenly it could be seen by all.

Michael wandered through the banquet room of this palace, a vast space illuminated by ten thousand candles, and gazed at Rudolf's intense face as he whispered with Rabbi Loew. Servants glided past Michael, carrying great platters of stuffed birds and thick steaks and soups in silver bowls, the air filled with the aroma of the feast. Michael listened to musicians play sad and melancholy music. He watched as jugglers and acrobats made the Emperor laugh. He saw the greedy assistant slink away into the night, surely never to return. The banquet was an astonishing success, and the Emperor returned to Hradčany Castle in the early hours of the morning full of amazement and respect.

"Before the Emperor reaches his own castle," Rabbi Hirsch said, "the angels, they carry the palace back to its original spot. Later, Rabbi Loew tells the Emperor about the angels and the tricky assistant that caused the problem and the Emperor says, 'Rabbi, next time I come to your real house.' And that's what he did. But ever after, nobody can ever question this miracle. If they do, they are calling the Emperor a fool."

Then, for the first time, the great villain named Brother Thaddeus appeared in the story. A big hulking man with no hair on his head and no beard and no eyebrows. As bald as Dr. Sivana in Captain Marvel or Lex Luthor in Superman. He was the greatest enemy of Rabbi Loew and the king of the Jew-haters. A lot of times, he told lies to stir up his followers. He was at his worst around Passover, spreading rumors that Jews killed Christian babies and mixed their blood with the unleavened bread called matzoh. Why? To start riots called pogroms, inciting mobs to kill or drive out the Jews, and take over their homes and shops. Rabbi Loew had to use all of his powers to foil him.

171

Michael was suddenly huddled in a door-way, as a mob marched on the Jewish Quarter, hurling stones at old men and young ladies, smashing windows, waving sharpened poles called pikes. Up the street, Brother Thaddeus smiled from a balcony. Then — *Shazam!* — the stones were changed in midflight into roses. Big, fat, white roses! Their petals dropping away like snowflakes! Brother Thaddeus frowned. His jaw dropped. He barked orders. The crazy people in the mob threw more rocks and stones, but they kept turning into roses, piling around Michael in the street as high as his waist. A group of young Jews appeared to face the mob. They bowed to the crazy people and thanked them for the flowers, while Rabbi Loew watched from the shadows of his study. Rabbi Loew did not smile.

Then, the scene shifted, and a second mob assembled in a square in the shadow of a cathedral, loading baskets with stones, sharpening knives, while Brother Thaddeus called on God to bless them. But the sky grew abruptly dark, lightning scribbled a warning, clouds burst across the city, and for more than an hour, dogs rained from the heavens. Thousands of them, landing softly on all four paws, barking and howling, their fangs bared. Brother Thaddeus rushed to the cathedral. His followers shivered in fear and cringed in fright, dropped their stones and knives, and ran home. Michael was certain some gallant ancestor of Sticky had been there in the rain and the howling.

Rabbi Hirsch explained that through the magic of Kabbalah, Rabbi Loew could speak to all dogs and many birds, and they often came to him with warnings of the evil plots of Brother Thaddeus. That is how he learned of the planned revolution against Emperor Rudolf. Brother Thaddeus was telling his followers that the Emperor had gone mad and must be overthrown. They were storing arms, preparing for the day.

Late one night, while Michael watched, Rabbi Loew wrote a long, detailed letter to the Emperor, warning him of the great trouble that was brewing and asking him to protect the Jewish Quarter. He sealed the letter with wax and asked Michael to deliver it to the Castle. After all, Michael was a Shabbos goy. Nobody would stop *him* on the streets beyond the ghetto. The boy took the letter and slipped into the Prague night, through narrow alleys, where buildings leaned at strange angles and rats scurried in the dark. He hugged the shadowy walls of deserted squares, crossed the river into Mala

Strana, and then began climbing climbing climbing to the walls of the Castle. When he came close, six guards appeared, their faces masked by iron visors, holding lances and giant axes. Growling and nasty, they yanked the letter from his hands and told him to go home. From the walls of the Castle he could see fires burning in the mountains. One guard laughed and said that these were happy fires. They are sending Jews to Hell, he said.

Michael reported this to Rabbi Loew, but a raven had already delivered the news. All over the kingdom, Jews found outside the ghetto were being killed. Next, the Jew-killers would breach the walls of the Jewish Quarter itself. We will wait three days, the rabbi told Michael, and then we will be forced to do something drastic.

Three days passed. More Jews were killed. There was no word from Rudolf. And then Rabbi Loew took his drastic action.

He decided to make the Golem.

"The what?" Michael asked, in the synagogue in Brooklyn.

"The Golem," Rabbi Hirsch answered. "The word, it means in dictionary English, like a robot. But the English word, you know, is not really true. Not good enough. Not *right*. To Rabbi Loew, the

Golem has another meaning."

The story of the Golem had really started a year earlier, when Rabbi Loew made a night visit to Emperor Rudolf in the Castle. Among the Emperor's collection of thousands of artifacts was a heavy silver spoon, almost eighteen inches long, with Hebrew letters engraved upon the handle. The Emperor asked Rabbi Loew for a translation. Rabbi Loew was astounded at what he saw, but gave Rudolf an incomplete version of the words. He didn't lie. He just didn't tell Rudolf all the words. For a good reason: he was afraid of what they said.

The object was laid aside, as the Emperor turned in excitement to show Rabbi Loew a monkey that could play the clavichord and then a portrait of the Virgin Mary that wept real tears. But when the evening was over, the Emperor presented the silver spoon to Rabbi Loew as a gift.

"He says, take it home, use it for soup," Rabbi Hirsch said. "Rabbi Loew takes it home. He doesn't make soup."

All the way home through the foggy streets, Rabbi Loew's heart thumped with excitement. He knew that he had been given the silver spoon that was mentioned in the Book of Creation. With this spoon, he could shape a man from mud. And by saying the correct words from the Kabbalah, he could bring the mud to life.

That is, through the wisdom of God, he could make the Golem.

The Golem, that huge creature whispered about in the secret books and hinted at in the Book of Psalms.

The Golem, who could not be destroyed.

The Golem, who was obliged to do whatever the Jews asked him to do.

"It's like *Frankenstein*," Michael said in a hushed voice. "You know, the movie? *Frankenstein*, with Boris Karloff?"

"I have not seen this movie," Rabbi Hirsch said.

Michael told him about the movie starring Boris Karloff as the monster who was created from the parts of dead bodies by Dr. Frankenstein. It played every year at the Venus.

"The Golem," Rabbi Hirsch said, "was not a movie."

He talked then about how Rabbi Loew fasted and prayed for three days, purifying his body and his soul. Then one moonless midnight, accompanied by two young and pure assistants, he slipped out of the ghetto through a secret passage. Michael saw him carrying the silver spoon. He noticed that under his coat, Rabbi Loew was dressed completely in white. The three men made their way to the banks of the Vltava. Sweating in silence, they began to shape the body of a man from the pure mud of the riverbank.

Then Michael saw Rabbi Loew take from his jacket a piece of parchment upon which he had written certain words in Hebrew. Letters only he understood. This was called a *shem*. It included the secret name of God. He inserted the *shem* in the Golem's mouth and leaned close to his ear and whispered a secret prayer. With the tip of a pointed tool, he etched a word in the Golem's brow, a word that Michael could not read. Then Rabbi Loew removed the *shem* and he and his assistants danced in a circle, moving one way and then another, chanting seven times the secret name of God. Michael could not understand the words.

But slowly, after the mud first turned very red, as if it were baking, and then cooled in a mysterious wind, the Golem rose from the riverbank.

Alive.

"The Golem, he's almost seven feet tall, his skin is the color of the clay," Rabbi Hirsch whispered. "He stands up naked on the riverbank and then one of the assistants gives to him a robe. They find out he can't speak, the Golem, but his eyes, and what he *does*, tell them he understands everything."

"Did he understand Yiddish?"

"Of course. And Hebrew. And German. And Czech, and maybe a little Greek too. He understands what he has to understand."

*Shazam!*

"It's like Captain Marvel," Michael said.

"Who?"

Michael was embarrassed. "A story in the comics." He leaned forward. "Tell me the rest."

"The rest?"

"What did the Golem *do?*"

Rabbi Hirsch looked uneasy.

"What the Jews need him to do," he said.

And then, leaning back in his chair, his eyes half-closing, Rabbi Hirsch transported Michael to Prague to witness the doings of the Golem. Michael could see the Golem lumbering through the dark nights to rescue a Jewish girl who was being baptized against her will. He could see the Golem summoning a million birds to darken the skies and shit on the heads of the legions of Brother Thaddeus. He could see the Golem in the shadowed doorway of Brother Thaddeus's house, filling the locks with mortar, so that for three days and three nights Brother

Thaddeus could not get out and his followers could not get in to plot against the Jews.

"Could he make himself invisible?" Michael asked, thinking of Claude Rains in
*The Invisible Man.*

"Sure. If Rabbi Loew says is okay."

But it was clear to Michael that the Golem
sometimes acted without orders from Rabbi
Loew. The creature knew he was a soldier
in a war, and he had a few personal ideas
about how to fight it. Once, the invisible
Golem entered the house of Brother Thaddeus on an evening when Thaddeus was
entertaining another big Jew-hater from Vienna. The Golem made Michael invisible
too, and took the boy along as he moved
through the huge kitchen. Michael saw him
piss in the wine bottles and switch the serving trays. And then saw the great uproar
when the gleaming silver dishes were un-
covered on the dining table and Brother
Thaddeus and his guests stared down at the
roasted remains of rats.

"Great!" Michael shouted, laughing out
loud.

"Yes, the Golem, he has a sense of humor," the rabbi said, looking merry. The
Golem had magical powers, he explained,
but he was not a god; in some ways he was
a large boy.

On another visit to Brother Thaddeus's house, they saw the hairless monk showing some visiting aristocratic ladies his private art collection, which was housed in a vast gallery full of nooks and crannies. The monk was very rich now, because all of the people who hated the Jews gave him money. Under his robe he wore polished leather boots, just like the Nazis, and they clacked as he walked down the halls. Then Brother Thaddeus turned into one corner, with the perfumed duchess and the silken princess and their ladies-in-waiting rustling beside him. All the time he was delivering a running commentary on the great works of art and his own great taste and how art would be better if only they could get rid of the Jews.

They paused in front of a work that even Brother Thaddeus had never seen before: two giant terra-cotta globes, protruding from a perfect rectangle in the wall. Brother Thaddeus began to expound on the glorious discoveries made in Italy of Etruscan culture, the delicate processes of glazing, firing, aging. The ladies leaned in closer, and then one of them reached forward to touch the terra-cotta globe.

It was soft!

"You see, she touches the Golem's ass!" Rabbi Hirsch said. "Sticking through the hole he chopped in the wall! And then he gives them — how do you say it?"

He flipped through the dictionary, stopped.

"Effluvium! He puts in the air, *effluvium!*"

"A fart!"

"Yes! Yes! A great big *fart!* And the ladies fall over, like with poison gas, and Brother Thaddeus begins to sob and the Golem runned away, laughing and laughing!"

They laughed together at the image of the Golem's triumph. And then slowly the rabbi's face settled. His eyes grew grave.

"Brother Thaddeus, he never gived, *gave* up," Rabbi Hirsch said. "But then, a terrible crime he planned. So terrible, this time he must be punished."

In the week before Passover, a small Christian girl disappeared, and in a dream, Rabbi Loew saw that this was part of a wicked plot for which the Jews, of course, would be blamed. Echoing through the rabbi's dream were two words: *Fünfter Palast.* Michael pictured him waking in his candlelit study from the dream, murmuring, "Fünfter Palast, Fünfter Palast . . ." Then he turned to Michael, played thoughtfully with his beard, furrowed his brow, and said that the words were the key to thwarting the evil intentions of Brother Thaddeus.

Those words, Fünfter Palast, were the name of the ruined Fifth Palace. It had once belonged to an emperor who went mad a century before Rudolf came to Prague. That forgotten emperor imagined all sorts of enemies coming to get him, so he had built a network of secret tunnels from the Fifth Palace to other buildings in the area. He lived to escape. One tunnel even reached into the cellars of the Old-New Synagogue, where he could disguise himself as a Jew and disappear into the fog. Another was connected to the Green Building, where Brother Thaddeus now lived. When the emperor finally abdicated, his enemies destroyed the Fifth Palace. Now the entrances were buried in the ruins, and no maps or plans had survived.

That night, Michael followed Rabbi Loew and the Golem as they dodged spies and policemen in the streets and went to the ruins of the Fifth Palace. The Golem lifted huge slabs of broken walls and collapsed beams, clearing a path, until they found steps leading underground to a sealed door. The Golem ripped the door off its hinges as if playing with a dollhouse. Rabbi Loew stepped inside. Ahead of them lay a dark, damp tunnel. Rats crawled at their feet. Water dripped from the ceilings. Michael saw it all, moving in the darkness of the tale.

Then Rabbi Loew lit two *havdalah* candles and he and the Golem eased into the tunnel. After a while, they came to a kind of crossroads, where other tunnels led away in different directions. The Golem paused, sniffing the air. Then he indicated with a nod of his head that Rabbi Loew was to follow him into the tunnel to the right. There was a coppery stench in the air. Rabbi Loew looked as if he were entering the outskirts of Hell.

Finally they came to a large room with glistening stone walls, filled with rotting tables, cobwebbed pots, beakers, tubes: the abandoned workshop of an alchemist. Rabbi Loew felt a chill that would remain with him the rest of his life. Even now, more than four hundred years later, it seeped into Michael.

And then the Golem became excited, growling, alert, his nose flaring. He made his way into a dark corner. He returned with two baskets. They were not draped in cobwebs. In one of them, Rabbi Loew found almost thirty vials filled with fresh human blood. Each was labeled with the name of a well-known Jew. In the other, wrapped in a Jewish prayer shawl called a *tallis,* was the body of a child.

"Right away," Rabbi Hirsch whispered, "he knows the plot."

It was obvious: just before Passover, Brother Thaddeus would have the body and the vials of blood moved through the tunnels to the cellar of the Old-New Synagogue. From there, under cover of night, his henchmen would plant the vials throughout the Jewish Quarter, and the child's body in Rabbi Loew's own house. Brother Thaddeus could then bring the police to discover them and "prove" that the Jews were engaging in human sacrifice.

A blood libel!

Rabbi Loew acted quickly. He told the Golem to carry the child's body back through the tunnels and hide it in the wine cellar of Brother Thaddeus's mansion. The Golem smiled and went away with the body, while Rabbi Loew prayed for the child's soul. When the Golem returned, Rabbi Loew ordered him to dig a deep hole in the earthen floor and bury the vials of blood. The Golem did what he was told, covering the hole with dirt, stones, and smashed beams. Then they retraced their steps. They noticed something new: the squealing of the rats had ended.

The next morning — it was the day before

Passover — the police began raiding houses all over the Jewish Quarter, using a list of names from Brother Thaddeus. Michael watched them arrive in horse-drawn carriages outside the house of Rabbi Loew, two detectives in plain clothes, one tall and gray, the other short, fat, and flushed. More than thirty uniformed policemen were behind them on horseback. And then a gloating Brother Thaddeus arrived in his own fine carriage, his leather boots clacking on the cobblestones.

The police found nothing. Brother Thaddeus was stunned. As he marched with the police past the ruins of the Fifth Palace, he suggested to the detectives that they search the cellars of the ruined palace and the nearby Old-New Synagogue. He reminded them that there were always rumors of secret tunnels.

The detectives did what he asked, and for hours they searched. They found nothing. Michael saw Brother Thaddeus grow pale. Beads of sweat appeared on his bald head. He blinked his hairless eyelids and scurried away, in search of his henchmen, to find out what had gone wrong. But, fearful of his rage, they had vanished into the hills when they realized the blood was missing.

And so the eight days of Passover ended

without the planned pogrom. And then it was Easter. Brother Thaddeus invited all the most important people in Prague to a lavish banquet, including the mayor and the chief of police, who brought his detectives as bodyguards. They were all assembled at table when Brother Thaddeus sent a servant to the wine cellar to bring up some of the oldest and finest bottles. After a few minutes, the servant returned, his eyes wide with horror.

"She's there!" he exclaimed. "There — in the cellar!"

Pandemonium!

All rushed to the wine cellar, except Brother Thaddeus.

When they returned, the police chief was carrying the dead baby. Michael saw its face, as white as flour. The detectives glanced at each other and then at Brother Thaddeus. The monk backed into a corner like a trapped animal. The mayor said: "It was you." And Brother Thaddeus began to weep.

There was a long silence in the basement of the Brooklyn synagogue.

"Did they hang him?" Michael said. "Chop his head off?"

"No. Him, they didn't need to make a martyr, and Rabbi Loew agreed. So Brother

Thaddeus was sent to prison for twelve years. He died there, blaming the Jews."

"And what happened to the Golem?"

"He — well, it's another story. And sad. Because it is a love story. And all love stories are sad."

For a moment, Michael Devlin saw his mother and father together, dancing slowly, like a couple in a sad movie. He in an army uniform, she in a gown. Dancing in marble halls. Rabbi Hirsch stared at his own fingers, and for the first time Michael noticed that he was wearing a wedding band on the third finger of his left hand.

"The problem is simple," the rabbi said. "The Golem is made of mud, yes. He is very large, yes. Very strong, yes. He can't speak and he have to obey every order from Rabbi Loew. But he also have his own thinking, does his own plans. Worse, worse — he have the feelings of a human being." He paused. "And after Brother Thaddeus is put in jail, after the great danger to the Jews is over — for a little while anyway — Rabbi Loew takes it easy. And so does the Golem. He looks so normal, gardening and that kind of stuff, Rabbi Loew even gives him a name: Yossel. Like Joseph. Joseph Golem."

In his relaxation, Joseph Golem began to notice a young woman named Dvorele. She was an orphan. Her family had been destroyed by Brother Thaddeus's followers, their house burned in one of those fires that had leveled so many Jewish homes in the countryside. After months of wandering, she had found refuge in the household of Rabbi Loew. There, she worked in the kitchen under the supervision of the rabbi's wife, Pearl. She helped clean the rooms. She did laundry. She began to learn how to read and write. Michael could see her clearly: small and dark, with huge brown eyes, like Rosalie Caputo in the sixth grade at Sacred Heart, and speaking very little, as if still paralyzed by the horror that had taken the lives of her parents, her three brothers and two sisters.

"Joseph Golem watches her," Rabbi Hirsch said, "and helps her with work, and soon — too bad! — love comes up in his heart."

Michael thought of Boris Karloff in the Frankenstein movie, playing with the flowers and the little girl beside the lake. He saw the Golem trying to explain what he felt to Dvorele, how he tried to get her to sense the great stirring within his heart. But he couldn't speak. He rolled his eyes. He looked sad. He put his hands to his forehead. He pointed at his heart and then at

Dvorele, trying to make her understand. But she shied away from him, busying herself with peeling potatoes or dusting the bookshelves in Rabbi Loew's study. Joseph Golem pined for her. At night, lying on his eight-foot cot in his cellar room, he sometimes wept.

One cold night, Rabbi Loew heard the great heaving sobs of Joseph Golem. He rose from his bed, lit a candle, and went down to visit the creature. At the sight of the Golem, turning and twisting in his bed, his teeth grinding and his hands kneading each other, the rabbi felt a great pity.

"Joseph Golem needs to say the words," Rabbi Hirsch said, "but he does not have language. Not Yiddish. Not Hebrew. Not German. Not Czech. And love, it's almost always about words."

That night, Rabbi Loew comforted the giant Golem, whispering prayers, soothing his addled heart. Finally, Joseph Golem fell into a deep sleep. Rabbi Loew stared at him for a long time before returning to his own bed.

"He is thinking, time is short for this poor fellow," Rabbi Hirsch said. "He needs to pray to find out what to do."

But the next day, Rabbi Loew had to travel to Pilsen on rabbinical business.

There was no time to pray for counsel from God. As soon as he departed, Joseph Golem approached Dvorele in the small garden of the rabbi's house. It was a day in spring. Bees feasted on blooming flowers. Water played in the fountain that one of the Sephardim had built from memories of Andalusia. Joseph Golem smiled and took Dvorele's tiny hand and pointed at the distant mountains.

Come with me, he seemed to be saying.

Come to the mountains of Bohemia, to their clear streams and green meadows.

Come, sweet Dvorele, and be with me.

But Dvorele had grown up beyond those mountains. And she thought that Joseph Golem wanted to return her to the horror she had escaped. She screamed. She screamed from deep within herself, from her heart and her lungs and her bowels. And she ran from Joseph Golem.

The Golem could not be hurt by knives or spears, but he suddenly erupted in rejection and rage. Michael pictured him toppling the fountain. Then he tore limbs off the beech trees. He smashed the shack where the gardener stored his tools. And in that wreckage, he found an axe.

Armed with the axe, he smashed the back gate of the garden and rushed into the city.

In his wordless, heartbroken anger, he chopped at the wheels of carriages and the doors of the rich. He destroyed the carts of the vendors of fish and vegetables. He broke down the doors of the Jewish Town Hall and reduced walls and masonry to powder and rubble. Michael saw people fleeing before him. And to Joseph Golem this became another rejection, more fuel for his blazing, wordless anger.

Michael hid behind a vegetable cart, as one of the councillors hopped on a horse to overtake Rabbi Loew, who was on the road to Pilsen. But Joseph Golem continued his rampage through the ghetto. Doors, windows, fountains, gardens: all were torn up, battered, destroyed. He saw a painting of the mountains and slashed at it with the blade of his axe. It was as if the great creature was looking in the quarter for something he could never find.

Finally, around sundown, Rabbi Loew returned. As he stepped from his carriage, he ignored Michael. His eyes were taking in the wreckage. The rabbi found Joseph Golem sitting in a deserted square, his axe resting on his giant thigh. The creature's eyes informed the rabbi that he was inconsolable. Rabbi Loew approached slowly, carefully, saying nothing. And for the first time, the Golem reacted in rage and rebellion against the man who had given him life. He threw his head back and released a wordless bellow that could be heard for seven miles. Then he snatched up his axe and began to march on Rabbi Loew. Michael thought: He must see Rabbi Loew as the true cause of his grief. If Rabbi Loew had not raised him from the mud of the Vltava, Joseph Golem would not be suffering the anguish of love.

The Golem stepped forward. He raised his axe. Before Rabbi Loew could give him an order, a small voice rang out sharply in the empty square.

*"Stop!"*

It was Dvorele.

She walked slowly into the space between the rabbi and the Golem. The great creature lowered the axe.

"Put it down, Joseph," she said softly.

The creature was wary, suspicious. He glanced at Rabbi Loew and then at the girl. But she was now fearless, as if God had put some iron into her. She came forward and took Joseph Golem's free hand. The axe fell from the other. She stood then on the tips of her toes, and reached up, and touched his face. The Golem fell awkwardly into a sitting position. Dvorele kissed his cheek.

The rage seeped out of him. He seemed to melt.

"Come," she said to Joseph Golem, turning finally to Rabbi Loew. "Let us go home."

Holding his hand, she led the Golem back to Rabbi Loew's house. The rabbi held open the door and the Golem stepped into the vestibule.

"You must sleep," Dvorele said to him.

The Golem nodded. Rabbi Loew led him upstairs to his own bedroom. He took pillows from the bed, which was too small for Joseph Golem, and laid them on the floor. The Golem was soon asleep.

Rabbi Loew moved quickly. He called for the two assistants who had gone with him that night to the banks of the Vltava. He took the silver spoon from a secret cupboard. He dressed completely in white. He removed the *shem* from its parchment case. Then he stood at the foot of the Golem, as on the Vltava he had stood at the head. He and his assistants prayed over the sleeping creature. And then Rabbi Loew slipped the *shem* into the Golem's mouth and in a grieving voice said the words from the Kabbalah, this time in reverse.

The Golem's huge body began to twitch. His eyes opened, full of fear and loss.

And then he crumbled into clay.

The assistants separated the clay from the creature's garments. They shook out the garments and folded them neatly. One assistant brought in two boxes resembling coffins. Rabbi Loew used the silver spoon to pack the clay into one box and tied it shut. The assistants lined the other with thick brocaded cloth, and Rabbi Loew placed the *shem* and the silver spoon on top. The assistants used nails to seal this coffin.

"Poor creature," one of the assistants whispered.

Rabbi Loew's eyes filled with tears.

"Yes," he said, glancing at the unsealed box. "You must scatter the clay on the banks of the Vltava. We must pray for him, the fine, sweet Golem."

"Will we ever see him again?" the other assistant asked.

"If we need him," Rabbi Loew said.

He took the small sealed coffin to the attic of the Old-New Synagogue, to rest among worn and discarded Torah scrolls and holy garments that had rotted with age. Rabbi Loew decreed that nobody could ever again visit the attic, except the chief rabbi. And that rabbi alone would know the secret of the creation of the Golem.

"And so it was," Rabbi Hirsch said, and

entered a long silence. "For centuries."

Michael cleared his throat.

"And Dvorele?" he said. "What happened to Dvorele?"

Rabbi Hirsch smiled.

"Along comes a handsome boy," he said. "Also an orphan. He falls in love with Dvorele and marries her, and nine wonderful children they have together."

Michael Devlin took a deep breath and exhaled hard, knowing that the story was over. Most stories and movies had happy endings, and this was a happy ending.

The rabbi glanced nervously at the door to the sanctuary.

# 12

Michael ran through the winter darkness down Kelly Street. His head was full of Prague and the Golem and the spires of distant cathedrals. Men moved through fog. Rats scurried in tunnels. Stones turned into roses. Love caused rage. He wondered who was wandering the streets of Prague at that very moment, and who was in the Old-New Synagogue, and whether the remains of the Golem were safe in their small, ancient coffin. He wondered about the magic words of the Kabbalah and the secret name of God.

And then, as he reached the dark alley that ran behind the Venus movie house, something hit him in the back and he was grabbed and spun and slammed against a wall.

Frankie McCarthy was an inch from his face in the darkness. He was so close that Michael could smell sour beer.

"Hello, Mr. altar boy," Frankie said.

"How's the little Kike-lover?"

Michael shuddered and said nothing.

"You were wit' that beard a long time, weren't you? What's *that* all about?"

"I'm helping him learn English," Michael murmured.

"Oh, you're a teacher now? I'm freezin' my ass off waitin' to talk to you, and you're a fuckin' *teacher?*"

Frankie lit a cigarette, grinning in the glow of the match. Then he stepped to the side, whirled suddenly, and slapped Michael hard in the face. The boy's ears rang. His face burned.

"You wouldn't teach that Yid anything he shouldn't know, would you, boy? I mean, you wouldn't, like, teach him about what happened to Mister G, would you?"

"No."

"But I hear you had some visitors, up your house," Frankie said. "I hear the bulls came to see you and stood there a long time. You didn't happen to teach *them* anything, did you, teacher?"

"No."

"How come I don't believe you, teach? How come I think you could be a perfect fuckin' canary?"

"The cops came to the house. My mother made them leave. I didn't say anything to them about anything."

Suddenly Frankie's hand came up and a four-inch blade snapped out at the touch of a button.

"You better not, boy. You better not say nothin' to nobody. Not to that old Hebe up the block. Not to no priest. Not to your mother. Definitely not to the fuckin' cops. You do? Something bad happens to me? I pay back. That's what Frankie McCarthy does. Frankie McCarthy pays back. I know where you live. So does every one of the Falcons. I know where your mother works."

Leave her out of this, prick, Michael thought, but said nothing. Frankie smiled in a mirthless way. Then he closed the knife.

"You remember that, teach," he said. "You remember what could happen, you teach the wrong shit."

He flipped his cigarette butt into the alley, then turned and walked slowly to the corner. Michael reached for the wall and steadied himself. His heart was thumping. He watched Frankie McCarthy cross Ellison Avenue and push through the steamed-over glass door of the Star Pool Room.

"You prick," Michael said out loud, using all those words he'd heard on the streets and almost never used. "You fucking shithead. You cocksucker."

All the way home, he wished he could summon the Golem.

# 13

At their afternoon sessions, Rabbi Hirsch said the words quickly in English and Michael returned them in Yiddish.

"Yes!"

*"Yoh!"*

"Thank you!"

*"A dank!"*

"You're welcome!"

*"Nishto . . . nishto . . ."*

*"Nishto far vos."*

*"Nishto far vos!"*

Rabbi Hirsch smiled. "Good, not too *goyish.*"

"It has to be *goyish,*" Michael said. "I'm a goy."

"Maybe it's true, that the Irish are the lost tribe of Israel." Then deadpan: "What?"

*"Vos?"*

"This!"

*"Dos!"*

"Where?"

*"Vu?"*

"Here."

*"Doh."*

"When?"

*"Ven?"*

"Now."

*"Itzt."*

"Who?"

*"Ver?"*

"Now the numbers," the rabbi said, holding up fingers as Michael said the words.

*"Ains, tsvai, drei, fir, finf, zeks, ziben, acht, nein, tsen, elef, tsvelf, dreitsen . . ."*

"Wait, wait, my shoes already I have to take off!"

The rabbi didn't take off his shoes to count, of course; he made tea. Michael was wearing a yarmulke, a satiny black skullcap that the rabbi had given him, explaining that some head covering must be worn in the house of God. This did not make him a Jew; Rabbi Hirsch made clear that he had no interest in converting Michael to Judaism. Wearing a yarmulke was just a sign of respect for the rules of this particular house of God. Michael told the rabbi that at Sacred Heart only the women were made to cover their heads, while the men held their hats in their hands throughout the services, and the rabbi shrugged. This made Michael wonder again why God had different rules for different people, but he didn't say this to Rabbi Hirsch.

"*Tai?*" the rabbi said, gesturing at the teapot.

"*Zaier gut,*" Michael said. "*A dank.*"

While the rabbi prepared tea, Michael went to the bookcase and examined some of the volumes, but he still could not read the alphabets. Rabbi Hirsch had explained some of the basic characters, but they would not stay in Michael's mind. This was a frustration, because after hearing the tales of the Golem, he had come to feel that the books in their ancient scripts contained secrets he must learn. The alphabets of God, he called them. The alphabets of the world.

He loved opening the volumes and seeing the beautifully designed pages; they were like the huge missals from which the priests at Sacred Heart sang Gregorian chant at high masses. They gave him a similar sense of order and perfection and mystery.

"Later, you can learn to read," the rabbi said, bringing two glasses of tea to the table. He moved an open letter out of the way. "First, speak. Men first speaked, uh, *spoke,* and then later they wrote."

"In the Ten Commandments, did Moses write like this?"

"Nobody know," the rabbi said.

"Knows," Michael said. "With an *s* at the end. Present tense."

"Nobody knows," the rabbi said, scooping three sugars into his tea, then handing the spoon to Michael, who did the same. "The original tablets, they have not survive. They might be just, how do you say? A legend. Like the lost tribe. . . . Some say Moses spoke Egyptian. He definitely didn't speak Aramaic. That is the language Jesus spoke. We know that for sure. Aramaic . . ."

So it went until they had finished the tea. Then the rabbi glanced at the letter and said he had to go into the sanctuary to recover a book. Michael followed him. The room was much smaller than the downstairs church at Sacred Heart, but to Michael it had an even more powerful sense of the sacred. A few weeks earlier in this basement sanctuary, Rabbi Hirsch had shown him the Ark, which contained the Torah scroll. That, he explained, was the symbol of the Tradition, a word he often used to describe the kind of Jew he was: a follower of the Tradition. When he said the word, Michael always heard it with a capital letter.

"All the centuries of the Jews?" the rabbi said. "Thousands and thousands of years? To this place, they are connected. That's what we Jews mean by the Tradition. That is what we have in a synagogue. Everything that ever happened."

"Is the word *synagogue* Hebrew or Yiddish?"

"Neither," the rabbi said, moving slowly through the pews, lifting prayer books, opening them to scan names, closing them. "It's Greek. This fact even most Jews don't know. *Synagogue* is Greek! Amazing! It means, uh, uh, place of assembly in English. I looked up it."

"Looked it up," Michael said.

"Yes: looked it up."

Michael loved these moments. The rabbi was a grown man, but he was always learning something new and becoming as excited as a ten-year-old when he passed the new thing on to Michael. One afternoon, he spoke in an amazed way about the Constitution and the Bill of Rights. Another time he discussed the building of the Brooklyn Bridge in the 1880s and how it changed New York, linking Manhattan to Brooklyn forever. Knowledge made his eyes twinkle, his face seem younger. He paced about the tiny room, he motioned with his hands, waving his fingers gracefully to describe music, making fists to express anger or passion. About some things, of course, Michael was the teacher. American things. Baseball.

Movies. Comic books. But most of the time, the rabbi led the class.

On an afternoon like this one, Michael wished he could tell his father about the things he was learning. His mother always listened patiently to his reports, but his father might have been even more excited. If Tommy Devlin had come home, he could have gone to college on the GI Bill, which Michael heard about from the rabbi.

"Imagine," the rabbi said, "the son of a carpenter, a farmer, a policeman, he can go to the university! Like any rich guy! Is a great country, *boychik*."

Michael imagined his father sitting in the kitchen, studying his college books at the same table where Michael was doing his homework. They could talk about how Judaism was the father of Christianity. He could tell his father about the synagogue and its three purposes. It was a house of worship, just like Sacred Heart. It was a house of the people, where Jews could spend time together. And it was a house of study. He wished he could explain all this to his father and let him know how sad Rabbi Hirsch looked when he talked about it.

"Almost nobody to this synagogue comes anymore," the rabbi said, waving a hand. "The Jews from around here? Dead. Moved away." That was why the upper sanctuary was kept closed, its doors locked and sealed. Michael had never seen it. "We have services there? Everybody is lonely. And another thing: we don't have the money to heat it up." Most of the congregation now was composed of older people, he said, who could not come easily to synagogue through the snow. "About Florida they are thinking more than about God," the rabbi said, "and who blames them?" He worried, he told the boy, that some Shabbos he would not have a minyan. The Tradition insisted on a minyan — a minimum of ten males — before worship could begin. "Nine men and one woman? Not enough. Not even one beautiful, intelligent woman. An old man with no teeth and a very little brain is okay, but not a woman. Sometimes . . ."

He sighed in the face of God's mysterious ways. Years ago, before Rabbi Hirsch came to Brooklyn, the upstairs sanctuary had been filled. "The old people told me this." There were services on Wednesdays too, and the synagogue was packed *all day* on Saturdays. "How wonderful it must have be. Like Prague when I'm a boy. Now? Not so wonderful. Not in Prague. Not here. I pray and pray but this does not become a house of the people. Not full of singing. Of praying. Of laughing. And you and me, we are the only ones who study." He shook his head. "The rabbi and his Shabbos goy."

Now Michael wandered to the back of the sanctuary, where double doors opened under the stoop on MacArthur Avenue. There were three locks and a plank wedged into two angle irons to keep the doors from being forced open from the other side. Hebrew tablets were cemented into the walls. And in the right-hand corner there was a narrow oak door.

"Where does this door go, rabbi?"

"Upstairs."

"Can I see it?"

"No, is closed," the rabbi said. "Well, someday maybe."

Then he stopped, a book in his hand. "Ah, here is the book. Greenberg, Yossel." He smiled. "Just like the Golem."

Michael came over, his stomach suddenly queasy.

"What's his name?"

"Greenberg."

"That's Mister G."

"You know him?"

"I was there when he was beaten up."

"You were there?"

"Yes," Michael said, and then realized he might have said too much. He turned away.

"Is very sad story," Rabbi Hirsch said. "His son writes to me a letter. He says his father is in — the word is coma? Yes. But maybe also he is given up on the life. He says Greenberg just lies in the hospital in the dark. The hospital, it don't help. His head is broke and hurts all the time. Tubes are in his arms. They give him medicine. They feed him. But Greenberg never says nothing. The son, to me he writes a letter that says maybe his father's old prayer book will help. The son, he says maybe the book will make Greenberg open his eyes."

Michael remembered the old man holding his head, the blood slippery on his fingers, the cash register held in the air, the breaking sound when it landed, and the shards of broken glass and ruined *Captain Marvel*s on the floor. He remembered Mister G lying in his own blood. He remembered Frankie McCarthy's sneer. The rabbi stared at him.

"Did you tell the police who done it, this beating to Greenberg?"

"No."

"Why?" the rabbi said softly.

*"Ich vais nisht."*

"You don't know *why?*"

Michael tried to face the rabbi, but gazed instead at the walls and the low ceiling.

"I can't tell the cops," Michael said. "Around here, you don't tell the cops anything. They're like, I don't know, the enemy. And I'm Irish, Rabbi. I talk to the cops, I'm an informer, and my mother says they were the worst people in Ireland." He struggled for control, pushing the image of Mister G's bloody face from his mind. "Around here, they call an informer a rat, or a squealer. I talk to the cops, and I get found out, they give me the mark of the squealer. They cut your cheek all the way to your ear, they —"

"You can't tell the police in secret?"

"No! I tell them and don't give my name, they do nothing. I give my name, they make me a witness, and then everyone knows my name. Look, I gotta go."

He started to walk out past the low railing. The world was suddenly blurry. Michael trembled, afraid he would cry, afraid he was about to lose Rabbi Hirsch.

"Wait!" the rabbi called after him.

Michael paused, and the rabbi came to his side.

"I didn't tell you go to the police," he said. "I want just to know why you didn't." He paused. "Now I know. You're, what's the word? Scared."

"Yes."

"Of the man who did this to Yossel Greenberg?"

"Not just him."

"Who else, then?"

"Everybody."

"Your mother?"

"No."

"Me?"

"No."

"So there's two people. Already we know it's not everybody."

Michael tried to smile, but his eyes were full of tears.

"Michael, you are a very good boy," the rabbi said. "You are kind. You are a worker, I can see. But you are young. You have not already learn some of the hard things in the life. One very hard thing? You keep quiet about some crime, it's just as bad as the crime." He paused. "Believe me. I know."

# 14

For two days, Michael walked on other streets to avoid the synagogue. The rabbi's words moved in and out of his mind, even while he sat in classes at school. *You keep quiet about some crime, it's just as bad as the crime.* He thought about talking it over with his mother. If he told the cops, would he really be an informer? He answered himself: Yes. Besides, if he talked, she'd be in trouble too. They might try to hurt her. They'd have to move. To go somewhere else. Maybe she'd even take him with her back to Ireland. Far from Sonny and Jimmy and games on the street and the Dodgers in Ebbets Field. Far from home. But suppose someone in Ireland heard about what he'd done? They might end up in even worse trouble.

At night, in his dark room, there was a jumble of images as he tried to sleep: Frankie McCarthy's knife, Mister G's broken head, Rabbi Hirsch's steady gaze as he asked him to explain his silence. What was done to Mister G was a crime. No doubt about it. So what was his own silence? To get rid of the faces, he tried to conjure other images, from comics or movies. But Frankie and Mister G and the rabbi kept returning. And then Custer appeared in his mind, right out of the West, and he sat again with his father in the balcony of the Grandview, and wished Tommy Devlin could be there to tell him what to do.

Walking to school in the morning, he thought about what it would be like if he never saw Rabbi Hirsch again. He was certain the rabbi was disgusted with him. After all, Mister G was from his synagogue and he sure couldn't afford to lose any more people. And maybe I can't fix Mister G's head, but I can help teach Frankie that crime does not pay. Just as the comic books said.

Except I can't be a squealer. Can't. I just can't. But I don't want to stop learning the rabbi's language, or hearing his stories either. If I never see him again, it's like finding half the pages in a book are blank. I need to know about Leah — how she died. And how he came to America, to Brooklyn. Maybe I can ask him all that, and then say goodbye and thank him for everything he taught me and tell him how sorry I am for the way it turned out. Yes. I have to see him. I can't just disappear. I can't be a coward.

That afternoon, after school, Michael knocked on the door of the synagogue. For a moment, he thought of running. But the rabbi opened the door and smiled broadly.

"Good, good," he said. "Today we learn the words for food."

It was as simple as that. There was no mention of the cops. There was no mention of Mister G, or crimes, or justice. The rabbi told Michael that bread was *broyt* and butter was *putter* and proper Jewish food had to be kosher. They had resumed their routine. Everything was as it had been. Except at night, when Michael saw faces in the dark.

Michael did not spend every afternoon under the tutelage of Rabbi Hirsch. Nor did his every waking vision turn on the menacing figure of Frankie McCarthy and his knife. As the snows melted and a chilly spring eased in, he and his friends were increasingly absorbed with the coming of Jackie Robinson. For Michael, such talk was a relief, a way to avoid discussing the images that stole his sleep.

"This is screwy," he said one afternoon, as they moved together through the raw weather of the Brooklyn streets. They were still wearing their winter clothes. "The Dodgers are training in *Cuba* this year, instead of Florida. Because of Jackie Robinson."

"How come?" Jimmy Kabinsky asked.

"Because he's a Negro, Jimmy," Michael said, using the word that his mother insisted was the polite way to describe colored people. "They don't let Negroes in the hotels in Florida."

"I don't know how they could get away wit' that in Florida," Sonny Montemarano said. "There's colored people all over Florida."

"How do you know?" Jimmy said. "You never been to Florida."

"My brother told me. He was down there durin' the war. He says, some places they got more colored people than white people down there."

"So where do they stay if they're driving someplace?" Michael said.

"They have colored hotels, I think. You know, only colored people."

"So how come Jackie Robinson can go to a hotel in Cuba?" Jimmy asked.

"Because they have a lot of colored people in Cuba," Sonny said. "I guess there's so many of them in that Cuba, they can go anyplace."

And so it went, as they wandered through the parish, avoiding the Star Pool Room, crossing the street if they saw a group of the Falcons moving along the avenue with their pegged pants billowing in the breeze. Michael noticed something about himself on these wanderings: when he was with his friends, he had to talk and act older, which was to say, tougher, more cynical, more knowing; when he was with Rabbi Hirsch he could act his own age. He even walked differently with his friends, falling into the rolling gait that Sonny had adopted from some of the Falcons.

This often made him feel like two people. He assured his friends that he was still keeping his eyes open at the synagogue, while teaching English to the rabbi, but so far there was no sign of treasure or a map. Technically, he was being truthful; there was no treasure to be found, except in the stories told by Rabbi Hirsch and in the books on his shelves. But Michael wasn't being completely truthful. He didn't tell them how much he liked Rabbi Hirsch. He didn't tell them about Prague and Rabbi Loew, Brother Thaddeus and the Golem. Those were his possessions: private, special, as alive in his mind as Sonny and Jimmy Kabinsky, but kept in separate boxes. They even rose from those boxes in his mind and came to him now in dreams. Besides, if he told his friends too much, they might suspect him of going soft, of shifting loyalties. They would treat him as if he were different. He could not imagine what they would do if they ever saw him in a yarmulke.

Baseball was easier to talk about. There was little argument about whether Jackie Robinson could hit big league pitching. All the sportswriters thought he could. They knew he could run too. And field. On Ellison Avenue, they talked about the color of his skin.

"The guy was in the army, right?" Sonny said. "Well, f' my money, if he can fight for his country he oughtta be able to play in the major leagues. Case closed."

"Why would he want to go where he ain't wanted?" Jimmy said.

"Because he can!"

They knew from the newspapers that Robinson had played the 1946 season for the Montreal Royals, the number one Dodger farm team, and tore up the league. Down in Cuba, he was still on the Montreal roster. The *Brooklyn Eagle* and the *Daily News* said the Royals would play a series of exhibition games against the Dodgers during spring training and then Branch Rickey, the boss of the Brooklyn team, would decide whether to bring up Robinson. But the newspapers were full of a word that was new to Michael and his friends: *dissension*. The sports writers used the word as if it were the name of a fatal disease.

"This thing, this dissension, you know, it could ruin a ball club," Sonny said.

"What do they need it for?" said Jimmy. "Why don't they just leave things alone and win the pennant? Last year, we was tied for first on the last day of the season. That's a pretty good team."

"Not as good as the Cardinals," Michael said. "The playoffs, suppose Robinson had played. The second game, he gets a triple, steals a couple of bases, maybe forces a third game. Then in the third game he homers in the ninth, and *we* go to the World Series in Boston, not the Cardinals."

"I don't like that dissension," Sonny said.

Dissension was all about the new colored player. The newspapers were reporting that Dixie Walker, "the People's Cherce," had asked to be traded if Jackie Robinson joined the team. Dixie Walker was a southerner. From Alabama or Georgia or someplace. "You know," Sonny said, "down there where they had that slavery all those years." Everybody on Ellison Avenue thought that

Dixie Walker was also the greatest right fielder in Dodger history. The boys knew that Walker had won the batting championship in 1944, when he hit .357, and Dodger fans weren't used to their players winning much of anything. But the newspapers now said Dixie Walker had caught the terrible dissension disease. And he wasn't the only one. There were others, including Eddie Stanky, the second baseman.

"That ain't dissension," Sonny said. "He's worried about his job."

"What do you mean?" asked Jimmy.

"He's a *second baseman*, Jimmy! And *Robinson's* a second baseman!"

"Jeez, I never thought about that."

"Think, Jimmy, think. Some of these guys got *angles!*"

Walking along the parkside, under the dripping trees, they talked about what position Robinson would play and how the manager, Leo Durocher, would never replace Stanky with a rookie. But maybe Robinson could play first, and there was always third, where the Dodgers were weak. And hey, maybe this wouldn't happen at all. Maybe dissension would get so terrible that Durocher would go to Rickey and say that as the manager, he couldn't do it, it was tearing the team apart, and Jackie Robinson would stay in Montreal. How could Dixie Walker put his arm around Jackie Robinson and say all for one and one for all?

At night, Michael struggled to make sense of this. He wished that Jackie Robinson was white, like everybody else. If he was white, they would bring him up and make him the goddamned first baseman and that would be that. No dissension. No trouble. No spring training in goddamned Cuba. Why did Jackie Robinson have to be colored, for Christ's sake?

But he was. And down on Ellison Avenue, they were predicting race riots at Ebbets Field. If Jackie Robinson struck out or dropped a ball or was hit by a pitch, it would be worse than Harlem in 1943, or the riots in Detroit or Los Angeles, where people were shot and stabbed by the hundreds. They said there'd be muggings at the ball-park. They said Robinson would ruin the Dodgers with dissension and they'd be lucky to finish fifth. Michael wondered if maybe Dixie Walker knew more about all this than he did. Maybe Dixie was afraid that more and more colored people would come to the big leagues and pretty soon even the white players would be calling each other motherfuckers.

Michael felt ignorant about the whole subject of Negroes. Except for Ebony in *The Spirit* and Fat Stuff in *Smilin' Jack*, there were no colored people in the comics. There were no colored people in the movies, except for Rochester and that guy in the comedies who was always seeing ghosts and saying, "Feets, get moving." There were no colored cowboys and no colored secret agents and no colored pilots. There were colored guys in the Tarzan movies, but they were natives, chasing Tarzan through the jungle; they weren't from places like Brooklyn.

There was only one colored man in the parish, a janitor who lived in the basement of an apartment house across from the park. He was tall and bony and his skin was very black, and they would sometimes see him setting out the garbage cans in the mornings. He had no wife and no children and never said anything, not even good morning, and certainly never motherfucker. But he worked very hard. None of them knew his name. He was a man in gray overalls with black skin.

For an hour on this rainy night, Michael tossed and turned, wracked with his own ignorance. Finally he got up, turned on the light, slipped into the living room, and found the volume of the *Wonderland of*

*Knowledge* marked *Min–Pea*. Back in his room, he read the one-page entry about Negroes. He knew they had been slaves, of course, knew that Arab traders had captured them and shipped them across the Atlantic. But he didn't know that the slaveholders would not let them go to school.

*The Negro entered America by the back door, and when freedom came to the slaves of the South, it brought with it innumerable problems that have not yet been entirely solved.* The worst problem, the book said, was that many Negroes weren't educated, and this hurt them when they started moving to northern cities after the Civil War. But Michael thought: That's a problem around here too; Frankie McCarthy isn't going to be a professor or work in an office. Neither are a lot of other guys. *In settling in the Northern cities, the Negroes occupied neighborhoods that had already been lived in by others, creating problems of housing that have become critical in recent years.* That's like us too, Michael thought. We live in neighborhoods that were already lived in by others, and we have problems too, especially since the veterans came home and found out there's not enough places for them to live. Last year, in a house on Saracen Place, the roof fell in, the building was so old, and three people were killed.

There are rats in a lot of buildings. There are six apartments in this building and only one of them has a gas stove and there's no steam heat. So what's the big deal? Life in New York isn't just hard for Negroes; it's hard for lots of people.

But even with such bad educations, the book said, Negroes had added a lot to the culture of America. *The native rhythm of the highly emotional Negro race has become a vital force in American music; and modern music, of which jazz is a form, has been profoundly affected, if not inspired, by the spirituals and "blues" which are entirely different from anything else found in music.*

That paragraph made him wonder. Suppose Count Basie couldn't play in America? Or Duke Ellington? Or Louis Armstrong? What if somebody said that they could only sell their records in Negro neighborhoods? What if Teddy Wilson and Lionel Hampton weren't allowed to play in Benny Goodman's band because they were Negroes? If they followed the rules of baseball, Negro bands would play for Negroes and white bands for whites and the musicians could never play with each other. Roy Eldridge couldn't play with Gene Krupa. That would be nuts.

But maybe baseball is different.

No, that's even more nuts.

Michael closed the book and returned to bed. He whispered: Trying to figure this out is one huge pain in the ass. I wish Jackie Robinson was white. But Jackie Robinson isn't white. And he can play ball. And he could help us win the goddamned pennant. Period. Case closed, as Sonny says.

Besides, skin color was skin color, right? It was just the color of your goddamned skin. There was nothing anybody could do about that. You were born with it. Like some people were born with big feet or blue eyes. You didn't make the choice. Your parents did. Or God did. God made Jackie Robinson a Negro. God made the choice, not Dixie Walker. What was it Rabbi Hirsch said?

*Vos Got git iz gut.* . . . What God gives is good . . .

In Michael's drowsy mind, they began to merge into a group: Jackie Robinson, the Jews, the Catholics in Belfast, Benny Goodman and Lionel Hampton, Gene Krupa and Roy Eldridge, Rabbi Loew and Dvorele. And coming out of the smoke, sneering and hard, the goddamned Nazis and Brother Thaddeus and Frankie McCarthy swaggering around with the Falcons.

*Vos Got git iz gut.* . . .

Mumbling his borrowed Yiddish, longing for the dazzling clarity of summer, he fell into sleep, dreamy with images of Jack Roosevelt Robinson playing second base under the sun of Havana.

# 15

Each day for a week, spring rains slapped against the stained-glass windows of Sacred Heart and the stained-glass windows of the synagogue. Each day, steady sheets of advancing rain, monotonous and soft, were followed by sudden twisted columns of water, skirling and dancing, destroying umbrellas, lifting hats off skulls, spattering the newspapers on the wooden stand outside Slowacki's until Mrs. Slowacki came out to cover them with a sheet of oilcloth held fast with a piece of angle iron. Basements flooded. Sewers backed up. Tree limbs snapped off and crashed into the yards. Shoes were ruined, their soles flapping like black tongues. Fungus seemed to sprout in clothes. In the apartments on Ellison Avenue, where the rain came pounding from the harbor like liquid ice, tenants stuffed towels into the sills of the kitchen windows and talked in the wet halls about how the weather was all different, wilder and fiercer, since the atom bomb.

For Michael, the raging spring weather was like something from a movie about the South Seas: a monsoon movie, a movie about hurricanes. With Jon Hall and Dorothy Lamour, and the evil prison guard, John Carradine, who looked like Emperor Rudolf of Prague. The power of the storms tested him, as it had tested Jon Hall, but it didn't feel like punishment. The storms had such a radiant brightness to them, such a newness, that they made Michael Devlin happy. He wanted to run through them, to dive into the little rivers along the curbs, to splash and roll and laugh and dance.

The snow was soon gone, washed down the Brooklyn hills to the harbor. On the radio, Michael listened to Red Barber broadcasting the Dodger games from Cuba through invisible barriers of distance and static. The words coming through the tiny speaker of the leatherette radio were often unclear, gouged, scratched, crunched, making abrupt loops and bends in the air. But when he could hear Barber, the announcer's voice was full of blue skies and palm trees. He never mentioned Jackie Robinson unless Robinson did something. There wasn't much argument about Robinson in those radio accounts of distant games, no alarm or anxiety, no mention of dissension; radio was not the same as the newspapers. But Barber's serene drawl was itself a guarantee that the season lay directly ahead of them. A season in which everyone knew that Jack Roosevelt Robinson would make history, just by showing up.

"I'll tell you why I want Robinson to come up," Michael said to his friends one afternoon. "Because it never happened before."

"There was never an earthquake in Brooklyn before either," Sonny said. "You want that to happen too?"

"Hey, maybe Frankie McCarthy would fall down a crack," Michael said.

"I wish he'd fall down the crack of his ass," Sonny said, and they all laughed.

Then one rain-drowned evening when his mother wasn't working at the movie house, Michael came upstairs and into the kitchen and saw a large cardboard box off to the side and his mother beaming. The room was loud with Al Jolson singing "April Showers," and though it wasn't yet April there had been a lot of showers, and Jolson made their annual arrival sound like an occasion of joy. While Jolson promised that the showers of April would bring the flowers of May, Kate Devlin pointed in the direction of the voice, and on a shelf between the kitchen and the first bedroom, shaped like a small cathedral, was a new Philco radio.

*So keep on lookin' for the bluebird,* Jolson was singing, *An' listenin' to his song,* as Michael's mother joined for the last triumphant line, *Whenever April showers come along. . . .*

"Up the Republic!" she shouted, as she always did when she was delighted. She had saved and saved and here it was: a new radio, and a Philco at that. An aerial emerged from the back of the radio and snaked around the wall molding to dangle out a window into the yards. No static distorted the voices; the sounds of human beings were as clear as water. The radio also had shortwave, and the names of distant places were printed in tiny letters on the glowing dark yellow dial. Copenhagen. London. Dublin. Paris. Moscow. And there, yeah, would you look at that? *Prague!*

"It's beautiful, Mom," he said. "I can't believe it."

"Neither can I," she said. "It was a real bargain down at Ginsberg's."

He didn't ask how much she had paid; he knew better than to try to get her to talk about money. Instead, he turned away from the new radio, listening now to Les Brown and His Band of Renown, and saw the peeling face of the leatherette Admiral, lying on its side on a chair beside the gas stove. The cord and plug dangled uselessly a few inches off the linoleum floor. The old radio looked as sad as a man without a job.

"What are you going to do with the old one, Mom?" he asked.

"God, who knows? Give it to the St. Vincent DePaul Society, maybe. Maybe some poor soul will find it there."

A pause.

"Can I give it to Rabbi Hirsch?"

"Och, Michael, it's a terrible oul' heap of junk. The rabbi might be insulted."

"No, no. He'd be — Mom, he's *poor*. He has almost no money. I *know* he wants to hear music. So . . ."

She smiled. "Do what you like," she said, and moved the dial in search of the *Lux Radio Theater*.

The next day, there was no rain. Michael rushed home after school, dropped off his books, picked up the old leatherette Admiral and went back up the hill to the synagogue. When Rabbi Hirsch answered the door, the boy handed him the radio.

"What's this?"

"It's for you," Michael said. "It's not the greatest, but it works."

The rabbi held the radio in both hands and for a moment didn't move. It was as if he were receiving something holy. Michael imagined him in the café in Prague when he was young, listening with his friends to the many languages of Europe.

"*A sheynem dank,*" he said. Thank you very much. He hugged the radio to his chest as if it were a treasure, and Michael saw his eyes water and his face tremble with emotion. "*A sheynem dank.*"

"You're welcome, Rabbi. *Nishto far vos.*"

"Come," Rabbi Hirsh said, his voice cracking slightly. "We listen to some music."

He moved some books and placed the radio on the bookshelf beside the photograph of his wife, Leah. They found an outlet and plugged in the cord. Then they stared for a moment at the Admiral. The rabbi gestured with a hand, urging Michael to turn it on. Michael was puzzled; this was not Shabbos, and besides, turning on a radio couldn't possibly be considered work.

"You turn it on, Rabbi," Michael said, putting his hands behind his back.

"*Neyn,* no, you do it, boychik."

"I refuse," Michael said. "It's your radio now, so you turn it on."

"Someday I want to tell somebody that a kid camed here and gave to me a radio and put music in my world."

"Okay. Just tell them *you* turned it on."

The rabbi sighed and reached reverently for the knob, the way Father Heaney might reach for a cruet.

And suddenly music filled the low-ceilinged room.

Bing Crosby.

*Let me straddle my own saddle*
*Underneath the Western skies . . .*

Michael started singing with him, the way his mother sang with Al Jolson.

*On my cayuse, let me wander over yonder*
*'Til I see the mountains rye-iiiiise . . .*

The rabbi hopped around, raising his leg, slapping his thigh, laughing, shouting, *"Vos iz dos? Vos iz dos?"* And Michael shouted, " 'Don't Fence Me In!' Bing Crosby!" And sang:

*Let me be by myself in the evening*
    *bree-ease,*
*Listen to the murmur of the cottonwood*
    *tree-ease,*
*Send me off forever but I ask you*
    *pleee-ease,*
*Don't fence me in. . . .*

More whoops, more jigs, and then Bing Crosby was gone. Michael had never before seen the rabbi so happy. They moved from station to station, hearing Nat Cole and Perry Como and Doris Day. Michael couldn't find Benny Goodman or Count Basie, but he showed the rabbi the numbers of the good music stations and how to find the news and the baseball.

"Again I want to hear Bing Crosby," Rabbi Hirsch said. "About don't put a fence around me."

Michael tuned in WNEW and heard the Goodman band. A trumpet player was offering "And the Angels Sing." The rabbi's head nodded to the rhythm. And then his face shifted into deep concentration.

"This music?" the rabbi said, his eyes widening. "This I know. From Prague, I know this. At weddings, we play this, only slower. And dance."

Michael glanced at the photograph of Leah. "Did you dance to it at your wedding?"

The rabbi's face twitched. "No. We never got to dance."

Michael suddenly pictured his father dancing with his mother. To "And the Angels Sing." A slow jitterbug, his father singing, *You speak, and then the angels sing . . . ,* and his mother laughing. He wished he could have seen them dancing and happy, and then tried to imagine the rabbi in the same way, with Leah. There was a hint of sadness in the air. Michael talked past it. He told Rabbi Hirsch the name of the song in English and explained that the trumpet player's name was Ziggy Elman.

"He's Jewish?" the rabbi asked, brightening.

Michael didn't know, but Ziggy Elman was in Benny Goodman's band, and he did know that Benny Goodman was Jewish. He had read that in some newspaper story. He told the rabbi that Goodman played the clarinet and his band was almost as great as the band of Count Basie, who definitely was the greatest. Goodman even had Negroes in his band long before baseball got around to it. Lionel Hampton. Teddy Wilson. The rabbi smiled and nodded to the music.

"This music," he whispered. "This I know."

At the end of "And the Angels Sing," there was a commercial.

"Ziggy Elman," the rabbi murmured, like a man saying a prayer. "Ziggy Elman! *Ziggy* Elman? Ziggy Elman . . ."

Then the six o'clock news came on and

Michael had to leave. Rabbi Hirsch ran a hand over the peeling leatherette radio and bowed slightly to Michael.

"Is the nicest thing happen to me in America so far," he said. "Please to thank your mother when you go home and study."

He went to the door with Michael.

"Ziggy Elman!" he said. "If my father only have called me Ziggy, I would have been a different person. Imagine a rabbi, name of Rabbi *Ziggy?*"

On his way home, Michael surged with the happiness that radiated from the rabbi. For an hour, the rabbi had been so happy, so full of delight, so overcome with the sounds of music and words, that the air of the tiny synagogue rooms seemed to sparkle. It was as if a deaf man had suddenly begun to hear.

That joy filled Michael's head as he passed the alley beside the Venus and started to turn into Ellison Avenue. Then it vanished. There was a small crowd outside the Star Pool Room. Two police cars and the Plymouth used by the detectives were up on the sidewalk. The front door was open. He could see that the green tops of the pool tables were empty. The Falcons were lined up against the wall with Abbott and Costello facing them. Michael drifted to the edge of the crowd, which was being held back by two uniformed policemen.

"What's going on?" he asked a man wearing a cap covered with union buttons.

"Da bulls are lockin' up that Frankie McCarthy," the man said. Michael trembled.

"What for?"

"Beatin' up some Hebe, I hear."

Then everyone backed up a few feet, and the detectives were leading Frankie McCarthy out of the poolroom. Frankie curled his mouth, like a gangster from a movie. His hands were cuffed behind his back and each detective had him by an elbow.

" 'Ey, Frankie boy," someone shouted. "See ya in an hour."

The crowd laughed and so did the Falcons, who were standing just inside the door of the poolroom. A few of them rested pool cues on their shoulders like baseball bats.

"This is a bum rap," Frankie McCarthy said, lifting his chin defiantly, like Cagney or Bogart. "They got nothin' on me."

Then his eyes picked out Michael on the fringes of the crowd. He said nothing, but his eyes chilled to the color of aluminum.

The detectives broke the look by shoving Frankie into the backseat of the Plymouth.

Abbott sat beside him, a dead cigar clamped in his mouth. Costello started the car and drove away. The crowd milled around, talking it over. One of the Falcons closed the poolroom door.

"He's some piece of work, that Frankie," said the man with the union buttons.

"Yeah: he's working overtime at being a bum," said Charlie Senator, who worked at the Bohack grocery store. He was a quiet, moody guy who didn't talk much but was liked by everyone. One reason they liked him was that he had a wooden leg and never complained about it. Michael had heard that his real leg was shot off at Anzio.

"You wouldn't say that to his face."

"Probably not," Senator said. "Guys like that jack you up in the dark. But he's still a bum."

"What'd he do was so bad?"

"Plenty," Senator said, and limped away.

Then Michael saw two of the Falcons looking at him from behind the plate-glass window of the poolroom. He turned and walked quickly home.

Going up the stairs, he realized how dark the halls were, full of shadowy places where Frankie McCarthy could jack him up. Why did Frankie give him that look? Why were the Falcons staring at him from the poolroom? Now Frankie was down at the precinct house and they'd want revenge. He remembered Frankie's knife. He saw Mister G with his broken head. Somebody must have talked. Michael knew that he had held fast with the police; he hadn't informed, he hadn't turned rat. But *somebody* had. And only he, Sonny, and Jimmy had been in Mister G's store that day. He felt vaguely sick. He thought he knew his friends. Maybe he didn't. Maybe Sonny or Jimmy had turned chicken and ratted out Frankie McCarthy. And if one of them did, why wouldn't the coward shift the blame, tell the Falcons it was Michael? Save his own ass.

But no: it couldn't be that way. They were his friends. All for one and one for all. They wouldn't turn informers. They wouldn't risk the mark of the squealer. The cops must have found another witness. Or maybe Frankie bragged in some bar about beating up Mister G. Or maybe they found his fingerprints on the telephone. It had to be something else. Not an informer. Not someone like Victor McLaglen in the movie about the informer in Ireland. Not a Judas. Maybe.

Still, Michael was afraid. He wished his mother were home, but she had another three hours, at least, to work at the Grandview. He locked the kitchen door behind him. He opened the bathroom door, his heart beating fast, poked his head inside, and was relieved that nobody was there. He tiptoed through the other rooms, turning on lights, holding his breath as he opened closets. Finally he felt safe. He turned on the new Philco, and lit a jet on the gas range to heat the stew his mother had left for him. While Ella Fitzgerald sang on the radio, he opened his schoolbag and laid his books on the kitchen table and gazed dully at his homework assignments. Boring goddamned crap. Why did they waste so much time in English with diagramming sentences? Sure, it came in handy, explaining things to Rabbi Hirsch. But it was so simple. They could get it over with in three days. They didn't need three weeks of dumb sentences. Why didn't they read Sherlock Holmes and see how A. Conan Doyle wrote sentences? Or Robert Louis Stevenson? They wrote beautiful sentences. Not this stuff. John threw the ball at Jane. Frank reached for his book. Shit. He thought about reading comics first and then doing the homework, but then he might be too tired and he had to get up at seven and serve the eight o'clock mass, and if he came to class without the homework he —

*The fire escape window!*

It was never locked. Anyone could get a boost up to the fire escape ladder on the first floor and walk all the way up to the top. Jesus Christ!

He ran to his room. The window was open about half an inch, with a towel jammed in the space to keep out the rain. He removed the towel and pulled down hard to close the window, but he couldn't get the crude lock to snap shut. He grunted and strained, but the lock was scabby with too many coats of paint. Still, the window was closed. He leaned a book against the window so that if it opened the book would fall and make a noise. Then he stepped back from the light of the street and looked down at Ellison Avenue. He saw nobody from the Falcons. Then the smell of burning stew summoned him back to the kitchen.

The stew was black at the bottom but the rest was all right. He scooped it onto a plate while Stan Lomax came on the radio, with the day's doings in the world of sports. Jackie Robinson was closer than ever to coming up to the Dodgers. In twelve games against the Dodgers and clubs in Panama he was hitting .519. Amazing. *Five-nineteen!* Babe Ruth never hit .519. Maybe Ted Williams or Stan Musial could do it, but they hadn't done it yet. Robinson was still a

Montreal Royal, said Stan Lomax, but it seemed sure he wouldn't be a minor leaguer for very much longer.

Finishing up the stew, wiping his plate with bread, Michael tried to imagine what it must be like to be Robinson. He examined his own skin, spreading it with his hand, then pinching it with thumb and forefinger. It wasn't really white. Paper was white. His skin was sort of pink. In the summer, it got red and then brown. It had freckles of a darker, reddish color. What must it be like to look at your skin and see that it was black? Or not really black. A kind of dark brown, really. What was it like to wake up every goddamned morning and see that skin and know that some shmuck looked down on you just for that? You hit .519 in spring training and some fat business guy in a suit, Branch Rickey or somebody, some prick who can't hit .019, will decide if you play or not? How could that be? Michael's anger rose in him and then faded. If I'm angry, he thought, sitting here, still white or pink, how must Robinson feel?

Then, in his head, he was Robinson, down in Cuba or over in Panama, eating dinner alone in some restaurant, a joint filled with all those girls who dressed like Carmen Miranda, bare bellies and tits bouncing and bananas on their heads. In a fancy place with candles and tablecloths and waiters, like all those movies about flying down to Rio, and here come Dixie Walker and Eddie Stanky. The restaurant is packed. There are three empty seats at my table, Robinson's table. I wave at them, my teammates, to come over and sit down. But Walker and Stanky won't sit down. They'd rather starve to death than sit with me. Like Englishmen looking at an Irishman.

And as Robinson, Michael was furious again. And then felt very sad. What the hell's the matter with those bozos? Why don't they try to get to know me? Maybe they could learn something. Hey, I went to college and they didn't, so maybe they'd find out a few things. How can they act the way they do without knowing anything at all about me except my batting average and the color of my skin?

Idiots.

Bums.

He spent an hour on homework, dealing quickly with grammar and arithmetic, taking longer to answer questions about a history chapter. This told the story of a heroic Jesuit priest named Isaac Jogues, who had his fingers bitten off by Indians and later had trouble saying the mass, because he couldn't hold the host. He wondered how he could tell this to Rabbi Hirsch without laughing. The goyim are crazy, he told himself. The goyim are definitely crazy.

For a while he listened to music on the radio. When he heard "Don't Fence Me In," he wished he had a telephone, so he could call Rabbi Hirsch and tell him the number of the station. But Rabbi Hirsch didn't have a telephone either. Almost nobody did. Not Sonny. Not Jimmy. There was a phone in the rectory at Sacred Heart. There was a pay phone in Slowacki's and another across the street in Casement's Bar, but there were always people waiting to use them. The cops had telephones too. All the telephones they wanted.

He got up from the kitchen table, brushed his teeth, and went into his room. He read comics for a while, and then heard his mother come in from work. She walked through the rooms and knocked at his door.

"You're all right, son?" she said.

"Fine," he said. "Good night, Mom."

He turned off the light and buried his head in the pillow. He remembered the rabbi's radiant face when he was listening to Ziggy Elman, and was trying to imagine what it was like to be Rabbi Hirsch when sleep took him.

# 16

By morning, everyone in the parish seemed to know that Frankie McCarthy had been charged with felonious assault in the beating of Mister G and was being held awaiting $2,500 bail in the Raymond Street jail. The old ladies whispered about it in the hallways. It was mentioned across the counter in Slowacki's candy store. Even Kate Devlin knew the story, although not a word had appeared in the newspapers.

"They should put him away for years," she said. "But, of course, they won't."

She explained to Michael how bail worked. The prisoner had to find a bail bondsman and come up with ten percent of the bail in cash. The bondsman would then put up the full $2,500, and Frankie McCarthy would be free until his trial. If Frankie didn't show up for trial, the bondsman would lose the $2,500.

"That idjit McCarthy," she said, "wouldn't have two hundred and fifty dollars, so he'll have to wait until his friends steal it."

Almost nobody in the parish seemed surprised that Frankie had been jailed. After all, they knew he had done it. But they also knew that the district attorney would have a hard time proving the case. If Michael, Sonny, and Jimmy Kabinsky said nothing in court, then it would be the word of Frankie McCarthy against the theories of the cops. From what Rabbi Hirsch said, Mister G might never talk again. But the boys knew there were few secrets in the parish. As the only possible witnesses they were the center of the parish's whispered attention. Michael most of all, because he had seen the worst part of the beating.

"T'ree times in a week, the bulls came up my house," Sonny Montemarano said that afternoon, as they stood beside the roof door of his building, gazing out at the rain. "Abbott and Costello, in person. They threaten you. They try to make you feel guilty."

"Me too," Jimmy said. "They come to see me day before yesterday."

"They did?" Michael said. "What happened?"

"Nothing," Jimmy said. "I didn't say nothing, I swear."

"What about your uncle?" Sonny asked, squinting now, staring into Jimmy's pale blue eyes. "Did *he* say something?"

"Nah. Just his usual."

"Whatta you mean, his *usual?*" Sonny said.

"You know, about the Jews and all."

There it was, Michael thought. The Jews and all. Jimmy's uncle was the rat. A rat so stupid he didn't even know he was a rat.

"Exactly what did he say, Jimmy?" Michael asked.

"I don't remember exactly."

"Try," Sonny said.

Jimmy gazed off at the rain sweeping through the backyards. It was as if he too now understood what had happened.

"You know, like, 'What's the crime, beating a Jew up? What's the big deal?' " His voice lowered in shame. "Then he says — I couldn't stop him, I swear — he says, 'So what, if Frankie McCarthy broke his head?' " He paused, but didn't look at Michael or Sonny. "Stuff like that."

Sonny moaned. "Jesus, Jimmy —"

"He didn't say *we* were there," Jimmy said.

"Maybe not *then*," Sonny said. "But they could grab him again on the street, when he's working, anyplace." He shook his head.

"They could beat the shit out of him until he told them what they wanna hear. They could threaten to deport him, send him back to Poland."

"One thing's for sure," Michael said. "The cops probably figure *you* told your uncle. He didn't pick Frankie's name out of the air."

"They will def'nitely call your uncle as a witness," Sonny said.

"And you too, Jimmy," Michael said.

"And *us*," Sonny said, looking at Michael in a trapped way.

Images of courtroom scenes flashed through Michael's mind. Oaths. Lies. Frankie McCarthy staring at them. The rows filled with Falcons. They knew where Michael lived. They knew where his mother worked. The wind suddenly rose, and rain lashed the roof above them, and backed them away from the open door. They stared out at the glistening black pebbles and the clotheslines and the chimneys.

"Frankie's boys must figure *we* ratted," Sonny said quietly.

"Nah," Jimmy said. "Why would they think that?"

"Because that's how they think," Sonny said. "They don't know us. They don't know your goddamned uncle either."

The rain faded again into a steady drizzle.

"We got to let them know it wasn't us," Michael said. "Without ratting on Jimmy's uncle."

"How? We write them a letter? We go to the poolroom and say, 'Excuse me, fellas, but we didn't rat you out, so don't do nothing to us, okay?' "

There was a silence. Michael felt cold.

"Maybe it wasn't my uncle," Jimmy said. "Maybe there was another witness. Maybe somebody was in the back of the store. Maybe a neighbor seen it from a window —"

"Yeah, wit' X-ray vision, like Superman," Sonny said.

There was another long silence.

"We're in deep shit," Sonny said.

# 17

One wet Tuesday after school, Michael entered the synagogue through the Kelly Street entrance. The door was open, awaiting his arrival, and he paused for a moment in the vestibule, feeling safe. As he shook the rain off his mackinaw, he heard a hard, almost braying sound from the far side of the door leading to the rabbi's rooms. The notes were familiar. *Braaah, braawp, brah-brah, bruh, brah-brah, braawp* . . . The first notes of "And the Angels Sing."

The sound abruptly stopped. Michael opened the door quietly and saw Rabbi Hirsch standing near the bookcase, deep in concentration, trying to blow on a curved instrument made of polished horn. His eyes were closed. He started to keep the beat with one foot, then tried again. *Braaah, braawp* . . . Then he paused, opened his eyes, saw Michael, and laughed.

"You catched me!" he said.

"Caught," Michael said.

"You caught me," the rabbi said. "I want to surprise you, but . . ." He brandished the horn. "I'm going to be a regular Ziggy Elman!"

Michael looked at the horn. "What *is* that in your hand?"

The rabbi explained that the instrument was a shofar, a ram's horn. It was used in ceremonies during the holy days called Rosh Hashanah and was the same kind of horn that Joshua had used in biblical days to flatten the walls of Jericho.

Michael started singing a song he'd heard a lot on the radio:

*Joshua fit the battle of Jericho,*
*Jericho,*
*Jericho.*
*Joshua fit the battle of Jericho,*
*And the walls came tumbling down. . . .*

"Wait, wait!" the rabbi said, signaling with the shofar. "Now, again!"

Michael sang the words more forcefully and the rabbi played a few notes in the thick, plangent tones of the ram's horn. *Joshua fit the battle of Jericho, Jericho, Jericho . . .* The sound of the shofar was fat, primitive, eerie, as if Rabbi Hirsch were reaching back across the centuries. But there was no melody from the horn. It was not mournful. It was not melancholy. It was just loud and brutal, like a foghorn.

When the rabbi finished, he shook his head sadly, his face drained by failure.

"Is impossible," he said. "A tune you can't get from a shofar, just a noise. You need —" He pounded his chest as if asking it to identify itself. "What's the word?"

"Lungs," Michael said. "So you have enough breath."

"Yes, yes, lungs."

He turned the shofar over in his hands.

"Why can't I make from it music?" he said softly. "Why can't I make from it *joy?*"

Michael could offer no answer.

"Why can't I make from a shofar like a regular Ziggy Elman?"

Rabbi Hirsch laid the shofar on a shelf of the bookcase and switched on the radio. It was tuned to WHN. Red Barber was explaining that with runners on first and third and none out, the Dodgers were sitting in the catbird seat.

"There's a bird in America that looks like a cat?" the rabbi asked.

"I don't know," Michael said.

"So why does Red Barber say the Dodgers, they are in the catbird seat?"

"He says it all the time, like he says *rhubarb*."

The rabbi was flicking through the dictionary.

"Rhubarb? That's like a fruit I see in Roulston's grocery store."

"Red Barber uses it to describe, like, well, a big fight. You know, if a batter gets hit by a pitch and he charges the mound? Or when Leo Durocher comes out to holler at the umpires. That's a rhubarb. And he says 'We're sitting in the catbird seat' when he means the Dodgers are in good shape. They have the upper hand. They're sitting pretty. Know what I mean?"

"No."

The words zipped through Michael's mind, and he realized what they must sound like to Rabbi Hirsch. Good shape and upper hand and sitting pretty. How did they come to mean what they mean?

"It's like to have an advantage," Michael said. "Like, you don't have to worry now. You can't lose. You can do it."

Rabbi Hirsch nodded, as if finally understanding Michael's fumbling attempts to explain. He went to the bookcase and lifted the horn again.

"If like Ziggy Elman I can play this shofar," he said, "I am sitting in the catbird seat."

Michael smiled.

"You said it."

# 18

One Saturday morning a few weeks before Easter, Michael, Sonny, and Jimmy were playing ball against the factory wall on Collins Street. The day was bright but still too cold for a full game of stickball; the other kids remained huddled in their apartments, and there weren't enough players to choose up sides. But Jimmy had found an old broom in his uncle's junkpile, and Sonny had saved a spaldeen from the previous summer, and they stripped the straw off the broom and then took turns whacking the ball off the factory wall. Home plate was chalked in front of the wall of O'Malley's Garage. Each player got ten swings at the ball, then they switched positions. The baseball season wouldn't begin until April 16. Nobody yet knew whether Jackie Robinson would join the Dodgers. As a Royal, he was now hitting .625 against the big club.

"They gotta bring him up," Michael said. "How couldn't they, the way he's hitting?

He goes one-for-three, he's in a slump."

"We'll know real soon," Sonny said. "Hey, Jimmy, throw me a curveball, you see what I do to it!"

Jimmy kept throwing fastballs to Sonny, who hit every one of them, while Michael moved around as the fielder, retrieving the ball as it bounced off the factory wall. When Sonny finished his ten hits and it was Michael's turn to bat, he discovered he was hitting the ball harder than he did the previous summer. He knew he was fifteen pounds heavier and two inches taller now, but for some reason he could also see the ball better. He watched the spaldeen leave Sonny's hand, and it really did get fatter and pinker as it came closer. Every time he swung, he made contact, and the ball rose high against the wall. He was finished quickly: ten pitches, ten hits. As good as Sonny. Then he pitched to Jimmy while Sonny played the field. Jimmy missed four of the ten pitches. And then they switched again. Around noon, a garbage truck wheezed up the street, its gears grinding, and stopped in front of O'Malley's Garage, blocking home plate. The boys stood around while the sanitation men heaved cans of trash into the truck.

"So what's the latest up there on Kelly

Street?" Sonny said. "You know, the synagogue?"

"I haven't seen a thing," Michael said. "I looked and looked," he lied, "but nothing."

"So where did the story come from?" Jimmy said.

"Three guys were playing stickball," Michael said, "and then a sanitation truck got in the way and —"

"Maybe we should go up there some night," Sonny said in a cold way. "Maybe we can find it."

"We got more important things to do," Michael said.

"What's more important than a fortune of money?"

"The goddamned Falcons, that's who."

Sonny gazed around the street. There was no sign of danger on this cold spring day.

"If we had a fortune of money," Jimmy said, "we could all move to Florida. You could take your mother, Michael, Sonny could take his aunt —"

"Your uncle stays here!" Sonny said.

"You know," Jimmy said, "if we do go in there some night, the synagogue, we better wait till after Passover. The Jews, during Passover —"

"They kill babies and put the blood in

the matzohs?" Michael said sharply.

"Well . . . yeah."

Michael thought of Brother Thaddeus and the tunnels in Prague and the Golem and he didn't want to play ball anymore.

"I gotta go wash the halls," he said, handing the bat to Sonny, who looked at him in a confused way. Michael drifted away from them toward Ellison Avenue. Thinking: You goddamned idiot, Jimmy. Because of you and your big-mouthed uncle, we have to look over our shoulders when we walk the streets, I'm scared shitless every time I go down the cellar to shovel coal, there's guys looking at us like they want to cut our goddamned throats, and you believe Jews put blood in the matzohs? Fucking imbecile. I gotta talk straight to them. Gotta. Got to tell them Rabbi Hirsch is a good man. Gotta tell them there's no treasure. Gotta come clean about what I'm doing there. Gotta gotta. Got to tell Rabbi Hirsch too. Gotta gotta gotta.

He turned into the avenue and then froze. His legs felt heavy, his hands cold. Frankie McCarthy was two blocks away.

Coming in Michael's direction.

With three other members of the Falcons.

All of them walking with a rolling swagger.

Grab-assing. Bumping each other. Smoking cigarettes.

Michael thought: Holy shit.

Frankie McCarthy.

He's back.

He's free.

Jesus.

Michael couldn't cross to his own house without being seen. He flattened himself against the windows of Pete's Diner, then inched around the corner into Collins Street, trying to look casual. He hoped Frankie and the Falcons were yelling at girls. He hoped they had gone to Unbeatable Joe's to drink beer. Most of all, he hoped they hadn't seen him.

The garbage truck was gone. Sonny was batting against Jimmy Kabinsky.

"Hey, let's go!" Michael shouted. "Frankie McCarthy's out of jail. He's coming up Ellison Avenue."

"Oh, shit," Sonny said.

He pocketed the ball and held the bat like a club as they trotted together toward Mac-Arthur Avenue, away from Ellison, away from Frankie. Only two blocks away to the right, on the corner of Kelly Street, was the synagogue. We'd be safe there, Michael thought. But how could he bring Jimmy to a place where he believed Jews mixed human blood into the goddamned matzohs? That would be what Rabbi Hirsch called *meshugge*.

So they ran another long block to the park, leaping onto the slats of the benches, then scaling the stone wall and dropping four feet to the ground. They were all silent, breathing hard as they moved through the debris of the winter: fallen tree limbs, pine cones, beer containers, overturned trash baskets, a lone shoe. They kept moving until they reached a stone transverse bridge, with a few cars moving over it, and found shelter in the darkness under the wide arch. They were now all breathing hard.

"He musta made bail," Sonny said. "The Falcons musta chipped in to get the two hundred and fifty bucks."

"You *know* he's gonna come after us," Michael said.

"Probably," Sonny said. "He's gotta blame *some*body. He's up on a felony. Maybe worse, if Mister G never comes out of the coma. That could be murder, for chrissakes. And he probably figures we're the only witnesses, that we could put him in the can for years." He shivered in the stony darkness. "We tell him about Jimmy's uncle, he won't believe us. Nobody's *that* fucking stupid." He glanced at Jimmy, sucked in deep breaths. "But you know, if he gets caught pullin' any shit while he's out on bail, they'll really hang his ass. So you ask me, he won't do nothin' *direct*, know what I mean?"

"In other words," Jimmy said, "the *Falcons* could get us, even though Frankie's not with them in person?"

"Exactly," Sonny said. "Frankie throws up his fucking hands when the cops come knocking at his door, and says, hey, I was home listening to the fuckin' radio and I got witnesses to prove it."

"Meanwhile, we take a good beating," Jimmy said.

"If we're lucky," Sonny said, "it's only a fucking beating."

A dozen cars roared across the stone bridge above them and then were gone.

"What the hell are we gonna do, Sonny?" Michael said.

"I don't know yet. I don't know."

# 19

For three straight nights, Michael dreamed of rooms that were both strange and familiar, full of many beds, with brown covers and blue pillows, and chairs draped with sheets. Above the beds there were frames without pictures. The beds were very short, then very long, so that there was no clear path from room to room, and when he came to the end of the rooms, the apartment did not end: other rooms opened, new and strange, filling him with dread. Dogs barked, but he could not see them. Then he was outside and saw white horses on the factory roof. In the dark doorway of Slowacki's candy store, a man with a sallow face and a toothy grin tipped his bowler hat and the top of his head was made of raw hamburger. Then Michael was alone in his own apartment, with his father's picture on the wall, and someone was shuffling through the darkness, heavy feet dragging, and his mother wasn't there and his father wasn't there and he ran into the bathroom and slammed the door, listening to the shuffling, and turned on the hot-water tap and red snow came from the tap and rose like tiny flowers into the air.

Each night, he woke up sweating and trembling and afraid of falling back into the dream. He could not call his mother. I'm not some little kid, he thought. This is a dream. That's all. It's not real. This room is real. That window. This bed. My clothes and my comics. Dreams are dreams. And then he'd drift off and the images would return, sometimes shifting their order: the white horses first, and then the man with hamburger for hair, and then the endless empty rooms.

He thought about asking for help from Mrs. Griffin on the second floor. She had a worn pamphlet called *Madame Zadora's Dream Book*, and Michael wondered if it would explain his dreams. She used the dream book to help her pick horses, or The Number. Kate Devlin didn't gamble; she said she worked too hard for her money; so Michael wasn't sure what was meant by The Number. But Mrs. Griffin went every morning to Casement's Bar to give Brendan the bookmaker her choice of numbers for the day, and it was said that back in 1945 she had won two hundred dollars. Maybe she would know.

One afternoon, he knocked at her door. Mrs. Griffin, small, wiry, and dressed in a quilted pink housecoat, smiled at the sight of him. She asked him in and started boiling water for tea. She did all this with a Pall Mall burning in her fingers.

"I've been having these terrible dreams, Mrs. Griffin," Michael explained. "I thought maybe your book would figure them out."

She looked wary. "What's your mother say about them?"

"She doesn't talk about dreams," he said. "And, I dunno, it's hard to talk to her about some things. Like dreams."

She took a drag on the cigarette, then tamped it out in a saucer.

"What kind of dreams?"

He told her. As she listened, horror spread across her face like a stain. "Oh boy," she said breathlessly. And listened more. "Oh boy. Oh boy. Oh boy oh boy."

Then they sat there for a long, silent moment. She peered at him.

"You're in trouble, Michael," she said. Her voice was burry from cigarettes.

"Maybe."

She popped a Pall Mall from her pack

and lit it with a wooden match. Her eyes glistened.

"But it's not trouble you caused, right?"

"Right."

"You're worried about somebody with a broken head, right?"

"Right."

"That's the hamburger head. And you're trying to make sense of something, like, you know, putting a picture in a picture frame."

This hadn't occurred to him, but he thought about Jackie Robinson's skin, and nodded.

"In a way."

"You're thinking of some other place, not yours, the furniture all covered up and stuff."

Michael thought: The synagogue? Prague? Rabbi Loew's study? The attic where they keep the Golem's dust?

"Sometimes."

"And you're thinking of moving away. Like getting on a white horse and riding off into the sunset like Gene Autry or something."

Michael laughed. She served tea, still smoking.

"From time to time," he said.

She went into another room and came back with *Madame Zadora's Dream Book*. It had a red-and-black cover with a drawing of a woman in a gown covered with symbols, caressing a crystal ball. The symbols made him think of alchemists.

"Well, we figured out some of it," Mrs. Griffin said. "But I'll be goddamned if I can make any sense of the bowler hat or the red snow coming out of the water tap."

She paused, squinting at a page. Michael sipped his tea, but it had a metallic taste and he wished he could have a cup of Rabbi Hirsch's brew.

"Let's see. Washing yourself with snow, that means pain will go away. Eating snow, that's you're leaving home. But — was it the *hot*-water tap?"

"As a matter of fact, yes."

"That's good, maybe. Snow in a warm climate means good luck. But that's not the same as a hot-water tap. Still, it's close."

She turned to another page.

"The bowler hat, the bowler hat. Let's see . . . a man's hat, that usually means, uh, emotional sorrow," she said. "Losing your hat, that means watch out for false friends. A new hat is a sign of wealth. A big hat means joy and prosperity. But a *bowler* hat? Jeez, I dunno. Even Madame Zadora doesn't get into *bowler* hats. You know anyone that owns one?"

"No. I've seen them in the movies, but never in real life."

She looked hard at him now.

"You got a lot of things on your mind, don't you, kid?"

"Yes."

"I don't blame you," she said. "Everybody knows what happened to Mister G." She sipped her tea. "And everybody knows Frankie McCarthy did it and could go up the river for a long stretch. Especially if you turned rat. So you're worried about that, which it's natural. And that's in all the dreams, I guess, that *worry*. And the ghost walking through the rooms? That's your father, Michael, God rest his soul. You wish he was here. You wish he could go with you and beat the crap out of that Frankie McCarthy." She put out the cigarette. Michael counted six butts in the saucer. "But he's not here. And you can't run away."

"So what do I do?"

"Pray," she said. "And keep the faith. You believe hard enough things'll work out, they will. Mark my words."

That night, he didn't dream. Each morning now, he prayed. He stayed alert to danger. And on the streets, nothing happened.

Michael was careful leaving the house. He watched the rooftops, fearful of falling bricks or garbage cans. He made certain the doors to the flat were always locked. He got permission from his mother to increase the wattage of the bulbs in the hallways. He took different routes through the parish on his journeys to see Rabbi Hirsch or to serve mass at Sacred Heart. Going to mass was always the easiest; Frankie McCarthy and the Falcons didn't get up until noon.

Sonny tried to keep the three of them calm. From his aunt's house next door to the Venus, he could see into the poolroom. Frankie was there, all right. Hour after hour. Smoking. Playing pool. Laughing with his boys. But Sonny never saw him go out on a patrol. Never saw him act as if he was looking for anyone.

"Maybe he figured out it's not us," Michael said.

"Nah," Sonny said. "He's a crafty prick. Like a snake. He knows if anything happens to us, the bulls will drop a fuckin' subway car on him." He chewed the inside of his mouth. "He'll wait. He won't forget."

The boys waited too. They went to school. They played in the street. Michael stopped in the synagogue to learn new words and phrases. He added *fressing* to his vocabulary, meaning eating like a slob. A *momser* was a bastard, a son of a bitch.

*Latkes* were potato pancakes, and the word for dirt was *shmootz*. But Frankie remained a presence in his mind, like a bad tooth in a jaw. Even when life seemed normal.

On the Sunday before Easter, while hundreds of people were strolling through the parish with palm crosses stuck in their lapels, Kate Devlin took Michael by subway to Orchard Street in Manhattan. The train was filled with women like her, taking their children to be outfitted for Easter. Most of them had saved for months to buy clothes, and the clothes on Orchard Street were the cheapest in New York. At the Delancey Street station, they emptied the train, and hundreds of them climbed the stairs, dragging their kids into the parish they all called Jewtown.

This was the first time that Michael had come to Jewtown with his mother, and he was excited by its jammed, narrow streets, tiny stores, bearded men, racks of clothing climbing ten feet above the sidewalks. He imagined himself into the Fifth Quarter in Prague. The ghetto. The air was pungent with strange odors. Men and women shouted back and forth in five or six languages. Music played from unseen radios, adding to the din. Everyone seemed to be bargaining, in a frazzled routine of declaration, rejection, compromise, fingers being used to emphasize numbers. Young men in yarmulkes, black pants and collarless white shirts, with straggly beards and sidecurls dangling over the ears, measured waists and chests and trouser lengths with worn yellow tapes, marked them with chalk, then shoved hanging clothes aside to allow a customer to stand before a mirror. Kids looked panicky at the sight of themselves in strange clothes. Mothers tugged at seams and felt the fabrics and told the kids to stand straight. Michael felt sure that if he stayed long enough he would see Rabbi Loew. Or Brother Thaddeus, his baldness disguised with a wig.

For an hour, he and his mother examined suits and rejected them. Too expensive. Too cheesy. Too small. Too big. They went slowly up one side of Orchard Street and back down the other. At the corner, Michael gazed down Delancey Street and saw the dark, ugly outline of the Williamsburg Bridge, its towers crowned with knobby pronged spires. He thought: *Prague.* Rabbi Hirsch must have seen the spires of St. Vitus this way, as he walked from the ghetto toward Old Town Square. Except our tunnels are subway tunnels. Not the evil tunnels of Prague, where fanatics seethed and babies were strangled in the dark. Here on Orchard Street, Michael thought, he was even safer than a Jew in the ghetto. Here, Frankie McCarthy would never find him.

Then his gaze fell upon a dark blue suit hanging just above sidewalk level in a small store across the street. Neat lapels, dark buttons. That was the suit he could wear when he was twelve. It would be fine for Easter, but it would be better after he turned twelve. In that suit, he would look older: thirteen, maybe even fourteen. In that suit, he could start looking like a man.

"Look at that one, Mom," he said, and led her through the crowds, suddenly anxious that someone else might find it first. A young clerk came out. His face was very thin, framed with red hair; he was wearing a yarmulke. Kate Devlin touched the fabric and asked the price.

"For you, fourteen dollars," the young man said, in an accented voice.

"It's very dear," she whispered to Michael.

*"Es iz zaier taier,"* Michael said.

The clerk looked startled.

"You're Jewish?"

"No," Michael said. "Irish."

"Irish? Ah, *ains fun di aseres hashvotim.* One of the lost tribes." The clerk laughed.

"Three dollars off!" he said, lifting down the suit.

"You're kidding," Kate Devlin said.

"Three and a half," the clerk said. "You are *die mutter?*"

It sounded like *mooter*, but she understood.

"Yes," she said, and smiled uneasily. "Can he try it on?"

"Yes, yes. In there." He pointed to a dark niche burrowed among clothes. Then to Michael: "Your mother wants *ain glazel tai?*"

"Mom, you want a glass of tea?"

"That'd be nice," she said.

"*Mit tzuker?*" the clerk said.

"*Bitte,*" Michael said, knowing his mother took sugar with her tea. "*Zait azoy gut.*"

While Michael changed, the clerk pushed through the bunched clothes and disappeared into a deeper part of the shop. Michael emerged first. The suit fit almost perfectly. His mother made him turn around, and nodded approval. He pushed aside some clothes and saw himself in a cracked mirror. It was like gazing at a stranger. Maybe even a sixteen-year-old stranger.

"I love it," he whispered. Kate smiled. Then the clerk returned, holding three glasses of tea. A wooden clothes hanger was tucked under his arm. He handed one glass of tea to Kate.

*"Azoy shain!"* the clerk said. Beautiful. "You look like a man."

"We'll take it," Kate said.

"The hanger is free," the clerk said, smiling and handing a glass of tea to Michael.

*"A dank,"* Michael said.

They clinked glasses in a toast.

*"Lang leben zolt ir,"* Michael said. Long life to you.

"God bless America," said the clerk.

"Up the Republic," said Kate Devlin, hugging her American son.

# 20

Back in the parish, Michael hurried to see Rabbi Hirsch to brag about his Orchard Street adventure. It was like a story out of a library book: he said the magic words and — Open, Sesame! — something amazing happened. It wasn't Shazam! The words were Yiddish. Words that came from Rabbi Hirsch. But they had worked.

The synagogue on Kelly Street was locked. The front door remained sealed. He hoped the rabbi was all right, but the day was so fine, with the sky blue and the streets washed clean by the spring rains, that it didn't seem possible anything bad could happen to anyone.

He walked around the front of the armory and looked at the bronze statue of the World War I hero with his small tin hat and wrapped leggings and wondered why there were no statues for the men who died in the Battle of the Bulge. Maybe it was too soon. Maybe they were making them in some studio or foundry, in Washington maybe, or in Paris, France, where the artists all lived. He sat on the steps and gazed at the green buds on the elm trees, and the sparrows chattering in the pale green branches, and wondered how far it was from Paris, France, to Prague. There must not be a ghetto anymore in Prague. The Nazis must have killed everybody who lived there. Then images of the camps unspooled in his mind, those newsreels he'd seen in the Venus, of hollow-eyed men and scrawny, skeletal women and bodies piled like the junk in Jimmy Kabinsky's uncle's yard. How could they have done that? How could anyone do that? And why didn't anyone help? And where was God? How could He let so many people die? Men. Women. Babies.

And suddenly he thought: They must have killed the rabbi's wife.

They must have killed Leah.

Of course! Those goddamned Nazi *momsers* must have taken her to the concentration camp. They must have put her in the gas chamber. Or starved her to death. Or shot her. Or buried her alive.

*Of course!*

That's why Rabbi Hirsch sometimes glances at Leah's beautiful face in that browning photograph and seems to feel such an awful sadness. And maybe that explains another thing. He told me once that when he was young, he tried to live without God. Then he went back to God and became a rabbi. He didn't make a big deal about it. But it must have meant something to him, or he never would have mentioned it. Maybe now . . . maybe because of what happened to Leah, what happened to millions of *other* Jews, maybe now he has changed his mind again. Sometimes, the look on his face is . . . well, it's not exactly confused. It's not even unhappy, because in a minute he can change back again and teach me a new word in Yiddish or talk about Ziggy Elman. No: in that little flash, that glance, he looks . . . bitter. Like he's pissed off at God. Or maybe even worse, like maybe he's a rabbi who doesn't believe in God.

Michael stood up, his stomach churning, wondering how he could have been so stupid, not to have thought of this before. He knew now that he had to ask Rabbi Hirsch about more than words, about more than distant Prague. He had to know what had happened to the woman named Leah, the rabbi's wife. Had to find out her story. And the rabbi's, too.

And then he saw Rabbi Hirsch in the distance, trudging heavily under the spring trees on Kelly Street in the block leading from the park. From that distance, he seemed small and vulnerable, in his black coat and black hat. Michael started to run to him. He wanted to tell him how sorry he was for failing to understand about his wife, Leah. He wanted to tell him a lot of things. And then he saw that Rabbi Hirsch was carrying two shopping bags. The rabbi's face brightened as he saw Michael running toward him.

"Hello, Michael. *Vos makhst du?*"

"Okay, good. *Zaier gut, a dank,*" Michael said, taking the first shopping bag and reaching for the second. The rabbi pulled the second bag away, saying they could each carry one.

"You'll never believe this," Michael said in an excited voice, "but we saved three and a half dollars on a suit today *because of Yiddish!*"

He told the story while the rabbi unlocked the door. The rabbi was chuckling, asking Michael to repeat the Yiddish phrases, as they went to the kitchen and placed the shopping bags on the table. The boy glanced at the photograph of Leah, but he could not ask about the way she had died. The rabbi seemed too happy. They unpacked two bottles of wine and boxes of matzoh and three cans of soup.

"What's all this for?" Michael asked.

"*Pesach.* How you say it in English? Piss-over?"

"*Passover*," Michael said. "*Piss*over, well, *piss* is the word for, uh, urinate. And —"

They briefly discussed the phrases *taking a piss* and *pissing in the wind* and being *pissed off.* And when they finished laughing, the rabbi told Michael about Passover. He explained about the time when the Jews were slaves in Egypt and how God sent a series of plagues against the Pharaoh to convince him to free the Jews. The tenth plague was the last one, and the worst of all. It killed only the firstborn children of Egyptian families. But the Angel of Death passed over the homes of the Jews. The angel knew which homes were Jewish because they had been marked on the doorposts and lintels with the blood of a lamb. Michael was thrilled at this tale; a magic sign had saved them. When this happened, the pharaoh finally got the point and decided to let the Jews go free. Michael tried to picture the Angel of Death, soaring above Egypt, with black wings and a ferocious, stern face, like the statue of Moses he saw in the encyclopedia. He pictured the weeping Egyptian mothers. He saw the Jews gathering at dawn, to head north to the land of milk and honey.

"Ever since, we gather on the . . . anniversary? Yes, the anniversary, to celebrate and to give thanks to God. Eight days it lasts. A big dinner we have the first night: a seder. The family, the friends, everybody eats and prays. Pesach — Passover, the great feast of the spring. The feast of the free."

"Maybe Jackie Robinson will have the same kind of dinner next year," Michael said. "A seder."

"If he lives in Brooklyn already, we tell him, Jackie, come here."

"Wouldn't that be great?" the boy said.

The rabbi tapped the *Brooklyn Eagle*. "See, he is coming to the other land of milk and honey: Brooklyn!" He balled his hands into fists and held them together as if gripping a bat. "This year in Jerusalem!"

They both laughed. The rabbi hefted the package of American matzohs.

"To Egypt, everything goes back," he said, opening the package, sliding out a matzoh, and handing it to Michael. "The matzoh, for example. The Jews, when they get the news from the Pharaoh they can leave, they don't want to give him time to change the mind. But they don't have time for the bread to —" He made an expanding gesture with his hands. "To get fat?"

"To rise."

"Yes: to rise. So they grab what's there already. Bread that haven't rise. This." He held up the cracker. "Matzoh."

Michael took a bite of the long, wide cracker. It was dry and tasteless.

"A Hershey bar it's not," the rabbi said.

He opened a cabinet and lifted a brown paper bag off a shelf. He placed it on the table in front of Michael.

"For you," he said. "For your mother."

Michael looked puzzled.

"Bread," Rabbi Hirsch explained. "Regular bread. What we find in the store here in America. *Hametz*, we call it."

Michael peered into the bag and saw some rolls and slices of rye bread.

"The Torah tells us to take away — what is it called? — *leavened* bread, or *hametz*, from our houses during the eight days of Pesach. You don't do this, you don't really observe Pesach. And to make matzoh even more important, the Torah tells us to find every scrap of *hametz* and scrub clean every part of the house. Some holy men, they say *hametz* is like pride: bread that's all big and empty, like — what's the word? — puffed up."

He smiled in a mild way.

"Not me," he added. "Bread is bread, except at Pesach."

He handed the bag to Michael.

"So this is a bag of *hametz*," he said. "Still good. Give it to your mother." He paused, as if trying to gauge the feelings of the Irish woman he'd never met. "Or you can do something else with it, if your mother, she would be insulted."

"She's always worried about insulting *you*," Michael said. "And she loves rye bread."

"What a *meshuggeneh* world," the rabbi said.

"Full of *meshuggeners*," Michael said, preening slightly as he used the Yiddish in a casual way.

As the rabbi cleaned the stove and the floor, with Michael helping him move the furniture to get at hidden *shmootz*, he told him about the fine seders they would have in Prague, at huge oaken tables crowded with generations of the Hirsch family. Michael could see the old people belching and farting on the couches and the children running back and forth, playing a game about hidden *hametz*, and cousins flirting and friends courting. All that, as the rabbi talked: and the reading of the Haggadah and the Four Questions and the dipping into the bitter herbs, all of them close and thinking they would go on for many more generations, the young burying the old forever.

"That was a happiness," the rabbi said. "All gone away."

"Will you have a seder here?"

"Maybe next year," he said. "We save up some money, maybe. Your mother could come, and you, and who knows? Maybe some from the synagogue even."

He tried to explain to Michael about how the last members of the congregation, old and bent, would wait at home and be picked up by their cranky children, the children embarrassed by the old people, and then be taken to strange places. Some of them would be flown to Florida. Some taken by car to New Jersey. Some would go by train to Long Island. But they would not be here. They would not be where they were needed.

"*Nu*, by coming for a seder, they make all the hard part okay, the hard part of a year, the hard part of a whole life," the rabbi said. "We are all together, means we survive again another year."

But nobody was coming this year, and Michael could feel the loneliness seeping through the room like a fog.

"Maybe you could come to our house, Rabbi," he said. "Have a seder with us."

"No," Rabbi Hirsch said firmly, and then sighed and grew lighter. "Next year, here we have seder. And we send to Jackie Robinson a note too."

They talked a while longer, the rabbi scrubbing and dusting while Michael, for the first time, prepared tea.

"How come Passover and Easter come around the same time?" the boy asked. "You know, just before Opening Day?"

The rabbi smiled.

"Opening Day, I don't know about," he said. "But the other is simple. The Last Supper? You know, the famous painting? The supper that it happened just before Easter?"

"Sure."

"Well, the Last Supper, it was a seder," the rabbi said. "Jesus and his friends were together to give thanks for the freeing from Egypt."

"You're kidding!"

"No. So you better take this *hametz* home. The cleaning I got to finish."

Michael lifted the grocery bag and went to the door. He paused with his hand on the doorknob and turned to the rabbi, who was opening a box of steel wool.

"Rabbi?"

"Yes."

"I have a question."

"Yes?"

Two questions. Not one. Two. Ask. No, don't ask. Yes, go ahead. Ask. Ask.

Michael took a deep breath, exhaled slowly, and asked his first question.

"If God sent a plague against the Pharaoh to save the Jews," the boy said, "why didn't he send a plague against the Nazis?"

The rabbi was very still. His hands were limp against his sides.

"I don't know," he whispered in a voice powdery with despair. "I don't know."

He sounded like a rabbi who didn't like God very much, and certainly didn't love Him. And maybe didn't believe in Him at all anymore. Michael did not ask his second question. He did not ask what had happened to the rabbi's wife.

# 21

On Easter Sunday morning, Michael kept
looking at his reflection in the store windows
as he walked along Ellison Avenue. The
priests told them at church that Easter was
about Jesus rising from the dead, proving
His immortality; everybody in the parish
knew better. It was about new clothes. And
in his new blue suit, white shirt, striped tie,
and polished black shoes, Michael thought
he looked older, more mature, whatever that
vague word meant. Not yet a man, but no
longer a boy.

He saw a girl named Mary Cunningham coming out of her building across
from the factory. She was thin, with long
brown hair, and was dressed in a light
blue coat and a straw hat with plastic
flowers around the crown. She smiled at
him in what he felt was a new way. She
was in his grade at Sacred Heart, but since
the boys were separated from the girls at
school, they only saw each other in the

schoolyard or on the street.

"Happy Easter, Michael," she said, smiling. Unlike some of the other girls in his grade, she didn't wear braces. Her teeth were as hard and white as Lana Turner's.

"Yeah, same to you," he said.

"That's a great suit," she said.

"I like that hat too," Michael said. "You going to mass?"

"Of course," she said. "We have to go, right? But I gotta wait for my father and mother."

His own mother had gone to the eight o'clock mass, which was all right with Michael. He didn't want her walking him to mass as if he were a first grader.

"See you there," Michael said to Mary Cunningham, and moved along more lightly in the bright spring morning. Suddenly Mrs. Griffin was calling to him from across the street. She was dressed in a tan coat and high heels and laughing hysterically.

"Michael, Michael, hey, Michael Devlin," she shouted, looking both ways for traffic, then scurrying across to him. "You heard the news?"

"What news?" She was more excited than she had been when the war ended.

"Your mother didn't tell you?"

"No."

"My horse came in!" she said. "What'd I tell you? You gotta have faith! And it was all because of you, Michael. You told me your dreams, right? And we figured out some of them. But I couldn't figure out that damned bowler hat. I thought about it for days and nights. Then yesterday I'm looking at the charts in the *Daily News*, I see there's a horse running in the third at Belmont, and get this: his name is *Bowler Hat!* I say to myself, I say, God used Michael to give me a winner! I knew it in my bones. I knew it in my heart! God says to Himself, That Mrs. Griffin, she needs a few bucks, she needs a gas stove, she needs some nylons. So He sends a dream through *you* to *me*. I run across the street, and I put five bucks on Bowler Hat with the bookie, and son of a gun if it don't come in by a lengt' and a half and pays twenty-two to one. I'm rich, Michael!"

She hugged him and put a bill in the palm of his hand.

"Keep the faith, Michael," she said, "and keep on dreaming, kid."

She pirouetted away and Michael opened his hand. A five-dollar bill. From a nightmare! He'd never had a five-dollar bill of his own before, and his head filled with objects as he hurried on to mass: flowers for his mother, a box of chocolates for her, comic books, maybe a hardcover book. Or he could give the whole five bucks to his mother to help save for a phonograph. Or maybe he could have a date with Mary Cunningham. Take her for a soda. Or to the Grandview when his mother wasn't working. He'd never gone out with a girl, but he knew about dates from the movies and *Archie* comics and *Harold Teen* in the *Daily News*. And Sonny talked about the things you did with girls. In the balcony. In the park.

He turned into Kelly Street, skipping along, thinking about girls and the things Sonny told him about them and the mysteries of their bodies. He wondered too what Mary Cunningham thought when she saw him in his new blue suit and what she would think if he talked to her in Yiddish or quoted Latin from the mass. Would she think he was weird? Or would she think he was the smartest guy she'd ever met? He wondered too what it would be like to touch her skin or play with her hair, and then wondered if such thoughts were sins.

And then stopped near the synagogue as he heard a low, angry, keening sound. A sound of deep, hopeless pain.

He followed the sound to the corner, and

there was Rabbi Hirsch, his face the color of ashes, anger and grief clenching his jaws. He had a coarse towel in his hands and was violently scrubbing the walls of the front of the synagogue. Someone had painted about a dozen red swastikas on the dirty white bricks. The words JEW GO were daubed on the sealed front door. Even the sight of Michael did not ease his pained fury.

"How could they *do* this?" the rabbi shouted bitterly. "*Who* could do this?"

Michael put his arm around the rabbi's waist, trying to comfort him, but the rabbi pulled away from the boy, seething with anger, and grabbed the picket fence for support. Michael backed away, feeling wounded and stupid, but also fearful that the wet paint would end up on his new suit. The rabbi reached for a mop and stabbed at the swastikas, smearing the fresh red paint.

"Wait here," Michael said. "Don't go away."

He ran all the way to Sacred Heart, fighting a stitch in his side, ignoring the sweat that was dampening his fresh shirt. Each time he faltered, gasping for breath, he saw Rabbi Hirsch in his mind's eye, and rage urged him on. Outside the church, the sidewalk was packed with people in flowered hats and new suits and newsboys selling *The*

*Tablet.* It was as if the whole neighborhood were converging on the 10 A.M. solemn high mass that was to celebrate the resurrection of Jesus. Michael pushed through them, thinking, Move, goddamn it, move, and took the steps two at a time into the church.

The nine o'clock mass was over, but the pews were almost full of those who wanted to hear the solemn high mass at ten, sung by three priests. Michael glanced up and saw that the choirboys were already assembled in the loft. An usher tried to stop him, but he pushed the man aside and hurried down the aisle and into the sacristy. He was relieved to find Father Heaney sitting on a chair, smoking a cigarette, finished with his own duties. The three other priests were helping each other don the gorgeous gold-embroidered white vestments used at Easter.

"Father Heaney!" Michael hissed. "Listen, there's — I gotta — you have to —"

"Take a deep breath, kid," the priest mumbled, "then tell me what you're trying to say."

Father Heaney listened as Michael told him the story, his voice hushed, to avoid distracting the other priests, who were busy dressing, talking among themselves. Father Heaney's face shifted. A deep vertical crease carved itself into his brow.

"I'll call the cops," he said, standing suddenly and going to the sink to quench his cigarette.

"No, you can't *do* that, Father. The cops don't care, we don't ever call the cops, they — *we've* got to help him."

"Why?"

Four altar boys suddenly entered the sacristy. Michael nodded hello. The altar boys went to the door leading to the altar and waited. Out in the sanctuary, the choir began to sing. One of the priests glanced at the wall clock, said, Let's go, and altar boys and priests went out to begin mass as music surged around them. Father Heaney stood looking at Michael. His eyes were more focused now, as if a film of indifference or boredom were being peeled away.

"We're not cops," Father Heaney said, when he and Michael were alone. Outside, the music soared. "Why should we get involved, kid?"

"Because Rabbi Hirsch is a good guy!"

"How do *you* know?" Father Heaney said, in the tone of someone who had seen too much evil.

Michael exploded. "How do I know? I'm the Shabbos goy at the synagogue! I help him turn on the lights every Saturday morning. I'm teaching him English. He's teaching me Yiddish. And his wife is dead and he's alone and he doesn't need some goddamned Nazi painting his synagogue!" The words clogged, as Michael realized he'd used the word *goddamned* to a priest, and then rushed forth again. "My father *died* fighting the Nazis. *You* saw all kinds of guys die in the war, you —"

Father Heaney's slits of eyes opened wider and he stepped back a foot, as if the words had pierced a part of him that had been numb for a long time. He raised a hand, palm out, stopping the flow of Michael's words. He reached for his coat.

"Come on," he said.

He walked out into the church, pointed at a few men and gestured for them to follow him. He grabbed one of the altar boys from the previous mass, a tall Italian kid named Albert. Some parishioners looked up from their prayer books at Father Heaney as if wondering why he was disrupting the mass. The choir reached a pitch and then stopped. Mr. Gallagher, the owner of the hardware store across the street, arrived late and was searching for a seat when Father Heaney took him by the elbow and guided him back outside.

At the foot of the church steps, Father

Heaney started giving orders like the military man he'd once been. He slipped two dollars to Albert, the altar boy, and sent him to buy some coffee and buns at the bakery. He convinced Mr. Gallagher to open the hardware store and hand out rags and scrubbers and solvents. On the corner near the schoolyard, he saw Charlie Senator, who had left his leg at Anzio, limping toward the church. He whispered a few words to him, and Senator gave him a small salute and fell in line.

Then all of them were marching down the avenue, carrying mops and rags, pails and solvents. People in Easter finery looked at them in surprise. A few more men joined the line of march, with Father Heaney and Michael out front, as the platoon crossed the great square at the entrance to the park and turned into Kelly Street.

Father Heaney's face was now clenched in righteous anger, his mouth etched tight, the muscles moving in his jaws. He didn't say a word. Michael wondered if he'd gone too far, mentioning his father. His mother never did that, not to the landlord, not to Michael, not ever, and he'd never done it before either. But it just came out, and it was true. Private Tommy Devlin had died fighting these *momsers*. These lousy pricks.

And he suddenly pictured his father marching with them down Kelly Street, going again to fight the Nazis. Then he realized he was the only boy among almost a dozen men. And saw himself with his father's platoon. Helmeted. Carrying a machine gun. Going to get these bastards who killed babies and old ladies and turned men into living skeletons. Heading for Belgium.

When they reached the synagogue, Rabbi Hirsch was still poking with his mop at the first swastika.

"Rabbi, I'm Joe Heaney," the priest said. "I was a chaplain in the 103rd Airborne. Most of these men fought their way into Germany two years ago, and one of them lost a leg in Italy. They are not going to let this bullshit happen in their parish."

"Please," Rabbi Hirsch said, "I can do it myself."

"No, you can't," Father Heaney said.

And so they went to work. Mr. Ponte, the stonemason, fingered the texture of the bricks, while Mr. Gallagher examined the paint. "Sapolin number 3," Mr. Gallagher said. "Every moron in the parish paints his chairs with it and then sits down before they're dry." Together, he and Mr. Ponte mixed the solvents in a steel pail. Others peeled off their Easter jackets, removed their ties, rolled up their sleeves, and grabbed rags and mops. Father Heaney stripped to his T-shirt. Albert, the altar boy, arrived with buns and coffee, then grabbed a cloth. A police car came along and one of the cops wanted to make a report, but Father Heaney said that he and Rabbi Hirsch would take care of the matter in their own way.

"We both believe in an Old Testament God," Father Heaney said. "He punishes all morons."

The cops shrugged and drove away. Michael hung his jacket and tie on the picket fence, on top of Charlie Senator's coat, and joined in the scrubbing. The men said little as they scrubbed and grunted. Their eyes seemed cloudy with memory, as if the things they had seen a few years earlier were driving them to finish. Michael was soon exhausted but pushed himself harder, thinking of the grainy black-and-white images from the Venus newsreels, the skeletal men, the hollow-eyed women, the mounds of corpses. Thinking of soldiers dead in the snow. He kept glancing at Rabbi Hirsch, but the man had retreated into himself, his lips moving inaudibly as he attacked the hated red paint. The word JEW vanished. Then the word GO. And another swastika.

He must be thinking of her, Michael thought.

His wife.

Leah.

At one point, Frankie McCarthy and four of the Falcons strolled up from Ellison Avenue and stood on the far corner beside the armory. For them, Michael thought, the hour was early. Usually, you didn't see them until noon. They passed around a quart of Rheingold beer and wore sneers on their faces and one of them said something that made them all laugh. But they knew better than to look for trouble from this group of men. Michael thought: Come on, Frankie, shout something about the Kikes, come on. These guys kicked the shit out of the *Wehrmacht*, Frankie, these guys beat Tojo. Come on, prick.

For a moment, Charlie Senator glared at the Falcons, as if he were thinking the same things, then went back to work, putting his weight on his good leg as he bent into the paint with his rags. Lighting cigarettes, jingling change in their pockets, the Falcons watched the Christians cleaning the swastikas from the synagogue and then went bopping away to the park.

Finally, it was done. The walls were lighter where the swastikas had been painted. But the light patches had irregular shapes and didn't indicate what had been put there on an Easter morning. Rabbi Hirsch walked back and forth alone, mounted the steps leading to the sealed front door of the upstairs sanctuary, examining the walls, then came back to the men. He was still shaking his head, his mouth a bitter slash. The men had finished cleaning their hands and pulling on their jackets and neckties. Most were sipping coffee and smoking cigarettes and wolfing down the buns from the bakery. They looked awkward now, saying little, staring at the wall or the sidewalk or the sky. In the war, Michael thought, they must have soldiered with Jews. But they certainly didn't know many rabbis. The synagogue was as strange a place to them as it was to Michael on that first morning of ice and snow. He saw Rabbi Hirsch flex his fingers as if to shake hands, but his hands were covered with paint.

"Thank you, gentlemen," the rabbi said hoarsely.

"Here, Rabbi, use this stuff to get the paint off your hands," said Mr. Gallagher, dipping a rag into the solvent. "It smells awful, but it does the job."

"Thank you, and thank *you*, Father Heaney," the rabbi said, cleaning his hands. "And Michael . . ."

His body shook in a dry, choked way, but he would not weep.

"I wish to the synagogue, you all could come," the rabbi said. "To have a big seder together. . . . But food we don't have here, just tea, and matzoh, and —"

"It's all right, Rabbi," Father Heaney said. "Some other time."

The rabbi bowed in a stiff, dignified way. Michael looked at his eyes and saw that he did not believe there would be another time. They would all go back to their world and he would stay in his.

"I'll see you, Rabbi," Mr. Gallagher said, and grabbed the pail, emptying the solvents into the gutter, nodding to the others to retrieve the mops. "Let's move out," he said. "It's a beautiful day."

Charlie Senator glanced at his watch and then at Father Heaney.

"Well," he said, "I better go do my Easter duty."

"You just did," Father Heaney said, popping a Camel from his pack.

# 22

That afternoon, after hanging up his suit and taking a bath to wash away the odor of the solvents, Michael handed his mother the five dollars. He explained about Mrs. Griffin but didn't tell her the details of his dreams.

"Och, Michael, you should keep it," she said, holding each corner of the bill with thumb and forefinger. "It was *your* dream."

"No, let's save it for a phonograph." He told her about the composers Rabbi Hirsch had mentioned, finding their names written into his notebook. Smetana, Dvořák, Mahler. "We can hear all the music they don't play on the radio."

"Fair enough," she said, and put the bill in her purse.

Then they sat down to an early dinner. Kate Devlin did not mention what had happened at the synagogue, so he knew she must have taken the trolley car to the eight o'clock mass at Sacred Heart. If she had walked, she'd have seen the swastikas. But

Michael did not want to spoil the meal by relating the events of the morning. The meal was the reason she'd risen so early to go to mass and had then rushed home to scrub potatoes and peel carrots, and prepare the small pot roast for the amazing oven of the new gas stove. That, and one other thing: although she had paid for a new suit for Michael, she did not buy an Easter outfit for herself. "I think I'll skip the fashion show at the eleven o'clock mass, thank you very much," she'd said before leaving. Now the kitchen was filled with the aroma of the roast, and before they sat down she toasted the *hametz* that Rabbi Hirsch had sent to them for Passover.

"Well, happy Easter, son," she said, "and to all the others who don't have food."

She said grace then, with Michael adding an "amen," and they began to eat. The meat was pink and savory and he cut off small pieces and tried to chew them slowly. He still ate much faster than his mother did. He slathered butter on the opened potatoes and the crunchy toasted *hametz*. He piled more carrots on his plate. She cautioned him about using too much salt. He sipped cold water. Then he told her what a seder was and how Jesus and the disciples were actually at a seder when they had the Last

Supper and how next year Rabbi Hirsch wanted them to come to a seder at the synagogue and was going to invite Jackie Robinson too. Kate Devlin thought that was a wonderful idea and said she would cook and they could carry the food up to Kelly Street.

But when dinner was almost over, he told her what had happened that morning. Kate Devlin was furious about the swastikas and thrilled at what Father Heaney and the men had done.

"At least they're not all a bunch of bigots," she said. "There's still a lot of decent people around here, no matter what you might think."

They talked about how the police had to find the people with the red paint and how it was probably the Falcons, since Frankie McCarthy had come by with his boys to see the results. They usually ate breakfast when other people ate lunch.

"You don't have to be Sherlock Holmes," she said, "to figure that one out."

But as this was Easter Sunday, and she wanted to make it special for the boy, she didn't dwell on the story. It was one more terrible event in a sinful world. After dinner, they walked together to the Grandview, where she was working that night. This was a big deal for Michael: because there was no school on Easter Monday, he could sit through the entire double feature, along with cartoons, the newsreel, and the coming attractions, while Kate worked in the box office. And he would go home with her when the pictures were over. She took him through the lobby to a side door, bought him a box of Good and Plenty candies, and then went to the box office.

The first movie was a western with Joel McCrea, and although he missed the beginning, he felt as if he'd already seen it ten times at the Venus, with different actors. The other movie was *13 Rue Madeleine*, with James Cagney, all about four OSS spies who infiltrated France to destroy a secret German rocket base before D day. The address in the title was Gestapo headquarters, and one of the OSS agents was secretly a German spy. Michael disappeared into the movie, training with Cagney, operating secret radios in barns and basements, moving bravely down dark European streets in a holy mission against the Nazis. When it was over, he felt uneasy. The swastikas were obviously symbols of evil, the Nazis were clearly the bad guys. How could anybody copy the Nazis by putting swastikas on a synagogue? Probably the Falcons. But maybe someone else. Maybe people right here in the RKO Grandview.

His feeling of unease worsened when the newsreel came on after the coming attractions, just before the Joel McCrea picture was to play again for the last time that night and he could see what he had missed. Part of the newsreel was about Jackie Robinson signing with the Dodgers. It showed Branch Rickey shaking hands with the smiling black player, and film of Robinson in Havana, slashing a ball to left field and dashing to first in a pigeon-toed way, his hat falling off as he rounded the base. Some people cheered. But about half the audience booed. In Brooklyn! They were booing a *Dodger!*

On the way home with his mother, he talked about the way Robinson had been booed, not because he was a Dodger, obviously, but because he was a Negro, and she tried to explain how there were all sorts of people in the world, and how some of them were ignorant or afraid or full of disappointment, and how you had to pity them and pray for them.

"They just don't know any better," she said. Then her voice lowered. "But, to tell the truth, some of them . . ."

She just shook her head, as they turned into Ellison Avenue for the last two blocks to home. The night sky was clear, bright with dense stars and a huge moon. There were more people in the streets now. The night was cool but not cold, with a brisk wind blowing up from the waterfront, and they were both glad they'd worn coats. A half-full trolley car raced by on its metal tracks. The bars of Fitzgerald's and Casement's were packed. They turned into the apartment house.

"We'll have a nice cup of tea," she said, "and then a good night's sleep."

On the second floor landing, as they passed Mrs. Griffin's flat, Michael could hear the squeak and bang of the roof door. He was suddenly wary. He remembered clearly hooking it shut. He stepped ahead of his mother on the last flight of stairs and turned cautiously on the landing. He could see a rectangle of sky through the open door.

"Why is that thing open?" Kate Devlin said, fumbling for her key. "Go up and lock it, son."

He went slowly up the roof stairs. When he reached the door, he could see it: a bright red swastika painted on the inside of the black door. Paint was splashed around the small landing.

"Mom! You better come up here, Mom!"

Coatless now, she left the apartment door

open and hurried up the stairs.

"Good God," she whispered.

She stepped outside, with Michael behind her. In the bright starlight they could see the words JEW LOVR painted on the outside of the door, the paint still wet to the touch. The words filled the door. There didn't seem to be room for the E in LOVER.

"Those cowardly bums," she whispered, then went back to the doorway. "Now be careful, don't get the paint on yourself."

She hooked the door shut and led the way downstairs. In the kitchen she pulled on her coat. Her face was cold and focused.

"That does it," she said. "I'm calling the police."

"They won't do anything, Mom."

"I'm calling them anyway. Lock the door behind me."

From the window, he saw her cross Ellison Avenue and walk into the back door of Casement's Bar, where there was a pay phone. I should have gone with her, he thought. Suppose they're down there? Suppose the Falcons are watching her? If they do anything to her, it's because of me. I'm the one who goes to see Rabbi Hirsch. I'm the one who went to get Father Heaney. Not her. He imagined men in black uniforms and polished boots coming out of the dark to hurt her. A phrase rose in his mind. *Got shtroft, der mentsh iz zikh noykem.* God punishes, man takes revenge. If they touched her, he would find them and kill them. No matter where they went, if they ran to the four corners of the world, he would find them. He didn't care if he was caught. He didn't care if they took him to the death house at Sing Sing and strapped him in the chair. *Got shtroft, der mentsh iz zikh noykem* . . .

And then he saw her come out of the back door of Casement's and step between two parked cars. She ran across the street. In the kitchen, he unlocked the door and peered down the stairwell. He saw her hand on the banister, heard her quick steps, and then she was coming up the last flight and he took her hand and led her into the kitchen and locked the door.

"All right," she said, removing her coat. "Let's have our cup of tea."

Two uniformed cops arrived about an hour later. One was beefy, gray-haired, and bored. He said his name was Carmody. The other's name was Powers. His skin was the color of oatmeal. Their polite boredom made Kate Devlin seethe.

"Whatta ya want us to do about it, lady?"

Carmody said. "Clean it off?"

"Investigate it!" she snapped. "There's paint all over the floor up there. These idiots probably took the can to the roof and threw it into the yards. Maybe you could find the can. Maybe you can find the brush. Maybe you'll even find fingerprints!"

"Well, well, a sleuth," Carmody said. "We've found ourselves a sleuth, Powers."

"Gee, we'd better do what the sleuth says," Powers said.

Kate's eyes narrowed to cold slits.

"Don't get sarcastic with me, Officer. You're here as a civil servant. You'd better be civil and you'd better be a servant."

Carmody sighed in a mixture of surprise and surrender. Kate Devlin wasn't like some of the Irish, who she once told Michael were far too docile in the presence of the police. Michael watched her with a kind of awe. Look at the way she was dealing with these shmucks. She was tough. Carmody took out a notebook and a stubby pencil and sat down heavily at the table, facing Kate Devlin. The other cop gazed around the apartment, peering into the darkened rooms off the kitchen.

"Name, age, employment, number of years in this apartment."

"Kathleen Devlin. Thirty-four. I work at

the RKO Grandview. We've been here since 1940."

"Where's your husband, lady?" the sallow cop said.

"In Belgium."

"Whatta you mean, Belgium?"

"He's buried there. That's where he died," she said, and pointed toward the roof. "Fighting people that used that sign."

Carmody saw the framed photo of Tommy Devlin for the first time, cleared his throat and looked at his partner. His face flushed. They were both more polite now.

"Yeah, well, ya know, Mrs. Devlin, this is really a matter for the detectives, and they can't do much at night." He closed the pad and stood up. "But we'll go up the roof and make sure everything's okay, all right? Don't touch nothing."

They went out and Michael could hear their heavy feet moving on the roof above the kitchen. His mother washed the teacups in silence. And he loved her a lot for what she had done. He had never heard her use her husband's death to make people feel sorry for her. Never. And she hadn't done it with the cops either. It was more like telling them that if her husband could die doing his job, they could try doing *theirs*.

She didn't weep in public. She didn't fly the flag like the patriots. She had a mass said every year around Christmas on the anniversary of her husband's death. But that was all. Some things, she always said, you kept to yourself. Now both of them had called up the memory of Tommy Devlin on the same day.

"Mom, could my father dance?"

"Why do you ask *that,* son?"

"I was wondering about it," he said. "Rabbi Hirsch told me that he'd never had time to dance with his wife. And, I, well —"

"He was a wonderful dancer," she said. "We used to go on Saturday nights to the Webster Hall in Manhattan. In the summer, we danced at Feltman's in Coney Island. He could jitterbug, all right, and he danced a lovely fox trot. But his favorite was the waltz. Mine too."

A waltz, Michael was thinking, what is a waltz? And was thrilled at the image of his father dancing. He had imagined him doing a slow jitterbug, smiling and graceful, but now that he knew that Tommy Devlin really *could* jitterbug, he had trouble imagining this other dance, a waltz. Kate seemed to read his mind.

"That's the dance that goes one-two-three, one-two-three," she said. "Here, I'll show you."

She took his hand and put another on his waist, and stepped, one-two-three, one-two-three, moving him in the tight space between the table and the sink, and then humming a tune. *Do-do-da-dee, da-da da-da, do-do-da-dee* . . .

"That's Strauss," she said. " 'The Blue Danube.' Sure, you've heard it before." He had. "They're always playing it on *Rambling with Gambling*, in the morning." He pictured his father dancing with her, in some ballroom out of a movie, and then Rabbi Hirsch offering a hand to his wife. And then saw a flashlight beam scanning the backyards.

He released her hand and moved to the window. The lights went on in one of the Collins Street apartments, and he could see an annoyed Mr. Rossiter gazing up at the source of the light beam. Michael opened the window and leaned out to see better. He could hear his mother turn on the hot-water tap for the stacked dishes.

"Be careful there, Michael. Don't, for God's sake, fall out."

"No way."

Then the flashlight beam held on something, and he could hear urgent voices from the roof, and sure enough, there it was, lying in some weeds. The paint can.

"Mom, you're better than Sherlock Holmes," Michael said.

She came over to the window, drying her hands on a dish towel.

"Glory be to God," she said.

"I better tell them it's Sapolin number 3."

"Of course, my dear Watson."

They both laughed, and after the flashlights vanished from the yards, they shut the window. Kate Devlin went to her chair and her book, and Michael went to bed. Lying in the dark, remembering the few graceful steps his mother had taught him, humming softly the melody of "The Blue Danube," he tried to picture a waltz. He must have seen many waltzes in the movies and didn't know their names. There were always dances in those boring movies set in earlier centuries, where Englishmen wore wigs and wrote with feathers, and the long, satiny women's gowns exposed parts of pale breasts. Those movies were hard to follow, because when the Englishmen talked so did all the kids in the Venus; they shut up only when the men were riding horses, dueling with enemies, or stabbing each other in marble castles. Certainly they must have waltzed in Emperor Rudolf's castle. And he remembered from geography class that the Danube flowed right through Vienna, where Rabbi Hirsch's mother went after leaving him behind. He wondered whether the Vltava itself flowed past Prague into the Danube.

Then he imagined his father in a tuxedo, like a bigger, darker version of Fred Astaire, waltzing with his mother across the gleaming floor of the Webster Hall. It was long before the war, even before Michael was born, and the music soared, and everybody stepped aside to watch, and his father and mother never got tired. Then, at the far end of the vast ballroom, Rabbi Hirsch stepped forward with Leah, and he was as young as Michael's father, his face blissful, and he bowed to his wife and started his waltz too.

At daybreak of Easter Monday, when Michael awoke, he saw two detectives in raincoats and porkpie hats down in the yards. They took the paint can away and then came to their house and made photographs of the door and some footprints and took another statement from Kate and Michael. They weren't the same detectives who had arrested Frankie McCarthy. Abbott and Costello must have had the day off. But they knew about the swastikas at the synagogue and they knew about what had happened to Mister G.

"You oughtta try to remember what happened that day, kid," one of the detectives said to Michael. "You're gonna need some help someday."

Michael said nothing. The detectives went away, and the next day, after school, Michael went to Mr. Gallagher's and bought some solvent and some black paint with money his mother had given him. She had cleared the costs with Mr. Kerniss, the landlord that Michael had never seen. While she was at work, Michael scrubbed the red paint off the floors of the hallways. Then he painted over the swastikas and the words on the door. But 378 Ellison Avenue felt dirty now. And somehow frail. He knew they would never feel safe there again.

# 23

For weeks, nothing happened. Everybody had heard about the swastikas, but there were no arrests. Frankie McCarthy drifted around the parish like a ghost, but he ignored Michael, Sonny Montemarano, and Jimmy Kabinsky. Even so, Michael didn't completely relax. The weather was warm and breezy now, and all the other kids of the parish were back on the streets. He played stickball on the crowded courts of Collins Street, hitting balls farther than ever, but often striking out when he glimpsed any of the Falcons coming along Ellison Avenue. If he was bigger this spring, so were the Falcons, and they moved like they were the true rulers of the parish.

Pushed by Rabbi Hirsch to study, study, study, Michael worked a little harder at his homework and his grades moved into the low 90s. He still traded for old comics and bought new ones and read them in his room. He found a magazine called *Hit Parader* and learned the words to new songs and passed the lyrics to the rabbi. Now he would hear the rabbi suddenly begin to sing "Zip-a-Dee-Doo-Dah" or "Cool Water" and, best of all, "How Are Things in Glocca Morra?," which he promised to sing for Michael's mother at next year's seder.

Michael did more of the sweaty work of janitoring, gladly washing the halls each Saturday morning, using a cream called Noxon to polish the brass mailboxes in the vestibule, feeding coal to the hot-water boiler in the basement. This meant he missed the first stickball games of the morning, but they always kept playing as long as there was light. He remained wary and was sometimes tense, feeling that Frankie McCarthy was like a bomb ticking away. At night, he still dreamed of blood-red snow rising from watertaps and white horses on rooftops and men with hamburger for hair.

He was glad to fill the hours with other matters, and for Michael the most important matter of all was the fate of Jackie Robinson. In a strange way, he felt that he was merging with Robinson. Whenever he was alone, he imagined himself into Robinson's mind, sharing his loneliness, feeling the way all eyes were upon him, trying to bring glory to Brooklyn while knowing that even in

Brooklyn there were people who hated him. That was the lesson of the newsreel at the RKO Grandview: even people who were bound together by a place like Brooklyn and a team like the Dodgers could be split apart by things like skin color. The bitter anger of Rabbi Hirsch on Easter Sunday morning showed that religion could do the same thing. The days of spring were beautiful, but Michael sometimes thought that the world was crazy. And scary too.

When the season had started, Michael read all the stories about Robinson in the *Brooklyn Eagle* and the *Daily News* and the *Journal-American*. He listened to Red Barber on WHN. Days passed. And he knew that Robinson was in terrible trouble. He was drawing sellout crowds to Ebbets Field. But he was 0-for-20 against major league pitching and there were some writers who thought he might go 0-for-the-season. Michael dutifully cut out all the stories and pasted them with mucilage into a large coarse-papered scrapbook he'd bought in Germain's department store for twenty cents; this was history while it was happening, he thought, and he wanted to keep it for the rest of his life. But each story about Robinson's failure made him feel worse, and he wondered if he would ever fill the book.

In some way he felt that if Robinson failed, he would fail too.

"Maybe the guy can't hit up here," Sonny said one gray afternoon, in Michael's kitchen. "Maybe it's like too much pressure, Michael. Maybe he'll be like a pinch runner or something."

"He's gonna hit," Michael said. "I tell you, he's gonna hit."

He believed this the way Mrs. Griffin believed in Madame Zadora. But the truth was that, except for a glimpse in the newsreel at the Grandview, Michael had never actually seen Robinson play. In fact, he had never even been inside Ebbets Field. With Sonny and Jimmy, he had walked around the ballpark during the last days of the 1946 season. But they never got inside; even if they'd had the money, the park was sold out. Michael believed that it didn't really matter; after all, he had never been in the Vatican either and was still a Catholic. But going to Ebbets Field cost money. Even the cheap seats in the bleachers cost fifty cents. Anyway, he had school during the week, when the bleachers were half empty, and on weekends the whole ballpark was always sold out. He could have used the five dollars from Mrs. Griffin to buy a reserved seat, but he couldn't just buy a ticket for himself. He'd have to buy one for Sonny and Jimmy, one for all, all for one, and three tickets would cost more than most people made in an hour. He was glad he'd given the five bucks to his mother but sometimes worried that he'd been selfish toward his friends. He wished that Mrs. Griffin would find a horse named Red Snow and win a fortune. Then they'd all go to Ebbets Field. He could even bring Rabbi Hirsch.

Meanwhile, all the Dodgers, including Robinson, were more vivid in his imagination than in life. He looked at the photographs in the newspapers, and listened to Red Barber, and imagined them into action. In his mind, he could see Robinson playing first base and Stanky at second, Reese at short and Spider Jorgensen at third. But he couldn't really *see* them, in the flesh, until the school term was over. Sonny said that's when the Police Athletic League, the PAL, started giving out free tickets. Sonny knew all about things like that. But June was a long way off. If Jackie didn't start hitting, they could send him back to Montreal. Michael wondered if he'd ever get to see Robinson, to be there in the crowd to defend him with his voice, to make him know he wasn't alone.

The need to be there for Robinson increased by the day. The Phillies came to Ebbets Field for three games, and they started yelling insults at Robinson. Sonny's cousin Nunzio was an usher at Ebbets Field and told him all about it. The Phillies manager was a southerner named Ben Chapman, who had been traded away from the Yankees before the war for calling the New York fans Kikes. Now that he was a manager, he could get the whole Phillies team to yell these things at Robinson. Kike didn't work for Robinson. He wasn't a Jew. So they called him a nigger. They called him snowflake. They said he should go back to picking cotton. Robinson did nothing. He had promised Mr. Rickey he wouldn't fight back. At least not that first year. And so he put up with it.

"That's the deal he made with Rickey," Sonny said. "He can't do nothing about nothing, for a year. They spit on him, he can't spit back."

Listening to Sonny, and reading the stories, Michael tried to imagine how Robinson felt. After all, he graduated from college out in California. He was smarter than any of the idiots on the Phillies. And he had to take this crap from them? They could say things in a ballpark, in *Ebbets Field,* that they wouldn't say to him out on the street?

Thinking like Robinson, Michael grew enraged. He saw himself walking into the Phillies dugout with a bat in his hand and breaking heads. He saw himself sliding into second with his spikes high. If you hurt me, I'll hurt you back.

And he thought: Jackie Robinson needs the Kabbalah.

Jackie Robinson needs the secret name of God.

Jackie Robinson needs the Golem.

Everybody else said that all the Dodgers really needed in the series with the Phillies was Leo Durocher. Leo the Lip was the Dodger manager since before the war, and he didn't take any crap. He was a tough guy. He'd go right over to the Phillies dugout and, as Sonny said, knock Ben Chapman on his dumb fucking ass. If Robinson couldn't do it, Durocher would, and that would be the end of that. But Durocher had been suspended before the season started by some fat southern bozo named Happy Chandler, who was the commissioner of baseball. Chandler said the reason was "conduct detrimental to baseball." Everybody in the parish learned the word *detrimental* on the same day, including Michael. And everybody knew it was a bum rap.

Michael tried to explain this to Rabbi

Hirsch one afternoon, as Red Barber described a game on the old Admiral.

"First, a bum rap, what is this?" the rabbi said.

"It means, well, that the guy is convicted of something he didn't do."

In Durocher's case, the detrimental conduct took place in Havana. The Dodgers were playing the Yankees. Everybody in Brooklyn hated the Yankees. They wanted to beat the Giants, but they flat out hated the Yankees. Anyway, Durocher had been warned to stay away from certain people. Gamblers. Guys he knew in nightclubs or something.

"This he didn't do?"

"No, no, he stayed away from them," Michael said. "But at this Yankee game he noticed that two of the gamblers he was supposed to stay away from were sitting in Larry MacPhail's box. Larry MacPhail is the president of the Yankees."

"This is — the word is hype . . . heep-oh-crazy?"

"Hypocrisy. And Leo told the sportswriters about it and they put it in the papers. But Happy Chandler didn't suspend MacPhail for having the gamblers in his box. He suspended *Durocher* for *talking* about it!"

"Hyp*o*crisy!"

"And here's the worst part, Rabbi. The reason behind it? I read it in the *Daily News*. The reason was that Larry MacPhail got Happy Chandler his job!"

"Corrupt!"

"A straight payoff!"

Oh, there were some other things too. Leo had married a divorced woman named Laraine Day. Last year, he was supposed to have beaten up a fan. But basically his detrimental conduct was in pointing out the truth. The result was that an old guy named Burt Shotton was managing the Dodgers in 1947. And Burt Shotton didn't wear a uniform. He wore a suit and tie. When he left his last team, he swore he would never wear a baseball uniform again, and he didn't. But he couldn't go out on the field. And he was too old to kick the crap out of Ben Chapman.

"*Crap,* what is this word?"

Michael was embarrassed but he explained what the word meant. The rabbi laughed.

"That would be good to see!"

Rabbi Hirsch was working hard at understanding baseball. On the table, there were sports pages marked with a red pen, and sheets of blank paper covered with names and numbers and Hebrew letters. He seemed to have chosen baseball as his key to understanding America. He had been listening to the games since the beginning of spring training, and even his language started to change. On some days, he almost sounded like Red Barber.

"Ho, boychik, you just missed some rhubarb," he said one afternoon, slurring the word in a southern way. "But don't worry. Higbe's sitting in the catbird seat!"

The games, and Barber's voice, made Rabbi Hirsch happy. But he also was disturbed by Robinson's slump. He shook his head one afternoon, as they listened to the game and Robinson grounded out to the shortstop. He said that soon they would have to *will* Robinson into hitting. He and Michael, if nobody else. They must pray. They must chant. They must light candles. They must believe.

"Why can't we use the Kabbalah?" Michael said. "There must be words there we can use."

The rabbi gave Michael a cautious look.

"We only go to the Kabbalah," he said, "if all else fails. That is not yet."

But Rabbi Hirsch did understand how important it was for Robinson to succeed.

"For the colored people, is very important," he said. "And for poor people, all kinds. And for us too, for the Jews."

Michael waited for an explanation, and it came.

"A man like this, he is a, a . . . I don't know the word. But he is there for others. Catholics, when they are hated, Jackie Robinson is a Catholic. Jews, when they are hated, Jackie Robinson is a Jew. You see?"

"Sort of."

"So Jackie Robinson we have to help," Rabbi Hirsch said. "We help him, we help ourselves."

"I see."

"You must talk to Father Heaney too."

"I will."

And he did. Father Heaney was very grave as Michael explained what Rabbi Hirsch had told him. He nodded his head and said he would offer up the seven o'clock mass the following morning for Jackie Robinson. That afternoon, Robinson went 0-for-3, with a base on balls. In bed that night, Michael whispered in Yiddish.

*A gefalenem helft Got.*

God helps the defeated. God helps the defeated. God helps the defeated.

And ended his prayers with ten Our Fathers and ten Hail Marys. He hoped the bad dreams would not come. He hoped he would dream of Robinson hitting a triple.

And then stealing home. Against the Phillies.

Please God, help the defeated, he whispered. Let Jackie Robinson hit.

# 24

In the midst of Robinson's awful slump, a rumor swept through the parish: Frankie McCarthy had copped a plea. The detectives had traced the cans of red Sapolin number 3 straight to Frankie and found a stiff paintbrush in the lot on Collins Street, six doors from Frankie's house. The rumors said that a clerk from Pintchik's paint store on Flatbush Avenue picked Frankie out of a lineup. "They even had fingerprints on the brush," Sonny explained. "And on the can. This guy is *dumb* as a cucumber." Frankie's lawyer told him it was better to plead guilty to the charge of vandalism than face trial for assaulting Mister G.

"And get this," Sonny said. "The lawyer was a Jew and the *judge* was a Jew!"

"They should've thrown him in the goddamned river," Michael said.

"We'll, he'da gone *up* the river on the assault charge," Sonny said. "For a couple of years. Copping to the paint thing, he's out in a couple a months."

It didn't seem right to Michael. Poor Mister G was in a bed somewhere with a broken head. His mind was gone. His store was gone. His wife must cry herself to sleep. His kids were trying to get him to read an old prayer book so they could talk to him before he died. Frankie was going to be all right, with a nice warm cell and all his meals. "Three hots and a cot," Sonny called it. And because of other things Frankie had done, Rabbi Hirsch had trembled with bitterness and Michael's mother had been driven to fury. In a few months, Frankie McCarthy would be back on the street. He'd sneer. He'd laugh. He'd hurt someone else. It wasn't right.

The rumors turned out to be true. But when Michael brought the news to Rabbi Hirsch, the rabbi said nothing. He made a sound. *Humf.* That was all. *Humf.* The sound of a man who knew that for some crimes, nobody ever truly pays.

Rabbi Hirsch did not brood, at least not in front of Michael. He was too busy mastering the theory and practice of baseball. Alone in the synagogue, he wrote pages of notes and consulted them while firing questions at Michael.

*A bunt is what?*

*How is explained a southpaw?*
*This Red Barber, he's a socialist?*
*What means picked off?*
*Harold Reese, why is called Pee Wee?*
*A double play, this is two runs?*
*Mr. Shotton, his name is Boit or Burt?*
*Who is an Old Goldie?*

None of this was easy. Michael had tried to teach baseball to his mother and had failed. After fifteen years in America, she still didn't know first base from third. But Rabbi Hirsch went at the task with Talmudic intensity. After hearing Michael's explanations, he copied the language of baseball from loose sheets of paper into a kid's composition book. He made diagrams. He insisted on knowing the rules. Much of this was abstract. The daily newspapers never showed photographs of the whole ballpark, but Michael had a drawing of Ebbets Field that he'd cut out of an old copy of the *Sporting News* and he used it to explain the positions and the bases. When they talked baseball, the sadness left the rabbi's eyes. They never talked about Frankie McCarthy. And for a few days they stopped talking about Jackie Robinson too. What needed to be said had been said. The prayers had been offered. God knew what He should do. But it was too soon to use the Kabbalah.

And then Robinson began to hit.

And then Robinson began to dance off second base, driving pitchers crazy, drawing throws from angry catchers, coming in a rush around third, with Red Barber's voice rising, saying, *And here comes Robinson.*

Robinson began to hit, and the Dodgers began to win. And in the synagogue on Kelly Street, Rabbi Hirsch was clipping stories too, from the *Brooklyn Eagle* and from the *Forvertz.* Michael brought his scrapbook to show Rabbi Hirsch, and the rabbi got one for himself.

"Is like a story," the rabbi said. "Each day, a new chapter."

"It's history," Michael said.

"And something else," the rabbi said. "In America, he is *new.* Just like me." He paused and ran his hand over one of the clippings. "With Jackie Robinson, the book I am not starting in the middle. In America, it takes so long to learn what happened before. But here, we are at a beginning."

When the game was on the radio, all that had happened before to Rabbi Hirsch seemed to disappear. He never talked about Prague. He didn't evoke the spires of the cathedrals. There was no need for the Golem, if Jackie Robinson was taking a long lead off first. There were too many questions to be answered, too much to learn. The rabbi wanted to know about Sportsman's Park in distant St. Louis, where a man named Country Slaughter — such a name! — hit one over the pavilion roof. He wanted to know about Forbes Field in Pittsburgh and Shibe Park in Philadelphia. Forbes, who was he? And Shibe? He was a ballplayer? The rabbi tried hard to imagine these sun-drowned places in the vastness of America. While he had baseball, there was no place in his mind, it seemed, for night and fog.

*Zip-a-dee-doo-dah,* the rabbi sang during a game, when Robinson scampered home from second on a wild pitch.

> *Zip-a-dee-ay,*
> *My-oh-my, what a wonderful day . . .*

Baseball made him sing. He was always out of tune, but it didn't matter. He learned the words to "Don't Fence Me In," all about straddling his own saddle underneath the Western skies, and Michael found the English words to "And the Angels Sing." These the rabbi sometimes changed. *You hit,* he would sing, *and then the angels sing . . .* and laughed at himself.

One warm evening in June, Michael was walking home from the synagogue, brooding about Pete Reiser. Nine more days until the end of the term, and then Sonny can help us get PAL tickets so we can go to Ebbets Field, and Pete Reiser runs into another goddamned wall! Ends up in a hospital. Unconscious. Just like '42. Reiser was hitting .383 that year, then he runs into a wall and hits .200 the rest of the season and we lose the pennant. In '41, he hit .343, led the league in doubles and triples, and we *won* the pennant. We need Pistol Pete. We need him. And where is he? In the goddamned hospital, just like Mister G, and he can't talk, and the sportswriters said when his head hit the wall, the sound was sickening. That's like Mister G too. When Frankie McCarthy hit him with the cash register. Sickening. We never saw Mister G again, and his wife left and his kids left and the store is empty, like it has a curse on it. Maybe center field will have a curse on it. The curse of Pete Reiser. Oh sure, they put Carl Furillo there for now. Great arm, but not Reiser. And they brought up this Duke Snider, but he strikes out too much. Shit. Jackie Robinson can't do it alone. The Dodgers need Reiser too. I wish I could go to the hospital and pray and pray and Reiser's eyes would open and he'd get up like nothing happened and take a cab to the ballpark. Maybe if I prayed hard enough, Mister G would get up too and go to the candy store and everything would be the way it was before. And summer would come, all hot and green, and we could go to see Reiser and Robinson. Watch Reiser steal home. Against the Cardinals. Cheer Robinson dancing off second base against the goddamned Phillies, just the way Red Barber describes him. *And here comes Robinson!* And *There goes Reiser . . .*

Michael was crossing the street beside the factory, his head full of green fields and roaring crowds, when they reached him.

His arms were grabbed and he was lifted and jerked sideways and shoved hard against the picket fence of the factory. The streetlight was out. But Michael saw the faces. The Falcons. Tippy Hudnut and Skids, Ferret and the Russian. He smelled sour beer. Stale sweat. He felt hard fingers digging right to the bone of his arms and his heart pounding. This can't be happening. Not now. No. Not tonight. No. Please, no. Then he was twisted around and one of them drove a punch into his stomach. His body exploded in pain. He couldn't feel his legs. His belly felt split. He couldn't breathe. He tried to speak, but no words came from his mouth, only a kind of whimper. A shameful kid's whimper.

Then he smelled shit.

His own shit.

No.

Then there was another tearing jolt, *No,* and he bent over, *No, no,* and something, a bat, a billy club, smashed against his legs.

"Little cocksucker," one of them snarled. "Singin' like a canary."

"Fuckin' Jew-lover," a second voice growled, panting as another punch smashed into Michael's stomach. "Half a fuckin' Hebe. How do you like *dat?*"

"This is from Frankie," a third voice said. "He sends you his best. He wants you to have a real good fuckin' summer. He'll think about you every night. You and your fuckin' friends."

Michael thought: I'm going to die. They're going to kill me.

Then the shit-stained world exploded into a high, white, ringing emptiness.

# 25

His mother's voice was soothing and whispery but her eyes were wide and anxious, and then she went away. A bald man with thick eyeglasses peered at him and used his smooth fingers to pull back one of his eyelids. Behind the bald man there were horizontal bars of light and dark. They went away too. Father Heaney's face peered at him and his lips moved but no words came out and then he went away. A tube of cold glass was slipped under his tongue and then grew warm and then slid out. Every time he tried to move, he hurt. He felt warm and wet and realized he had pissed in the bed and was embarrassed. His mouth tasted like nickels. There was something attached to his arm, and when he was alone and stared at the bars of light and darkness and then closed his eyes he saw purple lines and pink bars. Sounds came from a long way off. Wheels squeaking. Dishes clattering. A blurred loudspeaker voice. He heard rosary beads clicking smoothly against each other. He smelled something soapy. He was tossed, pierced, penetrated, moved, washed, handled.

He lost two days.

And then woke to his mother's face again, her eyes wide in relief, her cool hand touching his cheek. He said, Hello, Mom, and she exhaled and said, Thank God.

His tongue felt furry, and she held a glass to his lips while he sipped the cool water. The taste of nickels remained. After a while, her eyes narrowed, and her face was full of wrath, and she said, Who did this to you, son?

He tried to tell her. He described the Falcons. He tried to make them clear without naming them. He did not say the names of Tippy Hudnut and Skids, Ferret and the Russian. He wanted to tell what he could tell, without violating the codes. The Irish codes. The codes of the parish. Even though they had done this to him. Tippy Hudnut and Skids, Ferret and the Russian. Even though they had beaten and broken his body. Even though they had put him in this room.

But then he remembered the humiliating smell of his own shit, and he could not hold back. This wasn't the police. This wasn't the district attorney. This was his mother, right here in a third floor room at Brooklyn Wesleyan Hospital. He told her the names, as precise as a batting order: Tippy Hudnut and Skids, Ferret and the Russian. He didn't know their full names. He knew what they were called on Ellison Avenue. He told her how Ferret and Skids held his arms while Tippy and the Russian took turns hitting him. He told her about the smell of beer. He told her what they'd said about delivering a message from Frankie McCarthy. He did not mention the shit.

"Did they use a club on you?"

"Yeah. On my leg. I couldn't see what it was — a bat or a club or what."

"They'll not hit another boy around here," she said. "I promise you that."

Her face was a grid of lines, with her green eyes burning. She went away to fetch the doctor, and he came back with her, his face shiny and smiling. There wasn't a hair on his head. Unlike Brother Thaddeus, he had a mustache, eyebrows, and eyelashes.

"Well," he said, "you've got two badly bruised ribs, young man, a fractured bone in your lower leg, the tibia we call it, along with multiple contusions and a few loose teeth." He smiled in an insincere way. "Otherwise, you're fit as a fiddle."

Michael tried to laugh but his ribs hurt too much. He wondered if Pete Reiser hurt this much. Or Mister G. Kate told him to lie still. When the doctor left, Michael reached for his mother's hand.

"What about my friends?" he said. "What happened to Sonny and Jimmy?"

"Nothing," she said, a hair of bitterness in her voice. "Nothing that I know of."

"You're sure?"

"I'm sure," she said. "Why? Was something supposed to happen to Sonny and Jimmy?"

"The Falcons, they told me they were gonna get them, sort of," he said. His voice sounded disappointed. He didn't mean to sound that way. "They must think the three of us squealed on Frankie McCarthy."

"If anything had happened to them," she said, "I'd have heard about it."

"We didn't tell the cops anything, Mom," he whispered. "We're not informers."

She squeezed his hand in a comforting way and glanced at the cast on his leg.

"But Jimmy's uncle, he's so dumb, it could be he said something to the cops, and maybe —" His head hurt, trying to figure things out. "They might have taken something he said and added it to something else and, oh, who knows, Mom? But I didn't rat. I swear . . . I didn't. I didn't squeal."

There was a long silence, and Michael could feel confusion coming off his mother like a mist.

"Sonny and Jimmy — when I was, you know, *out* — did they come to see me here?"

"I don't know, Michael," she said gently, responding to the sound of abandonment in his voice. "They weren't letting visitors in to see you, because it was . . . well, a police matter, I guess. Of course, I know everybody here, from working here, so I had no trouble. And I *am* your mother. And Father Heaney came by. . . ." She turned away, gazing at the bars of the venetian blinds and the street beyond. "I'll let Sonny and Jimmy know you're okay."

"And what about Rabbi Hirsch?"

"I haven't seen him," she said.

"If they let a priest in, they should let him in."

"Who knows, Michael? I'll try to find out. You'd better rest."

Exhaustion moved through him like a tide. He tried to resist it, tried to force his eyes to remain open. His mother's hand felt warm. The tide took him.

# 26

With his lower right leg encased in a heavy plaster cast, Michael remained in Brooklyn Wesleyan Hospital for nine empty days. He did have some visitors. Father Heaney stopped by to tell him not to worry about his final exams; he'd be allowed to take them when he was feeling better, even if the school year was over. On another morning, he woke up to see Abbott and Costello staring down at him. The detectives wanted names. Michael said he didn't know any names.

"Come on, kid, don't bullshit us," Costello said. "Everybody knows the names of these bums."

"Get their names from everybody then," Michael said.

"You just don't want to be helped, do you?" Abbott said.

"It's too late now," Michael said.

They sighed and left. Michael wondered why he didn't just give them the names.

Tippy Hudnut and Skids, Ferret and the Russian. Just those names. Street names. Let the cops figure out their real names and where they lived. But he couldn't do it. Even though they had hurt him, hurt him real bad, he couldn't be a rat. He knew if he turned rat he'd be sorry for the rest of his life. He'd be walking down a street somewhere and remember the time he ratted to the cops and he'd be through for the day. He'd be in the army, where nobody knew him, and someone would want to know about his life and he'd have to keep this one thing secret. Or he'd take the cop's test and be assigned to some precinct and then run into Abbott and Costello and they'd remember that he was a rat and tell all the other goddamned cops and they'd freeze him out, because everyone knew that cops despised informers as much as the criminals did. No. If he ratted, he'd be as bad as them. Then they'd really win. Then they'd really ruin him. They'd make him as dirty as they were.

Every morning the bald doctor arrived at Michael's bedside, carrying a clipboard, flanked by an intern and a nurse. His favorite word was *fine*. Michael was fine. His progress was fine. He was healing up just fine. Then, feeling fine about himself, he moved to the next patient.

Every afternoon, before going to work, Kate Devlin came to visit, bringing him ice cream and newspapers and once, the latest *Captain Marvel.* The comic book now seemed childish to him. He had learned that there were truly bad people in the world, and when they went after you, you really hurt. He told her he didn't want any more *Captain Marvel*s. He was more interested in the newspaper stories about Jackie Robinson. And the condition of Pete Reiser. The great center fielder was conscious again, promising to be back playing soon, and the sportswriters were demanding that Branch Rickey come up with some money to pad the concrete walls of Ebbets Field. They called him El Cheapo and said that half the ballplayers didn't have enough money to take the subway to the ballpark. But Rickey had brought up Jackie Robinson when all the other owners wanted white players only, and Robinson always called him Mr. Rickey, so how bad could the old man be? Each day, Michael read every word of the sports pages and tore out the stories about Robinson. When his mother arrived the following morning, he'd give them to her to take home.

"You'll have a scrapbook on this fellow thicker than the blue books," she said.

"Someday he'll be *in* the blue books, Mom," he said. "This is history."

But when she was gone, and the doctor and the nurses moved to other rooms, he was left to think. And he began to feel alone in the world. There was no sign of Rabbi Hirsch. Not even a note. Worse, neither Sonny Montemarano nor Jimmy Kabinsky had come to see him. His best friends. One for all and all for one. He didn't expect the other kids from school to visit him. But he knew that if either Sonny or Jimmy had been hurt, he'd have visited *them.* He wished that they had telephones at home so he could call them from the booth down the hall near the nurses' station. But nobody he knew had a telephone, least of all Jimmy and Sonny. They would have to come to the hospital to see him. Obviously, they'd found better things to do. In the first few days, he tried to make excuses for them. Maybe they'd decided to study for the final exams that Michael had missed. Maybe they'd found jobs after school. Maybe Sonny's mother was sick or Jimmy's uncle. And yeah: maybe the Falcons had warned them to stay away from the hospital.

But maybe it was something else. Lying in the dark at night, he wondered if they thought he had squealed. Not about the beating but about Frankie McCarthy. They could have heard this on the street. Maybe Frankie had spread rumors that the DA was using Michael as a witness. Maybe the cops had spread the word that they had gotten Michael to talk, in order to scare Frankie. Why not? They all lie. Cops lied and judges lied and politicians lied. Everybody knew that.

The maybes warred in his head. And there was one other. Maybe they'd heard that Michael had shit in his pants. That would have meant that he was scared, that he had no heart, that he couldn't take a beating like a man. No matter what they knew about him, he could be just another momma's boy. Maybe that's what they thought. The worst maybe of them all.

He wished he could talk about these things with Rabbi Hirsch. The rabbi would come up with a Yiddish proverb that would make him feel better. He would ask Michael for the name of a good boy who could serve as the Shabbos goy, filling in until Michael came back. Like Carl Furillo was filling in for Pete Reiser. And because Michael didn't want to send Sonny or Jimmy into the synagogue, he would tell Rabbi Hirsch to ask Father Heaney. And Father Heaney was the kind of guy who'd go down and turn on the lights himself. Then Rabbi Hirsch would change the subject to Jackie Robinson and talk about the latest game and try out some new words he had learned from Red Barber. And maybe he would sing "Zip-a-Dee-Do-Dah" or "Don't Fence Me In" and make Michael laugh. Or he would talk about how punishment was the job of God. Even if Rabbi Hirsch was angry with God. Even if he didn't, maybe, believe in His goodness anymore, after everything that had happened in Europe.

But there was no Rabbi Hirsch coming down the corridors of Brooklyn Wesleyan. It was as if he had never existed.

And Michael felt more alone than he'd ever felt in his life.

On the fourth day, the nurses allowed him to go on his own to the bathroom in the corner of the room. This was an enormous relief; Michael hated the cold steel bedpans of the first days and thought he saw the nurses smirking at him, as if they knew what had happened on the evening of the beating. Now he was free to swing off the bed and hobble to the bathroom without a nurse's help. The cast felt as if it weighed a hundred pounds. But there was something worse. When he looked in the mirror for the first time, he saw a stranger. The stranger's face was lumpy and swollen. The skin on the right side of the stranger's face was the color of an eggplant. He touched the mirror and then his face, and knew that he was the stranger.

Later, dozing in his bed, he remembered the evening of his beating and the four Falcons stinking of beer, and he wanted to hurt them back. He wanted to cause them pain. To turn their faces purple. To break their fucking legs. Pricks. *Momsers.* And then he sobbed, because he could do nothing; even if he caught them one at a time, he could not hurt them. If his father were alive, *he* could hurt them, really badly, so they'd never hurt anyone again. But Michael was too young and too small. He could hit a spaldeen harder now, but he could not beat up men. And they were men. They were as big as soldiers. As big as the detectives. He could hurt them with a bat. Maybe. But if they took the bat off him, it would be worse than the first time. And a gun . . . the police would know, his mother would be shamed, and where would he get a gun anyway? He tried to imagine himself with a gun in his hand, making them beg. But he could not imagine himself firing the gun, shooting holes in their heads and their hearts.

His face was an hourly reminder of the

power of the Falcons. He wondered what Mary Cunningham would think if she could see his face now. After all, his new suit would do nothing for his face. Any more than a new suit could change Jackie Robinson's face.

And then he thought: My face, or most of it, is now as dark as Robinson's face. He got up and hauled his cast into the bathroom again and stared at the mirror. They made me into Jackie Robinson, he thought. They did to *me* what a lot of people want to do to *him*. They made me into him. Into Jackie Robinson. My blackened face is like Robinson's. I'm as helpless as he is. He can't fight back, because he promised Branch Rickey he wouldn't. Not yet. Not now. He can fight back with his bat, with his glove, with his speed. But not with his fists. Neither can I. Not now. Not yet.

Then, thinking about Robinson, he felt another wave of loneliness and isolation. He wanted to be home. If he was going to be alone, if his friends had truly abandoned him, he wanted to be alone in his own room. Not here in this hospital, with its strange odors of ether and medicine, and stranger faces. Home. Where he would read every book he could get his hands on. Where he'd study harder than he ever had in his life.

Yeah. And get the highest grades in the class. Yeah, yeah. The way Robinson fought with his bat and his glove and his speed. Wasn't a batting average really a kind of grade? You get an answer right in a test, that's like a hit. You get a lot of answers right, you get a higher grade, a higher average.

He could do that. And keep doing it. Get a high school diploma. Nobody around here ever finishes high school. They go to work in the factory. They shape up on the docks. They become ironworkers or cops or firemen. I'll get a diploma, Michael thought, then get the hell out of the parish. Go away to the army or the navy or — shit, maybe even college. Why not? The college boys in the movies all looked like shmucks. They wore short-sleeved sweaters with letters on the chest and said things like boola-boola and got drunk at football games. Michael thought: I could do better than those guys. I could get out of here and go to college. Ride the white horse over the factory roof. Live in Manhattan in a penthouse like the guy singing that song. *Just picture a penthouse, way up in the sky, with hinges on chimneys, for clouds to go by.* Yeah: a house with hinges on chimneys. And I'd go to work in an office where my hands never got dirty and have a closet full of suits and shirts and ties and shoes. More than any gangster, and I wouldn't have to break the law. Yeah: get out. Go.

Then Sonny and Jimmy would be sorry they walked away from him. He'd be a big shot. In his penthouse. Reading at breakfast about Frankie McCarthy going to the hot seat in Sing Sing. Reading about Tippy Hudnut shot down in a cheap holdup in Coney Island. Reading about Skids and the Russian being sent up for life, and Ferret's body washing up on the beach with two holes in the head. He'd run into Sonny and Jimmy someday on Park Avenue, as he walked out of his building, a building fifty stories high. There they'd be, throwing garbage cans into a goddamned truck, and they'd say, Jeez, Michael, we're sorry we were such shmucks back in the parish that time you got beat up, and Michael would raise an eyebrow, like Joseph Cotten did in the movies, and say, Pardon me, but what's your name?

Yeah.

Maybe he couldn't shout *Shazam* and turn into the world's mightiest mortal. But he could wait in silence, like the Count of Monte Cristo, and build himself up. First, get smart, just like Edmond Dantès did, studying his books in the dungeons of the Chateau d'If. That wasn't all. He'd lift weights and learn how to box and he'd handle the Falcons himself, one at a time. Maybe not this year. Maybe not next year. He'd hold it all in, for now, the way Jackie Robinson did, and then when he was ready, he would explode. They wouldn't even remember him anymore, but he would find the guys who had hurt him and he would hurt them back. All by himself. *Got shtroft, der mentsh iz zikh noykem.* God will punish them, but I'll have my revenge.

And *then* get out. Take my mother. Get her a house with her own yard. And steam heat. Far away. Out.

After the sixth day, the nurses gave him crutches and let him walk around the third floor, in a pale green bathrobe. The crutch made it easier to swing the cast behind him. In one room, he saw a man who'd been shot. He saw another man who'd had a heart attack on the F train. In one of the rooms, an ironworker was in a cast from neck to toe after falling off a building, and his friends laughed and whooped and held beer bottles to his lips. They had written their names all over his cast. Michael would look out the window at Ellison Avenue and wish that *his* friends would come and laugh and

347

whoop. He wished someone would write on his cast. Anyone.

Then, at last, it was time to go home. His mother arrived around nine o'clock with warm clothes and some old trousers with the leg slit so he could push the cast through it. She led him out through the lobby, carrying his newspaper clippings and comic books in a shopping bag, and they took the Ellison Avenue trolley car home. Boarding the trolley, he felt awkward with the crutch, clumsy and defenseless, as he passed it up to his mother and then took her hand to pull himself up two steps. Actions that once were easy were now difficult; he wondered how many times he'd jumped up those stairs without thinking about them for a second. The driver nodded as they boarded, then paused as Michael and Kate moved to the rear and started the trolley after they took seats in the row facing the back door. There were only a few people in the trolley. Michael stared out the window, afraid of seeing Tippy Hudnut and Skids, Ferret or the Russian. He didn't want to see them, and he didn't want them to see him. He just wanted to go to his room. And close the door. And get in bed. And read about the Dodgers. His mother glanced at him.

"You're thinking about those thugs, aren't you?" she said.

"No. Yeah. Sort of."

"Don't."

"Why shouldn't I?"

"They've been arrested."

He glanced around, afraid someone might hear them, even in the almost empty car.

"You didn't give up their names, did you?" he whispered.

"There were plenty of witnesses," she said. "It was a warm night, people were out. Lots of people —"

"Mom, they'll come after *you*. They'll give you the mark of the squealer. They'll —"

"Stop it, Michael!"

He felt as if he would fall. He'd made her cross, with his fear and his childishness. But she held his hand as the trolley approached their stop, and he took a deep breath and felt safer. Then she was pulling the cord, and standing, and taking his elbow, helping him to the door. The trolley stopped. The door opened. She went out first and then helped him down the steps. The trolley pulled away, steel wheels squealing on steel tracks, and she gave him the crutches. Then she looked warily around the avenue; so did Michael. There were familiar faces doing the usual things. Teddy polishing apples outside the fruit store. Mrs. Slowacki arranging newspapers on the stand. Peggy McGinty wheeling a baby carriage in a distracted way. But he saw none of the Falcons.

"The police have warned the whole rotten bunch," she said, leading Michael into the hallway at 378 Ellison Avenue. "If they lay another hand on you, they'll go away for a long, long time."

"Yeah, and what about you? What if they get bailed out? What if they wait for you outside the Grandview? They —"

"Och, Michael: they're pack of stupid cowards," she said. "But they are not *that* stupid. They must know now that they've gone too bloody far."

He was very quiet as she unlocked the door to the apartment. They went inside, and the kitchen looked exactly as it did before he went to the hospital. He gazed at his mother as she started a kettle for tea. He wanted to believe her, to be as brave as she was, but he was afraid of the Falcons, afraid for himself, afraid for her.

"Don't let them scare you, son," she said, looking at his drained face and touching his hand. "That's how they win."

He trembled in the warm, bright morning light.

# 27

With her son home at last, Kate Devlin took the night off from the Grandview, switching a shift with another cashier. She made a stew, thick with potatoes, carrots, and onions, and beef that fell to shreds with a touch of a fork. Michael ate two helpings. They did the dishes together and listened to the radio and talked about things that did not matter. The windows were wide open to the warm night, and from the dark yards they could hear dishes clattering, laughter, radios, the sounds of the Brooklyn evening. Kate suggested tea and her son said he would love some tea, and then there were two sharp knocks on the locked kitchen door.

Kate was suddenly alert. She switched off the radio, as if to hear better, then took a carving knife from the drawer beside the sink. Michael lifted a chair and shifted his weight to his good leg in order to swing it better. There were two more knocks.

"Who is it?" she said.

"Me. A friend of Michael."

When he heard the voice, Michael laughed and put down the chair and snapped the lock. He jerked open the door.

"Rabbi Hirsch!" he squealed.

The rabbi stood there in his black suit and black hat, his bearded face nervous and concerned. He had flowers in one hand, a small box from the bakery in the other.

"Hello to all," he said, and bowed deeply to Kate from the doorway. She sighed and laid the knife down on the sink.

"Mom, this is Rabbi Hirsch," Michael said. "Rabbi, this is my mother."

"Nice to meet you, Mrs. Devlin."

"Come in, come in, Rabbi," she said, offering a hand. He bowed stiffly again and handed her the flowers and the package from the bakery. She took the package by its thin white string.

"Thank you, thank you," he said, stepping into the apartment. Michael locked the door behind him, but the rabbi stood there awkwardly. His eyes took in the kitchen, but he avoided looking at Michael's bruised face.

"Have a seat, Rabbi," she said. "We were just having tea, and I know you like tea. Michael told me so."

"Thank you," he said again, taking one

of the chairs. Michael sat facing him.

"Pound cake!" Kate said. "My favorite!"

Her voice is a little high, Michael thought; she's actually nervous. She started a fresh kettle, ran water into a cheap vase, stacked the flowers in the vase, placed it on the table, and then found a plate for the cake, a knife, a cup and saucer for the rabbi. All in a nervous rush. Very few men came to this flat, and absolutely no rabbis.

"It'll be just a minute," she said.

"Forgive me, I don't mean to have you troubled," he said. The fragrance of the small purple flowers filled the kitchen, giving Michael a reminder of summer.

"Oh, it's no trouble, Rabbi. Michael always — did he tell you what happened in Orchard Street? With the suit?"

Rabbi Hirsch smiled. A summery smile.

"Yes, yes. That was very good. Another language, it's sometimes a good thing." A pause. "*Always* a good thing."

He still wouldn't look at Michael.

"Michael says he now has three languages: English, Latin, and Yiddish," Kate said, her back to the rabbi as she worked at the stove.

"He is a very good boy," the rabbi said. "He will learn many more languages. A diplomat, he could be."

"Wouldn't that be lovely," she said. "Maybe he could help unite Ireland."

"Or make Palestine the land of milk and honey."

She was smiling as the kettle whistled. She lifted it off the gas and poured water onto the black leaves in the teapot.

"You make tea the way in Prague we made it," the rabbi said.

"The tea leaves are cheaper," she said. "It's not a matter of principle."

He smiled. "Yes, but the balls of tea in America are very strange. The taste is not the same."

"How long have you been in America, Rabbi?"

"Nine months."

Michael looked at him now. This was news. Nine months? He had assumed that the rabbi had come here during the war.

"Michael says you are from Prague," she said. "Did you come here straight from there?"

The tea was steeped now, and she was pouring it into the cups. Michael thought: Keep asking questions, get the story, the whole story, the story of Leah. His wife's story. Ask the questions I can't ask.

"No," he said. "Another way, a long way to here."

Now, for the first time, he gazed directly at Michael's face. He removed his glasses and rubbed his right eye with a knuckle as if to focus it more sharply. His mouth turned down in a pained way. His eyes watered. Michael wanted to hug the man and ease his pain. But that pain also proved to Michael that he mattered to Rabbi Hirsch, even if he didn't come to the hospital. He had learned on Easter morning that the rabbi didn't cry easily.

"They did a terrible thing to you, Michael," he said hoarsely.

"It's getting better," Michael said. "A couple of days ago — in the hospital? — it looked terrible. Right, Mom?"

"Awful."

The rabbi turned away, clearing his throat, then sipped the tea.

"Three times, I comed to the hospital," he said softly. "But the police, they don't let me in." His eyes moved to the gas stove, then back to Michael. "I thought, maybe a Jew they don't see here much. But, no, is serious, the police said to me. Big case. Very serious. So I went to Kelly Street and said my best prayers."

Michael turned to his mother, as if for confirmation.

"I guess the police weren't taking any

chances," she said, turning to Michael. "Those buggers might have come there to get you."

Michael stirred with a kind of elation.

"Maybe *that's* why Sonny and Jimmy didn't come," he said.

"Maybe," she said, but Michael felt the pressure of words she preferred to leave unspoken. Rabbi Hirsch spooned some sugar into his tea, and nodded when Kate placed a slab of pound cake on his plate. The rabbi glanced again at Michael, and then his eyes drifted to the walls and the framed photograph of Michael's father.

"This is your husband, Mrs. Devlin?" he said. She turned, following his gaze.

"Yes. That's Tommy Devlin."

"Michael, he has the chin and nose of his father, and your eyes," he said. Michael felt a sudden dull ache, deep in his head, like a memory of someone moving through dark rooms. He sipped his tea.

"That's what they say," Kate agreed.

"A good man he must have been," the rabbi said. "And you, too, Mrs. Devlin. A son like yours is no accident."

"Thank you," Kate said, and smiled. "Do you have children, Rabbi?"

"No."

Don't stop, Michael thought. Go on,

Mom, get it all from him.

"But you were married?"

She heard me!

"Yes," the rabbi said.

A pause. Michael moved his chair to be able to see the rabbi without staring. The ache eased in his head.

"His wife's name was Leah," Michael said. "She died during the war."

"That damned war," Kate said.

A vagrant piece of music drifted from the yards. Bing Crosby, singing about faraway places with strange-sounding names, far away over the sea. Then Kate said: "Tell me about her."

Rabbi Hirsch stared at his tea the way Michael had often stared at the photograph of Leah. Small beads of perspiration appeared on his forehead. He held the teacup in a clumsy way.

"Forgive me," Kate said. "I don't mean to be nosy."

"Nosy, no, no, that you are not. But . . . a hurt, a bad hurt, maybe better we shouldn't talk about."

"Sometimes it's *better* to talk about things, instead of holding them all inside."

He glanced at her and exhaled.

"True," he said.

His eyes grew cloudy with the past. He

357

stared into the teacup.

"Well . . . it's in another life."

And then in the warm Brooklyn evening, with the sound of foghorns drifting from the harbor through the open window, the rabbi told the story to the widow from Ireland and her American son. And perhaps even to himself.

"We met in Prague in 1937," he said. "A Zionist she was, full of, how do you say it? *Passion?* She was from Warsaw. Eighteen years old. You know what is a Zionist?"

While Rabbi Hirsch tried to explain Zionism, Michael slipped again into Prague, a city where automobiles and trolley cars moved, where Rabbi Loew and Emperor Rudolf once held secret meetings in the fog. Michael could see Leah Yaretzky, slim and dark-haired, a student from Poland, speaking German and Yiddish and a little Czech, her eyes blazing. He stood beside young Rabbi Hirsch as he watched her at a crowded meeting at Charles University, everybody smoking, eyes intense, full of alarm and fear.

"It goes back before that night I seen her first time," the rabbi said. "It goes back to 1923, when the swastika we saw for the first time, in pictures from Munich," he said. "Hitler's name we heard in the wireless radio and the newspapers and the magazines, and in Italy, Mussolini already has came to power. Hitler, a *putsch* he tried already in November, out of a beer hall, and failed and everybody laughed at him. He's a Charlie Chaplin, who cares? But some smart people said: He is the future. My father said I would have to choice."

"Choose," Michael said.

"Choose. I can become more of a Jew, he said, or I can be no Jew at all. I choosed to be more of a Jew."

Before the end of the year, his father was dead. Michael could see Judah Hirsch at his father's hospital bed, promising to become a rabbi. Saw him in school. Studying holy books and listening to white-haired old rabbis explain Torah and Talmud. Working as an assistant in a modern synagogue in Prague. And then it was 1937, when Michael was two years old and his father was still alive and waltzing with Kate Devlin in the Webster Hall. And Michael could see Rabbi Hirsch going to the meeting where he first heard Leah Yaretzky speak.

Her words meant little to him. "A Jewish homeland, in Palestine, it was like a myth," he said. "Like something in a song. Nothing it meant to me. Jews had been in Prague for a thousand years. We were doctors, lawyers, businessmen. Jews were artists. Jews were writers. Why go to the desert to be farmers?"

But when Leah Yaretzky rose, she did not deliver a polite speech. Nor a sentimental speech. Certainly not a religious speech, and definitely not the kind of speech you would expect from a woman. Michael heard her speaking in beautiful Yiddish, silencing the crowd with talk about Hitler, who was in absolute power now in Germany. Hitler was not a Charlie Chaplin. She warned the audience about what was certain to come with Hitler to all of Europe, including Prague. Michael could hear her, as he stood beside Rabbi Hirsch, and Leah Yaretzky spoke about death and destruction. Her hands were waving as she insisted that they all must leave Central Europe for Palestine, so that the Jews could survive. She talked about Israel. She talked about Zionism. She talked about guns. Rabbi Hirsch had never heard a woman speak this way. Neither had Michael.

"She said if Jews were going to live they must be ready to die," he said. "And she was right."

"She wanted to use guns against the Nazis?" Michael asked in a thrilled whisper.

"Yes. And the British too, in Palestine.

The British, she said, they never understand anything unless you shoot them."

"Well, she was right about that," Kate Devlin said, with a faint smile.

The tea was finished now, and Kate Devlin stood up and went to a closet and took down the bottle of wine from the top shelf. She placed it on the table.

"A glass of wine, Rabbi?"

He peered at the label of the pint of Mogen David.

"You keep kosher?" he said in a pleased way.

"I like the sweet taste," she said, taking two clean water glasses from the rack on the sink. "Most wines are too sour. But this, I like this."

"Me too."

She poured the dark purple liquid into both glasses. The rabbi nodded and sipped, and his tongue grew even looser, the past more powerful, as he told about how he kept returning to the meetings, more to see Leah Yaretzky than to learn about Zionism. In private rooms, after the great meetings, Michael saw her charting the secret routes to Palestine. He saw her handing frightened men and women the lists of contacts along the way. He heard her arranging jobs in Tel Aviv. And he saw her late at night, rushing along the fog-slick streets, holding hands with Rabbi Hirsch, moving closer to him.

"It was, how do you say? A great love," he said, groping for words, but surprisingly — to Michael — not embarrassed. "For me, there was no mystery why I love her. She was good. Beautiful. She have, had, what I don't have, that *passion*. Still I don't know why she love me, a poor rabbi, who didn't believe what she believed."

"Nobody has answers to such questions, Rabbi," Kate Devlin said.

"No. We don't never know." He paused. "But there was one thing we could not to do. I saw her, I heared her, I loved her, my Leah. But I have in my head this one thing: to dance with her. Before I am a rabbi student, I love to dance. I love the cabaret, the music. I love when on the radio from Vienna we hear Strauss, a waltz. I love the jazz we hear too, Bix Beiderbecke? Paul Whiteman. . . . So I want to go with her to some place, not in rabbi clothes, some place with music and laughing and no worry about time and Hitler. Just to dance. Just that. To dance with Leah Yaretzky, to dance with my woman I love."

Kate Devlin's eyes watered. She sipped her wine.

"Could you waltz?" Michael asked, pic-

362

turing his father at the Webster Hall.

"Of course, boychik! We are only a day from Vienna, the world champion of the waltzes."

Judah Hirsch and Leah Yaretzky never found time to waltz. And Michael pictured the rabbi at a newsstand in Prague, reading that Hitler's troops were moving into the Saar. He saw him rushing about with Leah to meetings, dodging spies and informers. He was with Rabbi Hirsch on the steps of the synagogue as frightened Jews arrived in Prague from a place called the Sudetenland, to sleep on floors or in wagons, and together they heard Hitler ranting on the radio that the Sudetenland was German. Everybody wanted visas to America, like Ingrid Bergman in that movie *Casablanca*. But Michael heard them saying that the Americans didn't want any more Jews. And wondered if this was because in America there were also people who painted swastikas on synagogues.

Then there was a meeting of all the Jewish leaders in Prague. Michael listened as some of them said that they had survived all sorts of Jew-haters, all the way back to Brother Thaddeus; they would survive Hitler too. Besides, the major powers, England and France, they wouldn't allow this clown

Hitler to have his way. And Hitler wouldn't risk a world war over such a small country.

"On some days, even I believed this stupidness," Rabbi Hirsch said. "Only Leah refused to believe any of it."

Now Michael was watching newsreels with Rabbi Hirsch and Leah, in a dark, smoky theater in Prague, seeing Hitler taking over Austria, then watching a guy from England in striped pants standing beside a Frenchman in the city of Munich, saying that Hitler could have the Sudetenland. Everybody in the movie house was silent, except Leah. "Cowards," she was yelling. "Fascist bastards!" Now she was smoking furiously. Now she was sleeping on desks in grubby offices. Now she was jittery and irritated. Now she was losing weight. Michael saw her going away, two days here, three days there, to make speeches, to raise money, and there was Rabbi Hirsch, alone. Michael helped him pack his most precious books for shipment to an address in Palestine. He walked with him past a dance hall where the orchestra played and nobody danced at all.

He imagined the rabbi alone at night in his synagogue. Praying to God to deal with Hitler. Praying that the Jews would be saved. Above all, praying for Leah Yaretzky.

"You were married by then?" Kate Devlin said.

"Yes," he said. "On March 7th, 1939. But a very small ceremony. No party, no joy. We did not dance. She said such things — dancing, *lakhn*, uh, laughing — they are wrong when Jews are in danger. She said when together we are all safe in Israel, we will have a great party and dance for a week."

Then it was the day after their wedding. As Rabbi Hirsch spoke, Michael could see him at the door, as Leah said goodbye. She had to go to Lublin in Poland for five days of urgent meetings, and now she was asking Rabbi Hirsch to make a brief trip to Austria to deliver a package. They would meet again in Prague and then leave together for the south. To make their way to Palestine.

He saw Rabbi Hirsch arguing with her. This is foolish, he was saying. The Nazis are in power in Vienna. And Hitler is moving troops on the Czech borders. Open your nose, he was saying to Leah. You can smell death. And in such a time, he tells her, I want to be with my wife.

But Leah insisted. Rabbi Hirsch would go by car through the mountains to a certain hamlet. He would be met at a certain place by a certain man, would turn over a thick envelope, and then retrace his steps, back to Prague.

"I say, 'Leah, even a donkey takes one look at me and knows I am a rabbi.' She says, 'Not if your beard you shave off. Not if your clothes you change. Please,' she says to me, 'on this envelope, the money inside, depends hundreds of lives.' "

He paused. Michael leaned forward, his head full of James Cagney in *13 Rue Madeleine*.

"What did you do?" he asked.

"My beard I shaved," he said. "My clothes I changed." He paused. "We say goodbye. A joke she makes that with my shaved face and clothes from the university, she feels she's kissing another man. I kiss her again and say when we are safe, I never shave again."

And then Michael joined the beardless Rabbi Hirsch in a car driven by a blond Jew who spoke German. Racing through backroads, climbing into mountains, plunging into forests, until at last they reached a hunter's cabin. Two members of the underground were waiting, holding machine guns. Rabbi Hirsch turned over the package of money. The driver went on alone, to Vienna, and when he was gone, Rabbi Hirsch learned Hitler had marched into Czechoslovakia. Not a shot had been fired. The Wehrmacht was in Prague. The Nazis were securing the borders, including the border with Poland. And Leah Yaretzky was across that border, in Poland.

Now Michael could see Rabbi Hirsch turn and walk straight into the forest. Saw him as he walked and walked, avoiding the main roads, sleeping under bridges and in train stations and even in a chair in a public library. He walked with Rabbi Hirsch as they crossed together into Czechoslovakia and then saw thousands of German troops moving in trucks on main roads. Billowing in the wind were those scary black-and-red flags adorned with swastikas.

Then at last, Rabbi Hirsch was in Prague. He called the apartment across the street from the synagogue, the small flat where he was to live with Leah Yaretzky. Nobody answered. He saw men in black Gestapo uniforms driving around in polished black cars. An old man told him that some Jews had already been arrested, their names on Gestapo lists. He went to the post office, which was guarded by men in SS uniforms, but was told that nobody could place calls to Poland. From a café on Wenceslas Square, he called some other members of Leah's network. Nobody answered the first three calls and a German voice answered the fourth. The network had vanished, and so had Leah.

He finally risked going to the apartment. There were no Germans to be seen. A sign on the door of the synagogue across the street said that it was closed, but there were no guards posted on the steps. In the apartment, he packed a small canvas bag with pictures of Leah and his father, along with clothes and his basic documents. He burned the Zionist literature. Then he made two final packages of books, carried them to the synagogue, entered through a side door, and placed them in a storeroom in the basement. He rolled the Torah scroll and took it to the home of Mr. Fishbach, the beadle, who left immediately for the mountains, where the scroll would be hidden from the Germans.

"I wanted to go, right away to leave," he said, as Michael imagined his movements through Prague. "But Leah, she was out there, someplace. I knew this, I believed this, I hoped this."

Before leaving, Mr. Fishbach had told him there would be a final meeting at the Old-New Synagogue at four in the morning. The doors were locked, but there was a tunnel in the basement of a house down the street.

Then Michael was moving through the fog with Rabbi Hirsch, dodging Nazis, avoiding streetlamps, wary of informers, plunging into the ghetto, along the streets he knew so well. They went into the modern apartment house that had been erected on the site of the old Fünfter Palast. Then into the basement, where a man was waiting, showing him the hidden door, and then through tunnels, dripping and dank, and into the Old-New Synagogue. Rabbis were praying. Young rabbis were making disguises. Old rabbis stared at the walls. The leaders began making frantic arrangements to smuggle out the most holy artifacts from the Old-New Synagogue, to hide them in the mountains, or somehow move them to Palestine. Michael thought about the attic, the sealed room, the two tiny coffins, the silver spoon.

And then a young man from the underground appeared, explained what they all must do to escape, and at the end, called Rabbi Hirsch to the side.

"He tells me at the Polish border, Leah has been arrested. Leah and two others. By the Gestapo. They find two guns and Zionist writings."

He was quiet for a long moment. As if imagining what had been done to his wife.

"I never see her again," he said.

Kate Devlin reached out and touched his shoulder, to steady him. Then she quickly withdrew her hand, as if the rabbi might think her gesture inappropriate.

"Later, we heared that she died in a camp."

"Good God," she said.

"No, Mrs. Devlin. God was not good."

Michael thought: He doubts God. Here it is again. He's a rabbi and he doubts the goodness of God. Michael realized that he had been holding a piece of pound cake in his hand for a long time. He eased it toward his mouth. Thinking: How can he still be a rabbi if he doubts God?

"And you, Rabbi Hirsch?" Kate Devlin said. "How did *you* get away?"

"Very simple," he said, without pride. "I ran." Then he shrugged. "Or better, I walked. I walked to the mountains and traded my clothes with a woodcutter. I shave the hair off my head, so that now I am bald and without a beard." He turned to Michael. "Like Brother Thaddeus." A small smile. "Everything black, I throwed away. My identity papers I burned. My father's picture, this too. Anybody looking at him, he's a Jew. All I have is in my little bag, a picture of Leah, a few shirts, a toothbrush.

I walked and hid, like an animal that is lost."

He walked through Romania. He walked through Yugoslavia. He walked all the way to Greece. In Piraeus, he eventually boarded a ship going to the Dominican Republic, where a dictator named Trujillo was accepting Jews, because he thought there were too many black people in his country. Rabbi Hirsch lived in the Jewish colony the Dominicans called Sosua. He was one of the rabbis. The sun was hot. The beaches were white. He stayed for the duration of the war.

"And that's it, the story of my life," Rabbi Hirsch said. He smiled in a tentative way and sipped his wine. "Or like they say in Sosua, *la historia de mi vida.* Some Spanish I learned there too. I built some houses. I fished in the sea. I read all the time, newspapers in Spanish and English, *Time* magazine. My books, most of them were sent from Palestine, and so I have them there too, have Prague in the books." He tapped his forehead. "And here too."

He ran his tongue over his lips as if cleaning the residue of the wine.

"The colony in Sosua? A failure. City people, we are not good farmers. When the war ends, most of the Jews leave. I stay a little longer, but last year I camed here, when from Brooklyn the synagogue put a notice in the paper for a rabbi." He shook his head slowly. "How do you say? That's all there is to it. The ball game is over. *Nada más.*"

Michael glanced at the clock over the stove. Almost midnight. He was exhausted, but he wanted the night of confession and disclosure to go on and on.

"Are you absolutely certain, Rabbi, that your wife is dead?" Kate Devlin said calmly.

The rabbi was slumping now, his face drawn.

"One guy, I met him in Ellis Island, right out there," he said, motioning with his wine glass to the window and the distant harbor. "He tells me he is in the underground with Leah. And he says she shot three Nazis when they try to arrest her, and so they don't kill her. Killing her is like mercy. They keep her alive, in the Gestapo building. And when they are finish with her, they send her to the camps. Maybe Treblinka. Maybe Auschwitz. Nobody knows."

"But there must be some records," Kate said.

"After the war, letters I wrote to the Americans, the British, even the Russians," he said. "In German I wrote, in Czech, in my not good English." His body slumped lower in the chair. "To nobody I wrote in Yiddish. Nobody is left alive to read it." He took a deep breath, then let it go. "To Prague I wrote, to Vienna, to Warsaw, to the Jewish agencies in Tel Aviv. Everywhere, I wrote. All have her name on the same lists, just one name with millions of others. Dead, they say. No details. Just one word. *Dead.* In different languages. Same meaning."

The rabbi looked at Michael's face and touched his blackened skin and shook his head. Kate got up and went into the bathroom, closing the door behind her. Michael stared at the older man.

"Rabbi?" he whispered.

"Yes?"

"When you went to the meeting in the Old-New Synagogue?"

"Yes?"

"Why didn't you make the Golem?"

The rabbi turned his head and gazed out the open window at the nighttime city and the distant skyline of Manhattan.

"This I think about all the time," he said softly. "Maybe . . ."

He didn't finish the sentence because Kate returned from the bathroom and sat down facing him. Her eyes were swollen and pink. The pint bottle of wine was almost empty. She shared the last inch with Rabbi Hirsch.

"Your wife was a hero, Rabbi," Kate Devlin said in a consoling way. Michael noticed a slight crack in her voice, a tremble.

"Yes. You said it. A hero."

"And if you ask me, you are too," she said.

"No."

"Yes, you are."

"Leah, yes. Your husband, yes. But me? A hero? *Neyn. Keyn mol.* No."

She sipped the wine, her eyes full of concern and doubt, but in some way holding back. It was as if one question had been rising to her tongue across the long evening and she couldn't let Rabbi Hirsch leave without asking it. Michael watched her, waiting for her to speak.

"Do you still believe in God, Rabbi?" she said at last.

His face looked drained and pale. He shook his head from side to side.

"I believe in sin," he said, and finished his wine. "I believe in evil."

# 28

At the door, before setting out on his return journey through the parish, Rabbi Hirsch suddenly stopped and searched through his pockets. "*Vart a minut . . .* wait a minute. Ah, here!" He waved a small envelope, smiled, then removed two tickets. To Ebbets Field.

"For us," he said. "To see Jackie!" The rabbi's face brightened as he remembered a song from the radio. "We will buy peanuts and Cracker Jacks, and I don't care if we ever get back!"

Michael could only mumble his thanks, unable to speak up. The rabbi had told him that he'd never seen a baseball game, not even in the Dominican Republic. But Michael had never been to a professional game either; most kids in the parish saw their first game with their father. The boy had played ball. He had watched sandlot games at the Parade Grounds, on the far end of Prospect Park. But the great ballplayers of the Dodgers lived in newsreels, on the radio, on the other side of the gates of Ebbets Field. He had thought he would finally see the Dodgers with Sonny and Jimmy, once school was over. But things had gone wrong. He might never even see Sonny and Jimmy again. Now here comes Rabbi Hirsch. This wonderful man. With tickets to Ebbets Field. Together we'll see the Dodgers. And Jackie Robinson. Oh, jeez. He turned his head, afraid the rabbi would see the tears in his eyes.

"What a grand thing to do, Rabbi," Kate Devlin said, smiling in a beautiful way. Michael wondered if the rabbi saw her as beautiful too. She examined the date on the tickets and gave them back to the rabbi. Two weeks away. "But you know, he'll still have the cast on his leg."

"We'll get there, Mom," Michael insisted. "Don't worry."

Then he asked Rabbi Hirsch for one final favor: to sign his cast. The rabbi smiled and wrote on the smooth, hard plaster in chiseled Hebrew lettering. Michael thought: No ironworker has *that* on his cast. And they said good night.

"Please, Rabbi," Kate Devlin said, "be careful."

"Thank you."

"Mom, he got away from the *Gestapo*. He should be able to get away from the Falcons."

The rabbi smiled in a tired, knowing way and was gone.

"He's a good man," Kate said, as she locked the door behind him. "And very sad."

In the morning, Michael began his own version of spring training. He went to the roof and packed two Campbell's Soup cans with pebbles and taped the ends and started doing curls to build up his arms. He laid on his back and pedaled his legs in the air. The cast on his lower right leg was very heavy; he could only pedal it six times at first. Then eight. Then ten. After a few days, the weight of the cast lessened; he then tied the packed soup cans to his good left leg, to even out the weight. His foot sweated heavily inside the cast, and he had to scratch himself with a school ruler or a butter knife. But he was getting stronger. He could feel it.

Each day when his mother left for work, he laid out his schoolbooks on the table and studied, made notes, drilled himself in math and catechism and history. The radio played all day long, but he was able to concentrate on the schoolwork. He would take the exams soon; he wanted to do better than he'd ever done in the past. To hit singles and doubles. To race home, like Jackie Robinson. He even reviewed all the goddamned rules of English grammar and stopped himself when his mind wandered into the more adventurous terrain of Yiddish. In some weird way, trying to learn Yiddish made him understand English better. Grammar was like the frame of a building, he thought, the structure, what you had to build before you put in the floors or the walls or the roof. Maybe it was boring, but it was necessary. It was like playing baseball. The sportswriters kept talking about how Robinson knew the fundamentals. The basics. The rules. They really meant he'd learned how to play baseball the right way. Not like it was a goddamned hobby. For Robinson, baseball wasn't stamp collecting or model airplanes or something. It was his life.

There was so much to learn. Not just to pass tests, but to get ready for his life. Rabbi Hirsch had said to him once, translating a proverb from Yiddish: "The sea has no shore, learning has no end." Now, in his solitude, Michael knew what he meant. He looked up the proper nouns he'd heard from Rabbi Hirsch during the long night in the Devlin kitchen: Munich, the Sudetenland,

Piraeus, Trujillo, the Dominican Republic. None of them were in his schoolbooks and only the Dominican Republic was in the blue books. The entry explained that this was where Columbus was buried, on an island shared with Haiti, where everybody spoke French. It said that a guy named Trujillo was the dictator, just as Rabbi Hirsch said, and that he had brought the country good government.

He also found an entry in the blue books for Antonín Dvořák, who died in 1904 and wrote a masterpiece called the *New World Symphony*, which used music from Negroes and American Indians. But there was nothing on Mahler or Smetana. They were out there, in the sea without a shore. He wanted to know everything about them, but with the cast on his leg he still could not risk a trip to the library on Garibaldi Street, where there was a much larger encyclopedia. He would wait. And use his time in other ways. And when they finally got a phonograph, he would save up to buy the *New World Symphony*.

He did not go down to the street. News of the parish was filtered through his mother, or Mrs. Griffin, who stopped by every few days to talk about dreams. The worst news was that a fire burned out the orchestra section of the Venus and the disgusted owner just gave up and closed the place. There was talk that the Falcons had set the fire because the owner threw Tippy Hudnut out for exposing himself to a twelve-year-old girl. Nobody could prove it. Not the exposure. Not the arson. And Michael imagined a roundup of all the characters who had passed across the screen in the dark: Gunga Din and Dr. Cyclops, Ken Maynard and the Durango Kid, Humphrey Bogart and James Cagney, Bing Crosby and Edward G. Robinson, along with Tarzan, King Kong, Superman, the Masked Marvel, and Dick Tracy. He pictured them all together, coming off the screen, riding horses, driving cars, swinging from ropes in the jungle, and saying their goodbyes. All of them. Even Dracula. Even Dr. Frankenstein and his monster.

But there was no farewell, and from the rooftop Michael could see the marquee and the letters he knew said CLOSED. Sometimes, sweaty and tired after lifting weights, he would lie on his stomach on the raised canopy that rimmed the roof and gaze down into Ellison Avenue and his lost summer. He often saw Sonny Montemarano and Jimmy Kabinsky walking with other kids, drinking sodas, pitching pennies against the

380

wall of the diner. He could see part of their ball games. They never looked up. He did not call down.

Other times, he would lie on his back on the canopy and gaze at the clouds. He watched them shift and change, as if in the hands of magicians, immense gauzy sculptures in the blue summer sky. One day he saw Winston Churchill there, smoking his cigar. He saw CúChulainn shaking his fist at the English. He saw Indians peering from cliffs and soldiers holding hand grenades. He saw Pilgrims, lions, trucks, mountains, the bodies of women, the Hunchback of Notre Dame, huge galleons in full sail, deep-sea divers, dogs, igloos, and the mushroom cloud of the atom bomb. Once, in late afternoon, with the sun dropping toward New Jersey, and the clouds all mauve and lavender, he saw the Golem.

Immense.

Faceless.

His arms outstretched.

Waiting to be called.

One afternoon, after reading about Dvořák, he tried to imagine the *New World Symphony*. He had never heard a note of it, but he would try to make it up. He closed his eyes, and could see Columbus on the Atlantic, the waves higher than his masts, and the music was full of danger and the sounds of crashing waves, dark music full of fear too, for they must have been terrified, going where nobody had gone before. The fear of drowning. The fear of sea serpents. And then the music softened in his head. The sun appeared. The sea was like glass. And in the music he could hear birds. Calling them all. Gathering on the masts. Coming from land. Coming from America. The music was happy then and full of the sun and thick green jungle foliage and the sound of flutes and Indians coming to see them in canoes, bringing water and flowers. The New World!

Michael hummed his imaginary symphony, seeing fights with Indians then and arrows in the air and blood on the ground and more white people coming, from Spain and England, bringing colored people after them in chains, and then there were drums in Michael's head: drums from Africa; the drums of Indians; drums while Cortez conquered Mexico, and drums when the Pilgrims came to Plymouth Rock, and drums during the Revolution, and snare drums for the Civil War. He made the drum sounds: *BUM bum bum bum, BUM bum bum bum,* adding a trumpet to make the screams. And invented bugles for George Armstrong Custer, who died on the Little Big Horn and came back to life in the RKO Grandview, only to die there forever. He made great *ooooohhhhhhing* sounds and *awwwwwing* sounds when the land filled with wheat and corn and cattle and schoolhouses, when he could see the Grand Canyon and the Rockies, the sound of majesty, right out of all the cowboy movies when the wagon trains came to the Promised Land, to what Rabbi Hirsch called the land of milk and honey. He gave a sound to the sunsets, a little sad, and a happy sound to the sunrise, like Louis Armstrong. He tried to imagine the sound of the color red. He made a *whooshing* sound for a fast river, and threw in a train whistle as the railroad pushed west, and then the blues, sad and melancholy, and jigs and reels for the Irish arriving and "O Sole Mio" for the Italians, and was trying to imagine music from the Jews, when he saw Bing Crosby, as he wandered over yonder just to see the mountains rise. *Let me be by myself in the evening breeze. Listen to the murmur of the cottonwood trees. Send me off forever but I ask you please. . . .* And ended in Ebbets Field. The music for the color green sounded like *buy me some peanuts and Cracker Jack. I don't care if I ever get back.*

And opened his eyes. And saw two pigeons watching him from a chimney. He wondered what Dvořák's symphony really sounded like and vowed that if he ever lived in a place where there were hinges on chimneys he would play Dvořák at breakfast.

The makeup exams were scheduled two days before the ball game at Ebbets Field. He did not want his mother to escort him to school to take the tests. He wanted to go on his own. But she insisted, promising to leave after he'd walked into school. They took the trolley car. As they passed the poolroom, he saw Skids and the Russian standing outside, laughing, smoking, combing their pompadoured hair. He slumped down in the seat.

"I thought they were in jail," he said.

"They were," Kate Devlin said. "But they let them go."

"How come?"

Her face was troubled but she spoke in soothing tones, as if concerned about upsetting him before the examinations.

"The district attorney said you would have to testify against them. They came to see me at the Grandview, and I told them you couldn't remember much about the night. It was too quick. I said I was willing to talk to them, but they said anything I had to say was just hearsay. They needed you. I told them they couldn't have you. And that is bloody well that."

Michael remembered her cold fury when she saw him in the hospital. Now something had changed her. Maybe she just couldn't allow her son to be an informer. Maybe she was afraid.

"It's a terrible thing," she said. "Them getting away with it, I mean. But we'll talk about it after your tests."

"They can't get away with it forever, Mom."

"I hope not."

She dropped him at the school at five minutes to ten, and he swung into his classroom on the crutches. The room was completely empty except for Brother Donard, a younger teacher with curly red hair. Brother Donard told him to choose a seat and they could begin.

The exams seemed like the pink spaldeen that morning when he and Sonny and Jimmy were still musketeers. Big and fat. All you had to do was swing. He was finished with all of them before one o'clock. Brother Donard glanced at the clock and looked surprised; he picked up the papers and told Michael to enjoy the summer. The same to you, Michael said, and swung down the empty corridor on his crutches. Then he stopped.

Down by the double doors leading to the schoolyard, he saw Sonny Montemarano walking in. Sonny saw him too, turned slightly, and seemed about to run.

"Sonny! Hey, Sonny, wait a minute!"

Sonny looked vaguely ashamed of himself as he waited for Michael to reach him.

"Where you been?" Michael said. "What are you doing here?"

"Summer school."

"In what?"

"I'm not supposed to talk to you," Sonny said, his head and eyes moving around in search of witnesses. The corridor was empty.

"Says who?"

"Says everybody."

"How come?"

"They say you're a rat."

"That's bullshit, Sonny, and you know it."

Sonny said nothing.

"Sonny, the charges were dropped against those guys. I just saw Skids and the Russian in front of the poolroom. The reason they're out? I wouldn't *talk*."

"They say you ratted them out and then got ascared of them. That's what they say."

"The cops came to see me in the hospital, Abbott and Costello themselves. But I wouldn't say anything. I swear to God. Go ask them."

"Why would anybody believe *them?* They're cops!"

"Why would anybody believe the pricks who did this to me? Four on one, they held me, they beat the crap out of me, for *what?* What are they, goddamned *heroes?* You believe them before you believe me, Sonny, and you're supposed to be my *friend?*"

Sonny glanced at Michael's face, then at the cast, and stared into the schoolyard.

"I'm sorry, Michael," he said. "*I* think you didn't rat. But everybody else thinks you *did.*"

"They're all wrong."

"But we gotta *live* with them."

"Okay," Michael said, and pushed forward on the crutches to leave.

"Hey, Michael," Sonny shouted.

"Don't bother, Sonny," Michael said. "I heard what you were saying. I'll see you."

"Maybe later, you get the cast off, we could play a little ball."

"Where? The Bronx?"

He swung away on his crutches, angry and alone, feeling that a part of his life was over.

# 29

On the last Tuesday in June, with the sun high in the Brooklyn sky and a clean breeze blowing from the harbor, they went together to Ebbets Field. They met at the entrance to Prospect Park, the rabbi in his black suit, black hat, and white socks, Michael in gabardine slacks and a windbreaker. The boy made good speed on his crutches. His face was no longer black and swollen, but there were still purple smudges under his eyes and his ribs hurt when he laughed. In the pockets of the windbreaker he carried cheese sandwiches prepared by his mother.

"We should take a taxi," the rabbi said.

"It costs too much, Rabbi," Michael said. "Besides, I'm getting pretty good with these things. And I need the exercise."

As they crossed a transverse road into the Big Meadow, he gazed from a hill upon the long lines of fans coming across the swards of summer green. Kids and grown-ups, grown-ups and kids, in groups of six or seven, but following each other in a steady movement, carrying bags of food and cases of beer and soda. He and the rabbi moved to join the long lines, the rubber tips of Michael's crutches digging into the grass, slowing him down. Some fans wore Dodger caps and T-shirts, others wore the clothes of workingmen. Some carried portable radios, and music echoed through the great meadow, bouncing off the hill where the Quaker cemetery had been since before the American Revolution. Michael told the rabbi that George Washington had retreated across this park after losing the Battle of Long Island, and the rabbi looked around alertly, as if remembering other hills and other retreats.

The smaller groups came together at the path that snaked around past the Swan Lake. The voices were abruptly louder in the narrow space, the music clashing and then blending like the sound of a carnival. They went past Devil's Cave and over a stone bridge, with the zoo to the left, another lake to the right, the trees higher, the earth darker. There were no signs giving directions, but they were not needed; everybody knew the way to Ebbets Field.

"In the legs, you will have big muscles,

like a soccer player," the rabbi said, as they reached another roadway through the park and followed the thickening crowd.

"I never played soccer," Michael said. "Did you?"

"In secret," the rabbi confided. "My father worried too much, and then my secret he discovered. He stopped me."

He sighed and shook his head.

"My father said Jews don't play soccer, and rabbis never!" he explained. "Maybe he was right. I don't think so."

Then other lines of people were joining the throng, men and boys and a few women from other parts of Brooklyn, converging like pilgrims coming to a shrine.

"I love America!" Rabbi Hirsch suddenly exclaimed.

Michael smiled.

"Look at it! All around is America! You see it? Crazy people coming for the baseball, for the bunts and the triples and the rhubarbs! Look: Irish and Jews and Italians and Spanish, every kind of people. Poles too! I hear them talking. Listen: words from every place. From all countries! Coming to Abbot's Field!"

"*Ebb*ets Field," Michael said.

"That's what I said. Abbot's Field! Look at the fanatics, boychik. Up in the morning with nothing to do except see the baseball? What a country."

"Well, school is out and —"

"But the men! Look at the men! On a *Tuesday!* How can they not work? In every country, on a Tuesday, you work!"

"Maybe they work nights. Maybe they're on vacation."

"No. No, it's — they are *Americans.*"

The rabbi was inhaling deeply as he walked and talked, as if memorizing the odors of the brilliant Tuesday morning. He was free of the closed air of the synagogue basement, and he loved it. He was perspiring heavily in his black suit, wiping away sweat with a finger, stopping to drink from a stone water fountain. But his body seemed oddly lighter, and he walked with a joyous bounce.

And then up ahead, through two stone pillars, the trees vanished and the light was brighter, and they could smell hot dogs frying and hear car horns honking. They were pulled along in the human river, out of the park and into Flatbush Avenue. Now another great human stream was feeding the river, a darker stream, as hundreds of Negroes arrived, many of them with gray hair and paunchy bodies and lined faces. They were walking from Bedford-Stuyvesant.

They were coming from the Franklin Avenue stop of the IRT. They were hopping off buses. The older ones had waited decade after decade for a morning like this. They had waited for longer than Michael had been alive.

And he gazed at them, more Negroes than he had ever seen before, some of them coal-colored and some chocolate-colored and others with skin the color of tea with milk. There were flat-faced Negroes and hawk-nosed Negroes, men with wide eyes and squinty eyes, fat men and skinny no-assed men, men who looked like prizefighters and men who looked like professors. All greeting each other with jokes and smiles and hand-shakes.

"America!" the rabbi said. "What a place."

And then before them, rising above the low houses, above the umbrellas of the hot dog carts and the whorls of cotton candy, right there in front of them was Ebbets Field. Up there was the magnet pulling all of them through the summer morning. Up there was Jackie Robinson.

Michael felt unreal as he moved with the rabbi through the crowd. The scene was like Coney Island and the circus and the day the war ended, all in one. And Michael was in it, part of it, feeding it. Music blared from the concession stands. Men with aprons and change machines hawked programs and pictures of the Dodgers, pennants and posters. A grouchy woman stood beside a cloth-covered board that was jammed with buttons. All were selling for 25 cents.

"Pick one!" the rabbi said.

Michael chose a button that said I'M FOR JACKIE.

"Two!" said the rabbi.

They moved on, their buttons pinned above their hearts. They eased along Sullivan Street, staring up at the weather-stained facade of the great ballpark. It was more beautiful and immense than anything Michael had ever seen. Bigger than any building in the parish. Bigger than any church. He paused, balanced on the crutches, to allow the sight to fill him. So did the rabbi. They stared up at the structure, seeing people walking up ramps, and behind them, thick slashing bars of black girders and patches of blue sky through the bars. As they stood there, like pilgrims, the crowd eddied around them, and Michael felt a tingle that was like that moment in a solemn high mass when the priests would sing a Gregorian chant and the altar seemed to glow with mystery.

Then they turned another corner, into Montgomery Street, and found one more entrance, *their* entrance, and a guy bellowing, "Program, getcha program here!" The rabbi pushed his glasses up on his brow and squinted at their tickets.

"This is the hard part," he said. "To find the chairs."

"Seats, Rabbi."

"Here, you look."

Michael examined the tickets and led the way to the gate. A gray little man with a mashed nose like a prizefighter's was guarding the turnstile. Rabbi Hirsch handed him the tickets and he tore them in half and gave back the stubs.

"Enjoy da game, Rabbi," the ticket taker said brusquely.

The rabbi looked startled.

"Enjoy da game," he said to himself, passing through the turnstile after Michael, shaking his head in wonder. America.

Inside, Michael stood under the stands, not moving for a long moment. Savoring it. Inhaling the cool smell of unseen earth and grass. Feeling holy.

I am here, he thought, in Ebbets Field. At last.

Then they climbed and climbed on the

ramps, the crutch pads digging into Michael's armpits, the dank, shadowed air smelling now of concrete and old iron, ushers directing them ever onward, climbing until the street seemed far below them and Michael could see the church steeples scattered across the endless distances of Brooklyn. The crowds thinned. Then they passed through a final darkness. And Michael could feel his stomach move up and then down and his heart stood still.

For there it was. Below them and around them. Greener than any place he had ever seen. There was the tan diamond of his imagination. There were the white foul lines as if cut with a razor through a painting. There were the dugouts. And the stands. And most beautiful of all, there below him, the green grass of Ebbets Field.

Ballplayers were lolling in the grass, tossing balls back and forth, breaking into sudden sprints. They were directly beneath him and the rabbi. The Pirates. The rabbi gripped a railing for a moment, as if afraid of losing his balance and tumbling down the steps and out onto the field.

"Is very high," he said, his face dubious.

But an usher directed them to their section, and they found their seats, on the aisle, eight rows up in left-center field. The rabbi sat in the end seat. The seats beside Michael were empty. Behind them were three men wearing caps adorned with union buttons. International Longshoremen of America. Michael explained to Rabbi Hirsch that the game hadn't yet begun, that the Pittsburgh players were taking batting practice, getting ready for the game. Together, as they ate Kate Devlin's cheese sandwiches, Michael and the rabbi, like new arrivals in Heaven, explored the geography of the field. They could see the famous concave wall in right field and the screen towering forty feet above it, with Bedford Avenue beyond. Red Barber had helped put that screen into their imaginations, and there it was before them, as real as breakfast.

"An Old Goldie you could hit over the fence?" the rabbi said.

Michael said Yes, over the fence was an Old Goldie. He showed the rabbi the famous sign in center field where Abe Stark of Pitkin Avenue promised a suit to any player who hit it with a fly ball. "A heart attack the fielder would need to have for a ball to hit this sign," the rabbi said, and Michael laughed. There were other signs too, for Bulova watches and Van Heusen shirts, for Gem razor blades and Winthrop shoes, but Abe Stark's sign was the only one anybody ever remembered. Michael explained the distances marked on the walls: 297 feet to right field, 405 feet to center, 343 to left. He explained the scoreboard. He explained the dugouts. He was explaining the pitcher's mound, and its height, and the meaning of the word *mound,* when there was a sudden sharp crack and a ball sailed from distant home plate on a high, deep line to the upper deck in left field.

Then another crack, another ball flying into the upper deck while the crowd ooohed.

Then another.

"Jesus, that Kiner kid can hit the baseball, all right," a man behind them growled.

"No doubt about it, Louis," his friend said.

"Even if it's on'y battin' practice."

"He does it in games too, this guy."

Ralph Kiner! A rookie last year, out of the navy. Now the big young star of the Pirates. Driving one ball after another into the stands. At the lowest point, the drive went 343 feet; balls hit into the upper deck would go 450 feet. Michael was afraid for a moment, imagining Kiner doing it in the game to Ralph Branca, the Dodger pitcher. On this day, the Dodgers must win; he did not want to remember forever a Dodger defeat. Then he thought: The man's right, it's only batting practice.

Then Kiner was finished and behind him came another batter. There was a medium-sized cheer, and the rabbi asked why in Brooklyn they were cheering for a player from Pittsburgh. The growling man behind them gave the explanation.

"Here's Greenboig," he said.

And Michael then told the rabbi about Hank Greenberg, who spent all of his life with the Tigers in Detroit and was one of the greatest of all hitters. One year he hit 58 home runs, only 2 less than Babe Ruth's 60. Michael didn't know as much about the American League as he did about the National, but he knew these things from reading the newspapers, and he explained that Greenberg had been in the air corps out in India or someplace and this was his first year in the National League and might be his last.

"Okay, this I understand," the rabbi said, rising slowly to gaze across the field at the tiny, distant figure of Hank Greenberg. The rabbi stood so proudly that Michael thought he was going to salute. Greenberg lined two balls against the left-field wall. He hit two towering pop-ups. Then, as the rabbi sat down, he hit a long fly ball to center. The Pittsburgh outfielders watched it, tensed, then saw where it was going and stepped aside, doffing their caps and bowing.

The ball bounced off Abe Stark's sign.

There was a tremendous roar, with shocked pigeons rising off the roof of the ballpark, and everybody was standing and the outfielders were laughing.

"He hits the sign!" the rabbi shouted exultantly. "He wins the suit!"

The guys behind them were also laughing and discussing the sign, as batting practice ended and the Pirates trotted off the field.

"Dey can't give 'im da suit from battin' practice," one of them said.

"Wait a minnit, Jabbo, wait a minnit. Look at dat sign. Does it say, Hit Sign Win Suit, except in *battin'* practice?"

"No, but Ralph, da outfield went in da dumpch! Dey let da ball go pas' dem! Dey di'n't even *try*."

"I say Greenboig gets da suit, whatta ya bet?" said the one named Louis.

The debate was erased by another roar, as the Dodgers took the field and everyone in Ebbets Field stood to cheer. Two Negro men arrived at their aisle, carrying programs. One was very dark and wore a Dodger cap. The other was pale-skinned and wore a Hawaiian shirt and had field glasses hanging from his neck.

"Scuse me, pardon us," said the man in the Dodger cap. They were in the third and fourth seats. The one with the field glasses sat beside Michael. He glanced at the I'M FOR JACKIE button and smiled.

"Great day for baseball," he said.

"Sure is," Michael said.

"Enjoy da game," Rabbi Hirsch said.

A group of young men came up the aisle, laughing, posing, about six of them, and took seats across the aisle on the right, a few rows higher than Michael and the rabbi. They wore T-shirts with the sleeves rolled up over their shoulders and tight pegged pants. None of them wore a hat, and their Vaselined hair glistened in the light. They were all smoking cigarettes, and one held a pint bottle in a paper bag. They reminded Michael of the Falcons.

For a moment he felt a coil of fear in his stomach. But he turned away and gazed down at the field. This was Ebbets Field in broad daylight, not a dark street beside the factory. The Dodgers ambled to their positions. And Holy God, there was Pete Reiser! Going out to left field! Back from the dead. Furillo was in center and Gene Hermanski in right. But Pistol Pete Reiser was with them, down there on the grass. Michael pointed him out to Rabbi Hirsch.

"He looks okay, boychik," the rabbi said. "Maybe some prayers helped. And maybe some hits he'll get."

The outfielders were right below them, casually tossing a ball while the cheers faded and the organ played "Take Me Out to the Ball Game." Branca was throwing warm-ups to catcher Bruce Edwards. And the infielders were firing the ball, from Eddie Stanky to Spider Jorgensen at third, from Jorgensen to Pee Wee Reese at short, and from Reese to Robinson.

"He looks cool," said the man beside Michael, peering through the field glasses, talking to his friend. "Real relaxed. Like he been playin' the damned position all his life."

Everybody stood for the national anthem. The Negroes put their hands over their hearts. The men behind Michael took off their union caps, and Michael whispered to the rabbi to take off his hat. The anthem ended and there were shouts of "play ball" and the game started. Branca retired the first two Pirates on ground balls.

"He's got good stuff, dis kid," the union guy named Jabbo said. "Pray for your *paisan*, Ralphie."

"Let's see what he does wit' Kiner."

Kiner hit the first pitch into the upper deck. Foul by a foot. The whole park groaned at the crack of the bat. Michael explained foul balls to the rabbi, and then Branca struck out Kiner and everybody applauded.

"Scared da crap outta me wit' dat foul ball," the one called Louis said. "I thought it would land in Prospeck Park."

"In Prospeck Park, it'd still be foul, Louis."

Reese led off for the Dodgers and grounded out. That brought up Robinson. There was an immense roar. The two Negro men stood up and applauded proudly.

"Here we go," said the one with the field glasses.

Robinson dug in, his bat held high, facing the pitcher. And he was hit with the first pitch, twisting to take it on the back. The crowd booed.

"They ain't wastin' no time today," the man with the field glasses said. "Gahdamn!"

A voice came bellowing from the right. One of the young toughs. Wearing a black T-shirt.

"Don't hit him in the head: you'll break the ball!"

His friends laughed. The Negro with the baseball cap glanced at them and then returned his attention to the field.

"Forget it, Sam," the one with the field glasses said. "Don't you be gettin' riled, now, hear me?"

Rabbi Hirsch was staring intently at the field. Hank Greenberg was playing first base for the Pirates, and Robinson seemed to be talking to him. "I wish I could hear them," Rabbi Hirsch said. "I wish I could know what Henry Greenberg says to Jackie Robinson. A letter I should write him." Then Robinson took a lead off first, hands hanging loose, legs wide, focused on the pitcher. The pitcher glanced over his left shoulder at first, went into his windup, and before the ball reached the catcher's mitt, Robinson stole second. The place exploded. Michael's heart pounded. This was Robinson, doing what he had to do. They hit him with a pitch? Okay: steal second, and up yours, shmuck.

"Dat's da way," the union guy named Louis shouted. "Good as a double!"

"Hold on to your hat, Sam," the Negro with the field glasses said, smiling broadly.

Robinson was jittering off second base now, the number 42 on his back, taking short pigeon-toed steps, wary, alert, drawing a stare from the pitcher, waiting, now drawing the throw, and abruptly stepping back on the bag. The batter was Furillo. As

Robinson did his dance, Furillo took a ball, then another ball.

"Jackie's got him crazy," the man with the field glasses said. "He's losin' control."

Once more, the pitcher glared over his shoulder at Robinson. The park was hushed. The pitcher pitched. Furillo sliced it down the left-field line and Robinson was racing around third, his cap flying off, and fading into a hook slide as he crossed the plate in a cloud of dust.

Ebbets Field erupted into cheers and flying balloons and some brassy tuba music from a band near first base. The two black men were laughing and applauding. The union guys, Louis, Jabbo, and Ralph, shouted: *Way ta go* and *Dat's all we need* and *Call a doctor, da pitcha's bleedin'*. Michael felt like he was part of a movie. And Rabbi Hirsch was jigging, clenching his fist, waving his hat, dancing.

"What a beauty is this!" he shouted to Michael. "What a beauty, what a beauty!"

The man with the field glasses turned to Michael, glancing at the Jackie button.

"You ever see him before?"

"No. This is my first time in Ebbets Field."

"Take a look."

He handed Michael the field glasses.

"You got to adjust them," he said. "But don't try to read the writin' on them. I took them off a dead German."

After adjusting the lenses, Michael could see all the way to first base, where Furillo was taking a lead; all the way to the dugout, where Burt Shotton was sitting in a civilian suit and Robinson was standing alone, with one foot on the top step. He could even see the dirt on Robinson's uniform.

"Thanks," Michael said, handing the glasses back.

"You got to see a great play, boy," the man said, adjusting the lenses again for himself.

"I sure did," Michael said.

The man said his name was Floyd, and he shook Michael's hand and then introduced his friend, Sam — "We were in the army together" — and then Rabbi Hirsch reached across Michael to shake hands with the two men. "My first time in Abbot's Field too," he said. "Like Michael." There was a great sigh as Hermanski grounded into a double play to end the inning.

In the top of the second, Hank Greenberg came to bat. A few people stood to applaud. So did Rabbi Hirsch.

Then they heard the voice:

"Siddown, Rabbi, don't hurt your hands

clappin'." It was the youth in the black T-shirt. "This sheenie can't hit no more."

Rabbi Hirsch turned toward the voice and slowly sat down.

"This word?" he said to Michael. "What is it?"

"What word?"

"Sheenie."

"Ah, it's one of them dumb words."

"A word for Jew?"

"Yeah."

The rabbi turned again to glare at the young men. His face trembled. But then he turned back to Greenberg's at bat.

The voice again, shouting at the Dodger pitcher: "Give dis Hebe a little chin music, Branca. He'll quit right in front a ya."

Rabbi Hirsch turned again to Michael; his early joy seemed to be seeping out of him.

"What means chin music?"

"It means, like, throw the ball close to his chin."

"So they think, throw near Hank Greenberg's head, he will quit? Because he's a Jew?"

"That's what *that* guy thinks."

Greenberg took a ball, low and away.

"You said Hank Greenberg, he was a hero in the war. These young men, they don't know this?"

Floyd heard him and leaned over.

"They are ignorant, Reverend," he said. "They are stupid."

But the loudmouth in the black shirt wasn't going away. He bellowed: "Hit him in the Hebrew National, Branca. Let's see how big his salami is."

A few people in the crowd laughed, but Louis stood up.

"Hey, whyn't you bums keep y' traps shut? Yiz are insultin' people!"

"Ya wanta do somethin' about it?" the young man shouted. His friends were all laughing now.

"I'll come over dere and give you a fat lip, buster!"

"You and what army?"

Greenberg swung and lined a ball deep and foul. The whole park groaned in relief.

"His cousin caught it and sold it on da spot!" the young man shouted.

Now Rabbi Hirsch stood up and faced them.

"Please! The mouth, shut it up, please. This is America!"

The tough guys started singing the first lines of "America the Beautiful." Sarcastically. Out of tune. Full of the courage of superior numbers.

"Please," the rabbi said. "The big mouth!"

Then Greenberg walked.

"Whad I tell you?" the young man shouted. "Dis old Hebe can't hit no more!"

"All right, can it, shmuck," Louis the union man shouted.

"Kiss my ass!" the youth replied.

That was enough. Louis was up, leaping across the aisle. He grabbed the young man by his black shirt and smashed him with his right fist. The young man's friends rose as one, throwing punches, and the two other union guys piled in, and then everybody in the area was up. Floyd and Sam stood to watch, carefully, warily. Then they looked at each other. Without a word, Sam slipped off his glasses and his wristwatch and tucked them into his pocket. Floyd handed the field glasses to Michael, who thought: If I didn't have this cast, if I only could swing at them, hurt them. . . . But now others were diving into the brawl, and the young men were backing up as the union guys went at them. Jabbo knocked down a kid with red hair. Ralph kicked a sunburned kid in the balls. The one called Louis grabbed the loudmouth by the hair and whacked his head into the top of a seat. The young man squealed.

"I'm bleedin'! I'm fuckin' bleedin'."

"Wrong," Louis said. "You're fuckin' *dyin'.*"

And banged his head again on the seat. Suddenly Rabbi Hirsch hurried over and tried to get into it, but now it was all fists and feet and curses and he was shoved back. His glasses fell and he was groping for them on the concrete steps when two of the young men started kicking him. Michael grabbed one of his crutches and hobbled toward them, but then Floyd and Sam pushed him down in his seat. "Watch the stuff," Floyd said. He grabbed one of the young men attacking Rabbi Hirsch, spun him, and presented him to Sam, who knocked him down with a punch. The other one looked up, his eyes wide with fear. Floyd bent him over with a punch to the belly. And then kicked him in the ass, tumbling him down the steps.

Suddenly it was over. The six young toughs were ruined. Bleeding, groaning, whining. Rabbi Hirsch found his glasses and looked around in amazement. Floyd and Sam took their seats. The union guys sat down.

"Can't even watch a fuckin' ball game in peace no more," Louis said.

"Hey, Louis, want a hot dog?" one of his friends said.

And now the cops arrived, ten of them, beefy and pink-faced and Irish, all in blue with their batons at the ready. Rabbi Hirsch was still standing, baffled, his eyes wide. One of the cops looked at the battered youths and then at the rabbi.

"Did *you* do this?" he said.

"I wish," the rabbi said.

"They went dattaway," one of the union guys shouted. Floyd and Sam laughed for the first time.

"Who did it?"

"The Jewish War Veterans, officer."

The cops hauled the young men to their feet and led them away. The whole section burst into applause. Louis stood up, faced the fans, lifted his hat, and bowed.

"What a rhubarb!" Rabbi Hirsch said, laughing and making a fist. "What a great big excellent goddamned rhubarb!"

# 30

On the Fourth of July, Michael watched the fireworks from the roof, where grown-ups cheered and the noise was like an artillery barrage. Sonny and Jimmy were not there. They were in the streets, where they could believe what everyone else believed about Michael.

In the days that followed, Michael heard laughter from those streets and the *phwomp* of spaldeens and the rise and fall of arguments. But he was no longer part of it. His world had shrunk to the apartment and the roof, his room and the cellar, with occasional trips to the Grandview when his mother was working. In the dark theater, he saw *Double Idemnity* and *To Each His Own* and *The Spiral Staircase*, imagining himself scheming with Barbara Stanwyck or waltzing in wartime London with Olivia de Havilland or protecting Dorothy McGuire in a vast, evil mansion. When the movie was over, he was still on crutches, still facing the long hobble home through streets more dangerous than any in the movies. On that walk, he often felt like a five-year-old, guarded as he was by his mother.

Alone in the apartment, he read great hunks of the *Wonderland of Knowledge.* On the way to the Grandview with his mother, he stopped at the library and borrowed books and looked up names that were not in the *Wonderland of Knowledge.* He devoured *Howard Pyle's Book of Pirates* and *The Adventures of Tom Sawyer* and *Captain Blood.* But he could not share these imaginary adventures with any of his friends anymore, the way he did in other summers. He couldn't tell them the stories or debate the heroism of the characters. He couldn't try to make those books fit into the realities of the street.

On a few mornings, Rabbi Hirsch came by, always when Kate Devlin was there. They had tea. Michael and the rabbi worked on words. Sometimes Mrs. Griffin popped in, to quiz Michael about his dreams. She was always polite to the rabbi. He was always formal with her. But then, like a spy on a dangerous mission, the rabbi had to move out again without being seen. There were still people out there who loved swastikas.

When Michael received his grades from Sacred Heart, he was temporarily elated. His average was 99, surely the highest in the class. But only his mother celebrated the report card, with cookies from the bakery and rich, dark tea.

On the night he received his grades, he heard terrible news from Kate. Father Heaney was leaving Sacred Heart, to take up duties in distant South America. Michael's elation over his grades vanished, and he begged her to allow him to go alone to Sacred Heart to say goodbye to Father Heaney. Maybe he was going to the Dominican Republic, where Rabbi Hirsch had friends. And he was sure Rabbi Hirsch wanted to say goodbye too. But Kate Devlin insisted that Michael wait until her day off; it was still too dangerous for him in the streets of the parish. And when she finally took him by trolley to the church, Father Heaney had packed and gone. Michael felt as if an entire Allied army had left the field.

The priest wasn't the only one leaving the parish. They saw moving vans now on almost every Saturday, packed with furniture and clothes, bound for Long Island or Queens. The war veterans led the way, using the GI Bill to get mortgages on homes with driveways and grass and safety. Familiar faces disappeared from the streets. One Saturday morning, Billy Dorrian moved out of the first floor right to be replaced by a family named Corrigan, whose kids were four, three, and two years old. Then Michael heard from his mother that Charlie Senator had left, giving up his job, gone to a place called Levittown. He remembered the day Father Heaney and Charlie Senator and the other veterans had cleaned the swastikas off the synagogue and wondered who would be brave enough to do that job now.

Day and night now, his mind was full of the words and rhythms of Yiddish. He worked on his *aleph-bayz*, trying to master the alphabet. He greeted his mother each morning with *"Vie gehts?"* And she answered, "The top of the morning to you too." He learned the difference between a *shlemiel* and a *shlimazel*, explaining to his mother that a *shlemiel* walks into a living room, bows to his host, and knocks over an expensive lamp; the lamp falls and breaks the foot of the *shlimazel*. Harold Stearns from the second floor was a boring *shlub*. Tippy Hudnut from the Falcons was a *grob-ber yung*, a stupid young man, thick, as his mother would say. How many of the men at Casement's Bar were *gonifs*, and which among them might be the big *makher* they all so desperately needed? Lots of hustling *gonifs*, but no *makhers*. He told his mother that *sha* meant shush, and she said, "Well, doesn't 'shush' sound Yiddish too?" The Falcons were a load of *khazerai*, pig meat, eaters of garbage, or *behamas*, animals. They all ought to be put in the *bays oylem*, six feet under. And the cops? *Bupkis*, that's what the cops give you. Nothing. Zilch.

In the second week of July, Michael started visiting Rabbi Hirsch again in the synagogue. Tuesdays for now ("Thursdays we can do when your leg, it's better") and on Saturday mornings, so that he could once more serve as the Shabbos goy. Father Heaney had sent an altar boy to replace Michael, but the boy was leaving for summer camp, so Michael insisted on getting his old job back. There was only one problem: his mother insisted on walking with him, even on Saturday mornings, making him feel like a little kid. He protested that at such an early hour, the Falcons were still sleeping off beer.

"And suppose," she said, "they've stayed up all night and are just going home?"

So she went with him. But even with his mother beside him, Michael walked first in the opposite direction, away from Unbeatable Joe's, where the Falcons always seemed to be at the bar. That route also took him away from the stickball court on Collins Street. He didn't want to see Sonny Montemarano. He had nothing to say to Jimmy Kabinsky.

"This is aggravating," he said one morning, as they finally reached the synagogue.

His mother answered: "Getting beat up again would be a lot more aggravating, Michael."

Rabbi Hirsch was always happy to see him, talking in an excited way about the Dodgers and about Jackie Robinson and about how he wished they could get Stanley Musial away from the Cardinals. But he often seemed sadder than before their trip to Ebbets Field. It was as if he regretted the confession he had made to Kate and Michael about his own past. It was as if he knew he could not truly fit into this scary piece of America. He would sing along with the radio and now knew all the words to "Don't Fence Me In," but when he sang the part that went *Let me straddle my own saddle underneath the Western skies* his eyes misted over. He first heard the words before swastikas appeared in the Brooklyn night. Once Michael saw him glance at Leah's photograph as if he knew that she would never recognize him in his American disguise. Too often, he wore the expression of a man who expected to be struck. By a stranger. By America.

But there was fun too. Michael showed him how to play a tune on an empty Chiclets box, opening one end, leaving the cellophane intact. Michael played "Don't Fence Me In." The rabbi took the chewing gum box and played "And the Angels Sing."

"At last!" he exulted. "I am a Ziggy Elman!"

Michael brought a second empty Chiclets box one morning, and they played duets. "Don't Be That Way" and "Sing Sing Sing" and "One O'Clock Jump." They tried a Count Basie tune called "Open the Door, Richard," which sounded awful, and were much better on "How Are Things in Glocca Morra?" They finished with "And the Angels Sing," with Rabbi Hirsch doing the trumpet solo. They agreed that the yellow peppermint box had the best tone.

"On a shofar I can't play a tune," the rabbi said, his face beaming. "But on a Chiclets box I am Mozart! I am Ziggy Elman! My instrument! We practice hard, boychik, we go to the hall of Mr. Carnegie."

One Tuesday afternoon, Michael let himself into the synagogue and heard the rabbi playing alone on a Chiclets box. He had slowed down "And the Angels Sing." Now it was mournful and melancholy. Like the blue books described Jewish music. When he saw Michael, he changed the tempo and once again became Ziggy Elman.

"Music we get from everywhere," the rabbi said. "From the sky. From the air. From chewing gum even."

At night, Michael had trouble falling asleep. The bulky cast was a hard reminder of what had happened to him, and he always had trouble getting comfortable. He thought every night about Sonny and Jimmy and wondered if they ever thought about him.

In the rising summer heat, he wondered how his life would have been if it hadn't snowed so hard that day in December and he hadn't gone shoveling and if Unbeatable Joe hadn't paid them a dollar. He wondered how it would have been if they had gone to Slowacki's candy store that day instead of to Mister G's. Or if they had started an hour earlier or an hour later. They never would have been in Mister G's when Frankie McCarthy walked in and Mister G wouldn't have stuck up for Sonny, and Michael wouldn't have seen all the violence that came after that. Sonny and Jimmy wouldn't have run out. The cops would never have come to ask him questions. Nobody would have thought he was a rat. It would have been a different summer. Mister G would still be selling newspapers, cigarettes, and candy. Michael wouldn't have a broken leg. He'd still have his friends, and he'd be playing ball across the endless afternoons or traveling with them to the beaches of Coney Island. Ten minutes on a snowy winter afternoon had changed his life. It was so goddamned unfair.

Then one night, he was walking home from the Grandview with his mother, discussing a movie called *Boomerang*. A vagrant had been accused of murdering a priest in some town in Connecticut. The cops thought the vagrant was guilty and the newspapers wanted to put him in the electric chair. But a lawyer played by Dana Andrews proved that the man was innocent. What was different was that Dana Andrews didn't find out who really killed the priest. He'd never before seen that kind of ending in a movie.

"Life is like that sometimes," Kate Devlin said. "You think you know, and you really don't."

"But this is a true story."

"That's what they *say*. It's still a movie, son."

Then they turned into Ellison Avenue to

walk the final three blocks home. And Michael stopped moving, tightly gripping the handles of the crutches. Walking straight at them were five of the Falcons, including Tippy Hudnut, Skids, and the Russian. They were talking loudly, shouting at two girls on the far side of the avenue.

"Come on," Kate Devlin said, placing a hand in the small of Michael's back. She knew they could not turn and run. Not with Michael on crutches. So she walked straight at them. Defiantly. And then the Falcons saw them. Tippy, thin and long-haired, with tattooed arms, smiled and widened his arms in a gesture commanding the others to wait. They spread themselves across the sidewalk. Kate moved to the space between Tippy and the bulkier, blond-haired one they called the Russian.

Tippy stepped to the side, blocking her way.

"Well, looka who's here," Tippy said. Michael could smell the beer on his breath.

"Excuse me," Kate said.

"Nah, I ain't gonna excuse you, lady."

She glanced around, but the street was empty now. She stepped to her right, and Tippy moved again.

"The fuckin' troublemakers," the Russian said, his yellow teeth showing as he grinned.

"I want no trouble with you, young man," Kate said.

"She don't want no trouble," the Russian said, and the others laughed.

"But you'll have plenty of trouble," Kate said, "if you don't let us go home."

"Oh, wow: a threat," Tippy said. The word sounded to Michael like *tret*. Tippy's eyes were glittery, his nostrils flaring. "Are you scared, fellas?"

"Oh, yeah, I'm scared," said Skids, who was the shortest, with thick muscles bulging from his T-shirt and black eyebrows that met above his nose. "I think I'm gonna shit my pants."

"A broad and a gimp," Tippy said. "Very, very scary."

"The broad ain't bad-looking but," said the Russian.

"Great tits," said Skids.

Kate slapped him. And then Skids grabbed her blouse and tore it down. She started to cover herself and then Michael piled in, swinging his crutch, saying, *You bastards, you bastards, you fucking bastards.* Skids shoved Kate backward and then jerked one of Michael's crutches from his hands and swung it, hitting him in the back of the neck, and then the other crutch was gone, and he was toppled over on his side and one of the Falcons kicked him. Shouting, *Stool pigeon, rat-fuckin' stool pigeon* . . . He saw his crutches placed across the curb and the Russian stomping them into pieces. He started to get up and saw Tippy shoving his hand under his mother's skirt, while Skids held her from behind, squeezing her breasts. She was screaming now: *You pigs, you dirty pigs, you cowardly pigs.*

And then a window rolled up from one of the apartments, and another, and voices were shouting, *Hey, you bums, stop that you bums,* and then one of the Falcons said, *Awright, let's get da fuck outta here.* And they were gone.

Michael pulled himself up by holding a lamppost. His neck ached. His side was burning. He turned to his mother. Her face was a ghastly mask of anger and humiliation. She pulled her blouse together with one hand and hugged Michael with the other.

"Hey, lady, you all right?" someone shouted from the upstairs apartments.

"We've got to go," Kate whispered to her son. "We've got to get away from here. We've got to leave."

# 31

She didn't speak again that night, nor did she speak in the morning. He asked her a few questions: Did she feel all right? Did she want to see a doctor? She shook her head yes, then no. At breakfast, Michael made the tea. Then he went downstairs to Teddy's grocery store, swinging with one hand on the wall and one on the banister, and bought her some pound cake. Her favorite. She poked at it with a fork. He told her he was going to the cellar to look at the hot-water furnace. But he took a stickball bat from the back of the hall, to use as a cane, and kept going out the front door, heading for Kelly Street.

The parish was just waking up. There were shreds of morning fog. He took the long way along MacArthur Avenue, slowed by the cane, driven by the need to summon Rabbi Hirsch, to have him talk to his mother. Father Heaney was gone. He didn't want neighbors to know what had happened because his mother might be ashamed. He couldn't call the cops. He needed Rabbi Hirsch. His soft voice. His humor. His wisdom. Finally, he turned into Kelly Street.

And stopped in front of the door as if he had been smacked.

Someone had carved a swastika into the wood. The gouged edges were rough, as if they'd used a can opener. He banged on the door, called Rabbi Hirsch's name, used the bat to bang harder.

And then he saw him.

Lying in the gutter between two parked cars. Like that poor wino who died during the blizzard. Up at the end of the street, across from the armory, the corner where nobody lived.

"Rabbi Hirsch!" Michael hobbled quickly to his side.

But the rabbi could say nothing. His face was crusted with drying blood. There was a gash over his right eye. His jaw hung slack and loose. His lower teeth had been snapped off at the gums. There was a huge swelling on the left side of his head, and blood seeped from his left ear, puddling on the asphalt.

Michael raised his bat and began screaming at the sky.

*Noooooooooooooooooooooooooooooo.*

Then the world was red as rage, and he

smashed with the bat at the trunk of one car and the windows of the other, he swung at the air, he struck at the ground, he cursed and bared his teeth, and hammered again at the cars, while Rabbi Hirsch lay there, and people were shouting from windows, away down the block, and he wailed again at the sky, wolf howl, banshee wail.

*Nooooooooooooooooooooooooooooo.*

The ambulance came and a police car and a crowd of kids and women and the owners of the two ruined cars. An orderly said, He's alive. But as they lifted Rabbi Hirsch on a stretcher into the ambulance, Michael heard one cop asking him whether he'd done this to the rabbi, and someone was shouting, Lookit my cah! Who the fuck's gonna pay for my cah? And the other cop was saying, Your insurance company pays, pal, and the man said, I don't got any fuckin' insurance! And then Mr. Gallagher was there, on his way to work, and he said to the cop, This kid couldn't do this, this kid was with us when we cleaned off the last swastikas, this is a good kid, and look, he's got a cast on his leg, for Christ's sake, and there's no blood on the goddamned bat.

What about these cars? a cop said. Who did this to these cars? Mr. Gallagher said, Find the guys that beat up this rabbi and yiz'll have your answer.

While they talked, Michael's head filled with images of violence. He imagined Tippy and Skids and the rest of the *momsers*, kicking, stomping, laughing, while one of them gouged the swastika into the door; imagined Rabbi Hirsch fighting back, the way he tried to fight at Ebbets Field, and falling between the cars, while fists and shoes and sticks rained down on him; and wished he could have arrived when it was happening, shown up with his father, and Sticky the dog, and Father Heaney, and Charlie Senator. Then there would have been a fair fight. He imagined his mother telling his father what had happened on Ellison Avenue and how they had put their hands on her. And pictured his father getting his M-1 and going hunting for Falcons. I wish I could do that. Go and get them.

He said none of this to the police. And after Rabbi Hirsch was lifted into the ambulance, Mr. Gallagher drove Michael home. Don't worry, the older man said. The cops will get those bums. Michael did not reply.

As he climbed the stairs, he felt numb and slow, his strength drained away. He gripped the banister to steady himself, and then made an effort to finish the last flight.

His mother was sitting where he'd left her, but suddenly her own numbness vanished. She got to her feet and went to her son.

"Jesus Mary and Joseph, son. What's happened?" she said.

He told her. And dissolved in tears and then in rage again. He punched at the air. He shook his fists. He ground his teeth.

"I'm gonna get them!" he shouted. "I'm going over to the poolroom and I'm gonna *kill* them! I don't care what they do to me! I'm gonna kill them, kill them, kill them."

"Don't bother, son," she whispered, hugging him until the rage ebbed. "We'll be leaving."

Then she turned away from him, folding her arms, and for the first time since the news of the death of Tommy Devlin, she began to weep. The sound was full of a deep, grieving helplessness. And Michael thought: They have to be punished. Here. On earth. Not in Purgatory or Hell. Here.

And then he thought about the only way that punishment might be certain.

# 32

On the following morning, Kate Devlin was up early. Michael heard her say that she had lost one day of work, she could not afford to lose two; but the words were just words to him. Rabbi Hirsch was in the rooms, his blood on the walls, at the table, in the bathroom. He heard her say that they had to hurry to the hospital, it was the day his cast would be removed; but the words receded behind the screen of blood. He chewed cereal and saw the rabbi's teeth snapped at the gums. He heard the radio, and saw the blood leaking from the rabbi's ear. He turned on the water tap to wash his face and saw blood. He combed his hair and saw the great swelling of the rabbi's skull.

"I have to see him," Michael said. "I have to see Rabbi Hirsch."

He heard his mother say that if he was in critical condition, they might not allow visitors. Her voice seemed to be coming across a vast distance. He heard her say she would check with her friends who still worked at Wesleyan. Heard her groping for words of comfort.

"They say your leg could be as good as new," she said. "You know, when bones break, they heal harder than ever."

Michael wanted to believe this, wanted to believe that when he healed and his mother healed, and *if* Rabbi Hirsch healed, they would all be stronger than ever. But if Rabbi Hirsch died, he would not heal. The rabbi's face forced its way into his mind, and everything else seemed trivial. I am sitting where he sat that night, Michael thought. I am sitting where he told his story. He is here. I must try to believe.

They walked out into the hot morning, slowed by the plaster boulder of Michael's cast and the need to use the stickball bat as a cane. He could hear Harry James playing "Sleepy Lagoon" from an unseen radio and wondered what it would sound like on a Chiclets box. Or the shofar. And then saw Rabbi's Hirsch's face: the snapped teeth, the blood, the swollen skull. Try to believe, he told himself. Try to make him heal by believing.

In front of Casement's, a fat man sat in his undershirt on a folding chair, fanning himself with a newspaper. The asphalt felt soft. A lone pigeon circled sluggishly over the rooftops. Kate took Michael's hand as they climbed aboard the trolley car, and then, as they passed Pearse Street, he saw Frankie McCarthy.

"Mom, look."

"Holy God."

McCarthy was with some of the other Falcons, swaggering along the avenue, carrying a small canvas bag. He was out of jail for the second time. They could see Tippy and Skids, laughing and joking. They saw the Russian. And Ferret. Frankie McCarthy walked as if he were a veteran home from the wars. Michael wondered if they were telling him what they had done to the Devlins, mother and son, and how they had battered the rabbi from Kelly Street.

"Do nothing," he heard his mother say in a cold voice. "We'll be moving."

At the hospital, he stopped thinking of the Falcons while nurses directed them down corridors that Kate knew from her days working the wards. Rabbi Hirsch must have been rushed through these halls, he thought. With frantic nurses beside him and doctors shouting orders. They went to a tiny room on the first floor, and Michael lifted himself onto a gurney. Maybe he was on this gurney. Maybe they used this to wheel him into the operating room. A young intern in green scrubs looked at Michael's cast and the hospital records and reached for some large shears.

"You're Jewish?" he asked Michael.

"Irish."

"You got Hebrew written here, buddy. It says long life."

"Can I save that piece?" Michael said. That piece of Rabbi Hirsch.

"Sure."

Then the intern shoved the shears under the cast and started cutting. This was a simple thing to do; the cast that felt like cement to Michael turned out to be fabric and plaster. The intern first cut down the inside of Michael's right leg, and then did the same on the outside, cleaving the cast into two parts. He gently pulled them apart and they made a sucking sound where the fabric and plaster had stuck to Michael's skin. Suddenly, the odor of compacted sweat filled the tiny room. When Michael looked at his skin, it was white and mottled like grass that had lain under a rock. He expected to see worms.

"Can he walk on that?" Kate said.

"Why not?"

"Without a crutch?"

"Hey, it looks as good as ever," the intern

said. "But you gotta get it X-rayed before you leave."

"Can I wash it off?" Michael asked.

"Right in there."

Michael slid off the gurney and tried putting his full weight on the leg. The floor was very cold under his bare foot. There was no pain, but the leg felt weak and strange and very light, in spite of all the exercise on the roof. He went into the small bathroom, feeling unbalanced as he walked, and found soap and paper towels and washed his calf and ankle and foot. His soapy hands on the leg made him feel odd, slippery, thrilled. When he was finished, he stepped out and the leg felt fresher but not quite his. The intern was gone. Kate waited by the door, holding one sock, one shoe, and the piece of the cast that bore the Hebrew lettering. She forced a smile.

"You heard him," she said. "As good as ever."

They walked down the hall to have the X ray made. He was here, too, he thought. They must have X-rayed his skull. The room was crowded. Everyone was white. Doctors, nurses, and patients. As they waited their turn, Kate studied the classified advertisements in the *Brooklyn Eagle*, circling apartments with a blue pencil. He thought: She's serious, she's giving up, she wants to leave. And how can I blame her? I'm the guy who dreams of white horses racing over the factory roof.

"You're next, young man," said a nurse with frazzled blond hair. "Soon as we do this guy." He heard her bright telephone operator voice. He heard her speak to Kate: "Thanks for your patience, Kate. You know how it goes."

"I certainly do," Kate said.

"Nurse," Michael said. "Did you X-ray a rabbi here yesterday?"

"A rabbi. Yes, I believe we did. He was mugged, poor soul, wasn't he?"

Someone called her and the conversation ended before it had begun. He heard his mother say: "He's in the best hands here." He heard his mother say: "It's not like some city hospital." He heard her say: "They're just butcher shops." Michael wiggled his toes, massaged his skin and muscles, and measured one leg against the other. The damaged right leg was definitely thinner. He wanted to get out into the sunshine, to exercise the leg and let the sun brown his skin. And then take care of one big thing.

"Mom, I want to see Rabbi Hirsch," he said suddenly. "He's here somewhere, and I've got to see him."

She looked at him in an exasperated way, as if considering that the rabbi might be part of their troubles. Michael sensed this.

"It's not *his* fault, what happened," Michael said angrily. "He's a good man and they're not. You know it, Mom."

"All right," she said. "When you're in X Ray, I'll find out where he is."

Then it was his turn. He followed a nurse into the X-ray room, while Kate went out to the corridor. The X ray took a few seconds. He asked the dark-haired nurse operating the machine if she had X-rayed a rabbi the day before. "I was off yesterday," she said. Then called out: "Next." And told Michael to wait outside. With Kate gone, he sat in the back row, behind dozens of women and children and a few men, and felt his anger throbbing like a wound. Goddamned nurse. Maybe she's lying. Maybe she doesn't want to tell me about his broken head. Maybe there's brain damage. He saw the blood seeping from the rabbi's ear. He saw the slick red puddle on the asphalt.

Kate returned, shaking her head.

"He's up on the seventh floor," she said. "In intensive care. No visitors, Michael."

"I've got to see him," Michael said. "I don't want him to be alone, the way I was."

"I know that, son," she said, irritated.

434

"But he's in a coma. Do you understand what that *is?*" He nodded that he understood. "They've got a cop up there, keeping everybody away. We'll come back when he's better. Out of the coma. We'll bring him pound cake and iced tea."

That was that. They walked home together. Michael was still limping, but he kept increasing the weight on the healed leg, hoping that each step would make it stronger. It was almost noon. The sun beat down from a cloudless sky. Flowers wilted on the stands outside the florist's shop. The asphalt was softer. Dogs huddled against walls, their pink tongues hanging. Kids sat in the shade on the side streets, sucking on lemon ices and drinking red sodas. Michael felt sweat seeping down his back under his shirt, as slow and thick as blood. It must be hot in his room at the hospital, Michael thought. He must be sweating under the bandages. But he will not die. I have to believe that. I won't let him die.

"It's a scorcher," he heard Kate say, as if forcing herself back to normal conversation.

He heard his own voice, following her lead. "The radio says it'll be ninety."

"Human beings aren't made for such heat," she said. "When it's sixty in Ireland, we think we're in the tropics."

The hallway was cooler than the street, but as they climbed the stairs, Michael's stomach churned, and the heat grew clammier, as if it were pressing down from the roof. He paused at the first floor landing, touching his mother's forearm.

"Someone's upstairs," he said.

She listened. They could hear the muffled sound of a flushing toilet. In the Caputo flat, pots clanged against a sink. Jo Stafford was singing "I'll Be Seeing You" in Mrs. Griffin's. But there were no baritone whispers above them, no shuffling of feet.

"Come on, son," she said, leading the way.

And stopped as she turned on the second floor landing.

Sonny Montemarano and Jimmy Kabinsky were sitting on the steps.

"Hey, Michael," Sonny said.

"Some friends you've been," Kate Devlin said. "Move over and let us by."

Sonny stood to let her pass, and for a moment Michael was afraid that he'd completely turned against the Devlins and would strike her. He tensed, ready to attack.

"I don't blame you for being mad at us, Mrs. Devlin," Sonny said softly. "But we didn't have no choice."

"Yes, you did," she said, her anger pushing her up the steps. "You could have had guts."

Her keys jangled as she opened the apartment door. Michael started to pass Sonny and Jimmy.

"How you feeling, man?" Jimmy said, looking ashamed.

"Fuck you," Michael whispered.

"We gotta talk to you."

"About what?" Michael said, and kept going.

Sonny grabbed the back of his belt.

"About Frankie McCarthy," Sonny said. "He's got a gun." Michael gripped the banister. His mother appeared at the door above them.

"Are you all right?" she said. "Michael?"

"Yeah, Mom. We're goin' up the roof and talk."

"Don't go near the edge," she said, a look of disdain on her face for Sonny and Jimmy, and went back into the kitchen.

On the roof, they leaned against a brick wall. The air was thick with heat and chimney smoke. Ridges of shiny black tar pushed through the joined seams of tarpaper. A yellowish haze shimmered over the rooftops of Brooklyn. While he talked, Sonny wouldn't look at Michael, but his words came in an anxious rush.

"So you know Frankie got out, right? The lawyer talked some fucking judge into it, saying Frankie was too young to do time with all these bad guys in Raymond Street, being seventeen and all, and too old to go to Warwick or Youth House with the bad kids. So they give him credit for good behavior, and yesterday they tell him get the fuck out. First thing he does, he gets himself a piece. From the racket guys down President Street. I hear this from one of my cousins lives down there. Then last night, they all meet in the poolroom. Jimmy and me are hangin' out on the fire escape in my aunt's house, you know, by the Venus? It's so fucking hot we can't do nothin' but hang there. And here comes Frankie McCarthy and the rest of them, drinking beer from containers. They sit on the steps beside the Venus. It's closed now, you know? They always hang there. Right beneath us. And we see Frankie show them the piece."

"Looked like a .38," Jimmy said.

"Then they talk about having a big party," Sonny said.

"A welcome home party," Jimmy said.

"And Frankie says, 'Yeah, we'll get these fucking people out of our hair, once and for all.' "

"They mention you," Jimmy said. "They

mention your mother."

"The Russian says they gotta let everybody know what they can do or the cops will nail them all."

"And that Skids, you know, little guy with the muscles? He says they gotta do to you and your mother what they did to the rabbi. To set a fucking example. And Tippy Hudnut says they didn't go far enough, they shoulda killed the Jew bastid and burned down the synagogue with him in it."

"Then Frankie shows them the piece again," Sonny said. "He says they can grab who they want, take them out to Gerritsen Beach or someplace and blow their heads off. He says, 'These fuckin' people around here, they gotta know we mean what we say.' He says, 'I met some Mafia guy in the can, he told me how to do it.' "

"They're laughing all through this," Jimmy Kabinsky said.

"Frankie says the mafioso told him he could get them plenty of work, big money," Sonny said. "Robbing cars, muscling guys for the loan sharks, and getting people to pay protection. You know, the bars, the stores, they don't pay, you break their fucking windows. You burn the store out. You rob everything or kick over the stands or whatever. They could make a mint of money, Frankie says. But then he says, 'You gotta put fear in them to make it work.' "

"So he says he wants to have his welcome home party Friday night," Jimmy said. "At the poolroom. To make sure everybody knows he's back. To show the cops can't do nothing about nothing. A big party, with a sign and all, a fuck you to the parish. Let everybody know. Get drunk, get laid."

"Then get you. Get your mother."

"Burn the synagogue."

"Get the guys that cleaned the synagogue that time."

"Burn down the fucking hardware store," Jimmy said.

"All in one night," Sonny said.

"Jesus Christ," Michael said.

He turned away from them, looking toward the factory roof. The hard edges of the dark brick building were dissolving in the heat. He couldn't see the white horse. He took a deep breath, exhaled slowly, then faced them.

"How come you came to tell me?" he said.

Sonny's face was loose with emotion. His eyes welled.

"We don't want nothin' more bad to happen to you, Michael."

"You're still our friend," Jimmy said.

"Even though you joined up with the rabbi when you was supposed to find the treasure."

"I found the treasure, Jimmy."

"You did?"

Michael tapped the side of his head. "It's up here."

He started to leave, and Sonny grabbed him, heaving with emotion.

"I'm sorry, man," he said, and hugged Michael.

"So am I," Michael said, and pulled away.

# 33

After an early dinner, Michael went to his room, the window open to the humid August evening. He could wait no longer. Now he must do something. To save the life of Rabbi Hirsch. To make somebody pay for all the blood. He watched from the fire escape as his mother moved quickly along Ellison Avenue to the Grandview; from that height, she looked small and vulnerable. Before she left, he had heard her voice, bright and charged with hope, as she described the apartment she'd found in Sunset Park, a place with a garden, where she could grow geraniums and roses. He had heard her say that she'd already talked to the manager at the Grandview, explaining some of what had happened, and he understood why she wanted to move and would try to help her transfer to an RKO theater in Bay Ridge. He'd heard all that; heard her say she was sure she could borrow the money from the Dime Savings

Bank to pay for the moving expenses.

"We've got to get out of here," she had said. "There's a sickness here and we have to escape it."

But he kept thinking of Rabbi Hirsch in the gutter, and the Falcons grabbing them in the street that night, and his crutches being smashed and Skids tearing her blouse and Tippy reaching under her skirt. She spoke of packing dishes and hiring movers, and Michael saw Frankie McCarthy raising the cash register in the air over the fallen Mister G. She talked about leaving in ten days, so he'd be eligible for the Catholic school in Bay Ridge; he flashed on Frankie McCarthy's knife in the chilly darkness of the alley behind the Venus. He thought about the lost summer too, and his lost friends, while Kate tried to put the best face on moving.

"You've never lived anywhere else," she said, "and maybe that's not such a good thing."

Not true, he thought. I've lived in Prague. I've moved through fog-bound streets and secret tunnels, seen two-headed alligators and unicorns, watched angels carry palaces from distant cities. I've seen cathedral spires rise in the air like rockets. I've seen rocks turn into roses.

Then she asked him who, after all, he would really miss in the parish, and he said: "Rabbi Hirsch. He's my only friend."

"Well, we're not going to California," she said. "You can visit him. He can visit us."

And he thought: Not if Frankie McCarthy takes over the parish. Not if Rabbi Hirsch dies.

He waited until it was dark and then locked the door behind him. He went up to the roof and crossed the length of the block on the rooftops to the open door of 290 Pearse Street. Then, silent in his sneakers, he tiptoed down the stairs of that building to the vestibule. When he was sure nobody was watching, he darted into the street. His leg felt stronger now. Hugging the walls, ducking into doorways, trying to remember *13 Rue Madeleine*, he moved along Ellison Avenue to the hospital. When he passed bars, he turned his head away, afraid of being spotted by friends of the Falcons. His body felt as clenched as a fist. I'm a spy, he thought. A spy in my own country.

The bright, clean lobby of Brooklyn Wesleyan was crowded with visitors. About a dozen waited on line at a desk for passes, but he didn't bother trying to get one; they'd just say no. Then he saw the janitor from the parkside. His black face was shiny with sweat or fever, and he was standing in his striped overalls at the door marked Admissions. Nobody bothered talking to him. One nurse came out and beckoned a woman who was standing behind the janitor. It was as if he were invisible, and Michael remembered the way Jackie Robinson stood by himself on the dugout steps on that glorious day at Ebbets Field.

When a crowd of visitors started into an elevator, he joined them. They were carrying flowers or ice cream or books. Most looked concerned, but one beefy man acted like a department store elevator operator: "Fifth floor, ladies lingerie, household goods, rubber ducks . . ." He broke the tension. Three older women laughed. Michael wished he could laugh too, as he got off with a few others on the seventh floor.

He found Rabbi Hirsch in room 709.

He was lying in a murky darkness, and Michael could barely recognize him. There were heavy bandages around his skull. His face was swollen and distorted. His lower lip was split, and there was a blackness where his teeth used to be. One of his arms was encased in plaster from fingers to shoulder. There were tubes dripping fluid into his other arm. His eyes were swollen and shut. He had taken a terrible beating.

Michael thought: Never again.

He leaned close to the man's right ear.

"Rabbi Hirsch," he whispered, "it's me. Michael Devlin."

The rabbi's eyes fluttered and then opened slightly.

"Michael," he said. He breathed heavily and tried to smile. "Boychik."

The eyelids closed, as if exhausted by the effort. Michael held the rabbi's cold hand.

"Go away," the rabbi croaked. "It's not safe."

"I know," Michael said. "But we have to do something. We can't let them win."

He told the rabbi what he knew and what had happened to him and his mother and what was coming. He told him about the gun. He told him what Frankie McCarthy was planning for the synagogue. He told him that Father Heaney was gone to South America and Charlie Senator had moved away. He told the rabbi all this without knowing if the rabbi heard him. The man's eyes remained closed, his battered face unmoving. His breathing was pained and shallow. For a moment, Michael considered calling a nurse, even if she made him leave. Then the rabbi's eyes opened and he looked directly at Michael.

"We have to do something," Michael said.

The rabbi's expression said: *Such as what?*

Michael leaned even closer to the rabbi's ear.

"Tell me the secret name of God," Michael whispered.

The rabbi's eyes widened.

# 34

Early Thursday morning, Michael went to the park carrying a small, rusting spade in an old canvas *Brooklyn Eagle* bag. He'd found both in the cellar, beside the hot-water furnace. His mother was still asleep in the smothering August heat, and he left her a note saying that he was going to church. A small lie, he thought, but the less she knew, the better.

It was almost eight o'clock and already the heat was clamped upon the city. On Pearse Street, a water wagon from the Sanitation Department lumbered uphill, and as the water sprayed the soft asphalt, steam rose into the sullen air. At the entrance to the park, a gray-haired man in khaki shorts sat on a park bench, listening to a portable radio and drinking beer from a quart bottle. His eyes were glassy. His skin was blistered with sweat. He didn't seem to hear the news announcer say that the day's temperatures were expected in the high 90s and there was no end in sight. The man was very still, as if comforted by the rich dirt smell drifting from the dozing park.

Michael moved quickly across the moist meadows toward the dark smudge of the hill that was crowned by the Quaker cemetery. A few lone men slept on the meadow grass in a litter of beer containers. A woman walked a small dog. The ball fields were empty. Above them, clouds moved slowly but took no shape.

Michael hurried along, the canvas bag hanging from its shoulder strap. He crossed the deserted bridle path where men and women galloped on rented horses across summer afternoons. He saw two boys walking to the Big Lake with fishing poles. He paused to drink from a stone water fountain until the boys vanished past a shoulder of the hill.

Then he plunged into the woods. It was cooler here and the trees were taller, their dense foliage blocking the sun. He climbed and climbed, inhaling the deep odors of earth and rotting leaves, and then looked back. Nobody could see him here. No cops. No Falcons. Nobody. Few kids came this way either, afraid of the old graves and silent tombstones beyond the high iron fence. His mother had explained once that the cemetery had been there since before the Revolution, and when the land was laid out for the park the Quakers were allowed to keep their cemetery forever. Sometimes on foggy nights, boys traveled here and dared each other to climb the fence and walk among the dead. Michael had never joined them.

Now he turned his back on the graves and found an open spot beneath a giant elm. He cleared away a thin carpet of dead leaves. Then he began to dig. The dirt was heavy and black. As he shoveled it into the canvas bag he followed Rabbi Hirsch's instructions and cleaned out the twigs and stones and leaves. The dirt must be pure. When the bag was full, he stopped to gasp for breath in the sticky air. Then he placed the spade on top of the dirt and swung the bag onto his shoulder. His bad leg buckled under the weight, but he felt no pain. He adjusted the bag and bent forward, and he knew he could carry it. He started back down the hill.

He took a different route across the meadow, stopping every fifty yards to shift the bag from one shoulder to the other, and went out through the Pritchard Street entrance. There were more people on the street now. A man with a squeegee and bucket cleaned the show windows of the

Sanders theater. More kids entered the park with fishing poles. Nobody looked at him.

Michael walked down Kelly Street. His shoulders were sore now from the weight of the dirt. At the armory, he waited until he was certain nobody was watching. From his pocket he removed a key, taken from the rabbi's clothes at the hospital, and hurried to the side door of the synagogue. He quickly opened the door, entered, and closed it behind him.

He waited in the dark vestibule for a long moment and decided not to switch on the lights. The police knew that Rabbi Hirsch was in the hospital; if they saw lights burning, they might come in and find him. I don't want to see the cops, he thought. It's too late for them. It's too late for all of them.

He went up the three vestibule steps and unlocked the second door and entered Rabbi Hirsch's small apartment. He set the bag down and in the dim light moved books on the top shelf of the bookcase, behind the radio and the photograph of Leah. There he found the second key. It was about four inches long, made of iron, and heavy. It was attached to a painted wooden stick.

Michael used the key to open the tall oak door in the corner. The door that had never once been opened by Rabbi Hirsch in Michael's presence. At first the unlocked door would not open. He had to pull it hard, using all of his weight, until it squeaked on rusted hinges. Before him, a dusty stairway rose into darkness. His heart beating quickly, Michael went up the stairs, feeling his way near the top, thinking for just a moment that he should turn back, until he grasped the handle of another door. He turned it and shoved hard. The door made a scraping sound on the stone floor.

There before him was a great, vast, high-ceilinged room, illuminated by colored shafts of light from stained-glass windows and slashing bright beams where sections of glass had been punched out. He was in the abandoned main sanctuary at last, and the sight filled him with awe. The downstairs prayer room was like the downstairs church at Sacred Heart: low-ceilinged, plain, dusty, the pews full of prayer books. But this was like entering a secret room in a lost city.

He walked carefully along the wall, stepping over broken plaster and shards of smashed stained glass and stones that must have been hurled at the windows. He counted twenty-one rows of benches. There were prayer books at odd angles on every bench, some of them gnawed by rats. Thick cobwebs draped from the benches to the floor. The words KHAL ADAS JESHURUN were carved into the marble above the shuttered double doors that had once been the main entrance. Above the entrance was a balcony, like a small version of the choir loft at Sacred Heart.

Michael stood there, facing the sanctuary, trying to imagine what it had been like during the Holy Days when every seat was filled and there was a rustle of anticipation and wonder. He could see faces. He could see clothes. They had come here, assembled, embraced, and then left, some of them never to return. There must be places like this, he thought, all over Europe. In the feeble light, he could see on the far wall the carved wooden Ark where the Torah once was stored. It was huge, four or five times larger than the Ark in the basement sanctuary. Past the glass chandeliers, he could pick out the *ner tamid,* the eternal light, hanging from the ceiling, its candle no longer lit. And in the center, just as Rabbi Hirsch had told him, was the *bimah,* the speaker's platform.

Standing there in this desolate emptiness, from which even God seemed to have fled, Michael began to weep without control.

He wept for Rabbi Hirsch with his broken face and his losses and journeys and endless grief. He wept for Leah Yaretzky. He wept for Sonny and Jimmy. He wept for Mister G. He wept for all those bony people he'd seen in the newsreels, staring with dead eyes past the barbed wire. He wept for his mother, who had crossed an ocean to escape hatred and found that it followed her like a wolf. He wept for Father Heaney and Charlie Senator, who had gone to their own diasporas. He wept for those people who long ago had come here to this holy place to celebrate their survival and good fortune and then had moved on once again. And then he wept for his father. Who was taken from the balcony of a movie house to the snows of Belgium, carrying with him the memory of a waltz on the polished floors of the Webster Hall. Carrying a picture of his wife. Maybe even carrying a picture of me. Oh, Daddy. Oh, Dad. Please help me now.

He lost all power in his legs and slid down the side of one of the benches and sat weeping on the dirty floor.

He wept until he had no more tears to weep.

And then he stood up and gathered himself. After all, he had work to do. Work that he now believed only he could do. And Shabbos began the next day at sundown. So did Frankie McCarthy's party.

He went to the *bimah*. The raised platform was covered by a dark purple cloth that was speckled with plaster and water stains. He pulled the cloth aside and saw the wooden platform that Rabbi Hirsch had described to him from his hospital bed. Sunk into the wood was an iron handle. He pried it up with his fingers and then lifted. A door opened in the top of the platform. Below him in the darkness was a long, deep, tiled structure that resembled a sink, complete with a water tap and drain. On the floor of the sink was a gleaming wooden box, shaped like a coffin. About two feet long. Tied with rough twine. Michael felt his skin pebbling in awe and fear. "It's true," he said out loud. "True." The box once handled by Rabbi Loew had survived the centuries and then had been taken by runners and couriers from Prague to Palestine and finally to this building in this parish in Brooklyn. And here it was before him. He held the railing of the *bimah* to steady himself and then he reached down for the box. For such a small object, it was heavy, as if many things had been compacted inside its burnished wood. He placed it on the edge of the *bimah*.

Then he realized that the cords that tied it shut were almost new. The box had lain in its dusty attic for centuries, but someone had opened it in recent years. There were holes spaced three inches apart around the lid, and indentations in the wood, as if a claw hammer had been used to remove nails. Below the lid, the smooth sides of the box were rough in five or six places, perhaps from prying by a screwdriver or flat chisel. And in his mind, Michael saw him: saw Rabbi Hirsch, while the Nazis were marching through Prague, watched him opening it, and, yes, witnessed him falling to his knees in despair as he failed to do what he wanted to do. He thought: I must pray, so I don't fail. He untied the knots. He slipped the cord off the box and then gazed at it for a long moment. He lifted the lid. He was certain then that he could smell the mists of Prague.

Lying on top of a piece of crumbling purple brocade was the silver spoon. It was dull and tarnished in places, but Michael could see the Hebrew lettering on the handle, and felt the same eerie chill that Rabbi Loew must have felt when it was handed to him by Emperor Rudolf. Beside the spoon, in a small ceramic box, was the curled parchment. The *shem*. They're here, Michael thought, just as Rabbi Hirsch whispered they would be. After their long journey, they came to rest here. In this abandoned room.

Waiting until they were needed. Waiting for me.

Michael picked up the long-handled spoon, feeling weightless and formless, as if the bones had vanished from his body. The thick silver spoon must have weighed three pounds. His hand trembled in wonder. He rubbed his thumb over the Hebrew letters, and he felt suddenly connected to the distant past. I am as old as the world, he thought. I have seen many things. He wanted to pray, to speak in a thousand languages at once, to express some nameless feeling of connection to the nameless man who had cut those letters in some nameless place across the seas. He tried to conjure a face. He tried to invent a name. Neither would come to him, as the silver spoon shook in his hand. And he thought: No man carved these letters. These letters were carved by God.

He gripped the spoon in both hands to stop the trembling and then held it up, like an offering, to the empty Ark and its unlit eternal light.

# 35

Across the long, broiling day, Michael made nine more trips to the hill beside the Quaker cemetery. Around two o'clock, he went home to assure his mother that he was all right. He had a grilled cheese sandwich for lunch and washed it down with iced tea. After she left to look once more at the garden apartment in Sunset Park before going on to work, Michael rushed to the park. It was after dark when he carried his last load of dirt into the synagogue on Kelly Street.

He poured each load of dirt into the long, flat sink, packing it loosely with his hands. After the last bagful was transferred into the sink, he sat down hard on a dusty pew. He was so drowsy that he felt as if he were underwater. I need a nap, he thought. Just an hour, stretched out on this empty bench. Just to rest. Just ten minutes. Five. But then he imagined waking in the gray dawn, and his mother panicking and the police searching the parish for him. He couldn't let that happen. No. He stood up straight and slapped his cheeks to come fully alert, and thought of the great, ballooning shape of Rabbi Hirsch's battered face. No: I have to sleep at home tonight. In my own bed. I need to be strong.

The upstairs sanctuary was now very dark, its spaces illuminated only by light from the moon. He looked at the *shem,* waiting in its ceramic box. The spoon lay hidden under a pew. Everything is ready, he thought, even me. But it was time to go home. After all, this was still only Thursday. He had one more day to do what must be done. One more day until the party for Frankie McCarthy. On Shabbos.

At home, he soaked in the bathtub and scrubbed away the traces of dirt under his fingernails. He went to bed before his mother came home, and in spite of the relentless, clammy heat, he fell swiftly into a dreamless sleep.

When he woke on Friday morning, the bed was marshy with sweat. He could hear the radio from the kitchen and his mother's voice, singing happily along with the Ink Spots on a song called "The Gypsy." He pulled on his white baseball pants, as instructed by Rabbi Hirsch, and his white socks and sneakers and a white T-shirt. But he felt strange and dreamy. His mother's familiar voice made him think that maybe none of this had ever happened. She sounded as she always did in the mornings before Frankie McCarthy walked out of the snowstorm into Mister G's. Everything else was the same: his chair, his bureau, the cabinet full of comics, the window that opened to the fire escape. Was he really dressing in white, for purity, to spend a day summoning a living creature from dirt? Was he to be like Dr. Frankenstein? He lived in the real world, not in a movie. Then he saw the piece of his plaster cast adorned with Rabbi Hirsch's precise Hebrew letters. He picked it up and kissed it reverently. Everything had happened, all right; all of it.

"Good morning, young man," Kate Devlin said cheerfully, poking a spatula into a frying pan on the stove. He mumbled a good morning and stepped into the bathroom to throw cold water on his face and comb his hair. He left the door open while he washed. Everything was familiar.

"You had yourself a sleep, didn't you?" she said. "It's almost ten o'clock."

"Yeah," he said. "Slept like a rock."

He closed the door and urinated and washed his hands, examining the bathtub for signs of dirt from the park. There were none. When he came out, Kate had laid three slices of French toast on a plate on the table. He sat down, slapped butter on the fried bread, and sprinkled sugar over the top. He ate greedily.

"Well, it's done," she said, explaining her cheerfulness. "I rented us a place. The one with the garden."

"You're kidding!"

"No, we'll be in by the middle of August, so we'll have to start packing tomorrow."

"But you're still working at the Grandview?"

"For now," she said. "Tonight for sure. But there's an opening out at the RKO in Bay Ridge. Just great luck." She gazed out the window at the summer haze. "We'll be out of here soon. It won't be soon enough."

Her voice mixed with the radio, a tune called "The Anniversary Song." Al Jolson. He heard a phrase about how the night was in bloom though a word wasn't said. Kate was talking about getting boxes from Roulston's grocery, and how he could begin packing his own things on Saturday. But he didn't even try to imagine the move, the new apartment, a garden. He was thinking only about the night ahead.

"Sometimes bad times are really for the better," she said. "We can throw out a lot of junk, and —" She noticed his clothes and smiled. "You're dressed to play ball!"

"Yeah."

"Where?"

"Up the park."

His plate was already clear, and he got up to wash it in the sink and place it in the drainer.

"You've made it up with those two so-called friends?"

"Well . . . I don't know. I'll just try to find a game."

"Be careful with that leg, now," she said.

Off he went, wearing his I'M FOR JACKIE button as a badge of defiance. He took the long way to the synagogue. Walking fast on what felt like a brand-new leg. Off to Kelly Street. Through the door. Into the upstairs sanctuary.

Then he started to work at the long, deep sink, murmuring the instructions from Rabbi Hirsch as if they were part of the mass. He ran some water and stirred the dirt and water with the long silver spoon to make mud. He stripped off his shirt and trousers to keep them clean, because later he had to be dressed in pure white. Then he started shaping the mud. A torso. Arms. Legs and feet. A head. Stepping back to be sure the proportions were right. Shaping the details of the face with the handle of the heavy spoon. Making an opening for the mouth. Dividing fingers and toes.

He was on the banks of the Vltava. He was waiting for fog. He imagined a red moon. His sweat splashed into the mud. Hours passed as he refined and refined his work. The light in the sanctuary shifted with the sun.

When he was finished, he walked as instructed to the four corners of the sanctuary and gathered dust and dirt in his hands and sprinkled it over the mud. As the mud dried, he smoothed the rough spots on hands and face until he could refine them no more. Then he went to the loft above the front door and found a worn, paint-spattered wooden stepladder. Right where Rabbi Hirsch said it would be. He carried it down to the sanctuary floor, bumping into walls in the tight stairway, knocking a wooden collection box to the floor. He carried the ladder to the front of the sanctuary, opened it, and adjusted the brace. He climbed up the rungs, as the ladder swayed and creaked, and lit the fat, squat candle of the eternal light with a wooden match. A soft, golden light immediately suffused the room.

Now he was very hungry. He went downstairs to Rabbi Hirsch's room and washed his hands in the sink and took apple juice from the small refrigerator and drank straight from the bottle. The juice was cold and sweet, but the bottle shook in his hand and the perspiration would not stop dripping from his body. He dried himself again with a towel, but the sweat returned. He sat down at Rabbi Hirsch's table, trying to be very still, struggling to control his fear. He was afraid of what he was about to do. Afraid he would succeed. Afraid he would fail. No: he would not fail. He believed. He would make it all come true. God would recognize him, his belief, his need. It would happen. Yes. It would happen, it would happen.

"Believe," he whispered to the silence. "I believe."

His gaze drifted to Leah's photograph and he wished he could talk to her. He wished he could talk to Rabbi Hirsch too. But he was alone here in this place, and there was nobody to talk to except God.

Whispering an Our Father, he climbed the dark stairs to the sanctuary. There could be no more delay. Shabbos was almost here. He pulled on his clean white baseball pants and his white T-shirt. He stared down at the shaped mud. He opened the ceramic box and saw the *shem:* a rolled yellow parchment an inch wide, so old that the paper was leathery to the touch. He walked to the edge of the *bimah* and eased the *shem* into the hole he'd made for the mouth. Then he took the spoon in hand again and used the point of the handle to letter a single word on the brow of the head.

**'Emet.**

It meant Truth.

Then, standing behind the head, he took a deep breath, raised the spoon over the shaped head, and began to chant. The prescribed sounds were all letters. *A,* and *B,* and *C,* and *D,* right through the alphabet. First in English; then, to be sure, in Yiddish. The *aleph-bayz.* Seven times for each letter, followed by the letters that Rabbi Hirsch had told him stood for the secret name of God.

**YHVH.**
**YHVH.**
**YHVH.**
**YHVH.**
**YHVH.**
**YHVH.**
**YHVH.**

The secret name echoing mightily through the empty sanctuary.

Then he added vowels, *A-E-I-O-U*, seven times, again followed by the name of God. All the time moving, forming a wheel, doing a kind of dance around the sunken *bimah*, making a circle that traveled from right to left. Following the commands of Rabbi Hirsch. Feeling his own body charged with power and mystery. Believe, he thought. Believe. Here is the Kabbalah. Believe.

For the mystery was all about letters, Rabbi Hirsch had told him. Numbers too, in Kabbalah, but above all, letters; for from letters we make words, and words are the names of life. They name arms and legs and faces. They name men and women, insects and animals, and the creatures of the sea. They name oceans and rivers and cities. They name the grass. They name the trees. God gave letters to man and man made words from the letters and used them to name God's nameless world. And Michael remembered from catechism class, *In the beginning was the word, and the word was with God. . . .*

So Michael danced and chanted, repeating the letters in pairs and in triplets, then singing them as if they were sacred music, the room growing darker now as the sun faded, while Michael tried to will himself into the inert mud. He rose into a frenzy of words and letters, hearing sounds from his mouth that he did not think, moving to music that nobody played, rising into clouds, moving palaces across distant skies, speaking to birds, joining hands in a dance with Mary Cunningham and the Count of Monte Cristo, soaring and swooping and breaking for third, up, rising up, full of rain and fire and salt and oceans, all the way up, chanting the letters that named galleons and cowboys, pirates and Indians, borne by the letters, swept through golden skies, above the crazy world, above Brooklyn, above Ireland, above Prague, above the fields of Belgium.

And then fell to his knees in utter emptiness. He had no more words in him. He had no more letters. He had no more music. He wanted to vanish into a dreamless sleep. Here in the sweet dusty darkness. He could hear the cry of a bird like a sound of morning. And then the barking of a dog. But he did not rise. He stretched out on the floor, facing the Ark.

And then the mud began to glow.

A deep red.

Then a brighter red. Like something in

an oven. Michael rose to his feet, his heart beating in fear.

He stepped back, afraid to look into the sink, retreating into the shadows, but the glow grew more intense. Two minutes. Five minutes. Ten. Like something deep in the coals of a sacred furnace.

And then a chilly breeze blew through the sanctuary. The burning wick flickered in the eternal light. Dust lifted from benches, and cobwebs bent and snapped. Something clattered to the floor in the darkness. The windows rattled. Michael felt the floor tremble and heard a wild sound of birds rising from the roof and then a high-pitched sound like a dog whistle, hurting his ears, piercing his brain.

And then a sudden silence.

He could only hear the pounding of his heart.

The breeze abruptly died.

And then two dark hands gripped the sides of the tub and the Golem pulled himself up.

It was him.

The Golem.

Everything was true.

Sitting there, the Golem was as dark as Jackie Robinson, his hazel eyes full of sorrow. He looked from left to right, the sorrowful eyes taking in the desolation of the sanctuary. He seemed to have expected this sight. He leaned forward and looked at the palms of his immense black hands before turning them over to gaze at their blackness. Then he stared at Michael for a long moment. Michael did not move. The Golem bent a knee, shifted his weight, and stood up.

Michael backed up as the Golem stood naked in the tub, his muscles rippling like bags of stones. He must be eight feet tall, Michael thought; bigger than any man I've ever seen. Without a sound, the Golem stepped over the wooden framework of the *bimah* to the floor.

Michael needed words. The words did not come. He fought the impulse to run. Talk to him, he thought. Speak to him.

The Golem stared at Michael and then reached forward, touching his face. His hand felt like the sole of a shoe.

"I'm Michael Devlin," the boy said. "Can you understand me?"

The Golem nodded yes.

"Can you speak?"

He shook his head sadly. No.

Michael tried to control his trembling. When he first had heard the stories of the Golem from Rabbi Hirsch, he imagined a figure from comic books. Made of pen lines and brush marks. Simple, sometimes even humorous, sent on missions of justice by a good rabbi. He did not expect this naked creature, as large as a tree, as dark as night. Standing before him, waiting for instructions. For a moment, he wanted to reverse the process, to send the creature back to where he came from. But then he remembered his mother's humiliation and the battered face of Rabbi Hirsch and his own lost summer. No: he could not turn back. He had invoked the name of God. He must go on.

"We . . . we have to find you some clothes," Michael said, pulling on his T-shirt. "You understand? Clothes. Because we have some things to do out there tonight." He pointed at a broken stained-glass window and the visible fragment of the August evening. "Out there in the street."

The Golem understood. He gazed around the dusty sanctuary, as if looking for clothing.

"Come on," Michael said. "Let's see what we can find."

They opened closets and pantries, the Golem defeating locks and layers of cement-like paint as he effortlessly jerked them open. They found banners, books, old Ark curtains; but no clothes. Until the Golem suddenly emerged from a tight, small sub-basement with what seemed to be a cape. There were golden cords or tassels on the ends, and he tied them at his neck to make the cape. In Rabbi Hirsch's kitchen, he bent his knees to fit under the ceiling, and whirled the cape. The frayed tassels crumbled and the cape fell. He grunted sadly.

"Wait," Michael said.

He removed the I'M FOR JACKIE button from his T-shirt and jumped up on a chair in front of the Golem. He held the two ends of the cape together and fastened them with the button.

"Great!" he shouted. "It works." The Golem laughed without sound. Michael said: "You look like you could fly."

Michael went to the small bureau where Rabbi Hirsch kept his shirts and underwear and in the bottom drawer he found a sheet. Perfect. The creature could tie it around his middle like a giant diaper. Or, what did they call it in those stories about India by Rudyard Kipling? A breechclout. When he turned with the sheet in his hand, the Golem was holding the photograph of Leah in his leathery hands, staring at her face.

"She's part of the reason you're here," Michael said, as the Golem replaced the photograph on the shelf. "That's the rabbi's wife. Killed by the Nazis."

He showed the creature what to do with the sheet, and the Golem tried clumsily to wrap it between his legs and around his massive hips, the sheet slipping until Michael tied the ends as tightly as he could. Michael stepped back, smiled, and said, "You look like Gunga Din." The Golem did not smile. He moved a huge hand toward the framed photograph, and then Michael told him some of the story. About Rabbi Hirsch and Leah and Hitler and the millions of deaths. About Frankie McCarthy and the Falcons, Mister G on the day of the snowstorm, and what was done to Michael and to Rabbi Hirsch and to Michael's mother. The Golem listened in a fierce way, his brow furrowing, a gash deepening through the word for Truth, which was lighter against the black skin. His head moved slowly from side to side. As his anger built, his eyes receded under his slablike brow. He did not smile. He did not laugh. His immense hands kneaded each other. When Michael told him about Frankie McCarthy's plans, a bright sheen appeared on his black skin.

"That's about it," Michael said. "That's why we brought you here. We have to stop them. We have to make sure they don't do stuff like this ever again. We have to make sure they are punished."

The Golem sat there for a long moment. Then he gazed again at the photograph of Leah, and Michael was reminded of the story about the Golem in Prague and how he fell in love with the girl named Dvorele. That was a heartbreaking story, but it also showed that the Golem didn't simply follow orders. He had his own feelings, his own ideas. Michael began to worry that he would not be able to completely control the creature. Then he saw that the Golem's eyes had fallen on the shofar, which lay on a lower shelf. The creature rose and gently picked up the shofar in his giant thumb and forefinger.

"Rabbi Hirsch tried to play tunes on it," Michael said, and smiled. "But he couldn't do it. Maybe you could. . . . Maybe you could send them a message down at the poolroom. Let them know we're coming."

Exhaling softly, the Golem took Michael by the hand and led him upstairs to the sanctuary. Pausing, the Golem stood with the shofar in both hands and bowed his head to the Ark. Then, with Michael behind him, he moved to the rear of the sanctuary and up the stairs to the loft. He seemed to know the way. He found another door and jerked it open. They stepped out to a small flat roof. For a dazzled moment, the Golem gazed at the million lights that were scattered across the blackness all the way to distant Manhattan. This was not Prague. He grew very still. Michael said nothing. The August heat was deadening, and there was no breeze. From this height, Michael could pick out the glow of the Grandview's neon sign, the tower of the Williamsburg Bank Building, the arc of the Brooklyn Bridge, and off to the left in the black harbor, pale green and small, the Statue of Liberty. There were still some people waiting out the hot night on blankets on rooftops and fire escapes.

The Golem brought the shofar to his mouth.

He blew one long, terrifying note. It seemed to rip a hole in the heat-stricken night.

He blew another.

And then a third.

Michael backed away, frightened by the power and savagery of the three notes blown on the ram's horn. Notes as old as the world.

But the Golem placed a hand on his shoulder. Reassuring him. Cautioning him.

Telling him to wait. Telling him, without words, that something was coming.

Something was.

It began to snow.

Millions of flakes, radiant and beautiful, drifting down through the August night. Black when Michael looked up, brilliantly white as they passed the level of his eyes, melting as they touched the hot rooftops and the sweating foliage of trees and the soft asphalt and the torrid steel of parked cars.

Snow.

Driven now by a sudden wind off the harbor. Coming now at a harder angle. As birds rose in great flocks to tell the news and dogs barked and windows opened.

Snow in August.

The Golem smiled. He handed Michael the shofar and then the boy led the way back through the synagogue. Now we will do it, he thought. Ready or not, Frankie, here we come. He left the shofar on the kitchen table and went out into Kelly Street with the Golem behind him, bending his head and shoulders under the lintel. The August snow was falling hard. Kids ran through it, shouting and yelping. An old woman came out on a stoop, looked up at the dense snow, made a steeple of her hands and mumbled prayers. Michael heard the wolf wind, and wished for Arctic fury, and the storm grew more violent. In the churning, gyrating, eddying frenzy of the sudden storm, nobody saw the white boy and his giant black companion.

Michael prayed. In English and Latin and Yiddish. Prayed to God, to Deus, to Yahveh. Prayed in thanks, prayed in awe. But he did not turn back. He moved steadily onward, leading a procession of two, the Golem's bare feet crunching a soup can, his face grim, his cape unfurling in the wind. The snow was so thick now that nobody could possibly see them, and yet Michael wasn't cold. Screened by the blinding snow, they reached the alley behind the abandoned hulk of the Venus, where Frankie McCarthy once had threatened Michael with a knife. Then they came to Ellison Avenue. Across the street was the Star Pool Room, with a six-foot-long WELCOME HOME FRANKIE BOY banner draped above the front door. A stray dog came out of the snow and huddled in the doorway beside the poolroom.

"They're in there," Michael said, standing beside the abandoned box office under the marquee of the Venus. "We'll have to go and get them."

The Golem placed his hands on Michael's

head. His brow furrowed. The driving snow halted, then skirled and danced, before resuming with even greater fury. Michael glanced at the dirty glass of the shuttered box office, where he had once admired the look of his suit on an Easter morning. He could not see himself. He could not see the Golem.

Jesus Christ, he thought. We're *invisible!*

He stepped out into the street, the Golem behind him, and marched through the storm, directly to the front door of the poolroom. The stray dog came over, big, black, muscled, sniffing around them but not seeing them, growling in a baritone voice. "Sticky?" Michael whispered, and the dog barked an answer. Oh, Dad. Oh, Daddy: Thank you.

Michael gently opened the poolroom door, and he and the Golem stepped inside. The dog waited in the snow, as if for a command. About fifteen of the Falcons were bunched together in front of the six pool tables with green baize tops. All turned to the door. The wind howled. Snow scattered across the floor. But they could not see Michael and the Golem.

"Hey," a familiar voice said. "Close that fucking door!"

Michael saw Frankie McCarthy coming

from a room at the rear of the pool hall, buttoning his fly. He was dressed like a movie gangster, in pinstriped dark suit, thick-soled shoes, a white tie on a white shirt. Tippy Hudnut slammed the door shut, and turned to Frankie.

"You find out anything yet?" he asked.

"I'm on the phone ten minutes, calling up newspapers, radio stations, everything," Frankie said. "Nothing. Nobody ever heard of it, snowing in fucking August. They treat me like I'm a fucking nut."

The Golem opened the door again, and he and Michael stood to the side. The dog continued to wait.

"Hey, what the fuck *is* it with that door?" Frankie said.

"You seen me close it, Frankie," Tippy said, closing it again. "Maybe it's that dog out there."

"Then give the mutt a swift kick and *lock* the motherfucker."

"We lock it, how will the broads get in?" the Russian said, as Tippy shooed the dog and closed the door.

"They knock," Frankie said, glancing at his watch. "Where *are* the broads, anyway?"

Michael saw that they were all there. Not only Tippy, but the Russian and Skids and Ferret. Along with the other idiots who followed them around and laughed at their jokes. And Frankie McCarthy. Playing boss. Acting like a big shot. Snarling, giving orders. To the right, a table was laid out with cold cuts and cheese, baskets of rolls and bowls of potato salad, quarts of whiskey and gin, and a tub full of beer bottles. On a table in the rear, a phonograph was playing "Sleepy Lagoon." Frankie went to the windows, his eyes glittery, his lips curled, and stared at the driving snow.

"What the fuck *is* this?" he hissed. "I gotta fuckin' party to throw."

He slammed a fist against the doorframe. The door swung open.

"All right, which one of you fucking jokers is doing this?" He laughed in a weird way. "You got some kind of a fucking button or something?"

Michael thought: Now. We're going to do it now. No more waiting. We're going to wipe that smile off his face.

The Golem seemed to understand. Skids came over to close the door, taking a key from his pocket to lock it. The Golem placed his hands on Michael's head. The lights above the pool tables dimmed, then came back to full strength. Michael and the Golem stood there, visible to all.

"What the fuck?" Frankie McCarthy said,

backing up, his face twitching. The others inched to the side, looking at the huge black man and the kid they had tried to terrify out of the parish. "Hey, what — hey, Devlin, who is this guy?"

The Golem stared at him, then turned to Michael. A smile flickered on his face.

"That's Frankie McCarthy," Michael said, as if making a formal introduction. He took the key out of the locked door and slipped it into his pocket. "He's the one I told you about."

Frankie backed up, his hand darting inside his jacket but not finding what he was looking for. He's scared, Michael thought. Scared out of his goddamned wits. Without taking his eyes off the Golem, Frankie reached in a fumbling way for a pool cue, finally gripping it by the narrow shaft. The other Falcons began spreading out. Their hands went into their pockets. They picked up pool cues. Their eyes were wide and uncertain, as if calculating odds. Glancing at the other Falcons, Frankie McCarthy was suddenly a little braver.

"You're looking for fucking trouble," he said, "yiz'll find it here." His bravado was cut by the crack in his voice. "This is members only. So leave now. While you can still fucking walk."

Michael saw Skids slap the butt of his pool cue into his hand. The hand that had mauled his mother's body. Most of the others followed Skids's example. Michael could sense their thinking: Good odds. Fifteen to one. Or fifteen to one-and-a-half. Good odds, no matter how big the guy is that's wearing the cape. The Russian put his hand in his back pocket and whipped out a knife. Ferret eased around to the side, holding an eight ball in his right hand.

"Just so you know, Frankie," Michael said, taking a step forward, "I never said a word about you to the cops."

"Don't horseshit me, you fuckin' punk."

"I'm not horseshitting you, Frankie," Michael said. "I didn't rat. But you know what I learned? I should have told them everything. I should have told them right from the start what a goddamned coward you were, beating up poor Mister G." Michael remembered what the rabbi had said one night in early spring. "That's what I learned. I learned, you keep your mouth shut about a crime, sometimes that's worse than the crime."

"A rat is a rat." Frankie sneered.

"No, Frankie. A cowardly bum is a cowardly bum. And you are a goddamned coward and a goddamned bum."

Frankie saw that all of them had weapons now. He winked at Skids and moved to the side, turning his back on the Golem.

"How's your mother, kid?" Skids said, and then made a panting sound. The others made sucking sounds or sounds used to summon dogs. Some of them laughed.

Michael rushed at Skids, but the Golem wrapped a huge hand around the boy's chest and shoved him back.

"You prick, Skids!" Michael shouted. "You gutless bum."

Suddenly Skids came in a rush, swinging the pool cue like a bat. The Golem grabbed it in midair as if it were a twig. He yanked it away from Skids, used both hands to snap it in half, and dropped the pieces on the floor. Then he grabbed Skids by the shirt, whirled, and heaved him twenty feet. Skids landed between two pool tables.

Silence, except for groans from Skids.

"That's just a start," Michael said. "Now, Frankie, you want my friend here to take care of you too, or do you want to do what's right for a change? You know, go down to the precinct, ask for Abbott and Costello, and tell them what you did. To Mister G, to me, to Rabbi Hirsch. Tell these friends of yours to go and apologize to my mother. Tell *my* friends that I didn't inform on anybody and we can live the way we used to. Do something really goddamned brave, Frankie. For a change."

There was a pause.

"I'm warning you, Frankie. It's your last chance."

Frankie said, "Fuck you, kid."

He looked at the others as if saying, Hey, nothing to worry about. Saying it to them, saying it to himself. There were too many of them for these two. His mouth curled, then became a slit, but his eyes were glittery.

"We got us a couple of tough guys here, boys," he snarled. "Whatta ya think of that?"

The Russian didn't think. He whipped open his switchblade and dove for the Golem. He was hit in midair and fell to the floor, the knife clattering from his hand. The Golem stomped his neck with his leathery bare heel and then toed him aside as if he were a stunned rat.

"Get the kid!" Frankie said, backing up, panicky, then turning to run to the small office in the rear. "Get that fucking kid!"

Two of the Falcons charged Michael, but the Golem stepped between them and the boy, and hit each of them with short, savage punches, knocking them down. Okay, Michael thought. Now it's too late for mercy. I told Frankie what he had to do, and he answered with a fuck you. So now he has to be punished. It's too late for Mister G. Too late for a lot of things. Including the cops. Again the Golem seemed to read his mind. He looked down at the I'M FOR JACKIE button, figured out how it worked, unpinned his cape and let it drop to the floor. He stood there, wearing only his breechclout, and glared at the Falcons. From the side, Tippy Hudnut suddenly threw a cueball, but it bounced off the Golem's head and succeeded only in annoying him.

"It's Frankie we're after," Michael said. "The others are small fry."

The Golem gestured for Michael to go to the door and leave. Michael didn't move. He thought: I've been afraid long enough. I'm not running.

The Golem then upended a pool table, scattering the balls and kicking a hole through the green top. He shoved the other Falcons aside as if they were dolls. Michael had told him to get Frankie McCarthy; he was going after Frankie McCarthy. Michael saw that all of them were panicking now, muttering, *Oh shit, oh shit, this guy, oh man, oh fuck, hey let's* — And then Frankie stepped out of the office. He was holding a gun. His feet were planted, his lip curled, like a gangster from a hundred movies. Michael felt a tremor of fear; he had never seen a real gun before, except on the hips of cops.

"Don't fuck with me, Sambo," Frankie said. "I'll blow a hole through you, and no jury will ever send me to the hot seat."

The Golem walked straight at him, the muscles corded and rippling in his back. Michael could see Frankie's eyes change. Now wide and jittery. The Golem took another step, and Frankie backed up, his jaw loose, his eyes wild, and then he fired.

*Blam!*

The bullet hit the Golem and he kept coming.

*Blam! Blam!*

And the Golem reached Frankie McCarthy. He took the gun away from him, held the grip in one hand, and snapped off the barrel. He tossed the pieces over his shoulder. Then he grabbed Frankie by the lapels and heaved him ten feet against a wall. Frankie fell in a shambling pile. But the Golem wasn't through with him. He took him by one leg and dragged him the length of the poolroom to the front door.

"Enough!" Michael shouted. "That's

enough for now! We don't want to kill him."

The Golem halted, dropped the groaning Frankie by the door, and turned to Michael for instructions.

"Wait," the boy said.

Michael turned to the other Falcons. They were backed away, far from the door, drawing closer to each other, as if for warmth. They needed to be taught a lesson too.

"Hey, listen, man, we're sorry what happened wit' your mother that time, okay?" said Tippy Hudnut in a pleading voice. "You see, we was drinkin' and, you know, sometimes, you got your load on, you don't know what you're doing. And, hey, you know . . ."

"Take your clothes off," Michael said. "All of you."

"What?"

"I said take your clothes off. Everything. Shoes, socks, everything."

"Hey, man, it's snowing," Ferret protested.

On the floor beside the door, Frankie moaned.

"You take them off," Michael said, turning to the Golem, "or *he* takes them off for you."

Ferret was the first to unbutton his shirt.

Within minutes they were all naked, shivering in the poolroom, a cluster of pale bodies, tattooed, scarred, muscled. The clothes were piled on pool tables, along with brass knuckles, switchblades, a homemade zip gun, a length of pipe. The Falcons looked much younger now, stripped of their armor.

"Now what?" Tippy whispered.

"Go home," Michael said.

"Through the fucking *snow?*"

Michael went to the door and opened it with the key. The wind howled. The black dog waited at the curb, snow gathering on his pelt.

"Go." The naked youths started reluctantly toward the door.

But now the Russian was on his feet, his jaw hanging loose. He looked at Frankie, who was facedown beside the open door. He looked over and saw Skids in a sitting position.

"Hold on, everybody wait," Michael said, as if addressing prisoners of war. "Russian, you go over there and help Skids get ready for his outing," Michael said. "Take his clothes off. Then take off your own. Very fast."

"You kiddin', or what?" the Russian said.

"You're one of the Falcons, right? Look at them." The Russian looked at the pale shuddering mass of the others. "One for all, all for one."

The Golem picked up a pool cue, and casually snapped it in half, as if doing an exercise. The Russian did what he was told. Skids limped naked toward the door, held under one arm by the naked Russian. I should go over and slap their goddamned faces, Michael thought. I ought to make them crawl on their hands and knees to beg my mother for mercy. But no. Wait. We'll save it for Frankie.

"All right," Michael said. "Get outta here. Run home to your mothers."

The naked Falcons began to run now, crowding through the door, past Michael, past the Golem, past the stricken Frankie, out into the falling snow. The black dog snapped at them, barked, lunged for them. The groggy Russian staggered out last, holding his jaw, guiding the shivering Skids. Michael closed the door behind them.

Then they were alone: Michael, the Golem, and Frankie McCarthy. We should wreck this place, Michael thought. The way they've wrecked so many places and people. The Golem somehow heard him. He smashed each of the six pool tables, the phonograph, the wall telephone, the office furniture, the benches. He tipped over the table loaded with food and drinks, glasses splintering, bottles breaking, beers and ice and potato salad carpeting the floor.

Neither of them was watching Frankie McCarthy.

Suddenly Frankie was behind Michael. And a blade was at the boy's throat.

"Okay, stop right there," Frankie shouted at the Golem, gesturing with a knife. Michael saw it glint in the light. "You tell this rat stool pigeon to unlock the fuckin' door. You don't do what I say, I cut his throat."

Michael was terrified, but he forced himself to be calm. Nobody on earth would ever again make him go in his pants.

"It's not locked, Frankie," Michael said.

"I don't believe you. You got the key. I seen you put it in your pocket."

Michael slipped the key from his pocket and Frankie grabbed it. The knife remained at Michael's neck.

"Now, you, big boy," he said to the Golem. "You go in the back and lie down."

The Golem did not move. He stared at Frankie McCarthy. His concentration was so fierce that a halo of energy seemed to rise off his head. Michael could see holes in his chest from the bullets, but no blood. And he could see a smile flickering on the dark face. If he were Jackie Robinson, he would now steal home. The Golem's face became a hard grid.

And then Frankie McCarthy's knife began to melt.

Michael could feel the heat on his neck. Then a warm dripping that was not blood. And not molten metal either.

Frankie backed up. His hand was full of wax. His face was full of terror. He turned to the door, stabbing at the lock with the key, his hand palsied by fear. The Golem stepped between him and the door. Frankie backed away in surrender.

"All right, enough," Frankie whispered. "I don't get this."

"Sure you do, Frankie," Michael said. "Don't you ever read *Crime Does Not Pay* comics? This is the part near the end."

"Please," Frankie said, his face runny with fear. "Whatta ya want me to say? I'm sorry, okay? I'm sorry about all that shit. You know . . . Mister G . . . I lost it, know what I mean? Dumb Hebe, buttin' in. There I was, just havin' a little fun with your friend Sonny and — Please. And your mother, hey, man, I was in the can that night." The Golem took a step toward him. "And what's that rabbi doing around here anyways? We ask him for a few bucks, you know, 'cause the guy's got a secret treasure in there, and he gives us some lip. What's he expect?"

The Golem inched forward, no expression on his dark face, and now Michael could smell the odor he wanted to smell. Coming from Frankie's trousers. Tears of shame welled in Frankie's eyes. His voice rose.

"Please, kid," he said whimpering now. "Gimme a break. What's done is done, right? Let bygones be bygones. Come on . . ."

The Golem looked at Michael. The boy could hear Father Heaney's voice: *We believe in an Old Testament God.* He nodded, and the Golem went for Frankie. He slapped McCarthy three times. Each slap broke something. Then he bowed formally to Michael before kicking out the glass in the front door.

He shoved Frankie ahead of him into the blizzard. He reached for the banner welcoming Frankie home, pulled it down, and then tied an end of it around Frankie's waist, making a crude leash. The black dog tore at Frankie's trousers, shredding them. Michael stepped over the shards of broken glass and followed them into the street, carrying the Golem's cape.

Holding the end of the banner, the Golem pulled Frankie to the middle of the avenue. He smacked him again, knocking him down, then grabbed his ankles. He snapped each of them. Frankie's screams filled the air. Windows opened. Michael shivered, but not from the cold.

"Remember, no killing!" Michael shouted into the howling wind. "We save him for the cops!"

The Golem looked at Michael, inclined his head slightly. Then he grasped the end of the banner tied to Frankie's waist and swung him around. Around and around and around, like a hammer thrower. With Frankie's feet flopping loosely and his arms straight out as the speed increased.

And then, with one final, immense effort, the Golem let him go.

Frankie flew high through the driving August snow and landed with a skittering crunch on the top of the marquee of the Venus. His screams turned to moans. Well, Michael thought, he won't be hurting anyone for a long, long time. And now, barely audible above the howling wind was Frankie McCarthy's pleading voice. *Help me,* he called through the snow. *Please, somebody help me, please.*

The Golem paused and then turned to Michael, who was standing at the curb, holding the cape. The black dog howled in triumph and farewell and then disappeared into the snow. Michael walked to the Golem and handed him the cape, thinking: I'd better call the cops to pick up Frankie. And he now noticed that the Golem's eyes were like tombs, as old as the Bible. The Golem slung the cape across his shoulders and fiddled with the Jackie button until it closed. Then he put a huge hand on Michael's shoulder and together they vanished into the storm.

# 36

When they reached Garibaldi Street, they faced a border. Behind them was a blizzard. Across the street, there was no snow. Before leaving the safety of the storm, the Golem once again placed his hands on Michael's head. They walked without being seen by sweating men who were emptying the bars to look at the snow falling a few blocks away. Kids poured out of houses. Women called them home. Nobody had ever heard of such a thing. Snow that fell on six square blocks and nowhere else? Snow in August?

In the lobby of the hospital, interns talked about freak meteorological conditions and how hailstones often fell before thunderstorms, and then one of the nurses said that nothing had been the same anywhere since they dropped that damned atom bomb and all of them laughed. They did not see the white boy with the slight limp. And they did not see the huge black man who was with him.

Michael led the way up the back stairs to the seventh floor. He cracked open the stairwell door and looked down the corridor. The nurses were crowded at a picture window at the far end, trying to see the storm, chattering and giggling in an amazed way. Michael and the Golem stepped into the bright white hall and walked away from the nurses to the room of Rabbi Hirsch.

He was asleep. His battered face was bloated and raw. Tubes were still dripping into his good arm.

The Golem looked down at the rabbi and his eyes filled with pity and tears. Michael wished that the clock could be rolled back, the rabbi healed. The Golem gestured to Michael to close the door. Then he leaned down and kissed the rabbi on the forehead. He placed his giant hands to the stricken man's temples. He touched the word for Truth on his own brow and then touched the rabbi's lips.

The swelling instantly receded. The flushed raw color evaporated. The Golem gripped the bottom of the plaster cast and gently tore it apart and then dropped it on the floor. The rabbi's eyelids fluttered, his mouth tried to form words, to decode alphabets in the dark.

The Golem motioned to Michael to find

the rabbi's clothes, pinching the boy's shirt to explain, as the boy had explained to him. Michael opened the closet beside the sink. The clothes were on a hanger. He lifted them out.

Rabbi Hirsch opened his eyes.

He fixed the Golem in a steady gaze, without wonder or astonishment; his eyes seemed almost surgical in their objectivity. Then he turned to Michael.

"God exists," he whispered, and his eyes widened in wonder. "Not just sin."

The Golem carried him home in his arms. The snow was now gone without a trace. They could hear sirens in the night. Michael opened the synagogue door on Kelly Street, glancing down the block at the turning dome lights of the police cars and the blinkers of the ambulances, all clustered around the poolroom. The Golem carried the rabbi into his cramped room and sat him in a chair.

"A glass tea I need," the rabbi said, and Michael saw that his teeth were intact again. "Put the water, then tell me everything."

The Golem went to the sink. Michael tried to run the tap, but the Golem gave him an offended look and assumed the task.

"Let him be," the rabbi said. And ignoring the huge creature, he listened as Michael told him what the Golem had done. He nodded, he shook his head gravely, he chewed on a cuticle, he raised his black eyebrows in astonishment. He never once said "Good." Then Michael was finished, the kettle whistled, and at last he smiled.

"So what is Jackie doing?" he said.

"He went two-for-four yesterday."

"Home he has stolen again, like on June twenty-fourth?" the rabbi asked.

"Not yet. He will."

"I hope we are at the game," he said. His voice was weak and strained. "I hope he does it to the Philadelphias. That would be something. We'd be sitting in the catbird's seat."

He looked at the Golem's broad back and then glanced at Leah's photograph. For the first time, his eyes were troubled.

"Why now?" the rabbi said, more to himself than to Michael. "Why not then?"

Michael understood, remembering the cord on the ancient box. "Did you try then?"

"Yes."

"In the attic of the Old-New Synagogue?"

"Yes." His eyes glazed over. "I failed."

The night was warm again, August again, sweaty and hot. The Golem poured water over tea leaves.

"Why I failed, I think now I know," the

rabbi said. "I was not pure enough." He paused. "I did not believe enough. Maybe, God I did not love enough."

His mouth started to form other words, but they would not come. The Golem handed him his glass of tea.

"*A dank,*" he said.

The Golem passed another glass to Michael, who accepted it and added his thanks. The boy looked at the rabbi, who smiled in a sweet, sad way. He stood up, refreshed by the tea.

"You are safe now, no? And your mother too. *Di tsayt ken alts ibermakhn.* Time, it changes everything."

"*Der beste royfeh,*" Michael said. The best healer.

"And now we have to deal with . . . him."

He looked at the Golem, who was squatting beside the sink and gazing at them.

"What do you mean?"

"Him we have to send back," the rabbi said. "With men, he can't live."

Michael felt a stab of regret. To send him back was unfair; they hardly knew him. But the Golem understood; there was a fatalistic look in his eyes as he sat on the floor. He held up his huge hand and then pointed upstairs. Rabbi Hirsch nodded, Yes. Upstairs. The box was there, like a small coffin.

The Golem waited until they finished their tea. Then he stood up, bowed under the low ceiling, and picked up the shofar. They climbed the stairs together. The rabbi, the boy, and the Golem. On Shabbos.

At the top step, the Golem smiled as Rabbi Hirsch pushed open the door to the sanctuary.

And halted in astonishment.

The sanctuary was again what it had been long ago. A thousand candles burned in holders along the walls and beside the Ark. The Torah was unrolled. The carved oaken pillars gleamed with fresh oil. The copper flutings on the *bimah* were burnished. The chandeliers were constellations of light. The stained-glass windows were healed and the dust was gone and the plaster whole. And the rows were filled with men holding prayer books, young and bearded and vital and proud, safe in America, their tall sons beside them, together on Shabbos. Among them, Michael saw Mister G, with a full head of hair, and three young boys, holding their prayer books. But there were so many others. There seemed to be thousands of them, millions, all the dead, all those who had vanished, Jews from Poland and Romania and Austria and Prague. The loft above them was full of women, and as Rabbi

Hirsch walked out to face them, tentative and hopeful, hearing the old prayers in the old lost language, he gazed up through the dazzle of lights.

And then he saw her.

"Leah," he whispered.

She was among the women, her face pale and beatific, and Rabbi Hirsch walked quickly, almost running, to the rear of the crowded sanctuary, his jaw loose, his eyes wide, and scrambled up the stairs, with Michael and the Golem behind him. In the loft, the women were jammed together like a wall, and then Leah Yaretzky shouldered her way through, her face dissolving in happiness. Rabbi Hirsch embraced her, holding her fiercely, almost desperately, whispering into her dark hair, and then they stepped out through the open door to the small roof, where the spires of Manhattan blazed magically in the distance.

Michael could not hear the words Rabbi Hirsch was saying to Leah. He could not hear because now the Golem raised the shofar to his lips and aimed it at the stars.

He blew a melancholy tune, full of love and sorrow and joy. The rabbi knew it by heart. The notes were addressed to the angels.

And then the rabbi bowed gracefully to

Leah and took her hand.

Michael knew there would be time to send the Golem back to the place from which he had come, to stand above him and recite the letters and alphabets in reverse and invoke again the secret name of God. He knew there would be time to return him to dust. There would be time to fold his tasseled cloak and his button that was for someone named Jackie. There would be time to lay the silver spoon on top of this earthly mound and tie the cords around the *shem* and close the door and return the *bimah* to what it was. There would be time. There would be time.

For now, Michael stood quietly in the hot Brooklyn night while clouds tried to become angels and birds talked and stones became roses and white horses galloped over rooftops, and the rabbi, at last, danced with his wife.

# Acknowledgments

This is a work of fiction, a mixture of memory and invention. But the writing was immensely helped by the contributions of others.

Above all, I'd like to thank my friend Menachem Rosensaft for checking and correcting my idiosyncratic version of Yiddish and for advice about Orthodox traditions. Obviously, he is not responsible for any imperfections that might remain.

In addition, I'm indebted to Leo Rosten's two American classics, *The Joys of Yiddish* and *Hooray for Yiddish!* They are a marvelous mixture of scholarship and humor and should be taught in our public schools. While writing this book, I also read, learned from, and drew upon *Yiddish Proverbs*, edited by Hanan J. Ayalti; *Anglish/Yinglish: Yiddish in American Life and Literature*, by Gene Bluestein; *The Meaning of Yiddish*, by Benjamin Harshaw; and *Words Like Arrows: A Treasury of Yiddish Folk Sayings*, compiled by Shirley Kumove. They have all contributed to the task of keeping alive this amazingly vital and supple language, and they fed the inspiration for this novel.

My readings in Jewish mysticism included *Kabbalah for the Layman* (volumes I, II, and III), by Rabbi Philip S. Berg; *The Essential Kabbalah*, by Daniel C. Matt; and *From the World of the Cabbalah*, by Ben Zion Bokser. I heard many tales of the Golem during a visit to Prague, but also read *The Golem*, by Chaim Bloch (translated from German by Harry Schneiderman); the detailed and scholarly *Golem: Jewish Magical and Mystical Traditions on the Artificial Anthropoid*, by Moshe Idel; and various essays by Gershom Scholem. I urge these works upon interested readers, along with a marvelous book called *Magic Prague*, by Angelo Maria Ripellino, translated by David Newton Marinelli.

— P.H.